I0762048

The Blue Girl, Candy Lee Caine

MICKEY J. "MIKE" MARTIN

THE FOWBLE PRESS

This book is a work of fiction. Any form of reference to real people, events, establishments, organizations, or locales is intended only to evoke a sense of authenticity. All other characters and dialogue have been drawn from the author's imagination and are not to be construed as real.

ISBN: 978-1-7371406-3-4 (Hardback)
LCCN: 2024906938

The Blue Girl, Candy Lee Caine

1

CANDY, SWEETER THAN CANDY

I FIRST MET CANDICE WILSON in December of 1969, while we were at a conference for college-aged students hosted by a local congregation of our church. Their building was located just a few miles from Fresno State College, where I was a student at the time. Candice was one of many participants coming from towns up and down the San Joaquin Valley. At the time, I was a twenty-four-year-old in the final throes of finishing the coursework required for an MBA degree, and just beginning to start thinking about a thesis project. I started the program immediately after completing a bachelor's degree, and it was to be the last step of my formal education before I became an honest–to–goodness tax-paying member of the work force. I could hardly wait to get it behind me and take on a full-time wage-paying job.

Our first interaction took place about as casually as it possibly could have: I sat down behind her as we took places for the beginning of the conference. From my unplanned but highly advantageous perspective, I had a perfect opportunity to check her out closely without being overly intrusive. I watched as she and a friend talked and quietly laughed together. The program got under way, and I continued to watch her during the hours that followed.

When our moderator asked us to provide brief self-introductions as a means of kicking off the program, I heard her name for the first time. *Candy,* I remember laughing to myself. *What in the world kind of name is that?* Laughing along with the rest of us as she continued, she added that Candy was only a nickname, that her full name was Candice Lee Wilson, and that she had traveled up from Visalia, a town located about forty-five miles south down the San Joaquin Valley, where she was employed by the gas company. She ended by saying that she was an active member of her local congregation.

When I introduced myself as Mike Holder of Fresno and said that I was an MBA student due to graduate in a year or so, she looked down as I was speaking. My information didn't seem to be of interest to her in the way I had hoped it would be. I was taken by her anyway, recognizing right away, as any guy my age would have, that she was a truly beautiful young woman. Her smile and laugh lit up her face as she spoke, causing everyone sitting nearby to smile and laugh along with her.

I was so fascinated, in fact, that I hesitated to approach her directly during pauses in the program, even though that's what I really wanted to do. Instead, I struck up a conversation with her friend — who was, by the way, also quite attractive — just to create an opportunity to get a little closer to her.

All I could think of as the three of us talked was Candy. She had what some would describe as high, Indian-like cheek bones, full lips, and a wide beautiful smile. Her face beamed as she talked and laughed. She was tall and slim and had beautiful green eyes, long legs, and long brown hair that was thick and shiny. I could hardly take my eyes off her. Candy, it seemed to me, was a perfect nickname for a honey like her.

Eventually, all of us got comfortably acquainted as we visited and bantered throughout the day and during a great lunch. We were highly appreciative of the effort conference planners had shown on our behalf.

Near the end of the day as we began saying our farewells, I asked her friend for her phone number when the number I really wanted was Candy's. Then, trying to act as if I didn't want to leave her out, I asked Candy for her number as well. They both laughed, but they gave me their numbers.

I had been too timid to approach Candy without some other excuse, I had to admit later on. *Guess I'll always be a sophomore,* I remember thinking as I drove home after the meeting. Even so,

I left the conference feeling pleased that I had collected the numbers of not one but two beauties I could call in the future. I didn't remember much of what our speakers said that day, but I remembered quite a lot about those two girls.

Our church group was so strict that other fundamentalists could have come to us for instruction, but, as far as I was concerned, the conference had been a great success, the kind of get-together that truly warms a single guy's heart.

BY THE TIME MY college years were about over, I had already become something of an oddity for being twenty-four years old and still unmarried. Young marriages were so common within our immediate and extended family that my siblings and most of my relatives had gotten married in their teens or early twenties. Most of them had started families before I had serious thoughts about entering that phase of life.

Taking on that level of responsibility was not for me, I had always thought, as I attended one wedding after another and extended my congratulations, back when others tied their fateful knots. I had no interest in making an early marital commitment, mainly, I suppose, because working my way through college had not been easy and I was totally committed to becoming a *successful* first-generation student. Up till then, I hadn't been serious enough to consider making a new life with anyone.

That mode of thinking changed in a hurry after I met Candy. At that point, the whole idea of getting a place of my own and settling down suddenly seemed to be the most reasonable path that could be taken, despite the fact that many of the guys I hung out with at the time were still blathering on daily about how we hoped a lot more years would pass before we tied ourselves down with the responsibilities of maintaining a hearth and home.

AS IT TURNED OUT, I never did call Candy's friend; I called her instead, just as soon I thought it was seemly to do so. It seemed necessary to hold off for a little while, just so I wouldn't come across as overly eager or needy. I was exactly that, but I sure didn't want her to know it.

When I called, she said she couldn't see me at the time but that I could call back in a few weeks, explaining that she had contracted a case of the Hong Kong Flu. Although the illness really was being passed around at the time and lots of people had it, her response came across as an excuse being thrown out to politely but effectively tell me not to bother calling again. Her response flattened me out for a while . . . *but only for a while.*

I waited several weeks as suggested and then called her a second time. She put me off yet again, saying that she was going to be tied up for a while but that I could call back later on, if I still wanted to. Yes, I said, I would. And that's what I did.

Finally, after waiting for weeks that seemed more like months, I was invited to her home for a visit. The invitation seemed reluctantly offered, but I could hardly wait to see her anyway. I counted off the days before the trip as if my whole future depended on it, even though I was aggravated with myself over the way I was behaving. It was annoying to think I had come across like a sophomore when I thought of myself as a sophisticated fraternity man. There are some emotions, as I know now but I didn't fully appreciate at the time, that aren't easy for any of us to control.

As pleased as I was to have an opportunity to see Candy again, the downside of the visit was that it came with an obligation to meet her parents. I wondered whether I would come across well to Candy on her own turf, much less how I would come over to her folks.

Much to my relief, visiting Candy and her parents Ernest and Jewel Wilson turned out to be a far more pleasant experience than I expected. From the outside, their place was totally unpretentious, but on the inside, it was as warm and cozy and comfortable as any I could have hoped to find. It really *felt* like a home, a place out of which feelings of love and support and comfort seemed to flow in abundance, without any conscious effort. Tranquility permeated every room. Candy's parents were just as warm and friendly as their home, and they welcomed me with a lot more smiles and much more hospitality than I thought I deserved, given the not so noble initial designs I had in mind for their daughter.

Their home was a welcome departure from the sort of places I'd lived in up to that time — a space-deficient family home with a gaggle of noisy siblings, small rooms in private homes, an apartment shared with three other students, and a run-down college fraternity house.

Candy was even more beautiful and open than I remembered. Her eyes were brighter and more expressive in the surety of her own home, and her smile even more wide and genuine. She was a delight to be around, and it couldn't have been any clearer that an enormous amount of love existed between she and her parents.

We enjoyed a great dinner on our first evening together, partly because her mother was an excellent cook but also because I had gotten so used to existing on various kinds of canned food and other off–the–counter items that anything she made would have been delicious.

Later on we played cards and dominos and got to know one another as we talked. The evening passed by in a hurry. I don't recall the hour I left to head back to my oppressive little room near the university, but I do remember departing on a cloud, the proud possessor of an invitation to come back again sometime echoing in my mind.

On the way home, I realized that I had just met an exceptionally wonderful set of parents, salt of the earth folks who would be a pleasure to know under any set of circumstances. It had also become clear that there was no free milk to be had in their household, and that, too, pleased me greatly, since I was more than ready to put any vestige of thinking that way behind me forever.

That night as I quietly tiptoed into my rented room to keep from waking anyone, my setting seemed to be even more of a dismal dungeon than it had in the past. I had been tired of how I was living for a long time, but now I knew for sure that my little room was the last place I wanted to be.

TRIPS DOWN THE VALLEY to see Candy during the months that followed became something of a trial as my academic load and part-time work schedule became more time consuming and trying than ever. As she started to become the major focus of my thoughts, little else was going in my life beyond the seemingly never-ending struggle to stay in the financial saddle long enough to complete my degree program and land a permanent job. I went further and further in debt just to be able to stay in school. I visited her whenever I could, but the difficulty and expense associated with getting away was a real problem.

These problems notwithstanding, Candy and I hit it off well from the beginning. The thought of leaving her at the end of each visit became a misery, a change I came to think of as moving from pleasantness and light to darkness and stultification.

CANDY, I GRADUALLY DISCOVERED, was just as traditionally minded and as conservative as I was, perhaps even more so. She and I both craved order and structure, in her case (although it was unknown to me at the time) because she had never had any at all and in mine because I had had too little. We were more alike than I first imagined. It became apparent early on in our relationship that what we both wanted out of life was a conventional relationship and home, and that we were both equally ready to make a long-term, serious commitment. We simultaneously concluded that we were right for each other — that, in fact, we seemed to have been made for one another.

One weekend some months thereafter she made a trip home with me to meet Mom and Dad and the rest of my large and noisy group of siblings. She got along well with all of them, just as I thought she would, and from then on we were convinced that we really did have a relationship that could stand the test of time.

I wanted a marriage of the kind my mother and father and my grandparents before them had enjoyed for their entire lives — long and loving relationships that had made them stronger and happier than they ever would have been if they had stood alone. In my view, a good marriage to a loving spouse was the core of human existence and nothing less than a gift from God. Given her relationship with her folks, I was convinced that she felt the same way.

Once I decided for sure that Candy was the one for me, I made a vow that if He would let me have her, I would toe the line for the rest of my life. At the time, I had never even as much as imagined that we would be tested in the way we were during the dark days that we would have to endure later on. All of that was yet to come.

The night I proposed to Candy in the living room of her parents' quiet and comfortable home is one that both of us will forever remember. She knew what was coming and I was ninety-nine percent certain that she'd say yes, but the great decision was not official until the momentous questions was asked and our pledges were actually exchanged. When she said yes, I felt like I'd won a million dollars.

Actually, though, feeling like I had any dollars at all was truly and verifiably no more than a figurative expression, since the twelve cents in my pocket at the time, a dime and two pennies, was the full extent of my worldly fortune. And, as if starting out with only twelve cents and a promise wasn't a lean enough beginning, an even starker reality lurked in the background — the fact that before long I'd have to start paying off what seemed at the time to be a humongous student loan, a debt on which principal and interest payments were scheduled to begin immediately after my graduation from college.

As happy as I was about our decision to get married, I was actually embarrassed and, on a practical level, more than a little fearful, in view of the financial straits I knew we'd have to face right out of the chute. But, in the way of many young couples just starting out, we made light of our realities and moved ahead as if our situation could not have been any better than it was. We turned the evening of my proposal into a private memory that has been dear to us from that day forward, one that we've laughed about ever since. We had the dime mounted and placed on a key chain to create a locket that could be worn as jewelry. We still have the locket today, over fifty years later, and it is one of our most treasured keepsakes.

Our boldness at the time, I have since learned, could not have been any more on target, since we were as right about our decision as it is possible for two people to be about anything. No worldly possessions we have ever had or that we will ever have could be of any greater value than the understanding we've shared since that time.

Our marriage on August 1, 1970, therefore, was both white and about as traditional as it could have been. My belief has always been that the wonder and solemnity of our church ceremony set lofty standards and a positive course for both of us, standards and a course we have striven to live up to from that day forward. As far as I was concerned, our marriage had been made in heaven and I had been undeservedly honored and permitted to enter a blessed state of personal existence. It may come across as unsophisticated as well as a bit overstated to describe our relationship in this way, but that was how I felt during our early days together, and I've felt the same way ever since.

2

DIED AND GONE TO HEAVEN

WE STARTED OUR MARRIED life in a tiny one-bedroom apartment that was located only about one mile from Candy's parents' home. It wasn't much to look at, but we'd have been happy anywhere in those days and the little place suited us just fine. We settled in her hometown because she already had a job there, doing work that she enjoyed. I didn't have a full-time position at the time, which meant that we had to rely on her income for a living — supplemented, of course, by my meager and unpredictable earnings from occasional employment as an entry-level substitute teacher.

When the college term came to an end and the time for yet another of what I continued to refer to as my *summer vacations* arrived, for the first time in many years I didn't have to pack up all my belongings and move who knows where for yet another construction job. Instead, Candy's earnings were enough to keep us afloat until I could complete the final requirements of my master's degree program — mandatory coursework and a research paper.

Candy was of constant support as I labored on, encouraging my efforts as well as providing concrete help to hasten the successful completion of what I thought would be the end of my formal academic endeavors. She worked while I wrote and studied and planned for the day when I would take on a full-time job of my own.

At this early point in our married life, we still weren't getting by well from a financial perspective, at least not as far as I was concerned. I felt downright embarrassed about the large amount of student loan and other debt I'd built up during my struggle to stay in college. The twelve cents I had in pocket on the night I proposed didn't amount to a drop in the bucket, not when it came to covering the cost of my obligations.

Luckily, though, Candy had built up a bit of savings to draw on, due to having worked and lived at home for several years before we met. We were thankful she had put away enough to sustain us for a while, even though it bothered me a great deal that our life together had to begin with relying on her earnings rather than my own.

My lack of current income notwithstanding, I spoke confidently and excitedly about the new home *I* (not *we*, mind you) would build for us one day soon. There was no doubt in my mind that I would soon be able to turn our situation around. If she was conscious of the presumptive vanity inherent in how I carried on at the time, she showed no signs of it; instead, she simply encouraged my enthusiasm and shared in my excitement.

If it is true that pride, as is often said, comes before a fall, it's clear to me in hindsight that in those days, I most definitely was a student of business ripe for a hostile takeover. I was as blind as a bat to it at the time, but now I see that even way back then my sweet wife was thoughtful beyond her years. Because it helped make sure that both of us remained positive and whole, putting my needs and well-being above her own was wise under in the circumstances. I had done nothing to earn her deference, but she gave it to me anyway. As much as I hate having to admit it, one way in which our partnership was off track for us back then was the fact that I, too, always put myself first. I see that now.

My two major commitments as we started out together — complete my master's degree program and locating a permanent job — kept me busy, but life had become dramatically different from the way I'd been living it only a short time before. To begin with, we had enough time to enjoy being newlyweds, and that alone was a wonderful change. Secondly, the sense of financial pressure that had been crushing for so long had been lifted. I felt as though I'd just been released after serving a long sentence in prison, free and living out in the sunshine once again. There was no doubt about it; it was a joyful time of life for both of us.

WHEN I COMPLETED MY coursework and the time rolled around to start work on the dauntingly onerous task of writing the research paper that was to be the capstone project of my MBA program, Candy surprised me by buying an enormously helpful gift — an IBM Correcting Selectric typewriter, which, in those pre-computer days, was a truly marvelous machine. It was a notably extravagant purchase, but the machine had a correction feature which, in view of my propensity for making last minute changes as well as an embarrassingly high number of errors of style and fact, made it a timely and most helpful gift.

Candy, who was an excellent typist, spent many evening and weekend hours helping prepare my study, even after putting in full workdays on her own job. With her encouragement and ongoing practical support, I eventually completed my project and graduated with an MBA in hand in 1971. For me, it was yet another load lifted off my shoulders.

WITH MY DEGREE PROGRAM behind us, we felt even more free to enjoy our life as a couple. We basked in our still new and fresh relationship and continued to work and save for the home we looked forward to building at some point in the future. Our situation improved even more a short time thereafter when I finally landed a job of the type I had been searching for — an entry-level staff accounting position with a well-recognized corporation in our area. My new employer was a nationwide printing company, Consolidated Business Forms, Inc., a business that had a production operation in our town.

With me gainfully employed, we finally had enough income

to make our lives even more pleasant as well as a lot more secure. Soon, I found myself enjoying the new and highly invigorating experience of having a little jingle in my pockets as well as a bit of free time to take advantage of it. Life takes on a whole new feel when there are two wage earners in a household, especially when both partners hold down positions that pay reasonable wages.

NOW THAT WE HAD regular and predictable work hours, we were free to use our time off to do whatever we pleased. Taking long weekend trips whenever we wanted was a great luxury, one that we took full advantage of by thoroughly exploring as much of the state of California as we could. We behaved, in fact, as if we were two kids in a candy store, going from here to there as if we didn't have a care in the world.

Our relationship by this time had become the way that characterized and predominated it for the next thirty years — light-hearted and fun, yet profoundly uplifting, despite the problems, large and small, we had to deal with along the way. Living with Candy filled me with confidence and the joy of life, and, even now, I can't help but smile as I recall an episode of the carefree bantering we engaged in on a regular basis.

As we worked together in our kitchen one day back while we lived in Granbury, Texas, to prepare a lazy Saturday evening barbecue, Janice Joplin's hit song "Me and Bobby McGee" popped up on the radio. Both of us were fans, Janice being a Texas girl and all.

"Bobby McGeeHee," I said, "is my favorite of all of Janice's songs. She's a wild-eyed, big-haired Texas woman, but she really got that one right."

"Bobby McGee," Candy said in response.

"What?"

"You mean Bobby McGee, don't you?"

"No, of course not; I mean Bobby McGeeHee. That's what she sings in the song, and that's exactly what she meant to say."

"Oh, yeah," she responded, laughing. "Then why does every disk jockey in the country say 'Bobby McGee' when they play her song?"

"It's obvious. They just don't understand Texanese as well as I do, after having lived in state for a while. The way she referred to the song — and what she actually says when she sings it, if you listen very carefully — is 'Bobby McGeeHee.' The title is misstated by virtually everyone, but I know what she intended. You just haven't picked up on local pronunciations as well as I have. Keep at it, though; I'm confident you'll make it to my level one day."

"Oh, right. You know Texanese about like I'm a space cadet."

"Well, then," I countered, "I guess that makes both of us *space cadets out in Texas* — or, should I say, *spacey Texans*. Hey, you know what? I think we're on to something here; we've discovered a label that fits us to a T, one we ought to use all the time."

We referred to each other as *spacey Texans* or *space cadets* for weeks thereafter, whenever we had time to kick back, be ourselves, and laugh for a while. No special skills or tools or talents are required, after all, of those who live and play in their own private Eden.

IT WAS AN ABSOLUTE pleasure for both of us to be able to laugh and joke and be spontaneous with one another in the way we did.

Today we hear about how lives can be *lived to the fullest* only if we *stay energized* and *seek the gusto* and so on along those lines, but I have come to agree with those who've said that thinking along those lines is way off the mark. For us, the most meaningful and memorable times of our lives have taken place at unexpected moments, during seemingly minor events that have occurred without any advance thought about what they might mean in the future. In my opinion, the wonderful relationship we were fortunate enough to be enjoying was empirical proof that some of the best moments of life occur without any deliberate effort or planning at all. Good times aplenty have happened for us in this way, and our memories of them have lasted ever since.

Our married life surely would have appeared as ordinary as toast from an outside perspective, and, in fact, I suppose that's just what it was. It didn't seem commonplace to me, though; I considered it an absolute blessing.

Many years had to go by before I finally began to appreciate the full depth of Candy's commitment to our marriage. For her, our relationship was in every respect a sacred trust, a bond that would never be broken. Among the inner vows she made at the outset of our time together, one that she told me about later on but that I didn't grasp the value of until years later, was that if anything ever did come between us, it would *never* be due to any lack of effort on her part. As simple as that may sound, she meant it with all her heart.

High on her list of personal objectives, for example, was a commitment to behaving in an exemplary manner when it came to matters of daily interaction between us. The best way to sustain a great relationship, she believed, was to remain honest, open, and humble in her daily life. Behaving in accord with these standards sounds simple enough, but it's only *simple to say*; it's not in any way *simple to actually do*. Candy, however, *really did*.

Although she behaved in this way from the beginning, I really didn't give her full credit for it until much later on. We can be totally blind, I have discovered, to some of our partner's most wonderful qualities, even those that are manifested on a daily basis. This, I suppose, is just one more way of admitting how very easy it is to take a partner for granted, or to fail to give credit where credit is genuinely due.

While I tended to focus more on quantity of life issues, she was far more focused on matters of quality. I paid a lot of attention to observables such as a good house, savings in the bank, a good job, and so on, while she thought more about intangible matters that are harder to clearly describe or measure. Faith and trust, as we all know, can't be seen or quantified, but they are of incalculable value when it comes to maintaining a solid marriage and living a worthwhile life. They're worth their weight in gold, in fact, precisely because their true value *is incalculable.*

As our years together went by, I began to feel guilty about getting much more out of our relationship than I ever put into it. Thinking this way started out as nothing more than a vague and ambiguous notion, but it grew until I wanted to become more to her and to do more for her than I had in the past, just to live up to the high but unspoken standards she'd set for us.

Ever upbeat and charming, she seemed to operate under the power of some sort of internal self-adjustment mechanism, a mode of being that kept a smile on her face most of the time. Everyday occurrences seemed special and wonderful when she was involved, due to her ability to see the positive side of almost any situation. This was true not only with respect to our life at home, but also in terms of how she related to our friends, my co-workers, and members of our own extended family. There were no half-empty glasses for Candy; it was absolutely true that, as my mother–in–law had pointed out from the beginning, "she seldom met a stranger."

Ever so gradually and without any conscious understanding on my part with respect to what was happening, Candy became more than a wife and partner; she became the best friend and best teacher I'd ever had. She proved to be just as principled and hardworking as she was beautiful and warm. Without overtly pushing any particular agenda or directly suggesting any specific changes on my part, she caused me to rethink many of my own priorities and habits and values. I don't think she ever consciously intended to change or lead or remake or improve me in any particular way, yet that's exactly what she ended up doing; somehow or another, she ended up becoming a role model for her own husband.

Back when we lived in Texas, it was common to hear people refer to any guy who seemed to be excessively pleased with his own situation as being "a man who acts like he's died and gone to Heaven." I didn't realize it at the time, but this was an expression that described me perfectly. Rightly or wrongly, it really did —

and, in fact, still does — capture what I thought about Candy and the life we enjoyed together. To me, she was a dream come true, and I simply couldn't get enough of her.

3

AT WORK IN THE REAL WORLD

AT THIS POINT, OUR work lives had begun in earnest, with both of us starting out in conventional entry-level jobs; Candy continued as a secretary at the utility company, while I pursued my position as an accountant for the business forms design and printing corporation. There was nothing exotic or exciting about what either of us did for a living, but we tackled our responsibilities for all we were worth. Visions of a wonderful future danced in our heads, and we had dreams we could hardly wait to see fulfilled.

With both of us working, we were able to move out of our apartment and buy our first home — a small place aptly described as a *starter home* by the salesman who dealt with us. We didn't care what he called it; we were just thrilled to move into something we could call our own. We still had a long-range plan to design and build a home according to our own specifications one day in the future. Unfortunately, we hadn't saved enough to do it just yet.

From the get-go, employment in a corporate environment went well for me, mainly because early in my work life I was more or less an employer's dream, a company man with a passionate vengeance. Neither specific direction nor pointed encouragement was required to get me to dive in as best I could. Working long and hard each day, I poured my best efforts into the tasks that were assigned to me. My supervisors, our controller and the plant manager, were all hard-working and highly competent individuals when it came to their own careers, and that made them good mentors for a highly motivated young employee like me, right out of college and as green as a gourd.

Without ever being directly told so, I knew before long that I could make exponential progress within the company if I really wanted to. Excellent internal opportunities were available at our regional headquarters in the San Francisco Bay area, and ample training was available for those who had decent abilities as well as the requisite desire for future growth. There was a pressing need, in fact, to fill some of our more advanced positions, and I had the right academic background to make such a move. For excellent career progress and salary advancement to take place, all I had to do was prove myself and demonstrate enough commitment to convince my supervisors that I was worthy of a long-term investment. There was no doubt about it; Candy and I were well on our way to enjoying a very solid future.

CONTENDING WITH THE MYSTERIES OF MARRIED LIFE

IT DIDN'T TAKE VERY long for me to discover that by marrying Candy, I had effectively married two people rather than one. Our relationship and home life were every bit as wonderful as I have described them, but only when she was in what I gradually came to think of as *her normal self.* When she was in that mode, she was a delight to be around, and she was that way, in fact, almost all the time, behaving as she had when we were just starting out.

What I had learned, though, was that there were times when she would lapse into behavior that was as inexplicable as it was mystifying. Changes in her demeanor took place so gradually and unobtrusively that it was hardly noticeable at first, but then it became more noticeable as our months together flew by. I did my best to ignore or make light of any unusual behavior that occurred, but the real truth was that I didn't have a clue what to make of what I saw. There were times, for example, when for no discernable reason she would suddenly turn inward, sometimes even to the extent of coming across as another person altogether, occasions on which she would become quiet and detached and then drift off into a world of her own making. Early on, I found this kind of behavior more puzzling than actually worrisome.

Whenever she drifted off into one her funks, she would ask me to just leave her alone for a while, promising that she'd be fine after taking a little time out for a bit of contemplation and rest. It had been her nature forever, she explained, to become emotional and moody on occasion, justifying it as being nothing more than "a feminine thing that she had had to deal with all her life." She had "learned to take care of in her own way," she said, and "all she needed was to be left alone to recompose herself. I'll be just fine after a bit."

On occasion, sometimes even during social gatherings when others around us were talking and having a good time, tears would suddenly appear in her eyes and begin to roll down her cheeks, due to emotions that had welled up out of nowhere. Anything, it seemed, could set her off. Whenever this happened, she'd cover it up as best she could until she could excuse herself and step out for a while, using explanations such as having something in her eye or that she wasn't feeling well or whatever. When this kind of thing took place while we were alone together, which happened more often than I really want to admit, she'd say that she'd thought of something or another that had made her feel sad, and that she'd be fine in a minute. And, again, she usually was — if I just left her alone for a while.

The thought that there might be deeper causes behind these instances of maudlin and unusual behavior really hadn't occurred to me. There are people, after all, I said to myself, whose emotions really are easily aroused by various stimuli — sad songs, upsetting newspaper or magazine articles, tragic incidents reported in the news, or other things of that kind, anything that conjured up unsettling images or thoughts. Some people, I rationalized, really are more sensitive than others, and more than a few women do tend to be a bit emotional at times. *What's so unusual about that kind of behavior?* I would say to myself, mainly because I really didn't want to make a greater issue of it than I had to.

Basically, I learned through dealing with an ongoing series of small incidents that lots of adjustments have to be made by people who set out to live together as man and wife. Having never lived with a woman before, I had nothing to judge our experience by. As far as I knew, our martial relationship was moving along in the same way as those of others, with the exception of a few quirks and idiosyncrasies that were unique to us. *Others have their problems,* I said to myself, *while we have ours.*

I thought of learning to live with a partner's foibles as being the key to maintaining a successful marriage, so I was always more than willing to overlook or come up with other ways of contending with any problems that came up for us. Candy, it seemed to me, must have been thinking along these same lines, since both of us chose to approach our concerns by doing whatever could be done to accommodate one another's needs and differences.

Even so, as we learned more about each other over time, it became increasingly apparent that her quirks and foibles were more than just a few and that some of them were too unusual to be considered healthy. I worried about what was going on with her, but in the end I always ended up accepting her behavior as *just the way she was* and trying to live with it as best I could. *Why make an issue of her problems,* I reasoned, *if it wasn't absolutely necessary to do so?*

Overall, therefore, things would have seemed from any outside perspective to be going quite well, and no one in our circle knew of her problems. The accommodation we settled on without engaging in explicit discussion was to let matters ride along as they were. It had become clear to me that her parents, Ernest and Jewel, must have known about her unusual behavior all along, but, for reasons I had no way of understanding, they had never chosen to discuss it openly with me. It seemed to me that all four of us had concluded that if we just left well enough alone, her problems would sooner or later clear up on their own.

UNEASINESS INTRUDED AT HOME

SO, IT WAS IN this innocuous way that as Candy and I continued to live together on the straight and narrow path we had chosen to follow, an unexpected sense of unease was insinuated into every thought I had about our future. *Why should I spend an inordinate amount of time worrying about what I've chosen to think of as the minor adjustments that I've been having to make at home? Buck up*, I remember thinking, *and get on with life*. We did indeed have everything we needed, but, for some unknowable reason, it just never seemed to be enough. My feet became itchier with every day that passed, even though I wasn't aware of any real justification for them to be itchy at all.

4

AN ITCH THAT HAD TO BE SCRATCHED

THE FIRST REAL CONSEQUENCES of the vague sense of unsettlement I felt was that I gradually became discontent with the whole idea of staying on the corporate career track that had gone so exceptionally well for me. For reasons I could not have explained to anyone, not even to myself, I decided against pursuing any of the excellent and well-remunerated openings that were well within my reach at the time. From a long-term perspective, this wasn't the wisest thing I could have done, but I decided against pushing myself in that direction.

I chose to pursue a position I had only casually fantasized about a few years earlier — a college professorship in business administration. With a marketable MBA in hand, the possibility of landing a two-year college position wasn't an unrealistic objective, given the rapid expansion of publicly funded colleges taking place after the end of the Vietnam war. I knew, too, that my corporate job would provide a good base of practical experience for assuming the role I wanted to land — an instructional assignment in business administration, which had been my major field of study in college.

When I brought up the idea of changing my career track to Candy, she encouraged me without reservation to pursue the goal I had in mind. "Whatever you choose to do," she said, "I'll back you in any way I can. What's most important to me is that you continue to enjoy your work. If a change of direction is what you really want, you have no reason to be concerned about me."

Having made sure that Candy and I were on the same

wavelength, I waited until an opening in education of the kind I wanted was announced by one of the community colleges that served our local area. Upon applying for the position, it was offered to me after only a single interview, but at roughly only about half of the salary level that would have been available if I had stayed in my corporate environment. Without hesitation, I immediately accepted the college's offer, and, with that, I was off on a new career track.

MY CAREER IN EDUCATION BEGAN

SO, JUST THAT QUICKLY, in late 1971, I found myself holding down the instructional role I had idealized and hoped to find. The overriding thought I had at the time was that *good things really do come to those who wait*, because it appeared that that was exactly what had happened to me. In fact, though, I really hadn't waited long at all.

In eager anticipation of all the many positive changes I expected to flow from involvement in my new occupation, I thought of myself as being quite fortunate indeed. Why I had been so quick about rejecting the solid corporate opportunities that had been available in favor of a career that *might* turn out equally rewarding, I really wasn't sure. I ought to have been able to explain and justify my own reasoning, but I couldn't, not even to myself. All I knew was that I felt *I absolutely had to move on.*

THE 1971–72 ACADEMIC YEAR turned out to be far busier and all-consuming than I expected it to be. A surprisingly high percentage of my time was spent not on instruction or engagement in the kind of study or preparation I had anticipated but on the *other duties as assigned* section that appeared as a single line on the contract I had signed. Expectations in this realm — committee assignments, student advisement, course and program planning, advisory groups, college and community relations projects, and so on — took up a much higher percentage of my time than I had imagined they could. When all of the college's expectations were combined, my new job was more than busy enough to bring about a great deal of eager anticipation for the summer vacation that was due to start in June.

Teaching doesn't pay very well, but one major fringe benefit of the occupation is having summers off to pursue other ends. Many teachers use this time to stay current in their fields or to build salary points through taking summer courses for higher credentials, while others work at second jobs or start businesses or side hustles to bring in extra income. What I intended to do with my own first summer off was something I had never been able to do in the past, which was *absolutely nothing.*

During the second half of the academic year, I looked forward to a summer of lolling in the sun the way I had when I was young, back during the lazy, hazy days of childhood. I wanted my vacation to be just that — a time of contemplation and leisure, a time for doing nothing more than routine chores around our house, and to do even that only as the spirit moved me. Due to the grind I had been dealing with for so long, I could hardly wait.

When my summer off finally rolled around, I roared off into it like a lion, eager to pursue the sybaritic pleasures my free time would enable me to engage in. Surprisingly, though, in no time at all I wound up feeling so bored and lethargic that I felt half stunned. Hanging around home made me feel more like a lamb than a lion, even though it was a mystery why. Being able to stay at home wasn't rewarding at all; in fact, it became downright disorienting, a feeling that I immediately and mistakenly attributed to outright boredom.

Long before the summer was over, I could hardly wait for the new academic year to get under way. Time off work, I had discovered, was not all it was cracked up to be. Being as free as a bird, as far as I was concerned, was for the birds.

From that point forward, it became standard practice for me to avoid scheduling any more than short periods of time away from work. I took only enough time off to, as I put it back then, *recharge my batteries*. Long vacations became a thing of the past, one of the first casualties of a fundamental decision not to *waste any more of my valuable time on idleness or leisure or any other form of unproductive activities*.

As soon after the beginning of the new academic year as I could get around to it, I enrolled in a doctoral program at an out–of–state university. That was in 1973. I made this decision with the intent of booking up every bit of free time I had for the indeterminate future. I knew that getting involved in a program of the kind I signed up for would be an intense and time-consuming undertaking, but that just the kind of commitment I wanted to make.

FOR EVERY ACTION, THERE ARE REACTIONS

FOR THE NEXT SEVEN years, I taught a full load of courses at my home college during our nine-month academic term, then enrolled myself as a full-time out–of–state graduate student at the other college during my summer breaks. When the academic term ended on a Friday where I was employed, I would load up my car and head out of town for the summer session that would start the following Monday. In turn, when the summer session ended on a Friday, I would head back home to resume my assignment at the college I worked for, if possible, on the very next Monday.

While I was away each summer to continue my education, Candy stayed at home alone, working diligently to cover the expense of my graduate study. During my summers away, I would return when there was an opening in my schedule, and she would visit me whenever she could arrange time away from work. In no time at all, my life became an absolute blur of activity, either for my job or for my doctoral program. A substantial portion of any free time I did have was spent on the care and upkeep of our home, since we couldn't afford to have that kind of work contracted out.

Being away from each other wasn't what either of us wanted, but we thought of it as being a temporary evil that had to be endured. I felt compelled to keep us on the path we were on, even though being apart turned out to be much harder on her than it was on me. She never questioned my commitment or rationale for doing what I was doing, but it was impossible not to notice how wearing it was for her. Even so, I continued to plow ahead, thinking that biting the bullet was a price that had to be paid for the pot of gold that would be found at the end of my rainbow.

Before long, the increasingly onerous requirements of my graduate program and my ever-growing responsibilities at work along with the normal requirements of keeping up our home and relationship led to a blur of activity that became more stressful, onerous, expensive and, in a strange way, disorienting than either of us had expected it to be. A few students at my home college began to take notice, and then started talking about me as being "way too gung-ho for my own good." If I had understood up front all of the complications my career choices would lead to, I very might have decided against pursuing another degree at all, especially a program as involved as a doctorate. I met my residency requirement, for example, by taking a painfully expensive and memorably lonesome year off work without pay, a long absence that made things even harder on Candy at home. After that, I sat for and passed the set of oral and written examinations that were required as a capstone assessment of my efforts, examinations based on the coursework I had completed.

Even after these hurdles were out of the way, the most difficult and challenging phase of the program still remained — the completion of an acceptable dissertation, an in-depth research paper on a single topic that had to be endorsed in advance by my graduate advisor. The thought of getting involved in a project of that magnitude was extremely daunting, in large part because my advisor happened to be a highly experienced senior professor who held an advanced degree in, of all subjects, *Research in Statistical Methods*. I knew I'd be put through a grinder before he and the other members of my committee would approve any project I tackled.

By this point I was already feeling so ragged that it was difficult to think clearly. I carried on, but I had become a weary traveler indeed. Candy, too, had been worn down by what I was doing, probably even more than I realized. In all honesty, I was too preoccupied to take proper notice.

COSMOPOLITAN ME

WHILE I WAS INVOLVED in completing my doctoral coursework, for some unfathomable reason I made yet another inner commitment that had far-reaching effects on my career and our home life alike. In a few words, I decided to remold myself into an educator who had a broader outlook on his overall role in society. It sounds a bit high-minded and rather grandiose as I speak of it now, but back then this became a personal development goal that I took very seriously, one that led to a number of highly important career-related decisions. Graduate programs are designed to change a person's way of thinking, and, for better or worse, mine most certainly had that effect on me.

I began to feel stifled by the environment that only a short time before had been so highly satisfying and rewarding and that I had felt honored to be involved in. In what amounted to the blink of an eye, I decided that I had to avoid becoming *trapped* in what I had suddenly come to think of as *my provincial setting.* What were the loftier issues I wanted to tackle? What were some of the changes I wanted to bring about? Well, I couldn't have described any of this if I had tried. When it came to what I wanted to accomplish, I couldn't have explained that either.

Setting these new objectives had a number of immediate consequences, one of which was that I began to feel an urgent need to broaden my base of experience, to do whatever had to be done to turn myself into a professional among professionals. I felt a pressing need to build a base of experience and a level of expertise that would qualify me to deal with issues and ideas in education that were the focus of scholarly specialists and others in the world of books and professional research, people whose work I had been studying. I was no longer content to work with what I had begun to think of as routine and mundane matters, the kind of tasks I had been dealing with for years. The thought of ending up forever locked in a narrow and confining setting suddenly became oppressive in the extreme. I had convinced myself that I absolutely *had* to get out of it, *no matter what.*

ADMINISTRATIVE ASPIRATIONS

BY THIS TIME IT had become clear to senior faculty members of my department at my home college as well as to key members of our upper administrative team that I would soon complete the doctoral program I had enrolled in years earlier. Knowing that I would want to make use of the new credential I was about to earn, they encouraged me to consider taking on the position of head of our department, which was a generally thankless stipend-paid assignment I knew my colleagues — especially the senior faculty members who broached the idea to me — wouldn't have touched with a ten-foot pole. Even a fifty percent raise in pay wouldn't have persuaded any of them to take on the job.

Every faculty member in my department was senior to me, and the majority of them wanted nothing more than to kick back and enjoy what is well-known to be one of the cushiest ways of making a living in the whole world — the role of a tenured college professor. Theirs was an attitude, I may as well point out right now, I found repellant. My view was that teachers ought to behave like clergymen, professionals who are fully aware of the life-changing effects their efforts can have on students. For that reason, I didn't think they should ever speak or think of their jobs as roles that could be coasted along within.

Despite how I felt about my colleagues' states of mind, their suggestions made sense to me, partly because they were making them at a time when some of our students as well as many members of our faculty still routinely mistook me for a student. *Taking on the job might enhance my credibility,* I thought, knowing that doing so would make me conspicuous for being not only the youngest instructor on our campus but also the youngest department head. In the end, what clinched my decision was that I had convinced myself that I was not a person who would enjoy having more free time.

As inexperienced as I was at the time, my colleagues rightly recognized that I was also energetic, enthusiastic, and sincere with respect to our department's role within the college. They knew I was spoken of around campus as one "who might make a real contribution one day, given the right opportunity." Opinions of that kind were mentioned to me on more than one occasion, and, even though they were never anything more than unsolicited and unofficial remarks, I was influenced by them anyway.

For these and other reasons, I expressed an interest and was subsequently appointed chair of my college department — with, I was thankful to say, the endorsement of nearly every member of our faculty as well as the support of most of our college's upper administrators. That this was so made the appointment seem even more acceptable because it meant that I had been urged to take the job rather than having pursued it on my own. The new role was nothing more than a position compensated by means of a small amount of classroom release time and a modest stipend, but I still felt honored to have it.

In the blink of an eye after assuming the new position, I found myself serving on more campus-wide committees, selection teams, task forces, focus groups, and community liaison activities than ever before. The busier I became, the more satisfied I was with what I was doing.

It was unavoidable that all of the additional activity would further eclipse the time I had to spend with Candy at home. I chose to plow ahead anyway, effectively ignoring her very real and legitimate needs. Staying on top of my additional responsibilities required so much more of my time and attention that it seemed to justify becoming less involved in keeping up a functional household. Excusing my behavior by saying that I had too much going on at work, more and more of what I used to do in this area wound up being relegated to Candy. She accepted our changed circumstances without complaint. I was too preoccupied and busy to realize what I was doing.

BECAUSE I WAS PLEASED with how my job was going, it wasn't long before I decided that I wanted to go all out in terms of pursuing a full-time position in academic program administration. I had understood from the beginning that my stipend-paid role was unlikely ever to turn into a permanent assignment, but I had known all along that it could serve as a springboard for the kind of job I might want to have one day — an administrative post within my teaching discipline.

Once my appetite was whetted for change, landing the job I had in mind quickly became the all-consuming focus of my off-duty hours. An appropriate description of my state of mind in those days would be to say that I had become *overly ambitious, sublimely confident, and fully but not insightfully inspired to achieve.* I knew *what I wanted to do*, but it really wasn't clear at all *why I wanted to do it.* That was no clearer than my rationale had been for leaving behind a well-paying corporate career some years earlier.

Due to my relative youth and unusually high level of motivation, my efforts led to what would have to be described as total absorption in my work — or, perhaps I should say, work in general, since, for me, working had become as much a way of hiding out as anything else, even though I didn't realize it.

The prophets of old were right to teach that the world is diminished if young men do not dream dreams and see visions, but they ought to have gone on to point out that their dreams and visions should be meaningful as well as grounded in objective reality. Mine weren't, given any objective assessment of my personal strengths and abilities and, above all, *true interests*. Even so, once the kind of thinking I was doing took root at the back of my mind, it remained embedded from that point forward.

The dean who occupied the position directly above me in

our college's administrative hierarchy at the time, the person to whom I reported, was a relatively young man who had deep ties in our community and who was doing quite well on the job. Because it was obvious that his position was unlikely to become available any time soon, this became all the justification I needed to want to launch my administrative career by moving to another institution. In those days, good opportunities were readily available to academics willing to move for the purpose of taking on new responsibilities, since colleges throughout the country were in the midst of a period of significant expansion. I knew that if I really wanted to plunge into deeper waters, there was every reason to think I could be successful. All that remained was the matter of talking over what I wanted to do with my sweet but clearly troubled wife.

CANDY RISKS HER ALL FOR MY CAREER

A SHORT TIME THEREAFTER when I explained to Candy what I had in mind, she reacted just as I thought she would; she said she would do whatever she could to help me reach my career objectives. "That's what I've been doing," she declared, "and that's what I will always do."

"Your parents," I pointed out, "aren't going to be pleased to hear that we intend to move away, no matter where we go or what reason we give for going there," even though I knew she had immediately thought of that very thing and that I was only stating the obvious. Ernest and Jewel loved Candy every bit as much as I did, so both of us knew exactly how they would react.

"Well," she replied, "I certainly won't like that part of it, either. I'm married to you, though, not to them, and there are times when we have to do what we have to do. You're trying your best to build a better future for us, so you'll just have to leave it to me to figure out how to break the news to them. They knew before we ever met that I might end up having to leave one day, if not for one reason, then for another. I guess that time has finally come."

Candy did her level best to come across as determined and resolute when she made these declarations, but it was impossible not to notice how a twinge of trepidation had crept into her voice. Even though it was abundantly clear that her comments were more dutiful than truthful, I evaded any reservations she might have brought to the fore by not truly encouraging any further input. That's how I was in those days, always ready to move ahead at full speed, even though I really didn't know where I was going or why I wanted to go anywhere at all.

THROUGH STUDYING THE *Chronicle of Higher Education* on a weekly basis during the months that followed, it didn't take long to locate a college with an opening that appeared to be an appropriate step up for me. It happened to be at an out-of-state institution. I submitted my application, then impatiently waited to find out if I would survive their paper screening process. As it turned out, I did. I took time off to fly out for a personal interview. When a job offer came through a short time thereafter, I immediately accepted. Taking another step up the career ladder I wanted to climb had proven to be remarkably easy, much easier than I expected it to be, just as it had been once before.

All that remained was for us to complete our move from California to the city out of state where my new job was located. That was when the whole undertaking became a lot more complicated than I expected.

For as long as I live, I will never forget what happened in the early morning of the day on which we pulled away from the curb at the front of our place in Visalia, California, to depart for our destination. After selling our home in town, Candy's father Ernest had worked hand-in-hand with me for three days to load the twenty-six-foot U-Haul truck I had rented for our trip, while her mother Jewel worked inside, helping Candy pack our belonging in boxes. Her parents absolutely hated the thought of our moving away, but it had always been their way to help us in any way they could.

Ernest and Jewel had been our constant companions since the day Candy and I first met, but, on the morning of what was to be our last day in town, they were having a terrible time trying to keep supportive smiles on their faces. It was tough for them to keep up a false front, when they clearly saw every box that was loaded taking them another step closer to the moment when their beautiful, loving daughter would move away from them. Unavoidably, all four of us had been thinking along these same lines.

No one had to tell me that I couldn't have asked for a better set of in-laws, which was why I felt nearly as sad about our leaving as they did. It didn't surprise me at all when, just before we boarded up before our departure, Jewel gave it up and finally began to sob in the way I had feared she might, nor was it unexpected that Candy began to cry as well. What truly caught me off guard, though, was when her rough and tumble father Ernest began to tear up along with them. That, I had not expected.

Their heartfelt sobbing as they clung to one another before we stepped up into the truck for departure struck me so deeply that in only a few seconds, I was nearly as broken up as they were. It aggravated me all to hell that I behaved that way, since that was exactly what I had intended not to do. What sense would it make, I had reasoned beforehand, to get caught up in a tearful departure, when all four of us knew we would get together as often as possible in the future?

What I had discovered, though, was that *thinking about leaving* those two wonderful people behind was a whole hell of a lot different from *actually doing it*. I drove away kicking myself for having been the one who'd brought it about.

To make matters worse, I *sensed* in an indistinct and unspoken way that was quite different from *actually knowing* that Candy and her parents hadn't merely been *sad* that she was moving away; they had seemed to be *genuinely troubled by the thought of it* as well. This had to be ridiculous, I remember thinking, because I couldn't see any justifiable reason for them to be worried about us at all. As I saw it, we were two mature adults heading off so that I could take on an excellent new position. I found it very troubling that they were so worried at a time when worrying didn't seem the least bit warranted. For some unknown reason, the fact that I had started thinking along these lines turned out to be more than enough to embed a palpable sense of foreboding in my already uneasy mind.

OUR LONG AND WINDING ROAD BEGAN

AS SOON AS WE got settled in our new location, I tore into my new job as if my life depended on it. I had no more to sell at the time than driving ambition combined with a huge amount of confidence and energy, but these attributes counted for quite a lot, just as they would have anywhere. Even though I stayed busy all the time, the vague feeling I had had for a long time about the work I was involved in being too mundane and ordinary never went away; in fact, it grew stronger than ever. Being brand new in my role and still totally unproven, it really wasn't justifiable that I began thinking along those lines, but I did it anyway, almost as if no other choice could have been made. Then, after I began to think that way, I started putting in longer days than I really had to, knowing that if I ever really did want to move from point A to point B, that was what I needed to do.

Almost out of the clear blue sky and certainly without giving such an important matter the level of consideration that was warranted, not long thereafter I acted on the grandiosity of my thoughts by impulsively setting a lofty and grandiose new professional goal for myself — a college vice presidency for instruction or a presidency. I simply took for granted my own potential for growth within academia as well as my ability to become a successful upper-level administrator, even though I had no track record to speak of at the time. Setting my sights on a position of this kind amounted to an enormous leap of faith, since it assumed capabilities as well a greater depth of knowledge than I had had an opportunity to demonstrate.

Knowledgeable professionals would have considered it highly presumptuous of me to have set such a goal, but, even if I had known what others felt, it would have made no difference. Thinking boldly is easy for those who have no understanding of the forces driving their ambition. I had given only a minimal amount of thought to the aptitudes and abilities and interests that are required to do well in the kind of position I had targeted, and I had given no thought at all to whether my own true interests and personal limitations meshed with the kind of work I thought I wanted to do.

Even a minimal amount of investigation would have brought out that my social skills, for one thing, were all but negligible, and that I had no interest at all in becoming more proficient in that area. This finding alone would have been more than enough to disqualify me getting into the line of work I had targeted, but I charged ahead at full speed in pursuit of my goals as if I'd investigated them in the way that was warranted.

Knowing I would not be content to work my way up through the chairs at any one location, I decided that I would make a series of carefully calculated occupational changes to build up the breadth and depth of experience I clearly lacked. Because I was far too restless to wait for an opportunity to open up where I was employed, I was willing to do pretty much anything to jump start or otherwise hasten my progress toward the upper-level job I had decided I absolutely had to have.

CANDY DOUBLES DOWN ON HER COMMITMENT

WHEN I EXPLAINED TO Candy what I wanted to do and why I wanted to do it, she once again reacted just as I thought she would, even though I took pains to point out that it would lead to a lot of moving. "Moving," I reminded her, "isn't easy to do, and I'm sure you remember what happened to us the first time around."

"I recall our first move very well," she assured me, "because it almost tore my heart out. In the future, though, Ernest and Jewel won't be there for us to worry about, and I thank God for that. I intend to do whatever is necessary to help you reach your career objectives. And no," she added, "I most definitely don't expect it to be easy."

She said she understood what to expect, but I doubted that she really did. My impression was that she was doing nothing more than getting along by going along. Despite these unspoken concerns, I just assumed the best and moved ahead as I had intended to all along.

THOUGHTLESS AMBITION

WITH MY NEW PLAN of action firmly in mind, I became more involved than ever in the work I was doing for my current employer. In addition, I began to play more active roles in professional associations within my subject matter area as well as within other groups that existed to meet the professional needs of those who held academic administrative positions. In the interest of making a good name for myself, I prepared papers to present at conferences, participated in panel discussions, chaired numerous committees, served on task forces, took on various leadership roles, and wrote a few articles for professional journals. I also wrote and published three books on topics of interest to me. They had nothing to do with my areas of professional expertise, but they were *somewhat* scholarly efforts, nevertheless. On top of the foregoing activities, I also spoke to local business and civic leadership groups whenever I was invited to do so, served on various town and gown activity planning committees, and participated in a wide variety of community-based events.

In short, I did everything I knew how to do to demonstrate my readiness, willingness, and motivation for moving onward and upward toward a higher-level administrative position, first within my academic discipline and then even further up the line. As the national market for the services of effective educational administrators continued to grow, I intended to grow right along with it.

Success, it would be correct to say, had become an end in itself, and success, to my way of thinking, had come to mean one thing and one thing only: *moving a step closer to my ultimate objective.*

So, it was with the intent of building a broad base of experience that I embarked on what was intended to be a carefully calculated series of career moves that would get me where I wanted to be. Each new job would be selected to provide a higher and broader level of experience, all for the sake of qualifying myself for the kind of position I really wanted to occupy. In no time at all, making this happen became the all-encompassing focus of my professional life. *We have to work to live,* I remember saying to myself at the time, *so why shouldn't I go for broke and try to make as much of my labor as I could?* It felt good to have a clear-cut goal and to be ambitious.

As I impatiently waited to move into a new environment, I took for granted that any new job I took on would be more interesting as well as more rewarding than the one I was in at the moment. I also took as a matter of faith that every more advanced role I took on would move me one step closer to the objective I had targeted — a vice presidency or presidency.

Candy, just as I expected, was fully supportive of every move I made, always taking on faith that I knew what I was doing and that every move was being made for the purpose of professional advancement; in fact, she seemed to be just as willing as I was to make changes and take risks. She never complained, that's for sure.

After a few years of hard work and near total immersion in whatever I was doing at any given location, I deemed myself ready to take on yet another somewhat higher-level administrative challenge. Because I did not expect to get something for nothing, I put in long hours day after day to pay my dues wherever I happened to be. Doing well was never automatic or easy, but I managed to turn in decent performances every place I went.

I made a series of additional moves during the years that followed. During my travels, one strong conviction I latched onto had to do with the attainment of academic tenure. Having it, it seemed to me, did reduce fear of being unseated for taking on unpopular stances or holding unconventional beliefs, but I had also noted that it all too often led to stagnation on the part of many of the teaching professionals I dealt with on a daily basis. In my view, their tenure had been bought at the price of becoming forever stuck in a debilitatingly boring and dead-end work situation. Other administrators I knew gave lip service to this same sentiment, but it wasn't the idle chatter for me that it was for them. By contrast, I earned and then gave up academic tenure, or the opportunity to return to a classroom if my administrative work happened to go badly, on three separate occasions, back when I knew a good number of professionals who would have given an arm or a leg to earn it just once.

Days and weeks and months and years flew by, but I hardly noticed their passage. My time was too taken up by meetings, task forces, publishing, speaking, community-sponsored activities, miscellaneous leadership roles, and the activities and projects of various professional associations on top of my main job to pay attention to anything else.

My life eventually ended up becoming one of near total absorption in work, so much so that the home life and relationship I still considered more wonderful than I had any right to expect were simply taken for granted. Every move I made was conveniently justified as being required for the sake of making dogged progress toward the highly specific personal professional goals I had in mind — first a general academic deanship, then a campus vice presidency, and then, finally, a presidency. My career, as far as I was concerned, was moving along swimmingly.

RAIN BEGAN TO FALL ON MY PARADE

MY CAREER WENT ON as described for years, even as our home situation continued to deteriorate. I uprooted us again and again, rationalizing each move in the same way but without ever considering the full impact of it on me or on Candy. Gradually and without my knowing it, moving from one job to another, which I always justified of as *advancement,* became more of an end in itself than anything clearly beneficial or that would accomplish anything truly worthwhile on behalf of myself, a given employer, or my profession at large.

Basically, I gradually lost track of what I wanted to do. Eventually, my thinking grew so terribly muddled that I became more and more confused about everything. It wasn't long before I ended up so far out in left field that I was totally lost, even though I didn't fully realize it at first. The one thing I did know, though, was that being out of sorts would inevitably lead to one thing or another going wrong on the job, and, as would be expected, that's exactly what eventually ended up happening; and, when the job I held at the moment began to go badly, it went *very* badly, *very* quickly. Soon thereafter I learned that it isn't possible to win them all, even for a person willing to expend his best effort to prevent the worst from happening.

My downfall began while I was at a larger and more prestigious college than I had been employed by in the past, a school that was widely thought of as being more progressive than most publicly funded institutions of its kind. I had taken a job there only because it appeared to be a higher-level notch to move up to. It did pay better, but that really hadn't played much of a role in my decision to relocate.

Because my duties and areas of responsibility at the new college were nearly identical to those of my previous assignment, I expected a relatively straightforward and easy readjustment. Much to my surprise, it turned out to be the first job ever to go poorly for me, and it went that way for me only because of the scattered and unsettled state of mind into which I had fallen. Things went downhill very quickly, even though I put in ten- and twelve–hour workdays six to seven days per week over a period of several years trying keep the worst from happening. It didn't help. Once the various cats got out of the bag, so to speak, I was never able to get them back in again.

I learned a short time after I became an insider at this

particular college that my instructional division had long been burdened by a history of serious personnel problems, most of which had festered for years. Extreme philosophical differences existed between various faculty members, differences that had led to open animosities, taking of sides, and the formulation of so many alliances that the various departments had become hopelessly Balkanized. My faculty, as a matter of fact, were more at odds with one another than any professional work team I had ever linked up with, and I had joined them at a most inopportune moment for me — a time when I was beginning to have serious personal problems of my own.

The faculty members who reported to me argued and fought incessantly, not uncommonly over the most inconsequential of issues. The less something mattered, the more they argued about it. On matters big or small, they did whatever they could to make mountains out of molehills. I felt sorry for how aggravatingly miserable they'd allowed their professional lives to become, even though I knew all too well that I, not they, would be held responsible if our ship sunk any further. To a person, each one thought of himself as a chief, never as a member of a team. If there was any opportunity to argue or fight, they always found a reason to argue and fight.

What made matters worse for all of us, especially me, was that three of the more senior members of the faculty had already tried their hand at the division leadership role I accepted as an outsider. Each one had done his best to persuade his peers to work together in a constructive way, but over time each of them had either gone down in flames or been pushed out of the assignment. One by one, when their personal approaches to solving the problems of the division ended in abysmal failure, they had angrily returned to the classroom. Now, feeling embittered and resentful due to the way they had been treated, each one was determined to get even in any way they could. Because getting even had become the order of the day, the chips they carried on their shoulders were harmful and, of course, highly counter-productive, but they were as real as hollow-point bullets.

My new *team*, therefore, was as fragmented and dysfunctional as any work group I could have hooked up with. Because each one was a capable and confident faculty member who had been effectively beaten up by their own warring colleagues, they were in the market for any means of settling scores that could be found. Worse still, because they were all tenured, nothing short of their molesting or murdering someone would change these internal dynamics, not if they didn't want them to be changed. They were stuck with one another, whether they liked it or not, so they blasted away at each other in any way they could, at every opportunity arguing over anything that could be argued over, even though most of their differences stemmed from nothing more than wounded pride dressed up as great concern over issues of high professional significance.

Most of them had dug in and taken sides to the extent that they no longer bothered to make any pretense of wanting to move toward cooperation and reconciliation; instead, they unabashedly preferred to malign and find fault with one another's motives whenever they could. Our environment became so toxic that agreeing with any one individual or department on any given issue was easily and all too frequently equated with taking a position against another. I was bitterly criticized and determinedly undermined any time I tried to control a controversy through taking a firm stand, yet I was blamed without hesitation when bickering wasn't brought under control in a way that was acceptable to the antagonists of the moment. It was a truly negative situation to work in, one in which I could do no right.

Sadly, it was at this point that matters became even worse, even though they were bad enough already, when I grew so discombobulated that I started making lots of stupid mistakes. Trying to blend in and, hopefully, become better accepted, I could hardly believe some of own my lapses in judgment. I made lots of them, though, just as big as life.

As I began to feel more detached from the argumentation that was taking place, I began to make more serious mistakes. I couldn't see my way clear to take even the most obvious of steps that might have moved our agenda forward. All I could do was watch, listen, think deeply about problems as they came up, then nod sagely from time to time, as if I knew how a given matter ought to be handled. I fiddled, in other words, just as Nero is said to have done, while my professional setting caught on fire and burned.

Unable to remain a prime mover within our little pond, I began to look at our situation as being a sad one for *all of them, the faculty,* to be caught up in, rather than as *one I was caught up in myself.* Behaving as if it didn't really matter how our problems were resolved, I felt genuinely sorry for every member of our staff; but when it came to making working conditions better for them or for myself, I couldn't come up with any new ideas to place on the table. I found it understandable when some of my faculty as well as our vice president, the person one step above me in our administrative ladder, became annoyed by my behavior, because I was annoyed by it as well.

After three years that seemed more like a decade, I was forced out of my position in exactly the same way as the three faculty members who had held it before me. I had never believed that the same thing might happen to me. The official story was that I resigned.

The transition from being a *star performer* to *an administrator with a problem* was distinctly unpleasant, especially in view of the fact that it had happened on the heels of a long string of highly successful appointments. Life, I was forced to admit, isn't always fair, not even for a hard-working go-getter like me.

CANDY'S DIFFICULTIES INCREASE AT A HIGHLY INOPPORTUNE TIME

IT GOES WITHOUT SAYING that Candy's special needs were eclipsed by all of the twists and turns that were taking place in my professional life. While I was hanging on by my professional fingernails, it hadn't been possible for me to be as attentive to her as I ought to have been. When she needed my help more than ever, the sad fact of the matter is that my mind was always elsewhere.

Moving away from the loving parents who had been her mainstays had been an enormous mistake, one that had greater negative effects than I realized while I was caught up in the fog of administrative warfare. On top of that, I made yet another serious mistake by suggesting that she stop working and stay at home. I was doing well enough at the time for us to get by on my earnings alone, so I thought being able to stay home would take some pressure off her back and make her daily life a little bit easier. All it did, though, was give her more free time to worry about this and that and everything else.

The sense of unease that had been detectable within our home all along quietly and unobtrusively grew more pervasive than ever. Even so, her support of my efforts to grapple with the many problems I was having at work never wavered.

Being able to say this became a major justification for my tendency to minimize the significance of the problems she was having at home. I figured that if she could put up with the angst caused by the problems I was having at work, my perplexing career moves, and my many personal piques and behavioral quirks, then I damned well ought to be able to find ways of contending with what was going on with her at home.

Turnabout, I thought, *was fair play*; I had my problems, and she had hers. *Whatever problems my dear, sweet, beautiful wife might have,* I decided, *I'm going to do my best to deal with them, in the same way she had, come hell or high water.*

Even though I was deeply worried by what was taking place with her at home, I remained as doggedly determined as ever to reach my occupational objective — a vice presidency or a presidency. In the way of a lemming on a mindless quest for better hunting grounds on the other side of a dangerous stream, I was oblivious to any of the adverse consequences that might stem from the career path I was so blindly committed to following. For me, there was no middle ground. I sailed along on autopilot, pursuing my career objectives even as Candy's personal problems as well as my professional dilemma became ever more pronounced.

BACK IN THE SADDLE AGAIN

WHILE THE LOSS OF my position was a serious setback, I knew even in the midst of my gloomiest days how pointless it would be to allow what happened to have an unnecessarily adverse impact on my career. I could have and should have done better on the job I'd just lost, but it was equally obvious that I had taken on an extraordinarily difficult assignment, one that had proven to be just as ruinous for others as it had been for me. So, after wasting only a short period of time on unhelpful self-flagellation and pointless mourning, I collected my thoughts and proceeded to make yet another fresh start.

The next job I landed was a step backwards in the sense that this school had a lower profile than the one I'd just left and my assignment was a step lower, but it turned out to be a good move anyway. The small college that hired me was located in a fairly remote community, but it was notable in one highly significant way — it was exceptionally well funded. It enjoyed not only the high tax revenues that came with being located in a county that had many high income-generating oil leases but also had been the recipient of a some exceptionally generous donations made by members of wealthy families who owned some of those leases.

What these facts meant on a practical level is that ample capital funding had been available for the construction of beautiful new buildings and the purchase of state–of–the art computers and software, classroom fixtures and furniture as well as many kinds of laboratory machinery, tools, and equipment. Even better, solid sources of funding meant that generous allowances were available for staff conferences and various other kinds of professional development activities. For the college's instructional deans, this amounted to living about as close to Fat City as we were ever likely to get.

Our college rightly boasted of having among the most

modern physical plants and best instructional equipment in the state in which it was located. This helped make the school an especially pleasant place to be employed, since the role of an instructional dean is considerably easier to handle when faculty are provided with current and well-appointed work environments. Most of my previous employers hadn't been even close to that well-funded.

As refreshing as this college turned out to be as a place to work, my long-standing professional goals remained just as compelling as ever. As soon as my feet were back on solid ground, my quest for the golden grail resumed as if I hadn't experienced a reversal at all. Given the fall from grace I'd experienced and in view of what was happening with Candy, it would have been very reasonable to have put down roots right where I was, a place where I was doing very well, rather than head back out on the road.

I didn't, though.

Strangely, I wasn't willing to stay put *anywhere.* Wherever we were and regardless of how my work was going, I always felt unsettled and discontent. From the outside, our home life as well as my career would have appeared to be going along reasonably well, when, in reality, I was wandering around in the dark.

6

LIFE WITHOUT A CENTER

THE SITUATIONS WE HAD to worry about — mine at work and Candy's at home — were on the verge of getting totally out of control, but I was too distracted and shaken by what had been going on in terms of my ability make a living for us to be of much help to my dear wife when she needed it. It's tough to be supportive when all you're able to do, figuratively speaking, is walk around in aimless circles, wringing your hands as you wander.

Candy was becoming more troubled every day that passed; there was no doubt about that. I knew she was struggling, but I couldn't muster enough strength to do much of anything to buoy her up, not even to provide the limited amount of support I had in the past; I was too much in need of being buoyed up myself to do anything that constructive. Because I had no better ideas for dealing with her mysterious afflictions at home than I had for contending with my own problems at work, her situation ended up becoming just another entry on a long list of others for which I didn't have a single answer to place on the table.

It was miserable to head to work every morning sick with worry over the possibility that either my job or our marriage, or both, might come unglued at any time. Negative thinking of the most draining kind began to dominate our daily lives.

So, there we were, both of us at the same time, desperately fishing for answers as we bumbled though our daily lives as if we were sleepwalkers, praying that we would be able to find effective ways of dealing with what ailed us on our own. We were too proud to seek out what we really needed, which was outside help delivered by professionals who knew how to deal with convoluted predicaments like the one we were caught up in. *Damn*, I remember saying to myself, *what a mess*.

In an effort to come to grips with my problems on the job, I fell back on the only method of dealing with difficult situations that had ever worked for me in the past. Hard work, in my view, was a fail-safe way to behave during any time of crisis, and most any problem, I reasoned, could be solved by falling back on this simple but rock-solid and praiseworthy tactic. *What could possibly be wrong*, I thought, *with trying to improve my situation in such a laudable and time-honored way?*

Well, as it turned out, quite a lot turned out to be wrong with the whole idea of becoming ever more deeply buried in work at that juncture. More of the same, I discovered rather quickly, wasn't the right prescription for dealing with what ailed me on the job, and *working harder* did not prove to be the equivalent to *working smarter*. Extra effort doesn't help much when problems are poorly defined.

WHAT BECAME OF "HOME"?

AS I CONTINUED TO struggle with my own personal problems as well as those Candy was having at home, I began to think of more differences between the values I bought into back when I became an aspiring member of the *cosmopolitan class* and those of my colleagues and our friends and relatives. I took note of the overall fact that that my professional colleagues had, in effect, taken off in one direction, while I had taken off in another. Our acquaintances had often warned, I had to admit, that my movements had become excessive and were difficult to understand, and now, for the first time, I began to see that they'd been right all along.

As committed as I had been for years to the grandiose concepts of pursuing *universals over particulars* and *great truths over localisms*, I wished I had spent more time on family, hometown, and down–to–earth activities and associations. Doing so may have staved off some of the coldness that enveloped me at work, and it probably would have of great help to Candy.

Then, at a time when I was already scraping rock bottom and had nearly reached the end of my emotional rope, my boat came close to sinking altogether. It happened when I was blindsided by the highly upsetting revelation that *there was no longer was a place I truly thought of as home.* When I tried to think of where I wanted to *go back to*, I couldn't define where that romanticized location might be. For me the whole idea of *home* had become nothing but a construct, an idealized location that no longer existed.

I behaved in even odder ways after making this sad admission. I wrote letters to cousins and aunts and friends I hadn't talked to for years, for example, asking how they had been doing and apologizing for not having kept in touch. In addition, I continued to ask former associates to fill me in on how well institutionally hosted community events had gone in recent years — fund raisers, festivals, and the like.

That I had so determinedly avoided social activities by labeling them as *excessively parochial, narrow, non-career enhancing* and therefore a waste of my valuable time now seemed quite amazing, considering that they would have been of benefit to both of us, especially to Candy. *Why hadn't family affairs or activities sponsored by my places of employment or the communities in which we'd lived not mattered more to me? Why hadn't I ever felt a desire to participate, to get involved, and to settle down anywhere, in the way my professional colleagues and friends had?*

What rang most loudly in my ears were the words of those relatives, colleagues, and friends who had said to me, in effect, "I really can't imagine what your life must be like, with all the relocations and changes you've had to put up with. It must be quite a challenge." Up to this point my reaction had been to laugh at their comments and counter by saying, "Don't you ever get bored, doing the same thing in the same place with the same people, day after day after day? That kind of life is not for me." Now, though, in view of the discoveries I had been making about myself, I found that I no longer felt that way.

MATTERS CONTINUED TO WORSEN AT WORK

I KNEW MY ANXIETY would sooner or later upset my applecart at work, and, sure enough, that's what eventually happened. Every other task I attempted began to either go wrong altogether or ended up being poorly completed, typically due to my inability to stay focused long enough to do anything well.

Professors, especially tenured ones, tend to see themselves as generals rather than as lieutenants, their true levels of expertise and ability notwithstanding, and they have all the latitude they need to be highly outspoken about anything and everything. Team members working in an academic setting are quick to note when others aren't doing their homework, and they typically aren't hesitant about making their displeasure known. Like sharks in the water, professors are quick to pick up on vibrations being sent out by a weakened administrator, and it didn't take long for my crew to catch on that my head wasn't in the right place. It was mortifying when I first began to overhear grumbling about how I was making way too many mistakes, knowing how unlikely it was that I would be able to get myself back under control.

In the same way that had happened once before, I truly began to stumble on the job, and this time it wasn't caused by long-standing or intractable problems within our academic division; it was caused by the emotional turmoil that was going on in my head. Before long, I gave up the pretense of trying to do excellent work; instead, my focus shifted to doing only what was required to get by from one day to the next.

Small colleges don't have the luxury of a deep bench, which means that every player's contribution is essential. Even though I knew the mistakes I was making were too significant to be ignored, the thought of being called on the carpet after all my many years of successful service and given a negative performance evaluation or, even worse, not being offered a contract for the following year, left me feeling weak-kneed and wobbly. Clearly, I was headed for a major derailment, and I doubted I would be able to survive the wreck.

I clutched after any ray of hope that could be seen. Unhappily, though, regaining my equilibrium on the job just wasn't in the cards. It's impossible to get out in front of a problem that can't be defined, and I couldn't even figure out *what* was wrong, much less *why*.

As troubled as I was, though, I never stopped putting in long hours in an effort to do my job well. Knowing what a positive impact a good educational experience can have on the lives of our students, I never stopped thinking of my work as being of high importance. It wasn't in my nature to give short shrift to even the most routine of my administrative duties — planning budgets for various programs and departments, participating in course development and curriculum planning, interviewing applicants for positions, conducting performance evaluations, helping to resolve conflicts between students or between students and teachers, or other tasks of that kind. My problems on the job were emotional rather than attitudinal, even though this distinction didn't matter to anyone but me. For as long as I occupied my position, I tried to do the best work I was capable of doing.

CANDY'S CONDITION ALSO CONTINUED TO WORSEN

IT IS OFTEN SAID that when it rains, it pours, and that seemed to be exactly what happened to us during the interval that followed. Even as I struggled to stay on top of my situation at work, Candy continued to slide further downhill at home. Her behavior took such an ominous turn that I worried about her day and night. Some of the changes I noticed were subtle and seemingly minor, others were clearly out of the ordinary, and still others were truly strange and mystifying. In the past, her unusual behavior had never seemed alarming, most likely because I was always too focused on my problems at work to give it the attention that was warranted.

The changes I noticed came about gradually, and, as always, never seemed to be directly caused by anything I did or failed to do. I never sensed any irritation or disappointment toward me, much less any outright anger. Her problems seemed to arise from within herself and appeared to be caused by whatever was going in her mind. She continued to put off any discussion of what was going on with her, no matter how insistently I prodded.

Her moodiness, for example, had become more pronounced than ever, until there were more frequent and longer lasting retreats into our bedroom for time under the covers. Then, because she slept more fitfully than ever, she began to have more bad dreams. These changes had caused her to become more distant and removed than she had been in the past. There are times, I soon discovered, when silence can be as loud as the Bells of St. Clements.

Despite all this, her bouts of depression and withdrawal were typically interspersed between periods of normal behavior, intervals during which she behaved like her normal vivacious self and during which she was a pleasure to be around. Now though, her mood swings had progressed to a point where I no longer knew what to expect. She could be as delightful and as loving as ever for days or weeks at a time, only to suddenly lapse into a black period of unexplainable remoteness and self-isolation.

My anxiety level was so elevated in those days that I was more than willing to downplay the severity of what was going on with her. *Given my own pathetic condition*, I reasoned, *how could I possibly justify finding fault in her*? In the overall scheme of things, I rationalized, *What does it matter if she retreats into silence once in a while? She always gets over it, doesn't she?*

I can learn to live with any change I see in her, I recall thinking, *if it is doled in small enough doses for me to get used to it a little at a time.* The only excuse I have to offer is that I wasn't my real self when I was thinking this way, not by a long shot. I was so confused and frustrated that I could have buckled under at any time; my condition was just that shaky.

A GROWING SENSE OF DESPERATION AT HOME

AS THE CONDITIONS WE were grappling with worsened, an unbearable sadness fell over our formerly tranquil and happy home. Candy's strange behavior was becoming more pronounced, but I refused to think of it as being symptomatic of any unmanageable or irremediable emotional problems. Because I blamed her difficulties on myself, I self-servingly continued to characterize them as being *relatively minor.*

The last thing either of us wanted was for anything to detract from the wonderful relationship we had enjoyed for so many years — especially at a time when my job was close to going on the rocks. We were still enjoying many good days, too, it must be pointed out. When she wasn't in a funk, our life together was just as rewarding and as pleasant as it had ever been — much better, as a matter of fact, than I thought I deserved.

If the most threatening problem facing us at the time was the fear that I might fall apart at work, I reasoned, *why make a greater issue of the problems she was having at home than I absolutely had to? Didn't we have enough to worry about already? If I were to fail on the job,* I asked myself, *then where would we be? Without my income, how would we get by? How would we pay our bills?* Viewed from this perspective, her problems seemed to be a lot more manageable than my own.

Time and time again over the years I had been asked how our marriage could have possibly been as wonderful as I described it to be, given the many changes and adjustments our lifestyle had forced us to make. It was a fair and reasonable question, and my answer to it had always the same emphatic *YES*; our marriage really had been as wonderful and fulfilling as I described it to be, no matter how hard that might be for outside observers to believe. My response had been the same: "When our relationship was good," I would tell them, "it was very, very good — as good, in fact, as it possibly could have been, and when times were bad, well, we just did the best we could to deal with our problems in our own way, knowing that our life would soon return to the way it was meant to be for us."

Now, though, for the very first time, my feelings about how things were going for us had definitely begun to change. When anyone asked how we were doing, what I really wanted to say in response was "I wish to hell you would shut your obnoxious, intrusive mouth and tend to your own damned family."

DOCTOR, HEAL THYSELF

SO, A LONG AND torturous road had to be traveled down before I finally admitted that professional matters had long since become as powerful a stimulus for me as the bell for Pavlov's dog. It really was true that I had marginalized every non-professional aspect of our lives.

As I struggled to get a better grip on myself, I recalled a few comments that had been made by a psychologist whose work I'd read but whose name I could no longer remember, a specialist who'd written that "a meaningful existence requires true emotional continuity" as well as "connectedness to family and place." I had dismissed his thoughts as being nothing more than catch-phrasing, but I had never forgotten them. Now, it had become clear to me that his observations had been right on target.

With painful clarity, it dawned on me how, in earlier years, back when I had a fresh doctorate in hand, it had made some sense to try to climb the academic ladder by moving from one institution to another, but that I had continued along that path long past when it was truly justified. The more I thought about this, the more I realized that a very high price had been paid for my lack of commitment to the down-to-earth intangibles of home and family and place.

The majority of my professional associates had stayed at one institution throughout their careers. Early on, I had privately sneered at those who chose safety and security over their active pursuit of career enhancement; I had, in fact, even gone so far as to publish a short journal article under the title of "Portable

Pensions and Professional Burnout." I didn't openly say so to anyone, but my intent had been to deride the provincialism and lack of ambition I saw in too many of my peers.

Most of my professional acquaintances had spent their entire careers at one or a few colleges and sunk deep personal roots in the communities in which their institutions were located. For reasons that were still unclear to me but that now seemed highly flawed, I had always *chosen the road.* Now, I envied those who had been able to happily vest at one location, especially those who had built solid reputations within in their service areas.

It had taken years for it to happen, but I had finally discovered that it is indeed possible for an ambitious person "to wake up one day feeling like a stranger, lost and out of place." Above all else, I realized how badly I had failed to satisfy Candy's innermost needs and that I had caused her way too much needless pain. Clearly, it was way past time for this particular doctor to get serious about healing himself.

GRASPING AT STRAWS

LIKE A MAN CAUGHT up in a desperate search for a miracle cure for his cancer, any snake oil treatment that promised relief from what was going on for Candy and me soon commanded my full attention. When I chanced to read a quotation in a newspaper about a book in which an author pointed out how easy it is for career professionals in a society like ours to "become systematically blind to some of the crucial elements of a balanced and well-integrated life and to the value of connectedness to place," for example, I reacted to it as if the words had been written expressly for me. This was another example of the kind of comment that I once would have dismissed as little more than psychobabble, but his wording so precisely described what I was thinking at the time that it resonated like a gong and cut like a knife. His overall observation so aptly characterized my condition that it was painful to contemplate.

His book was in my hands as soon as I could find it, and

before long I was off on a whole new tangent, immersing myself in an intensive study of every word he'd ever written. His comments turned out to be meaningful indeed, even to the extent of his entire analysis coming across as if it had been expressly written for me.

"There is undeniable educational value," he wrote, "in the whole process of moving from one place to another, adjusting to new circumstances, and going through the process of redefinition in the workplace, but it is also true that excessive moving about can result in a destructive form of personal indifference, one that erodes the fundamental sense of belonging we all need to be comfortably located in space and time."

Oh, doc, I remember muttering to myself as I read those words; *if you only knew.* What the good doctor did not add, though, it ought to be noted, is that by the time a person gets into such a situation, it's usually too late for him to do anything about it. In the way of a smoker who has decided to quit, I found it hard to stay disciplined enough to work my way out of the rut I'd lived in for years.

Basically, I began to do what so many others do after they learn they need to change their ways; I began to rationalize away the most negative aspects of my behavior and to exaggerate the importance of its positives. Smokers do this when they begin to claim, for example, that their habit is of some benefit to them, in that it helps them relax or keep their weight down. In my case, I continued to advocate the merits of the gypsy lifestyle to which I had become accustomed, even though I really no longer believed it myself.

"Some negative consequences are associated with any lifestyle we adopt," my sage wrote on, "even for those in professions such as mine, educational administration, that are generally viewed as *responsible* and *respectable.* Some feelings of loss are to be expected, it must be said, in any lifestyle we choose to live. A reduction of parochial attitudes requires some detachment from place, just as a higher-level professionalism does require some lifting of roots. Educators and school administrators, for example, are not exempt from same kinds of career crises that are faced by corporate employees. They are expected to live their lives in such a way as to be acceptable role models, but such exacting expectations can leave them feeling exposed and vulnerable. It is not surprising, therefore, for some of them to wake up one day in a situation they never wanted to be in."

There was no doubt about it, I concluded; the writer was talking directly to me. What he did not go on to point out was that it really doesn't help much to learn about a problem if the knowledge isn't accompanied by a prescription for doing something about it.

As I continued to beat myself up, I became more of an emotional wreck than ever. I slept badly, ate poorly, and thought more crazily every day, all of which made our overall situation even worse. All I seemed to be able to do was keep asking myself the same debilitatingly plaintive question: *How on earth could I have allowed such unpleasant things to happen to me, cosmopolitan soul that I am?*

AN EYE-OPENING SELF-INQUISITION

WHAT HAD BECOME OF the carefree way we lived back in the early years of our marriage? I wondered. *Why are we so uptight and tense all the time? What in the hell had changed?*

Why, I asked myself, *had I allowed the pursuit of my professional activities to dominate my decision making so completely that matters at home had become secondary? Life isn't meant to be lived that way,* I realized, *and it definitely wasn't what I wanted for us, so how and why had I allowed ours to get that way?*

Before long, a new and highly disturbing question floated into my troubled mind, one that threw me even further into despair. *Why,* I wondered, *hadn't my wonderful and dutiful partner ever questioned a single one of my many career moves?* No matter how strange or unconnected some of them surely must have sounded, she hadn't objected to any of them.

She had never taken issue with any move I wanted to make,

no matter how inexplicable some of them surely must have seemed when they were first brought up. Instead, her reaction had always been one of unconditional acquiescence, of automatically accepting the same career-relation justification for moving I always offered — lock, stock, and barrel, as if I couldn't possibly be wrong. M*ost people*, not just *most women*, it had occurred to me, would at least have insisted on hearing how and why another move would be advantageous. Candy, though, had never asked more than a minimum about what I wanted to do or why I wanted to do it; she had simply started planning for moves as they came up, without ever really questioning why they were necessary in the first place. The more I thought about all of this, the stranger it seemed.

Had what I thought of as her unwavering and admirable support of my career aspirations really not been that at all? *Had I,* I wondered, *been so outspoken that she had just taken for granted that she had no choice?* Had my own behavior, in other words, been the cause of her ongoing suffering?

A STRATEGY RUN AMUCK

LOOKING AT OUR SITUATION from this new perspective made it impossible to think of any of my past career moves as having been worthwhile. *They damned well couldn't have been*, I said to myself, not *if they had contributed to my precious wife's emotional decline.*

Arriving at this conclusion was as painful for me as a stiff punch in the gut, but my discoveries didn't end there; yet another question that had equally revelatory implications popped into mind as well. *If my career gyrations (including two job changes I'd been forced to make) hadn't been steps in a carefully thought-out career strategy*, I asked myself, *why had I made them at all?*

I had become dissatisfied with one job after another, no matter how well they went or where they happened to be located. I left most of my positions because I felt I *had to*, not because I really *needed to.* More often than not, in fact, the upper administrators to whom I reported had done their best to persuade me to stay on. Recalling that I left most of my posts feeling that I literally *had to move on* was what I found most disturbing. There was no way that kind of behavior could be described as rational or reasonable, not by any stretch of the imagination. There was no doubt about it; my career strategy had clearly run amuck.

7

MY OWN PROFESSIONAL NIRVANA

OVERNIGHT IT HAD BECOME clear not only that a change of course was necessary for us but also that it ought to be made as quickly as possible and from the top to the bottom.

I didn't need to talk with a shrink to know the possibility of an emotional collapse was staring me in the face. *How in the world had I managed to transform myself from the confident, happily married professional person I used to be into the troubled drone I had become?* Not only had I put in jeopardy the wonderful relationship we had enjoyed for over thirty years, I had also moved only a hair's breadth away from ruining what I had always thought to be an excellent academic career.

HANGING ON BY A THREAD

THE PRESSURE ON ME became even more pronounced when dealing with the kinds of prickly situations and aggravating difficulties that are part and parcel of any administrative position continued to become more difficult. My long-standing habit of immediately tackling work-related problems had flown out of the window, to the extent that I began to avoid or put off any duty that might further upset me.

Even though my professional and personal worlds were in turmoil, I tried to keep up a positive front and behave as if they were under control. If anyone had asked about my state of mind at the time, I'd have answered in the same way as the cool dude in the beer commercial who says with smug satisfaction that "Life can't get any better than this," when, really, it was all a sham.

MY UNUSUAL SEARCH FOR A WAY OUT BEGAN

BECAUSE MY STANDING PRACTICE had always been to turn to library research when I had a serious problem to deal with, that's what I did in this instance as well. I continued to immerse myself in self-help books that promised insights of benefit to those who wanted to deal with their psychological problems on their own. Before long, a few authors captured my attention so completely that I became obsessed by what they had to say.

The writers whose work I turned to were specialists who had seriously studied the kind of problems I was experiencing at the time. As mental health experts, they placed a lot of blame on what they referred to as "over-adaptation to work, of striving so hard to be successful in a demanding occupation that fundamental human needs end up being dangerously sublimated. This is a phenomenon," they declared, "that can cause feelings of guilt or self-betrayal — even anger — due to trading off too much to achieve career success." *Oh hell yeah,* I remember thinking to myself at the time; *that sounds exactly like what I might have done,* so I dug into this line of thinking more deeply.

"This is a condition," one of them wrote, "that is not always visible on the outside, but it is one that is nevertheless serious and real because inner conflict can be caused by the values, roles, and behaviors that are voluntarily taken on in order to succeed. One consequence of falling into such a state," several of these writers pointed out, "is that making too many small compromises in order to fit into an organizational niche may lead to feelings of guilt or emptiness that can cause depression, anxiety, and even rage — even in a person who appears to be a highly successful professional."

Wow, I exclaimed to myself as I read those words. *The man is talking about me, not about clinical case studies that have no bearing on what I'm experiencing right now.*

In the end, though, unfortunately for me, the only help I got out of my self-help reading was the discovery of a series of painfully accurate theories that helped describe many of the problems I was having; I did not find any usable solutions.

After calming down a bit, what I chose to do as a means of getting us out of trouble would have come as no surprise to anyone who knew of my past behavior. Even though I was burdened with gnawing guilt over having discovered that I had unintentionally become an aimless academic gypsy, I opted to use the means of getting us out of trouble I knew the best: As incredible as it may sound, I resolved to make *yet another move.* It was hard to justify this time around, given what I had learned about myself, but I decided to go that route, anyway. Flight, my decision made clear, remained my solution of choice for every major problem.

I knew my next move had to be different from all the others I'd made. First, I intended for it to be my last; second, it was to be made without any thought of career advancement or achievement. We needed a fresh start in a new setting, but I was determined to make sure this move would be to a location where both of us would be happy to put down permanent roots. If such a place existed, I intended to find it. It was with this resolution firmly in mind that I launched my last professional search, this time to what I intended to be the last job I would ever occupy.

A MOVE TO END ALL MOVES

MY TAKE ON OUR situation was in some ways akin to Neville Chamberlain's view of the international situation before World War II broke out in Europe; our move was to be a move to end all moves, a change that would not only solve my immediate problems but that would also restore us for the future. There were no Nazis nipping at my heels like there were for Neville, but there may as well have been, given the way I felt at the time.

Having settled on a course of action was enormously

relieving, even though the only determination I had made as of this point was just that we were going to move to a place where we could be content to actually settle down and stay. Come hell or high water, I intended to stay there forever, even if my new job bombed out miserably and I ended up having to pump gas or sweep floors for a living. Both of us were sick of moving.

I wanted to find a location where we could recover, an environment that would aid and abet our own rejuvenation as a couple. To restore the sense of connection and rootedness we had known during our early years together, it seemed critical to reestablish our connection to the kinds of intangibles I had ridiculed and rejected as if they didn't matter a whit. In my view, we needed to reconnect with the very kind of community involvements and attachments I had for so many years endeavored to minimize or totally ignore.

GETTING DOWN TO SPECIFICS

WITH THE AFOREMENTIONED RESOLUTIONS firmly in mind, I shifted my focus to identifying *where* we might resettle, a decision that wasn't the least bit easy to make at the time. Why? Well, because all of my former ties had been severed, and it was as real as a heart attack that there was no place in the country I genuinely thought of as *home*. The fact that so much was riding on the outcome of the decision — my own emotional stability, the salvation of my career, and our future happiness as husband and wife — made it enormously difficult. If this really was to be a move to end all moves, my search had to be conducted as carefully and as thoughtfully as possible.

My credentials as well as the academic job market were still strong at the time, so I was confident that I would be able to find what I was after.

Was the frenetic way in which I conducted my search yet another indicator of how close I was to losing control altogether at the time? *What I did* during the process wasn't so unusual, but *the way I did it* definitely was. For one thing, I felt an overwhelming compulsion to research not only the background of any institution that had an opening in my field of expertise but also the history of the state, vicinity, county, city, and even the neighborhood in which it was located.

Because I no longer felt proud of my own employment history, I made a subconscious determination to associate myself with an employer and a location that had histories I could identify with and be proud of. I intended to expropriate the history of my new employer as well as the area in which it was located as my own, without fully understanding what I was doing or why I wanted to do it. Basically, I was looking for a new sense of purpose and place. My goal, it would be correct to say, was to create a new definition of *home*, and, despite the fact that my search was conducted while I was somewhat detached from reality, I eventually found just the kind of place I was looking for.

TEXAS AS A STATE OF MIND

AFTER A PERIOD OF intense and careful deliberation, I decided to limit my search to colleges in the state of Texas — to schools *out in the heartland*, as I saw it, as far away from big city life as it was possibly to get. Employment by a small college in a small town, it seemed to me, would be the best environment in which to bring about the new approach to life and work I thought Candy and I desperately needed. In that kind of setting, I was convinced, I would find my own Walden Pond, my own professional Nirvana.

So, from then on, whenever an administrative opening at a small college in rural Texas appeared in *The Chronicle of Higher Education,* I checked it out in great detail.

Why, of all places, Texas, one might reasonably ask? I asked myself the same thing, in fact, not once but a great many times as my search was under way. The answer, I suppose, comes down to my belief that I needed to bring about a change of image, a complete change of personal style — to adopt a pose I truly respected, an attitude I wanted to assume, a way of life I wanted to live, and a set of values that stood for something solid. Our new location had to *feel* as well as *look* different from anything we had experienced in the past. If the move was to mark the beginning of a fresh new approach to life, then it had to be made for a job in an environment that would be new and special for us. Because it really was true that there was no place I thought of as home, I wanted to identify a new location that would serve us just as well.

Texas had long seemed attractive as a place in which to live and work, mainly because I so strongly identified with its lore and uniquely individualistic mystique. During trips to various cities around the state to attend work-related conferences over the years, I had been struck by the wide-open feel of the land and sky outside the larger urban areas. Driving through these spaces created a sense of peace I felt nowhere else. Lots of good academic opportunities were available there too, due to rapid population growth and the consequent expansion of educational institutions that had been taking place there for a number of years.

To my way of thinking, Texas was a state that could be accurately described as offering enough different living styles and settings to satisfy any taste. Through my past travels, I knew about the sandy beaches of the Padre Islands, the valleys in the Guadalupe Mountains, the California- and Florida-like citrus groves of the lower Rio Grande Valley, the bay at Corpus Christi, and the pine forest area of the eastern part of the state. I also knew about the wilderness area known as *The Big Thicket* that had been set aside as a refuge for migratory birds and other animals, and I had visited many cities within the state. I liked what I had seen.

Most appealing to me were the seemingly endless miles of open rolling prairie I traveled through during some of my visits. Large areas of the countryside had been lit up by bluebonnets as captivatingly beautiful as they surely must have seemed to the state's early settlers. The sense of openness I had felt made me feel free and unencumbered, and it was that kind of feeling I hoped to capture through our relocation.

It seems fitting, I thought as my search went on, *that*

monuments had been constructed at places like the Presidio at La Bahia, the Battlefield at San Jacinto, and the Alamo in San Antonio, because those places really did serve as great reminders of the state's unique and inspirational history.

I had long been captivated by the history of Texas and the way it became a state of the Union. It was inspiring, for example, to read the stories of the battles of San Jacinto, Goliad, and the Alamo, the results of which were the establishment of first a Texas Republic, a political entity that was recognized for ten years as an independent nation by the United States and by such major governments in Europe as England, Holland, and France, before it finally gained statehood. The thought of associating myself with a state that unabashedly celebrated an inspirational history of this kind was grounding and reassuring as well as immensely appealing.

Rural Texas, in particular, had a definite mystique for me. The idea of living there was as alluring as it has been to many other seekers of peace, escape, refuge, and, above all, a sense of personal space and privacy through the years. To me, the state represented more than a physical place; it represented a set of values and a state of mind I wanted to assume as part of my strategy for getting our home life back in order. Texas was more than just a state I wanted to live in; it stood for the way I wanted to redefine myself at the time. I didn't say anything to anyone, not even Candy, about what I was thinking, but thoughts of this kind were the driving forces behind my effort to relocate.

Week after week I watched for openings at small colleges in rural towns, the kind of environment I had identified as being suitable for effectively tackling the kind of problems that had come to dominate my professional life as well as my relationship with Candy. I knew from past experience that she would not object to any location I settled on, since she would accept on faith my word that my range of choice would be limited by the availability of suitable employment.

BEFORE THE ACADEMIC YEAR was over, the right job opened up at just the sort of college and in just the kind of setting I envisioned for us. Immediately after seeing the announcement, I launched an intensive investigation of the institution as well as the area in which it was located. It seemed vitally important for me to learn as much about the place as I could, since so much was riding on what would happen if I went there.

The employer I targeted was Weatherford College, an institution located in the Parker County city of Weatherford, just off Interstate Highway 20, about thirty miles west of what everyone in the area referred to as *the Dallas–Fort Worth Metroplex.* It was a comprehensive community college, an institution accredited by the Commission on Colleges of the Southern Colleges and Schools Association, or SACS, and the Texas Higher Education Coordinating Board to offer two-year associate degree programs, and the history of the school and the area around and about it was just as fascinating as I willed it to be. It was at this point that my obsession with all aspects of institutional, city, county, and state history took center stage.

Parker County, in which the City of Weatherford and Weatherford College are located, as it turned out, was a sparsely populated area of the state surrounded by miles of green grass prairie and low rolling hills — 426 square miles of it, to be exact. It was created in 1885 by a special act of the Texas legislature, and it is in an area "that looks," as city fathers and other promoters of the wider area said in their online promotional literature, "the way Texas is supposed to look."

Many other attributes of the city and county seemed equally attractive, notably some of the local historical facts I read. As examples, it turned out that the graves of Oliver Loving, a pioneer cattle drover, and Charles Goodnight, another local cattleman, were located there. Texas author Larry McMurtry, who was hot back then, derived settings for books such as *Hud* and *The Last Picture Show* from the general area. I also learned that numerous homes and other historical sites around there were old-timey enough to draw in thousands of visitors year after year. The bed and breakfast business, I discovered, was well established in Weatherford and surrounding towns.

Weatherford was also the birthplace and hometown of Broadway star Mary Martin, whose son Larry Hagman achieved so much public acclaim due to his starring role in the television program *Dallas*. Weatherford, it seemed to me, was a city that had a fascinating history.

Enrollment at Weatherford College, as I knew would be the case, was primarily local, consisting mainly of students who were there to complete two years of general education coursework before transferring upward to complete bachelor's degree programs at regional senior colleges, to earn two-year degrees or certificates in various occupation fields, or to qualify for entry-level employment or advancement opportunities at their present places of work. Yet another large group of students attended solely for purposes of personal fulfillment and self-enrichment. Basically, the college was just what I thought it would be — an institution designed for the specific purpose of delivering flexible, affordable, community-based educational offerings to local people.

My interest in the college was captivated from the first day I began to research it with the thought of applying for an administrative opening they had open at the time. What I found impressive was that those who had managed the institution in the past had a fascinating early history of having struggled not just to *serve*, but to *survive*. From the first day the college came into being, its path was never easy.

It was started after the Civil War, back when settlers were flooding into the state and towns were in competition with one another to establish institutions similar to those the new arrivals had enjoyed in their home states back east. In those early days, getting a new school online was not something that could be taken for granted.

The institution was born in March of 1869 when forward-thinking brothers of a local Masonic organization, Phoenix Lodge

Number 275, decided to extend the availability of educational opportunities in Weatherford through the construction of a Masonic Institute. They had in mind an entity that would do double duty as a lodge meeting place and as a public high school.

The cornerstone of their new lodge and school was laid on July 5, 1869, but their plans were set back when construction costs unexpectedly jumped so high that those who supported the effort were unable to meet their pledges of financial support. Construction had to be put on hold until the property could be sold to a single well-heeled member, a man who then promptly refinanced the loan back to his own lodge. Eventually, the building was completed and a school was finally opened for business. The first graduating class consisted of six students, whose diplomas were received on June 15 of 1876.

In 1884, the name of the school was changed to Cleveland College in honor of Grover Cleveland, the first Democrat elected president after the end of the Civil War. It operated for a decade under the new name, offering classes that ranged from grade school level through the senior year of college and maintaining an average yearly enrollment of around 300 students.

In June of 1889, the Masons sold the school to the Weatherford District of the Methodist Episcopal Church (South). From that time up until the early 1900s, the college struggled through a series of changes of ownership, name, and oversight as it tried to maintain a place in the community. Enrollment continued to decline for several years after the turn of the century, until by 1912 the size of the graduating class was only ten students. Such low enrollment forced the college's board of trustees to close the institution down on multiple occasions; from 1903 to 1921, for example, it operated only intermittently.

After a closure that lasted from 1912 until 1915, the school was reopened once again. Even though the college had changed ownership several times and had teetered on the brink of financial collapse, when it got back underway its future seemed much more certain. What happened is that plans had been put in place to reorganize the school as a private junior college, a new kind of institution designed to offer college courses leading to two-year Associate of Arts degree programs in addition to courses required for a high school diploma.

It was when the institution was officially reorganized as a publicly funded junior college in 1921 that Weatherford Junior College was first accredited by the Texas Association of Colleges. It acquired a sound financial foundation at this time as well, largely through grants from the estates of two prosperous citizens of the City of Weatherford, J. R. Couts and Edward D. Farmer.

After enrollment dropped yet again during World War II, the college was forced to accept a 1944 merger proposal submitted by Southwestern University of Georgetown, Texas. After the merger, the name of the institution was changed once again, this time to Weatherford College of Southwestern University.

This relationship lasted until 1949, when Southwestern's board of trustees notified the City of Weatherford and Parker County that they could no longer afford to continue to operate Weatherford College and asked the city or county to accept ownership. The City of Weatherford and Parker County took over at that point so that public junior college operations could be continued, and the university continued to manage and operate the college as a branch institution.

When it was determined that the City of Weatherford did not have the financial ability to support the college, the Parker County Commissioners Court called a special election to create a public junior college district. Southwestern University transferred ownership of the college to the county when voters approved the new district by a margin of nearly three to one. At this point, the school officially became Weatherford College of the Parker County Junior College District. It opened for its first session under the new name in September of 1949.

When enrollment increased between 1950 and 1965 and attempts to purchase additional property surrounding the college were unsuccessful, the Board of Trustees of the new college district called for yet another special election — this time to seek approval of issuing general obligation bonds for the purpose of purchasing additional land and constructing the necessary buildings for a new campus. When the bond issue passed in 1966, a ninety-acre site in the southeastern part of the city was bought for the new campus they had in mind. Construction began in 1967, and the campus I was researching as a possible place of employment had opened in the fall of 1968.

The college continued to expand during the late sixties and early seventies. When Fort Wolters, a local military base located on the eastern edge of the town of Mineral Wells in the college's jurisdiction, was closed down in 1974, the site was acquired as a facility for the college's first off-campus Education Center. Eventually, the reach of the campus was further expanded, this time through creating out–of–district centers at public school facilities in sparsely populated neighboring Wise, Jack, Palo Pinto, and Erath counties. By the mid-1980s, additional extension centers were added in the towns of Bridgeport, Granbury, and Jacksboro. On top of all this, the college also bought a 300-acre farm near the main campus in Weatherford as a site for instruction in the field of agriculture.

By November of 1992, Weatherford College employed 105 full-time faculty members, a large number of adjuncts, and had a regular enrollment of around 2,200 students each semester. In addition, the college drew in a summer enrollment of over 1,300 students and over 800 enrollments in continuing education courses. Even then, enrollment continued to grow. For a college in a sparsely populated rural area, these were respectable numbers.

As enrollment grew, more sites and buildings and programs were added over the years to meet the demand. A state–of–the–art fine arts center was opened in April of 1998, featuring classroom, performance, and exhibition spaces as well as a state–of–the–art performance hall with comfortable seating, a professional recording studio, a fully appointed art wing, and an exhibition space. A new technology building was added as well, a building equipped with computer laboratories and workstations, classrooms, a lecture hall, and space for the college's distance education facility.

By forming a partnering Economic Development Corporation in the nearby town of Decatur, yet another extension center was opened, this time to meet the needs of residents in nearby Wise County. Ultimately, the college ended up opening even more extension centers, new ones in the local communities of Aledo, Alvord, Azle, Bridgeport, Coleman, Decatur, Gordon, Granbury, Jacksboro, Tolar, and Lipan.

THROWING MY HAT IN THE RING

WOW, I REMEMBER THINKING as I completed my research prior to applying the administrative opening at the college, *what an amazing record of effort to serve in the face of such a long series of down and dirty challenges*. What was not to be respected about the gritty determination to succeed against the odds that had been exhibited by former administrators and board members and community leaders? Without a doubt, the institution had a record of struggling to serve that most any educator would have found impressive, which was just the kind of history I wanted my new employer to have.

Having learned that the college as well as the general area in which it was located also had histories more than intriguing enough to exceed my hopes and expectations, I eagerly threw my application for their administrative opening into the hat. I was truly delighted when, several months later, an invitation to interview for the position arrived at our home. I showed up for it fully informed, wearing my game face, intent on putting my best foot forward. I wanted that job so much I could taste it. The interview went off without a hitch, but, of course, nothing was said to me at the moment.

While I was in the area before and after my interview, I used some of my accumulated vacation time to explore the area in greater detail before heading back home. Thrilled and excited by everything I saw, I would have agreed to any reasonable terms to land their opening. When a job offer was extended a short while later, I literally jumped at the opportunity, accepting it immediately and without reservations or pre-conditions of any kind.

I felt enormously relieved when the deal was clinched and the position was finally mine, and I felt honored to have been offered an opportunity to play a small role in the many good results I knew the college was certain to accomplish in the years to come. Absolutely convinced that the new job and job setting would lead to a much better life for Candy and me, I was confident that that the college would be the last fresh start of my professional life.

WEATHERFORD COLLEGE

I REPORTED FOR WORK for the Fall term of the 1999–2000 academic year, eager and excited about tearing into my new assignment. There was nothing extraordinary about the main campus of the institution where my office was located, but the place had a western, down-home feel I found highly appealing. It was situated in an especially pleasant and attractive location on the outskirts of town, tucked in among the kind of low rolling hills that are common in that part of north central Texas. The campus consisted of sixteen buildings, one of them the administrative complex in which I was housed. The workspace assigned to me was good-sized, light, open, comfortable, and well-equipped.

The campus also had a student center that included a bookstore, cafeteria, and meeting areas; an appropriately equipped technology building; a fine arts center; an athletic center; a student services building to house our advisement, counseling, housing, financial aid, career center, continuing education, and other student resource programs; a centrally located library; a faculty office building; and a business building that also housed an advanced manufacturing laboratory. Other buildings on campus housed programs in agriculture, the natural and physical sciences, liberal arts, and allied health. I became a regular user of our physical activity facilities, which included indoor and outdoor basketball courts, heated indoor and outdoor swimming pools, a volleyball sand pit, a weight room, and lighted tennis courts.

It was satisfying to observe that college and community leaders alike had firmly (and, I thought, wisely) committed to promoting the western heritage of the area, which was, as would be imagined, exactly the kind of thing I came in wanting to see and hear. It was around this particular theme, in fact, that many solid town and gown partnerships had been founded over the years.

Agriculture and ranching were major activities in the area, which meant that our ranch management and animal husbandry were popular majors on campus. Western activities such as rodeos, horse shows, roping events, fairs, and related kinds of events were much enjoyed by students and local resident alike. Western dress was commonplace among students and faculty, as well as in the larger community. Equestrian and rodeo competition were among the most popular student activities on campus.

To meet all of these student needs, our main campus employed a staff of seventy full-time faculty members and a large and constantly fluctuating cadre of adjunct instructors. An appropriate number of support and administrative staffers were in place to back up the faculty, and I was one of those administrators — the Division Dean for Business and Social Science programs, to be specific.

By the time I arrived on the scene, our annual enrollment was 5,500 students, mostly for college credit instruction. In some semesters, we enrolled students from as many as sixty-seven Texas counties, fifteen states, and twenty-three foreign countries. Our student to faculty ratio was around eighteen to one, and the ratio of male to female students was about four to six.

It is no exaggeration to say that our college was a place where faculty members and administrators were devoted to the personal development of students, particularly those who needed a bit of extra help to succeed. For those students, an extensive array of support services was made available to increase their odds of success, including a highly proactive advisement program, assistance in becoming part of the academic and social life of the college, counseling assistance for setting personal, career, and academic goals, and effective procedures for securing financial aid. In and out of the classroom, our staff put forth great effort to support and encourage even the most uncertain and undirected of students. We did whatever we could to help them succeed.

Weatherford College turned out to be a great place to work, and I was as pleased as punch to be on the staff. I considered it an honor to be employed by an institution that had been and would continue to be such a tremendous asset to the community it served. I strongly identified with the up–by–the–bootstraps history of the place, especially when it came to the struggle to sustain the institution during difficult times. I truly wanted to help our college grow and prosper, admittedly for reasons that were to a large degree self-focused on my part, since, from that point forward, the success of the institution would be my success as well. In short, being on board created the sense of purpose and place I had wanted for a long time. I'd be the first to admit that I needed the college far more than it ever needed me.

As proud as I was to play a role in all the good work that was being done by our institution, there were times when the administrative job I held down really got to be a handful, mainly due to the wide array of courses and programs we had to offer. On top of that, we offered courses not only on the traditional academic calendar but also on weekends, at night, online via the Internet, by two-way video via the Virtual College of Texas, and in a concentrated *mini-semester* format. We did whatever we could to accommodate the varying work schedules of our students. My division was also intensively involved in providing courses and other kinds of support for the many educational centers the college sponsored at off-campus locations. There were times when I became so wrapped in the administrative work required to deliver our offerings, I didn't know whether I was coming or going.

As one senior faculty member jokingly put it shortly after I arrived, "Potential students can run from us, but they can never hide; if we don't get them one way, we'll damned sure get them another." It wasn't long before I discovered that the old professor wasn't far from wrong. On a practical level, what his statement meant for me personally was that I had to wear a lot of different hats and work on many more weekends and evenings than in the past. Even though I was a company man and a true believer, there were times when my job was truly wearing. The college got its pound of flesh out of me, that's for sure. Be that as it may, my work was just as worthwhile as I thought it should be, and I was doing it in exactly the kind of setting I wanted to be doing it in.

GRANBURY-MAYBERRY

I VISITED THE TOWN of Granbury for the first time when I drove about Parker and Hood counties while I was in the area for my job interview at Weatherford College. The town had a remarkable, impressive, inspirational story of its own, one that added greatly to the attractiveness of the area as the kind of place I had envisioned for us. It represented the West just way I wanted it to be, the way I wanted *us* to be — gritty and rugged and determined. It had grown from a small, private business venture centered on a simple, natural prairie springs and watering hole to the attractive place it was at the time.

Through further reading and study before accepting my job at the college, I learned that agriculture — not cattle ranching, as I had imagined — had been the leading industry around Granbury and, in fact, in all of Hood County back in the early days, and that cotton had been the leading crop. Later on, the county had also become known for pecan production, especially for the overall quality of the annual harvest. Even today, Hood is still one of the larger pecan-producing counties in the state of Texas.

The home we bought was in a development located in the middle of one of those commercial orchards, and it, too, wouldn't you know it, was a place that had a captivating story behind it. In the same way as our county and city, it had come into being only after yet another gritty but fascinating series of events.

The story of the town began with a dramatic economic decline that nearly brought about the end of the Granbury area and, for that matter, nearly all of Hood County during the late 20s and early 30s as a viable place to live. These, of course, were the years of the Great Depression, a period of economic downturn that devastated Granbury and Weatherford in the same way that it had many other areas of the country as well.

When both of the local colleges failed and had to be closed down, young people were forced to move away for access to educational opportunity and, at the end of their college training, for proximity to employment. By the early 1960s, Granbury had all but become a ghost town, and nearby Weatherford hadn't fared much better. With the failure of the agricultural economy, the loss of its educational institutions, and the lack of business or industrial employment opportunities, more and more people had to move to larger cities to find work. As this trend continued, many buildings in the two towns fell into a state of dilapidation and disrepair. Both places looked to be right on the verge of drying up and blowing away.

Then, just when local prospects looked darkest from an economic standpoint, the DeCordova Bend Dam was constructed on the Brazos River during the late 1960s. The dam created Lake Granbury, which, in turn, enabled the construction of the Comanche Peak Nuclear Power plant at a site located just a few miles outside of town. When these changes occurred, Granbury entered yet another significant period of transformation, one that everyone described as a significant revival of the local economy.

What began to take place at that point was a gradual but continuing movement of people from the Dallas–Arlington–Fort Worth metroplex back to rural Granbury. Once again, the area had come to be viewed as an attractive place in which to live. Retirees, in particular, were among the first to be drawn in, attracted by low tax rates, a quiet and slower way of life, and, above all, relatively low land and property prices.

Before long, working couples started to move to the area as well, in their case for an opportunity to live a tranquil country lifestyle and to send their children to schools that had few of the big city problems they were worried about. For many, commuting back and forth between Granbury and the metroplex to work became a normal part of their daily life.

It was due to this change of fortune that restoration and redevelopment of the old downtown area and historic square got underway in Granbury. Many of the old buildings and homes that were still standing and that had local historical significance were bought up and then lovingly restored by entrepreneurs, preservationists, and various categories of retirees. Real estate developers and other booster-type professionals soon got into the spirit of change, and before long the economy of the area was significantly revived. Since that time, more and more people moved into the area, to the point that gentrification and yuppification are now well-established facts of life in Granbury and Hood County.

In the way that a drab caterpillar gradually turns into a colorful butterfly, Granbury eventually evolved into a picturesque town situated on the shores of a new lake, the body of water that had been created by the construction of the dam on the Brazos River. The town encompassed an area of 4.5 square miles and had a population of over 11,000 citizens when we moved there, and many more lived just outside the city limits in rural parts of the county. The old town square became a popular tourist attraction, a place where country inns did quite well for themselves by catering to weekenders out of Dallas, Fort Worth, and Arlington. Due to the rustic atmosphere that was present in abundance at Granbury, the whole town became a great draw for family-oriented Texans

Over time, additional attractions had sprung up to draw in even more people, businesses such as miniature golf courses, batting cages, an old-fashioned drive-in movie theater, a playhouse, antique shops and boutiques, consignment shops, ice cream parlors, and boating, swimming, water skiing and fishing operations. One enterprising entrepreneur started offering scenic dinner cruises on a paddle-wheeler on Lake Granbury, and others opened retail shops offering items ranging from antique furniture to gourmet coffees and foods. The area also became a popular getaway location for golfers, partially due to weather that permits nearly year-round play. Near this one small town, there are five public and four private golf courses.

Granbury gradually eventually came to exemplify what could be called Texas style down home country charm. That's what attracts most people to the town, and it was definitely what attracted Candy and me. It was the ambience of the place we were after, as intangible as that might be. We loved the town from the first time we saw it.

I was so completely captivated by the lore and legend that made up the histories of the towns of Granbury and Weatherford, Weatherford College, and Parker and Hood Counties that I couldn't imagine more storied and interesting surroundings in which to live and work. The histories of these places represented the west the way I wanted it to be, and they offered the kind of environment I had hoped to find.

Was I guilty of romanticizing what I saw? Sure, but that was exactly what I wanted to do at the time; I needed *a place to believe in*, much more than I needed *a place to live*. In the way of a history buff who goes in search of heroic figures he knows are out there, I found just what I wanted to find.

Whether it was fuzzy-headed or not, this was the kind of thinking that clinched my decision to accept the job at Weatherford College as well as our choice of Granbury as a place to live. There wasn't a doubt in my mind that I'd found exactly what I had been looking for, and I was so happy to be able to move out there that I felt like waltzing on the town square.

OUR HOME AMONG THE PECANS

THE HOME WE BOUGHT on the outskirts of Granbury in July of 1999 just before my first year of employment by Weatherford College was in a private development fittingly named Pecan Plantation, due to its location among and beside one of the best known and most successful commercial pecan orchards in Hood County. In keeping with the fascinating histories of Hood County, the towns of Weatherford and Granbury, and the college by which I had just been employed, our upscale residential subdivision had a uniquely fascinating history of its own.

The residential development is located right in the middle of a farming operation called Leonard Farms, which is a 4,700-acre privately owned working pecan orchard located just southeast of Granbury. The development grew in prominence over the years, as more and more people were attracted to the peace and privacy of its beautiful setting within the farm on a seventeen-mile green-bordered loop of the slow-moving, tranquil, picturesque Brazos River.

People from the nearby Metroplex gradually evolved into the habit of visiting the area before the Thanksgiving and Christmas holidays, just to take advantage of the quality of the annual pecan crop, which was considered one of the best in the area. For some, making a seasonal pilgrimage out to Granbury to buy fresh pecans for holiday baking, pies, and gifts became a not–to–be–missed occasion, and the company store built up quite a loyal following over the years. The store became so successful, in fact, that it ended up creating its own website, *www.leonardfarmspecanstore.com.* Visitors and locals alike used it to mail seasonal gift packages from the shop to family members, friends, and relatives around the country.

Predictably, all this activity caused enterprising individuals to take notice of how much public interest the area was drawing. Among the earliest of those who saw commercial potential was a man by the name of Jim Anthony, who bought a large tract of prime but then still fairly inexpensive orchard land along the river. Shortly thereafter, he converted these acres of what until then had been mature pecan orchard land into a development of estate– and traditional–sized lots he made available for sale as home sites. From this quiet beginning, the beautiful country club residential community known as Pecan Plantation — or simply *Pecan*, as the locals call it — grew into being. Geographically speaking, it is located within commuting distance, about thirty-five miles, southwest of the edge of the Metroplex, and about eight miles southeast of Granbury proper.

As time passed, more and more features were added to the

development, until, finally, it could boast of having a wide enough range of living arrangements and amenities to appeal to the tastes, interests, or needs of most any potential investor. Buying in required adherence to a set of rigorously enforced deed restrictions that had been designed to protect the interests of property owners, but a quick overview will confirm that the developer's boasting was truthful, not just trade puffery.

Pecan is a gated community. Around the clock security was provided for residents who want privacy, safety, and protection of themselves and their physical property. Easy access to Lake Granbury and as well as to the town square is available through manned front and back gates. Excellent facilities for golfing, swimming, exercising, and white tablecloth dining are available at the country club, where attractive and reasonably priced guest rooms and conference facilities can be booked for private events such as weddings, anniversaries, business events, golf tournaments, etc.

The Orchard, a separate area within the overall development, is a 2,300-acre development of estate-sized lots under the pecan trees where horses are permitted and miles of riding trails are available, along with boarding facilities and a private equestrian center. The Retreat, another area of even larger and more beautiful estate size properties located in the orchard but nearer to the Brazos River, boasted of *elbow room galore for families that want their own personal space.*

The needs and interests of aircraft owners — serious commuters as well as hobbyists — are met by yet another area of the development, a unique selection of home sites that have direct access to a 3,600-foot lighted and paved runway. Supported by a private fuel station, homes in this area back up to the landing strip, and many of them come with hangers for private planes. A good number of these homes have been bought by working pilots who fly from Pecan daily to their employment at the Dallas–Fort Worth International Airport.

Yet another separate area of home sites at Pecan, The Estates, offers smaller lots for those who prefer patio homes that require little upkeep and convenient access to the golf course. For those who want even less to take care of, reasonably priced condominium units are available in another area of the development.

Two exceptionally well-maintained eighteen-hole championship golf courses snake through all of Pecan, one on each side of the development. The oldest and best known of the two courses is at the Pecan Plantation Country Club, a beautiful course that meanders through acres of trees and well-maintained homes. The club's facilities include a driving range, a pro shop, a snack bar, a white tablecloth dining room that offers a great Sunday brunch, a low-key but enforced dress code, twelve reservable guest rooms for visitors, and catering services with conference facilities for group activities.

Adjacent to the clubhouse are five lighted tennis courts and a Texas-sized swimming pool that holds 195,000 gallons of water and offers pool-side snacks and drinks. Lifeguards are on duty during summer months when the pool in operation. The second of the two private golf clubs, The Nutcracker, is located in the middle of another area of mature pecan trees. This club offers a snack bar and a complete health club, another highly popular residential amenity. Golf course lots, as one might well imagine, are a major drawing card at Pecan.

Among the other facilities in the development are a marina on Lake Granbury equipped with full boat launching facilities and stocked, as would be imagined, with gas, picnic supplies, basic food and beverages, fishing supplies, and a sandwich grill for casual lakeside dining; skeet and trap shooting ranges; and four attractively maintained beach and park areas along the stretch of the Brazos River that encircles the development, each park equipped with picnic tables, barbecue grills, playgrounds, and restrooms. Campsites are available for anything from tents to motor homes, and all of them are equipped with electric and water hookups, dump stations, restrooms, and showers. Wild deer and turkey are not an uncommon sight at these locations.

To help residents make the most of all these great facilities, a large number of clubs and other activities organized by members of the development are readily available. Golf and tennis tournaments, for example, are common, as are many different kinds of social organizations. Corporate and other group tournaments of various kinds have become well-established annual events.

All in all, there really isn't much to dislike about Pecan Plantation as a place to live, other than its distance from the Dallas-Arlington-Fort Worth metroplex. People bought homes there because it offered quiet country living in the midst of wide-open spaces, just the kind of setting I thought would enable Candy and me to get our lives back in order. I fell in love with the development during my first visit there, and, when I returned with Candy for a second tour in advance of accepting my position at the college, she was taken by it as well. We were as pleased as punch to have an opportunity to move there.

OUR DOWN-HOME LIFE BEGINS

IN WAS IN THE way that has been described that on July 15, 1999, during the twenty-ninth year of our marriage, Candy and I officially became Texans and residents of the gated golf course development known as Pecan Plantation and our down-home life began. For the first time in a long time, a positive future seemed to be in the offing for us.

The house we bought was one of the oldest and most run-down places in the development, but, again, we thought it had real prospects. It's a good thing that we felt that way, since it was about the only place at Pecan we could afford on my salary as an educator. Our closest neighbors, John and Eva Janssen, who were secure in their own prosperous retirement, looked down their noses at what we were doing. They would have liked nothing better than to have seen the old eyesore of a house we planned to restore torn down, just so it wouldn't detract from their own beautiful home.

The home had endured many years of neglect at the hands of its previous owner, an elderly widow who lived alone in it for most of her senior years and then let it run down before she passed away. She'd lived there, in fact, for over ten years with her *family* of two large dogs, without putting any more time or money into maintenance or routine upkeep than was absolutely essential.

It was depressing, in fact, to move into such a dilapidated and smelly old house after the string of nice homes we had owned in the past, but, after we got moved in, we tore into its restoration with a vengeance. In all honesty, restoring the place was not an optional undertaking; most of the work we did was absolutely essential, just to make it habitable.

In my case, I was so motivated by our shared vision of what the home could be made into that I approached my work with abandon, slinging around lumber, nails, caulk, paint, wiring, roofing, landscaping, and all the rest of it as if I were a seasoned professional. The project required so much hard, hot, dirty, and tiring work that it ended up becoming an integral part of my evenings and weekends for quite some time thereafter.

As far as I was concerned, we were doing much more than restoring an old house; we were restoring *us*. Each problem solved and upgrade made was immediately apparent, and I found it immensely satisfying to be able to see the tangible results of our own hard labor.

Candy approached her interior design and remodeling responsibilities with an equal level of diligence. We differed and argued over her selections of colors and styles for all kinds of interior items, from paint colors to the carpeting and draperies and blinds that were installed. Knowing that I couldn't visualize end results as well as she could, she won most of these arguments, usually leaving me grumbling about but still accepting the choices she made.

Fortunately, though, Candy's interior finishing turned out much nicer than we had dared to hope. While the finished restoration wasn't a Taj Mahal, everyone who looked at the results we wrought said that we had done a wonderful job. In short order, we began to think of it as our delightful sanctuary under the pecans.

OUR NEWLY RESTORED HOME was located right in the heart of the geographical area in Texas where the Comanche Indians (including the renowned Quanah Parker) and their raiders used to operate out of when they committed depredations against early Anglo and Spanish settlers. One of the most prominent landmarks in the region is the flattop mountain known as Comanche Peak, which was once used as a rallying point by their raiders, including Quanah and his band.

Even though the famous peak still stands out as a highly visible landmark, today it is known more for its proximity to the ultra-modern nuclear power plant that was named after it or for the new ranch-style house development that is being built around it than for anything of an historical nature. The nuclear power plant, which sits near a new development of estate-sized plots that are being gobbled up by well-off modern settlers from the metroplex, is one of Hood County's most notable employers. Even the famous peak itself, the Indians' rallying point, is being commercially developed. Chief Parker, I'd be willing to wager, would roll over in his grave if he could see the goings-on taking place today in his old stomping grounds.

Even with the additional development, there were still only around 21,000 households and a little over 58,000 people living in Hood County, which made it more sparsely populated than any place we had lived in the past. Because some seventy-five percent of the households in the county were located outside the limits of any incorporated city, the whole area is more or less dominated by a rural way of life. From my perspective, I'd gotten us as close to living a *down-home* lifestyle as any place we might have gone.

I sought out Hood County as a place to live for the same reasons as many infamous outlaws had in the days of the old west: I was a desperate man in search of a good place to start over. Jesse James was believed by some to be buried in a local cemetery, and some thought he'd lived out his life there in the same kind of peace and quiet people like me desired. If we had ever met face to face, I'm sure we would have understood one another quite well. In fact, our neighbors in the development would have been surprised to learn how much Jesse and I had in common.

The truth was that I had become just what Jesse and other outlaws had been in their own day and time: men with pasts they wanted nothing more than to forget. In the same way as the desperados of old, I thought of Hood County and the town of Granbury and, in our case but, of course, not theirs, the gated development of Pecan Plantation as a great place to begin anew, a setting where I could practice my trade and make an honest living as I lived out my final days in a quiet and peaceful environment. The outlaws found the place first; I merely followed in their footsteps.

Had a wanted poster like those that were circulated for Jesse and his kind back their day been written for me during this period of time, it would have to have been worded along the lines shown in the following poster.

An overstatement? Well, maybe . . . *but not by much!*

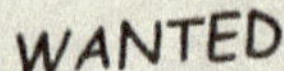

WANTED

PROFESSOR-ADMINISTRATOR
MIKE HOLDER

FOR CAUSING UNDESERVED EMOTIONAL AND PSYCHOLOGICAL DAMAGE TO HIS FRAGILE AND LOVING WIFE!

CAUTION!

Do not attempt to apprehend; suspect is confused and therefore extremely desperate. His anxiety level is more than high enough to make him harmful to unsuspecting members of the human race!

8

SETTLING IN FOR THE DURATION

WHEN ALL THE HARD work was completed and we finally got settled in our lovingly restored and beautiful new home, Candy seemed more at ease than she had been for years. At the same time, I, too, felt invigorated, mainly due to the relief of getting away from the pressure of my former position. The combination of my promising new job and the beauty of our new surroundings filled us with hope of a brighter and better future, and our prospects moving toward full recovery seemed be in the making. We were happier than we'd been since the early days of our marriage.

More than enough diversions and services were available at Pecan to meet our basic needs as well as to satisfy many of our personal interests. Contrary to our initial expectations, we began to make regular use of amenities we hadn't expected to utilize. The small library at the center of the second-floor guest rooms located above the main lobby and foyer across from the entrance of the clubhouse, for example, became one of my favorite places. It was well stocked with good novels, home improvement guides, and computer reference guides—just the kinds of books I wanted at the time.

We also appreciated the availability of the delicious take-out pizzas that were prepared from scratch by the dining room cook, especially when we had one on Friday evenings at the end of a busy work week. In addition, we found the Sunday morning brunch that was available in the formal dining room of the club to be so pleasant and the food so well prepared that it became a regular weekend stop for us. On weekdays while I was at work, Candy frequently went there alone, either for breakfast or for lunch.

Another highly welcomed benefit of living at Pecan was the friendliness and supportiveness of our neighbors, who proved to be warm and trusting as well as exceedingly helpful. Unexpectedly, we found ourselves surrounded by the friendly faces of people who understood the wisdom and value of building solid community relationships, even with neighbors who lived outside of their more intimate social circles.

Back when we were restoring our home, for example, one neighbor voluntarily helped me do the hard and dirty work of hauling away a huge stack of brush I had pruned from overgrown trees and bushes on our lot, another brought over hot soup for dinner at the end of a long workday, and yet another helped me adjust and remount some interior doors that wouldn't swing freely after new carpeting was installed — all without any request on our part. All this help was offered without any thought of reciprocation, by neighbors who were supportive even though they remained unobtrusive and discrete enough to allow us all the personal privacy we could have wanted. It was a pleasure to get to know them as they stopped by.

As the days passed by, the rural charm and peace and safety of the community slowly worked its magic, until we were quietly but thoroughly overcome by the ambiance of the place. Pecan — as we, in the same way as the locals, had come to call it — was in all respects exactly what its boosters and local real estate professionals had said it would be, a wonderful environment in which to live. We really had begun to think of our new location as a case of paradise found, our own little Eden on the Texas prairie.

Having floated around the country for so many years, we realized without having to explicitly say so, that Pecan could indeed become our final destination, a place where we could enjoy a good retirement, when that time finally rolled around. Living at Pecan delivered a level of peace and tranquility that most anyone would have appreciated. More than anything else, it was exactly what Candy needed. Knowing right away what a good thing we'd found, we prayed that we would be able to stay put for as long as possible — hopefully forever. We had every reason to think we were well on the road toward getting our lives back on track, back to the way things had been for us when we first got married. With these wonderful thoughts in mind, we settled in to enjoy the remainder of our lives, praying that we would never move again.

9

AN INNOCENT BUT FATEFUL DECISION

WHILE WE WERE ENJOYING our new life at Pecan Plantation, the time to celebrate my parents' fifty years of marriage rolled around. Because my brothers and sisters and I wanted their golden wedding anniversary to be special and different, we decided to do it up in a big way. With this thought in mind, we decided to include a detailed retrospective on their childhood days, a look back into their pasts that would begin even before they met one another and began courting.

We wanted to surprise them with pictures of people and places they would recognize from back when they were kids, shots they hadn't seen for years as well as new ones they had never seen. That kind of thing had never been done on any of our family occasions, so we thought it would be a lot of fun for all of us. We thought Mom and Dad, in particular, would love it, especially if it could be brought off as a total surprise.

Because I was the eldest sibling in our surviving birth family of five boys and three girls, Candy and I took on the responsibility of planning the event, even though we lived in Texas rather than in California where my parents and most of my family lived and where, therefore, the event was to be held. All of the necessary arrangements had to be made by telephone and through the mail anyway, so distance was of no real concern.

Candy and I lived closer than any of my siblings to our folks' childhood hometown out in rural Oklahoma, so it was obvious that it would be much easier and a lot less expensive and time consuming for me to collect data for the retrospective than it would have been for any other member of the family. I took the task on willingly and enthusiastically, and from the outset I truly put my shoulders to the wheel. I made a private vow, in fact, that we were going to put on the best golden wedding anniversary celebration in the history of golden wedding anniversaries, one that Mom and Dad and everyone else who attended would remember for a long time.

As it turned out, though, laying hands on the material needed for the retrospective segment of their anniversary bash wasn't as quick and easy as I thought it would be. A few years before their marriage, our folks had moved away from the town in which they'd been born and raised and where they first met. They had lived away from their rural hometown, in fact, for nearly all of their fifty years together, which meant that most of their hometown ties and relationships had been severed long ago.

To solve this problem, I wrote literally hundreds of letters, sent an even larger number of email messages, and made many long-distance telephone calls, all to distant relatives who lived back near their old hometown or still had some ties to the area. Each live contact was given a careful explanation of what we wanted to do for our parents, and then sworn to secrecy until after their anniversary bash was held. Using this approach, I found the names and addresses of a good number of people Mom and Dad had known before and after they got married — teachers, school administrators, coaches, preachers, merchants, various long-lost relatives, family friends, and so on.

Through mail and telephone and email messaging with these folks that went on for over a year, I was able to put together a collection of outside–the–family information to add to the–inside–the–family material my brothers and sister supplied — more than enough to create a montage consisting of old photographs, various anecdotes, graduation programs, facts about our parents' courtship and marriage, and other items of that kind. Using this material, I was able to assemble an interesting and poignant retrospective segment for our overall anniversary program. All in all, I thought it turned out exceptionally well.

I packaged key parts of the material into a narrated video, one that included pictures of people and places as well as videotaped comments that had been contributed by friends and acquaintances our folks had grown up with as children. To create a scrapbook to accompany the video, I bound into a hard copy booklet many of the old family photographs and other mementos I'd been able to beg or borrow from my contacts, including contributions made by lots of people who'd once lived in the hometown of their childhood. Both of these items were presented to them during their anniversary ceremony and banquet.

All this sounds straightforward and simple as it is explained now, but in actuality it was a time-consuming and challenging undertaking. By the time the retrospective was finished, I had mailed over five hundred letters (most of them copies), made no telling how many long distance telephone calls, and sent more email messages that I could remember, all in search of material. On top of all that, I had also put in an untold number of hours at various libraries, doing the research and reading that had enabled me to create a historically accurate framework into which the material that had been accumulated could be packaged.

When the event finally came to pass, the golden wedding anniversary party and banquet we put on for our parents turned out to be an exceptionally memorable occasion, an affair those who attended would recall for many years to come, just as my brothers and sisters and cousins and I had hoped. Our folks really got a kick out of their limousine ride to the banquet hall, and they were touched to the point of tears by the video and photo scrapbook we presented during our post-banquet program. The evening was made even better by the fact that a large number of friends and family members turned out to enjoy their special occasion with them. Enough money was spent on videotaping and still photography that evening to keep Eastman–Kodak in business for at least another year or two.

EVEN AFTER OUR FOLKS' golden wedding anniversary was over and done with, I carried on with the research I had been doing. The subject matter turned out to be so interesting that I decided to write a book about the history of my mom and dad's now long defunct hometown, an account that would subsume and then go far beyond their personal involvement there. Somehow or another, the project had gradually evolved into something I felt I absolutely *had to do* rather that something I merely *wanted to do.*

In addition to the data that was needed for my folks' anniversary retrospective, I collected a lot of other material as well — much of it about my parents' parents (my grandparents), their parents, and their grandparents on both sides of my family along with a great deal about their hometown and area in which it was located. These people, of course, were all long deceased, but their stories had turned out to be fascinating enough for me to want to pour a lot more time and effort into learning as much about them as I could.

Before long, I found myself up to my elbows in data having to do with the lives of ancestors on both sides of my family. My most fascinating discovery had to do with how my grandparents and, to a much greater extent than I imagined, my own mom and dad, lived through one of the most unforgettable episodes in our recent national history — the Dust Bowl and the Great Depression. As I learned more about what they experienced, my interest in learning more about my own extended family grew exponentially, eventually to the extent that doing this kind of research blossomed into a full-fledged personal hobby.

It was in this totally unplanned and grow–like–Topsy way that I embarked on an effort that took years to complete, a local history of the areas my folks grew up in out in rural Oklahoma. When it was finally done, I titled it *The Legacy of the Great Oklahoma Land Rush: A Photographic History of Hoffman Townsite and School in Okmulgee County* (but then retitled later on to *Hoffman, Okmulgee County, Oklahoma: Doing Business on the Indian*

Territory Frontier) and published it as a product of *The Fowble Press.* It didn't sell well, of course, due to its narrowness of scope and my total lack of experience in writing, publishing, marketing, and every other aspect of book publication that could be mentioned, but I was proud of it anyway. It had been an enormously rewarding undertaking, especially for an academic in sore need of something to occupy his private thoughts and get away from his many problems. Researchers, I suppose, just love research.

PUMPED UP OVER WHAT I considered to be the resounding success of my two forays into family research, I could hardly wait to tear into another effort of the same kind. This time, though, I decided to do a family history project I knew better than to get involved in at all. Really, it wasn't so much *what I did* that became a problem; it was *how I chose to do it.*

For my next foray out of the literary chute, I decided to write a short history of the Caine side of our family, an account just like the one I had completed about my side, the Holders. *A similar effort,* I thought, *would be a great way of demonstrating how much Candy and her adoptive parents, the Wilsons, meant to me.*

I had in mind a fairly straightforward repeat of the same general approach that had been used before, modified in a few ways to help deal with the peculiarities of the new undertaking. The first peculiarity had to do with the obvious fact that I knew next to nothing about Candy's life before she went to live with the Wilsons; the second was that I knew from the outset that she and her parents would not welcome or cooperate with any form of probing into her pre-adoptive past. Because there was no way to get around these two stark realities, I knew from the beginning that different tactics would have to be employed to gather the material that would be needed. Simply put, I knew that if the project wasn't done in secret, it couldn't be done at all; when it came to details having to do with Candy's childhood, she and her adoptive parents had always been close-mouthed.

From the early years of our relationship, Candy and the Wilsons had been crystal clear about not wanting to talk about any aspect of her pre-adoptive years. The topic was made off limits through never bringing it up on their own and by immediately changing or downplaying it any time I attempted to do so myself.

So, even though I knew before I got started that Candy and the Wilsons would strongly disapprove of any effort to delve into her past, I decided to pursue the project anyway. I simply took for granted that, when the history was done, they would appreciate and enjoy it just as much as they had my earlier projects.

I had long been offended by the fact that they'd made a mission of concealing her past from me, and I thought it had been very wrong of them not to have taken me into their confidence. Pursuing the new project, therefore, seemed justifiable as a back-door means of asserting my right to know just as much about my own wife's past as they did.

At the time I saw no legitimate reason *not* to do my work in secrecy. As a husband who loved his wife dearly, I knew in my heart there was nothing that might be discovered about her past that would change the way I felt about her in the here and now. *What, then,* I thought, *would be the harm? Besides, she hadn't complained — and, in fact, had actually helped — when I prepared the same kind of surprise for her in-laws, my own parents.* It was with these not entirely laudable or fully above-board thoughts in mind that I embarked on an unforgivably intrusive secret effort to learn as much as I could about my own fragile wife's childhood history.

10

IN SEARCH OF CANDY'S LOST CHILDHOOD

STARTING WITH NO MORE than the facts that Candy had been born on June 21, 1949, that her place of birth had been Phoenix, Arizona, and that her birth family name had been Britt, I intended to probe backwards until I could collect enough information to put together a brief history of the Caine family.

I intended to find the basics about her birth parents — who they were, what they did for a living, what had become of them, and so on. I wanted to know where they lived when Candy was a child, whether she had had any siblings, and, more than anything else, why they had put her up for adoption. With this information in hand, I intended to contact as many members of her family as could be located. After that, I planned to identify the school or schools she had attended as a child, the names of at least a few of her teachers and classmates, and to gather a few pictures of those people and places. This approach had worked well for my earlier projects, so I took for granted that it would be equally effective this time around.

Why wasn't I more thoughtful about what I was doing, inquiring minds might want to know? Well, in the first place, I had no actual experience or knowledge at all when it came to the kind of research I was doing. As a rank novice, I didn't know what I didn't know. In all honesty, I saw my endeavor as being more of an academic exercise, as a study of dusty records and, hopefully, old photographs, than as an activity that could lead to direct interaction with a bunch of strangers, much less strangers who might be troublesome or even outrightly hostile. I gave little to no serious thought to any adverse ramifications that might ensue from coming in contact with real people. Remember, nationally televised programs that might have served as cautionary models for what I wanted to do were not as common then as they are today. Basically, I went about my research as naively as if I were a walking, talking, blundering cliché of a bull in a China shop, setting out in search of a new set of fine tableware.

With the intention of swearing to secrecy any contacts that could be made, I planned to ask for contributions from anyone who was ready and willing to participate. I intended to pull together whatever facts I could locate about Candy's pre-adoptive years — anecdotes, mementos, stories, old pictures, and so on — so they could be linked together by means of an appropriate narrative. After that, I intended to combine my findings into a photo-scrapbook that could be presented to her and her folks. The finished product was to be presented as a total surprise, hopefully as a gift the three of them would greatly value.

BEGINNING WITH THE FIRST step that was taken, however, it became clear that my new project wasn't going to go nearly as smoothly as the one I'd done for my parents; false leads, forced tangential investigations, and a number of other unexpected twists and turns combined to make sure of that. For one thing, I found it aggravating to no end when I discovered that a deliberate roadblock had been put in place to prevent anyone from doing exactly the kind of investigation I wanted to do.

My first attempt to locate a birth certificate for a baby girl by the name of Candice Lee Britt, which Candy told me was her birth family surname back when we first started dating, who was born in Phoenix, Arizona, on June 21, 1949, for example, led to nothing more than a series of dead-end inquiries. No female child by that name had been born on that date, according to records searches for which had I paid good money and for which I had waited a long time to receive.

This false lead was just the first in a series of aggravations that cropped up during my efforts to find information about my dear wife's hidden past. Candy's birth hadn't been recorded under that surname, nor was it recorded under Wilson, her adoptive parents' last name. She and the Wilsons had given a phony surname for her — and, for that matter, maybe even a phony hometown. I had accepted this information as being factual since we started going together during my college years.

Learning that Candy and the Wilsons had deceived me provoked two immediate reactions on my part. First, it caused me to become even more aggravated that her past had been concealed from me at all; second, it made me more determined than ever to find out as much about her past as I could. The way I looked at it, keeping me in the dark amounted to a way of saying that I hadn't been worthy of their full trust and confidence, and, in my opinion, not having fully confided in me amounted to a direct violation of the pledges we had made not to keep secrets from each other.

THROUGH INNOCENT-SOUNDING PROBING I had engaged in over the years with members of the Wilsons' extended family, I had learned that not a one of them knew any more about Candy's pre-adoptive life than I did. The same was true of all of their close friends. Every one of them had been told, just as I had, that her birth family name had been Britt and that she had been born in Phoenix. Beyond that, not a one of them knew anything further about her pre-adoptive past. It was as if Candy had had no childhood history before she was adopted.

As Candy grew older, their questions about her past were always shunted aside, until, eventually, they finally stopped asking about it. The Wilsons, you see, were deservedly admired and esteemed by just about everyone who knew them, which had resulted in their motives rarely ever being questioned and their wishes being fully respected. Family members and friends alike tried their best to discourage me from doing any further probing in this area, knowing without asking that the Wilsons definitely would not approve of my delving into this off-limits topic.

Even after I solemnly assured them that anything they said would be kept confidential, no one could (or would) provide any additional details about Candy's birth parents or pre-adoptive life. The Wilsons, I discovered, had done everything they could to keep facts of that kind entirely to themselves. From the beginning of their association with Candy, it had been decided that she needed a total separation from the past to make sure her new life with them would be successful.

The more roadblocks I found in my way, the more resolute I became. *I'm her husband, for Christ's sake*, I remember exclaiming to myself. *If I don't have a right to know about her past, then who does?*

MY PROGRESS STAYED STALLED until a random thought led to a back door opening that finally got me back on track.

What I excitedly thought of at the time as a huge stroke of luck during what had turned out to be an annoyingly frustrating project occurred as I pondered what might have taken place back when the Wilsons decided decision to conceal Candy's past. *What if,* I wondered, *they had simply come up with a false family name for her, thinking that that step alone would be enough to keep her true surname a secret from then on?* Handling it that way would have been a simple way of keeping what they'd done under wraps, since nothing else about her past would have had to be changed or falsified to assure the privacy they had so clearly deemed essential for Candy's fresh start. *They weren't experts in identity concealment, for crying out loud,* I thought. *I'll bet they did nothing more than that*, and, as it turned out, I was right.

To test this straightforward supposition, I queried the public records database anew, this time going through birth records in search of a baby girl born in Phoenix, Arizona, on the given date but ignoring last names altogether. Phoenix was a populous city even then, but it was highly unlikely that many baby girls would have been born on that exact date. If such a birth record turned up, I knew a surname would be shown as well — unless, of course, that too had in some way been concealed.

Without too much effort, it wasn't long before what I was looking for turned up — a birth record for *Candice Lee Caine*, a child born to indigent parents *Luther Jackson and Pirley Mae (Hicks) Caine* at 7:37 p.m. on June 21, 1949, at the Maricopa County Hospital. In the blocks for their places of birth, her mother had listed McAlester and her father listed Hoffman, two towns close to one another out in rural Oklahoma.

Curiously, no first or middle name had been entered for Candy until over twenty years after her birth. They weren't added until 1970, the year Candy and I got married. When I asked by telephone how that could have happened, I was told that the parents just hadn't given their daughter first and middle names when she was born. They couldn't say why. The record had been updated all those years later at the request of the child herself. First and middle names had been added when she ordered a copy of her own birth certificate. Until then, she had remained *Baby Girl Caine.*

It was the *Eureka* moment I had been hoping for, the time when, at long last, I learned my own wife's true family surname as well as the names and hometowns of her birth parents. *They tried to throw me off*, I thought, *but they failed; now I'll be able to get down to the brass tacks of learning what I had wanted to know all along.*

Armed with her true family surname as well as the names of the state and towns her birthparents were from, I hurried back to the drawing board to resume my investigation of Candy's mysterious past. The fact that her birth record also listed her mother's maiden name would enable me to track down her birth mother or members of her birth family, or both.

I began with writing letters to the postmasters and superintendents of public schools in McAlester and Hoffman in search of current contact addresses for members of the Caine and Hicks families. In addition, I made telephone calls and conducted a whole series of internet searches for the purpose of identifying families with those last names still living in or near these two cities. I wasn't able to turn up a single member of the Caine family who would talk with me, but it didn't take long to locate a good number of people by the last name of Hicks who still lived in or near McAlester. Others, I was told, had moved away years ago, some of them to cities in Arizona.

I felt certain that when contact was made with members of all the families that had Hicks as a last name, one or more of them would be able to tell me more about Luther and Pirley and their daughter Candice. Using the facts these folks would provide, I thought I would finally be able to complete the project I had in mind — a detailed sketch of Candy's early life with her birth parents. It seemed to me that finding her birth certificate had opened the door to a whole new series of exciting discoveries about their mysterious past. It was a real shot in the arm to think that my future efforts would be blessed by much smoother sailing than had been the case up till then.

Much to my disappointment, my subsequent efforts didn't go nearly as smoothly as I expected. The members of the Hicks families I was able to contact knew a good deal about Pirley Mae's young life when she lived at home with her family, but not a one of them could tell me anything more about what became of her after she left home to marry Luther Caine.

FRUSTRATION QUICKLY TURNED INTO aggravation when my research from this point forward did not go as I expected it to. In some ways, in fact, it became more exasperating than ever. It hadn't been difficult to locate some members of the Hicks family, nor had it been difficult to identify a few who were ready and willing to talk with me; some of them, in fact, were anxious to do so, since they were intrigued by what I wanted to do.

After living in McAlester for only a year or two, they said, the couple had moved away without leaving a forwarding address and then simply never returned, not as far as any of them knew. All contact with them ceased at that point.

Both sets of parents, Luther's and Pirley's, had already passed away, but the relatives who were willing to work with me — brothers and sisters and aunts and uncles and cousins on Pirley's side of the family, people who normally would have been the couple's confidants — didn't have a thing to say about what I most wanted to know.

Working with various members of the Hicks family had turned out to be quite easy, since a good number of them still lived in or near McAlester and were readily accessible by email or telephone. Even some of those who had moved out of Oklahoma were willing to talk with me. What I found odd, though, was while some of them were ready and willing to talk, others were either reluctant to open up or really didn't want to interact. Instead of making an issue of this, I simply ignored any recalcitrance that was encountered. Why worry about those who wouldn't open up when there were plenty of others who would?

In the end, I was able to interact with a sufficient number of relatives on the Hicks side of Candy's family to pull together a good deal of information about her parents Luther and Pirley before they got married and moved away from McAlester for some unknown destination. Talking with members of the Hicks family confirmed what I had already surmised, which was that Luther and his people were about as rough a bunch as you might ever meet. Not a single member of the Hicks family had considered Luther a good match for someone of Pirley's talents, upbringing, and prospects. After meeting him only once, her parents had thrown a fit that everyone in their extended family still remembered hearing about. To a person, they said that life started going badly for Pirley when she met Luther, and her downhill slide never stopped.

Members of the Hicks family provided more than enough material for me to put together a good overview of what childhood and youth had been like for Candy's mother Pirley Mae. Even better, a few of them allowed me make copies of family photographs that had been taken while she lived with her parents before she met Luther Caine. This was a poignant moment for me, since they were the first pictures of my wife's

LEARNING THE BASICS ABOUT her father Luther's younger years turned out to be an entirely different matter, mainly because the few relatives on the Caine side I was able to locate were unwilling to talk with me at all. They didn't hesitate to tell me where I could get off, either, usually in no uncertain terms. Some made a point of slamming phones down in my ear, just to be make it unmistakably clear how frivolous and unworthy they considered my project to be. My impression was that they were people who would have reacted in the same way to any inquiry that might have been made of them, regardless of its merit. Not only were they an exceptionally rough bunch, but they also weren't the least bit close to one another. Talking with them wasn't just frustrating; it was nerve-wracking and, surprisingly, at times even a bit scary.

WHEN EVERY ATTEMPT TO contact members of the Caine family failed miserably, it became clear that reliance on members of the Hicks family as sources of information would be my only option. That would have been perfectly acceptable if any of them had, in fact, been able to provide more data about the period of time I most wanted to investigate — Candy's years with her birth parents. Unfortunately, none of them could offer any more than bits and snatches of second-hand information about that period, and none of what they did have to say could be corroborated. A few of them knew or had heard that the couple had had a child, but, beyond that, they couldn't tell me more because they just didn't know any more. They all automatically assumed, just as I had, that my wife Candy had been the child they'd heard about, and that she, therefore, had to be the reason I sought them out.

Luther, I learned, had from an early age been a black sheep in his own family, and, not long after she met him, Pirley became a black sheep in her family as well. After they married, they simply disappeared from the scene. The couple, everyone assumed, had moved away to raise their child in whatever way they deemed appropriate. They had already alienated or rejected every member of their family, anyway.

Bumping up against a roadblock of this kind was extremely disappointing. Worse still, it became apparent rather quickly that those who did know a little about the couple were not nearly as open or willing to comment as I had hoped they would be. With eyes averted and heads looking downward and slowly turning from side to side as they spoke, their body language made it clear that I was bringing up a painful family memory, one they didn't want to share with others. Worse than that, several of them acted as if they could have cared less about knowing any more about the couple than they already knew. It seemed clear that what they did know about Luther Caine was more than they had ever really wanted to know. Just mentioning his name was enough to make frowns or pained expressions appear on their faces.

Despite the paucity of information members of the Hicks family were able to provide, I wasn't about to give up on my search. Probing and questioning as if I actually knew what I was doing, I squeezed out every item of information they could be persuaded to divulge.

A research trail that seemed exciting and promising only a short time before once again became as cold as a cucumber. *Why*, I stormed and fumed, *had a project that ought to have been simple turned out to be so damned difficult*?

THEN, JUST AS I was sinking further down in the dumps than I'd been in a long time, there was another turn for the better. The only one of Luther's relatives (a distant cousin) who had been willing to talk with me for a while unexpectedly called me back, saying off-handedly — and, it seemed to me, somewhat grudgingly — that what I really ought to do was get together with Uncle Clarence, a man who, he assured me, knew more about Luther as a child and about Luther and Pirley as a couple than anyone else. Luther's cousin's comment was the first time I heard Clarence's name.

In the cousin's own words, "Clarence's health ain't good no more, but he'll come closer to helpin' you than anybody else. He's old, but he's still as sharp as hell. He can remember by accident more about stuff that happened in the Caine family a long time ago than anybody else can on purpose. I can't help you much myself," he said, "because I never could get along with them people," referring to the members of the Caine family as if they were opponents or strangers rather than his own relatives.

Clarence, he explained, was not a true birth uncle of the Caines. He was a just a neighbor who lived near Luther's father's home, back when Luther and his siblings were growing up. Upon asking their neighbor's name when they first met, the kids had been told "Y'all just call me *Uncle Clarence*, and that will be fine." Luther and his siblings had called the man Uncle Clarence ever since, even after they learned that the term was a local honorific and that they weren't blood relatives at all. The kids liked Clarence, who wasn't a whole lot older than they were.

Maybe the trail into their past wasn't completely dead after all, I thought.

"I'd love to," I said to the cousin right away. "Do you think he'll be willing to talk with me if I go see him? Will he be available?"

"Oh, hell yeah, he'll be available," I was assured. "He'll be there when you show up, you can bet your ass on that; he can't go nowhere on his own no more." Uncle Clarence, I was informed, was old and in bad health, and had moved into the Sunrise Assisted Living Center in Stigler, Oklahoma just a few years earlier.

"That old bird will talk your butt off, once you get him goin'. Your trouble will be gettin' him to put a clamp on it. Once he gets wound up, you can't git the old buzzard to stop."

"Thanks for the tip," I said. "And, by the way, do you happen to have a few old photographs of Luther I can borrow and copy?" Luther's cousin was the only person on his side of Candy's birth family I'd been able to reach, so I thought it would be wise to go for broke while I could.

"Yeah," he replied, after balking for a while to decide whether he wanted to fuss with me any further; "I guess I got a few shots you can use. Stop by my place when you can, and I'll go dig some up."

"Thanks a lot," I said, when I stopped by to see him, after he handed over a few ragged family pictures. "I'll return your originals as good as new, just as soon as I've made some copies."

"Hell," he responded, "I ain't worried. You gave me your address, so I know where you live." He threw back his head and laughed when he saw me blanch and start blinking, knowing that his point had registered and he'd been clearly understood. Believe me, it had been; he was a rough-looking and even rougher-talking character.

Lordy, I thought after we parted. If all the men on Luther's side of Candy's family are like this guy, a man obviously willing to threaten me without giving it a second thought and who clearly had been pleased by his ability to put a scare into person he hardly knew, I could well imagine what living in the same household with one of them must have been like. I was pleased that he had condescended to work with me, but I couldn't help but wonder what he'd be like if he really got mad at somebody. Because I didn't want to find out, I returned his pictures just as quickly as I could, and via registered mail at that. Even then, I mailed the letter only after making back-up copies, in case the post office happened to fail me.

If Candy's father Luther was anything like this character, I remember thinking to myself at the time, *no wonder Candy's birth mother's family, the Hicks, had been so put off by him.*

HOPING AGAINST HOPE THAT Uncle Clarence would become my best source of new facts about Candy's father's side of her birth family, I immediately checked an atlas to find out how to get to where he lived. Stigler, I discovered, was a small town up in Oklahoma, just over five hours of driving time north of our home in Granbury, Texas. I decided to make an unannounced weekend trip to visit with him in person. Writing or telephoning in advance might have provided an opportunity to decide against seeing me, and that was the last thing I wanted to happen.

As it turned out, that weekend trip up north to Oklahoma did indeed become the turning point I had been hoping to find. Clarence was the fount of information Luther's cousin said he would be. He was able to provide many new and helpful facts about Luther's childhood years as well as about his marriage to Pirley Mae Hicks.

My first meeting with the old man was so productive that I made two more trips back to his retirement home, just so I could sit by his bedside and listen to his recollections of the past. He had so much to say about the Caine family that my main line of research had to be placed on the back burner for a while, just so I could process it. It took quite a while to sort out his comments, place them in chronological order, verify them through library research, and then convert them into a readable narrative that could be inserted in my overall story.

It turned out to be a good thing that I went to see Clarence as quickly as I did, since he'll never be able to say anything further about the extended Caine family in general or about Luther and Pirley in particular than what he shared during my three visits. He died not long after our time together.

Clarence was an individual who told it like it really was. He had no academic training or professional title — he wasn't a genealogist or historian; he was just one of those enviable souls who are clear minded right up until their last days. Because he had been blessed in this way, he was able to recall many events from his own past as well as a great deal of the oral history of his hometown out in rural Oklahoma, a small town called Hoffman that used to exist in Okmulgee County. On several occasions after talking with him, I recall praying that my own senior years could be lived out in the same way as his, filled with lucid memories of younger, happier days.

He recalled many of the significant events that had impacted the town of Hoffman over the years, even though he admitted to being a little fuzzy on exact names, ages, and dates. He matter–of–factly suggested that I ought to tie down some of these details by means of a visit to the Hoffman Cemetery, up on the north side of town. When I followed up on his suggestion later on, I discovered that every person he'd talked about was right there, lying in repose just where he said they'd be. It couldn't have been more obvious that Clarence, without even trying hard, could have been a far better researcher than I would ever be, if he had been inclined to go that route.

Clarence knew a great deal about Luther's family situation from back when Colonel George Jackson Caine, Luther's father, had been his neighbor back in Hoffman, a fair amount about the Hicks family of McAlester that Luther married into, and more than anyone else who spoke with me about how married life had gone for Luther after he moved from Hoffman to McAlester to establish a household with Pirley Mae Hicks. He knew and clearly remembered how the early months of their marriage turned out, but, as had been the case for all of my other contacts, he was unable to shed any light on what became of them after their departure from McAlester.

"How is it that you know so much about Luther and Pirley's marriage," I asked, "when no one else on the Hicks side of their family knows much of anything about either one of them? That," I said, "seems odd to me."

"Them two didn't take up with nobody in her family because not a one of them Hicks could stand Luther,'" he replied. "It was because her family rejected him," he said, "that Pirley rejected every damned one of them. It was as simple as that. I got to know them two only because the old house they rented in McAlester was right next to the one I lived in. We had the same landlord. It wasn't nothin' but happenstance that we ended up livin' right next to one another, after us bein' neighbors over in Hoffman.

"Not a one of them Hicks, as far as I know, ever visited Pirley and Luther, and I never heard of or saw any member of his family, the Caines, ever comin' to town to visit them neither, even though Hoffman wasn't over sixty miles away. As far as I know, not a single member of his family ever stopped by. Them two was on their own from the very beginnin'.

"I never was close to any of them Caines when I lived in Hoffman, even though we was neighbors. Luther's father owned a barbershop and beer joint over there, and he thought he was a notch or two higher than everbody else. He was a crooked character that people stayed away from if they could. I seldom ever talked with Luther's father, whose first name was George, even though everbody always referred to him as T*he Colonel*. We never really got acquainted, the way some neighbors do. We got started that way, and that's how it stayed from then on. The Colonel wasn't never friendly, not to me or to anybody else, except with his cronies down at his bar.

"George Caine, Luther's father, if you want to know God's truth, was a mean sonofabitch, and his mother, who was a Creek Indian woman, really didn't have no choice but to live her life like a recluse, because that's what her husband wanted. Their kids didn't look to be half Creek, but they was. Both parents let the kids run wild and do whatever the hell they wanted, whenever they wanted. Whenever they got in enough trouble for word of it to get back to their father, he'd beat the hell of them with the leather belt he always wore. I could hear them kids howlin' from all the way over at my place. I got along with the kids okay, though, so none of them never gave me a bit of trouble. Thank God for that.

"Everbody was always too hard on Luther, back when he was a kid as well as after he and Pirley got married, especially them damned holier–than–thou Hicks. They thought they was a notch or two above everbody else. Luther's father treated him and his brothers and their sister as rough as hell, back when all of them was kids. The boy wasn't no angel, but, hell, I wasn't neither, not back in them days. I stayed drunk a lot of the time back then, the same way his daddy did. Even so, it always irritated me to hear people run the boy down.

"From the get-go, them Hicks never wanted nothin' to do with any of the Caines, especially their new son–in–law, Luther. They was religious, and they were damned proud of it, if you know what I mean. They never gave the boy a chance, much less any help. Whether or not that was what caused all his and Pirley's problems, I don't know for sure. He never had no problem causin' plenty of trouble for hisself, that's for sure, even without all the bitchin' by members of his or her family.

"Hell, that boy never was right," Clarence continued. "He never would've been able to plow a straight line, even if he'd been willin' to drive a mule. He and his brothers and sister never had a chance. Their mother passed away young, and their father never paid no attention to any of them, except to whip the hell out of them when they done somethin' wrong.

"Everbody always acted like they know'd from the beginnin' that Luther wasn't never gonna amount to nothin', and, wouldn't you know it, that was just how he turned out. Some people think they can tell all that needs to be known about some kids, just from watchin' them grow up."

Listening intently and making lots of notes, I eagerly lapped up every memory the old man could recall about Candy's birth parents.

It became apparent during our first conversation that Clarence felt a compelling need to say a few words in defense of Luther, when no one else I talked had a single word of good to say about him. He said more than enough to clarify why Luther and his brothers and his sister strayed so far off the high road. It was all due, he declared, to the poor start they got off to back in their hometown. He thought their time in Hoffman had warped the kids for life.

I'm sure he didn't think of himself as such, but Uncle Clarence was a natural born storyteller. Some of the happenings he told me about were so fascinating that they eclipsed Luther's immediate personal story for a while, in the same way that they eclipsed my overall research topic, Candy's time with her birth parents. As unlikely as it may sound in view of all the frustrations and distractions I had had to put up with up, the entire focus of my research *temporarily* turned on a dime, to the extent that I took off on a whole new track for a while. In the sense of feeling absolutely compelled to learn all there was to know about Luther's birth family, a hook had been irretrievably set.

Before I knew what was happening, I found myself caught up in a study of not only Candy's birth parents' lives but also of the lives of his parents and their parents before them. This was an obvious diversion from looking for information about Candy's young life with her birth parents, of course, but it still seemed to be the right direction to take for a while.

By the time I finished talking with Clarence, I had a huge amount of new information to sort through — so much, in fact, that transforming it into a comprehensible narrative ended up becoming a major effort in and of itself. After carefully piecing together his recollections of Candy's family history on her father's side, I was able to confirm through my own library research that everything he told me was verifiably true. I wound up having to limit what I wrote about Candy's side of our family to those relatives who had the greatest impact on him as a child, just to keep his part of my Caine family history manageable.

Because I had only a passing interest in genealogy, I made no concerted effort to look into the stories of Candy's cousins or aunts or uncles or any other family members outside of direct lineage on her father's side. Instead, I restricted my efforts to the stories of the significant others who, it seemed to me, had had the greatest long-term influence on the way Candy ended up being raised as a child. This, I figured, was the best way to stay close to the topic I'd set out to study.

Candy's childhood years were colored far more by happenings on her father's side than on her mother's. Several folks on her father's side made quite a splash while they were around, due to having committed deeds they were never able to live down. One of them, for example, got in enough trouble for a newspaper article to have been written about him, an article that detailed many of his nefarious exploits. In their own separate ways, other members on her father's side had been equally disreputable.

Unlike what usually happens in studies of the past, I was able to find more, not less, information about Candy's extended family lineage on her father's side than for her own immediate birth family. Enough data was available to describe for three generations back how these folks had lived, right up until her father married her mother. That, though, once again, was where my research trail petered out.

Clarence told me everything he'd ever heard about the Caine family, which turned out to be a quite a lot. Most small country towns have residents with keen eyes and ears — old-timers just like Clarence, for example — who tend to recall all kinds of facts about their neighbors. That's how it is in small towns everywhere, places where lives are lived under a microscope and not much of anything can be kept secret.

Using the data he provided, I was able to summarize the life stories of three generations of significant others on Candy's father's side of our family — Early and Etta (Burnham) Tiger; her maternal great-grandparents, George and Bonnie (Tiger) Caine; her paternal grandparents, and Luther and Pirley (Hicks) Caine, her birth parents. Through focusing on the roles of lineal *caregivers* rather than on *antecedents* per se, I discovered that, when life went wrong for one early member of Candy's lineage back in early 1880s, her disaster seemed to have created ripple effects that extended downwards through subsequent generations all the way up to the here and now. Altered only in the sense of placing events in proper chronological order rather than in the disjointed way he told them to me, Clarence's comments have been condensed into the three utterly fascinating stories that follow.

11

EARLY AND ETTA (BURNHAM) TIGER

ACCORDING TO CLARENCE, CANDY'S paternal great-grandfather's parents traveled with other members of the Creek tribe to the Oklahoma Indian Territory during a phase of their *removal* from the southeastern part of the United States. Their relocation was similar to that of the Cherokees, whose removal journey ended up being memorialized as the infamous *Trail of Tears*. The Creeks were *relocated* to a large tract of treaty land the federal government set aside for them in exchange for the land they lived on back east. Their new location was widely thought of as a highly undesirable and lawless wilderness at the time, not just by whites but by Indians as well. If the Creeks had had a real choice in the matter, according to the record, they would never have agreed to give up their ancestral land.

Through a careful search of cemetery and other public records, I confirmed Clarence's assertion that Candy's great-grandfather on her mother's side was a Creek Indian fullblood. Born on February 15, 1840, he lived out a rustic life in his remote part of the country. Under ordinary circumstances, next to nothing would be known about him today; he became an exception to the rule only because he got into a series of scrapes of sufficient local notoriety for brief written records to have been made of them. Had it not been for this, he would have remained an obscure and totally anonymous figure.

EARLY TIGER

THE FIRST MEMBER OF my wife Candy's birth family that Clarence told me about was her great-grandfather on her father's side, a man by the name of Early Tiger. His mistakes and misfortunes, as it turned out, had an enormous negative impact on multiple generations of Caines.

Early Tiger was an American Indian, a Creek, to be specific, a man who lived out his life in the Indian Territory, back before Oklahoma became a state of the Union. He lived in a sleepy little farm community in the northeastern quarter of the state, about seventy-five miles south of Tulsa and roughly fifteen miles southeast of the Creek Indian Nation capitol city at Okmulgee.

According to Clarence, Early Tiger was known to be an angry, bitter, cruel human being. His original Creek name (or, more likely, nickname; nobody knows for sure) was thought to be *Crippled Hawk*, which was later shortened to *Hawk*, according to what Clarence said he'd heard as a boy when he was growing up in Hoffman. The name was given to him, so it was said, by his father, who named him after a sight he saw shortly after his son was born — a hawk with a broken wing jumping from limb to limb up in a tree, desperately trying to stay out of the sight of human observers. It would have been owl-like for a hawk to have tried to stay out of the line of sight of the Indians of those times, since it might have end up in a pot if it had been caught. Back when Early was a young man, many of the Indians in his neck of the woods were living lean and hungry lives, and large numbers of them depended on government assistance for much of their existence.

Early's original Indian name or nickname wasn't needed for long, as it turned out, since *white* — or, as it was put back then, *civilized* — names were assigned to many Indians during the years that followed. A good number of them, as a matter of fact, had voluntarily adopted Anglo names years before, back when they still lived in the southeast, hoping in vain that doing so would help them co-exist with whites and hold on to their land. Early probably ended up being known as *Early Ray*, a citizen of the Creek

Indian Nation of the Oklahoma Indian Territory because he was renamed in one of these ways. His last name, Tiger, which was a well-known and respected Creek family surname, stayed the same as it had always been.

Well, I recall exclaiming to myself upon learning about the unexpected existence of Early Tiger and his relationship to Candy, *that explains how she got those high cheekbones*. I had always thought her round face and slightly rounded cheeks gave her, for lack of a better description, a vaguely *Indian* look. This particular attribute, along with her large and expressive eyes, were among her most becoming features.

Through additional library research, I confirmed Clarence's assertion that much of Early's life took place during trouble-filled years out in the Indian Territory, years that were a challenge for all Indians in his part of the country but that were even more troublesome for him personally. Because his problems were passed on to his descendants, I made it my business to get a better handle on what made him tick. His anger, I discovered, might well have been inherited through his genes.

THE TRIALS OF EARLY TIGER'S PEOPLE

MOST OF THE PEOPLE Early Tiger grew up living around were Indians or the offspring of Indians who had been *relocated* to Oklahoma after their eastern land was expropriated for white settlement. Resentment over this remained a sore spot for them from that point forward. Even today, there are still Indians around who don't have much of anything good to say about Anglos or the federal government.

Yet another reality that may have kept Early stirred up during his younger years had to do with conflict that was taking place within and among the Indians themselves. First of all, differences existed between what were called the *native* Indian tribes, members of the tribes that had once roamed free in and around the Indian Territory, and the various *relocated* tribes, such as Early's, the Creeks, who were resettled on land that until only a short time before had been the exclusive reserve of the natives. Broadly speaking, all the tribes of the Territory while Early was growing up could be divided into these two groups. Among the many problems the Indians had was that the native tribes were less advanced than those who were brought in from the east, and most of the tribes had different languages as well as different traditions. These problems and others like them made cooperation and communication between various tribes even more difficult, in a setting where it was already difficult enough.

We don't hear much about it today, but there also were class distinctions that existed between and among the various tribes. Many of the native Indians truly were wilder than some of the relatively well-educated and more politically aware Indians of the tribes that were moved into the Territory from the east. When many of the native Indians were uneducated and still living primitive lives, some of the resettled eastern Indians had already learned to read and write in the way of white people. When they were moved out west, some of them brought along enough personal wealth to build good homes and acquire various other kinds of valuable personal property; some, in fact, were even prosperous enough to own their own slaves. The majority of the resettled Indians, however, including members of the extended Tiger family, were not among those Creeks who had been blessed by a good education or material wealth. Like most of the so-called "wild" Indians, they were also poor.

The *wild* versus *civilized* distinction was only one of many differences that led to political divisions and splits among Indian people as a whole, people who would have been a whole lot better off if they had worked together on behalf of Indians in general. The multitude of differences that existed between and among the various tribes led to quarrelling that at times was on par with their arguments with whites. Many of the tribes had no understanding or affinity or liking for any of the others, but they were forced to live uncomfortably close together anyway. Internal bickering got to be fairly common, both between and within the tribes.

Early grew to adulthood during times that had to have been threatening, confusing, and aggravating for all of the Indians. It's understandable that people who had been effectively overwhelmed and then rolled over by tribal outsiders such as soldiers, white and black settlers, missionaries, various government agencies and officials who then wound up controlling most significant aspects of their lives might harbor a high degree of anger and resentment. All the forces arrayed against them combined to create the mechanism by which the Indians were *contained* and then crowded into ever smaller contiguous areas. *Why wouldn't Early's people have been angry*, I thought as I contemplated their situation, *when their whole way of life had been turned upside down?*

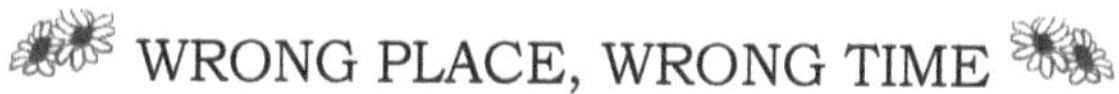

WRONG PLACE, WRONG TIME

THE FEDERAL GOVERNMENT'S APPROACH to helping the Indians included the funding to missionary societies to help pay for the construction and maintenance of new Indian schools and for the salaries of teachers, efforts intended to help the Indians pursue a *settled* way of life. In return for this, it was taken for granted that the missionaries would be supportive of various government measures and programs designed to uplift the tribes. It was through this mutually beneficial arrangement that missionary societies effectively became semi-official agencies of the federal government.

No matter how the pill was coated, only the strength of the forces that were pitted against them made the Indians swallow their frustration and anger and, ultimately, begin to convert to the white way of life. The outright abuse they had to tolerate was substantial, but they were forced to fall into line whether they wanted to or not. Because they were powerless, many of them were abused, ridiculed, cheated, and mistreated in all sorts of ways by white authorities, illegal settlers, and even some of the Christian missionaries. The record also shows that some Indians were routinely bullied and mocked and mistreated by soldiers of the United States Army, who, in many cases, hated them altogether, due to depredations of the past.

Even with government assistance, homelessness and near starvation became part and parcel of everyday life for many Indians. The fact that they were no longer in charge of their own lives caused some Indians to behave as dependents, people too reliant on government distributions of meat, seed, flour, corn, blankets, and other commodities. In this sad way many of them eventually ended up totally dispirited, to the extent that they began to live ever more dissolute and aimless lives. Alcoholism, for example, grew among them until it became — and in fact still remains — an absolute plague, and many of those who fell prey to it evolved into pitiable specimens indeed. Early, I discovered, was one of those who became a slave to this particular addiction.

FALLING INTO THE MIRE

NOT MUCH READING WAS required to confirm Clarence's assertion that Early had lived during what were clearly dreadfully troubled times for Indian people, nor had it been difficult to confirm that life got way out of control for him personally. His own comments were on file to confirm that he lived a depressingly miserable existence. He and many of his contemporaries had to contend with circumstances that were more tragic and confusing than we are able to appreciate today, due to our superficial and misshapen notions about Indians in general.

I had no problem confirming his assertion that Early was one of the many Indian fullbloods who fell into a dissolute way of life. I learned, for example, that he was controlled by a whole wide range of harmful vices. After using tobacco for the first time, he smoked or chewed or dipped from that point forward; once he tried alcohol, he was addicted to it from then on; and, after receiving his first handouts from the government authorities through the Bureau of Indian Affairs, it appears that he was unwilling to work for a living from that day forward. Long before he was mature enough to give any rational thought to his own future, his pattern of life seems to have been irretrievably set.

Some would attribute all of Early's vices and subsequent

shameful behavior solely to his own personal failings, but not me. I couldn't help but believe that a good amount of his many problems had to have been caused by the circumstances of his times. It doesn't seem far-fetched to think that some of his misfortune would have stemmed from growing up during a time when his people had little choice but to live a second-class existence, to live according to rules and values they didn't believe in. At the risk of romanticizing his many faults, it seems to me that he might have been one of those Indians who just didn't respond well to being physically and emotionally overwhelmed by white authority and power, perhaps to the extent that he, in the same way as many of his peers, gave in to a sense of hopelessness that had been created by the situation they were caught up in.

But, regardless of how or why his problems came into being, what's certain is that Early's life eventually become one of alcoholism and indolence, to the extent that he became thought of as a total wastrel and a completely dissolute character. He was quite well known by local law enforcement officers, community leaders, and all other authority figures in his neck of the woods. When he *went on a toot*, as some referred to a prolonged drunk in those days, and proceeded to make a public nuisance of himself, they'd haul him off to jail so he could sleep it off. When he recovered, they'd let him go, knowing full well that it wouldn't be long before he'd get drunk again and the whole process would be repeated.

Over time, Early evolved into a notorious neighborhood pest, a man who lived his everyday life in a haze of drunkenness and dissolution. To local whites, he was just another aimless, drunken Indian; to Indians who had their lives under control, he was considered a man without character. That he was viewed in these ways is a well-known fact, as attested to by Early himself in a newspaper article that was written about him later on. At first locals had only laughed at and made fun of his antics behind his back, but in later years his offensive behavior became too serious to be laughed at.

While I didn't want to set myself up as an apologist for his appalling behavior, it really did appear that the conditions he had to contend with would have been a lot for any man to swallow. Today, psychologists might say that his circumstances could have made him *act out* the way he did. It's too late now to do any more than speculate about what drove his negative behavior, but it isn't hard to imagine how he might have been embittered toward white and tribal authorities alike — the powers that effectively controlled his everyday life.

A FAR FROM NOBLE INDIAN

THE ONE OVERRIDING FACT Early's record made crystal clear was that his temperament and personality belied the patronizingly romanticized image of the *Noble Indian* so commonly portrayed in books and movies today. He wasn't the least bit noble or brave, not even in the broadest sense of the terms. Over the years, in fact, he turned into a highly dangerous person, someone you had to, as they put it, *watch out for*, a man who was known to be wound up tight and, therefore, never to be fully trusted.

As he aged, Early built up quite a reputation among his peers, not just due to his proclivity for drunkenness and carousing but also because he came to thought of as an unusually cruel human being. The latter side of his reputation came about as a result of one kind of work he did to earn goods in trade and, on occasion, a little cash income. He trained horses. There wasn't anything unusual about the kind of work he did, but the way he went about it certainly was. He employed training techniques that were admired by a few but that were repulsive to most people who knew about them.

His techniques were labor intensive and required quite a lot of time and patience to employ, but they were effective without fail. When an unbroken horse ended up in his hands through trading or for hire, he would start by securing the animal to a solid post using a rope halter thrown over its head and muzzle. With the rope surely gripped in his hands, he would gradually pull it ever closer, always keeping the post between them as a safety barrier. On the ground beside the post was what he referred to as his *training stick*, a three–foot–long switch that was around three-fourths of an inch thick at its base and tapered down to a finer point.

Steadily and carefully, he'd pull an *untrained* horse closer and closer to the post that stood between them, watching it become increasingly panic-stricken as the space between them narrowed. Once the horse was up close to the post and tightly secured by a short tether, he would beat it about the mouth, face, neck and flanks. The more the animal was struck, the more terrified it would become. It would fight back and struggle to escape, which, of course, was always impossible, as the trainer knew but the poor animal didn't. He'd continue the switching for as long as it took for either the trainer or the horse to require a moment of rest. Basically, the beating would stop only if the horse stood still. Whenever any resistance was shown, he'd resume the beating until there was another pause.

Sooner or later, every animal would get so bruised and battered and exhausted that it would stand in place, panting and shuddering and glaring in terror at the stick held upright in the trainer's hand. As soon as it was reduced to such a state, it would be hobbled and released and allowed to stumble off to pasture. At feeding time the next day, it would be re-harnessed and the training would start all over again, just as brutally as before.

Early knew that sooner or later, any horse would eventually begin to react in the same way; they'd learn to freeze and cower in abject fear at the sight of the upraised stick, so terrified that their eyes would follow it's every movement until it was totally out of their line of sight. With continued *training* of this kind, animals learned if they made as much as a twitch without Early's command, he would start beating them again. With enough exposure to this severe but highly effective regimen, all horses learned to move only when and where they were commanded.

Horses were saddled and broken for riding using similarly appalling techniques. In Early's eyes, the ends justified the means. He produced thoroughly well-trained animals, horses that could be ridden or harnessed for drayage or sold for a profit. They were more *broken down* than *trained*, but that didn't bother him in the slightest; he was quite proud of the quality of his work.

Every horse that fell into his hands was eventually successfully trained, although on occasion some of them ended up with broken bones in the occipital orb of an eye, an eye partially or fully damaged, or a broken ear hanging limply at the side of its head. Early wouldn't hesitate to beat an animal bloody, especially if he lost his patience, and he was known to have precious little of that. His perspective on training was that there would always be more horses, so what did it matter how the few that were untrainable and, therefore, of low value, were treated. That was only the beginning of why he earned his reputation for cruelty.

There were some who admired his training techniques, but most people were put off by them, just as they were by the man himself. If and when Early did happen to take note of this kind of reaction, it made him even more edgy and explosive than he already was, especially when he was drunk.

Over time, he had to get used to living his life as a loner. As he grew older, his social status caused him to become ever more bitter and venomous. He declined to the point that he drank to excess whenever he could, stole whatever he could get his hands on, and worked as little as possible. He had no education or training to build on, and, in the same way as other men in his situation, was easily angered as well as highly superstitious. The combination of all these disadvantages made reasoning with him next to impossible.

When he was angered or threatened or drunk, he was prone to lash out violently, sometimes without much provocation. As his alcoholism continued to worsen, his overall condition worsened as well. Over time he transitioned from being thought of as a harmless drunk into a man who was a real danger within the community.

Despite his bad habits and lousy reputation, Early married two Creek Indian wives and fathered a number of children over the years. Both wives divorced him after being beaten and abused. After each divorce, his angry outbursts became worse than ever, until he became more or less emotionally unhinged, a truly irrational person. He tried to constrain himself in order to stay out of trouble, but he was never able to keep his temper and his other vices under control. Each new run-in with the law became a little more serious than the last, until, over time, what to do with him became an open question within the community.

ETTA "MOCK" BURNHAM AND THE INCIDENT AT THE CREEK

EARLY TIGER'S MANY PROBLEMS came to a head one evening as he stumbled toward home in a semi-drunken state after attending one of the stomp dances that were common among the Indians of his time and place. It happened when he unexpectedly crossed the path of one of his neighbors, a young and unmarried Creek woman by the name of Etta Burnham. Etta, whose nickname, for reasons Clarence could not fully explain, was *Mock,* was also on her way home from having attended the same stomp dance. When he tried to take advantage of their chance encounter by attempting to strike up a conversation, she promptly and forcefully turned him away.

Angered at being rebuffed, Early grabbed her by an arm and, before Mock could get away, pulled her off to the side of the trail and threw her to the ground. Once she was down, he pulled up her skirt and, as drunk as he was, attempted to fondle her. Further angered when she continued to resist, he started slapping and backhanding her. When she still refused to calm down, his slaps quickly turned into closed fist punches, which he continued until she became so terrified that she was essentially rendered helpless. At that point, after dragging her into a stand of trees, he not only raped but kicked and slapped her around a little more as well. When he was through, he simply walked off and left her there, lying in a heap on the ground, crying her eyes out, with her skirt pulled up over a bruised and bloody face.

Under normal circumstances, an act of such unprovoked violence against a woman would have led to an outraged reaction within any community, but that's not what happened on this particular occasion. Instead of immediately reporting what had happened, Mock decided not to tell anyone about her having been raped, not even members of her own family. Her own family, in fact, were among those she most wanted to keep in the dark about the episode. Her problem was that she had a well-known reputation for behaving promiscuously and flirtatiously within the community, and it was just that kind of behavior that her folks had warned her against earlier that evening before she left for the dance. Her response had been to laugh and tell them to mind their own damned business, but, now that the chickens had come home to roost, she was far too upset and embarrassed to be willing to talk about the attack.

Instead, Mock concealed what happened by saying that "a drunk had tried to force himself on her but that she had successfully fought him off." To further embellish her story, she even bragged about having won the struggle against her drunken attacker. The lie was designed to impress as well as to put off questions by her family and friends, but most of them doubted her story from the first time she told it. Members of her family were among her greatest doubters, including her own mother and father. Their daughter had lied to them many times before, and they knew she was lying to them then; they just couldn't figure out how or why.

Months later, Mock, to her great surprise and dismay, discovered she'd become pregnant as a result of Early's attack, and, as time passed, it became impossible for her to conceal the fact that she was going to have a baby. As soon as her family became aware of her condition, they knew immediately that she'd lied to them several months earlier. Worse still, they were convinced that Mock wasn't as innocent as she claimed. If she was truly blameless, they reasoned, why in hell wouldn't she have spoken up at the time?

Now, long after the fact, when Mock cast all blame for her pregnancy on Early, it didn't do much to change their minds. They barely knew and certainly did not respect or trust the man, but their daughter had a bad reputation of her own to account for. They knew very well any further investigation would boil down to her word against his, since it was too late to prove exactly what had happened — especially if Early denied the charge or claimed that their relations had been consensual, as they knew he most certainly would.

Mock's family's first reaction was to altogether reject her allegations of unprovoked rape against Early, saying that she ought to have known better and that she should go back to her lover and plead for him to accept her for marriage. No child, they screamed, should be brought into the world without a father.

At this point, Mock suddenly panicked and saw that she had no other option but to wrap her mind around doing what her parents were pushing her to do. After summoning up every ounce of courage she could muster, a miserably dejected and thoroughly unnerved but determinedly dutiful Mock trudged away from her family home. She set out on miles of unpaved road, walking the dusty miles through her rural community that had to be traversed to reach the isolated piece of property that belonged to Early, the man who had so greatly wronged her only a few short months before. She knew right where he lived, as did everyone else in the area. She knew, too, that he lived alone, in a run-down old shack of a place that was even more scraggly looking than the unkempt land on which it stood.

After a few hours or so, she arrived at Early's front door. She paused for a few minutes on his stoop, her chin down on her chest, her heart beating a mile a minute, and her mind spinning in trepidation. After pulling herself together as best she could, she began to knock, timidly at first but then more forcefully.

Just as soon as Early opened his door and stood before her in his entry way, Mock launched into a tearful and emotional explanation of what she had deluded herself into believing he would think of as *their* tragic situation. Bawling openly as she spoke, she told him about her condition. Then, in terms as forceful as she could summon up, and in the tone her parents had instructed her to use, she demanded that he accept the responsibility of patrimony and take on his rightful role as the father of their child. Beginning hesitantly, but then with greater stridency as her story flowed out, she pleaded with him not to leave her to deal with *their* situation alone.

Early was as knocked back on his heels upon learning of her condition as Mock had been herself, back when she first became aware of it, only a few months earlier. In shock over what she said, he stood before her in open-mouthed amazement, wondering if what she was saying might really be true. *How could it be, though?* he thought. He'd been with the damned girl for only a few minutes on one miserable evening, minutes he could hardly even remember. The only thing he did remember well about that evening was how blasted angry he had been after she cold-shouldered him as if he were a total stranger. Who the hell did she think she was? he had asked himself.

Early had to tax his mind before he could recall much more about what had taken place that night at the dance, but, after he did begin to remember, the central thought that jumped into his mind was how she had been only one of a series of stuck-up women who snubbed him that evening. Thinking about how they treated him outraged him even more. *The last thing I ought to do,* he thought, *is start feeling sorry for any one of those sorry bitches.*

Why in holy hell, he thought after collecting himself for a while, *does stupid stuff of this kind always happen to me?* How did his drinking buddies Jack and Dub and Dempsey always manage to dodge these bullets, when he never could? Getting involved in *her situation*, he swore, was the last thing he intended to do.

Mock had seen in an instant that Early would never be the kind of accommodating and understanding mature man she had prayed to encounter. He bluntly claimed that he hardly even knew who the hell she was, then said did not want to have a damned thing to do with her. "There's no way under the sun that I'm the father of your kid," he yelled, "and you have a hell of a lot of nerve making that kind of accusation against me."

When Mock attempted to persist, he responded, "You behave like a whore. Any man in town could be your baby's father."

Then he slapped her hard in the face to make her to stop wailing. After that, he spun her around by the shoulders, kicked her in the butt, and told her to get the hell off his property, and slammed his door shut behind her.

When Early slammed that door on her, Mock felt like her head was going to explode. She stood for a while on the walk that led away from his porch, nearly overcome by a gut-wrenching combination of embarrassment, grief, worry, and fear, all rolled up in one devastating package. It was the worst day of her life, second only to the day of the rape itself.

After standing a little longer on his walkway as if frozen in place, she turned around and slowly began the dusty trudge back to her parents and home, sobbing more with each step she took. Her situation seemed so hopeless that she thought seriously about jumping off a bridge.

It was not until this miserable juncture that Mock took full note of the reality of her situation. All of her appeals for help had been rejected, and she had appealed to every person she thought might be able to help. Unfortunately, she had enthusiastically burned as many bridges as she could think of — *and then some* — before she got into trouble, which meant that no one was willing to go to bat for her when her life started going badly. She could not see even as much as a flicker of hope that might mitigate or stave off her all-enveloping gloom; all she saw before her was abject hopelessness.

What a mess, I thought as Clarence recounted her dismal story. Poor Mock, it seems, was literally surrounded by rejection, no matter which way she turned.

THE ONLY SENSIBLE SOLUTION

FEELING HOPELESS AND SEEING no other way to turn, Mock eventually ended up pouring out her miserable story to the only authority figures in the community who were willing to listen — a Baptist missionary couple that had long been active among the Indians of her area. They were a well-known man and woman, people who commanded quite a bit of local respect. Begging for their assistance, she repeated her accusation of forcible rape against Early.

Her story was convincing enough for the couple to get involved, even though she had not reported the rape until months after it happened and even then not until she had become visibly pregnant. They felt more than a little bit skeptical about her version of what had happened, especially after talking with her parents, who clearly didn't believe it themselves. Everyone, it was clear, was well aware of Mock's reputation in the community.

Because the need for her baby to have a father and for its mother to have a husband took precedence over taking sides with either Mock or Early, the two missionaries did their best to arrive at what they considered to be a reasonable solution under the circumstances. Basically, they used all the influence they could bring to bear to pressure Early to do what they considered to be in the best interests of the unborn child, the mother, and the community as a whole. They made it clear that they expected him to marry Mock.

After pulling together a group of local leaders and a few other influential people to apply additional pressure, they called Early and Mock in for a questioning and counseling session. After only a brief period of probing, the domineering and highly influential missionaries extracted a confession from Early that he had, in fact, had *consensual* sex with Mock that evening many months before. He adamantly denied having committed a rape. Everyone in attendance was skeptical of his protestations, especially after Mock brought forth a series of relatives who described how she'd been beaten on the night of the incident.

Before long Early got the message that formal charges of some kind might be brought against him if he refused to accept responsibility for what he'd done. Perhaps fearing yet another long stay in the bug-infested local jail or a threat of violence against him by one of Mock's relatives, he finally saw the wisdom of agreeing to accept his responsibility for her pregnancy. In effect, the powers that be shamed, cajoled, and threatened him into marrying and promising to provide for Mock, all for the sake of the unborn child.

Later, when I read the write-up of this sad affair, it seemed clear that it had been handled with a great deal of disdain for the veracity of both principals. But, the realities of the times being what they were, the missionary couple and other local authority figures must be given credit for having orchestrated a solution that promised some small chance of Mock and her unborn child being provided for over the long haul.

It seemed that forcing the two antagonists to get married was viewed as a viable means of solving two thorny local problems with one blow: Mock needed a husband and a home for her unborn child, and Early, for the sake of the community at large, needed a concrete reason to get his boozing and overall dissolute behavior under control. Marriage, everyone seemed to have figured, might provide the incentive both of them needed to come to their senses and grow up a bit. Regardless of what Mock and Early thought of the solution that was forced upon them, Early Tiger and Etta *Mock* Burnham were officially joined as man and wife on November 22, 1882, out in the Oklahoma Indian Territory.

THE FAMILY LIFE OF TIGERS

ACCORDING TO CLARENCE, the relationship that evolved over the years between Early and his unfortunate wife Mock not unsurprisingly turned out to be more accurately described as *hanging around together when it couldn't be avoided* than as an actual marriage. Without doubt, theirs was a pitiful union, one that overflowed with unhappiness. Everyone in the community knew all about their relationship, but no one in the area was *on their side*, so to speak, and thus there was no one around to help or guide or support them in any appreciable way. For better or worse, from the first day of their marriage, they were entirely on their own.

When all the dust of their conflagration finally settled down, Early's perspective on their situation remained the same as it had been from the beginning: He had been forced into a marriage he did not want, and to a woman he hardly knew and for whom he had not even an ounce of respect. Through twisted logic that only he could justify, he blamed everything that had happened to them on her alone and refused to accept any responsibility for having committed a travesty against her.

Moreover, Mock's family continued to believe that she must have been partially responsible for what happened, no matter how vehemently she denied it. Knowing that she had behaved promiscuously in the past, they were convinced she had encouraged Early's bad behavior. They thought the way she had carried on had dishonored their family, so they responded by cold-shouldering her from that point forward.

When her time finally rolled around, Mock gave birth to a squalling baby girl she named Bonnie. The child was born one month prematurely on January 15, 1883, when her father Early was forty-three and her mother Etta was twenty-one years old. The baby, as if some sort of plan had been put in place to make a bad situation even worse, was unhealthy from the day it was born, and it stayed unhealthy nearly all the way through childhood. Members of Mock's family were said to have marveled in later years that she had been able to get it through infancy and childhood, due to its poor health and the fact that her worthless husband had provided little to no support and always treated his wife and child as if they were dirt under his feet.

Although her daughter's first name was Bonnie, she was so whiney and irritable during childhood that Mock started calling her *Tiger*, after her own married surname. The nickname stuck.

The little girl grew up in the midst of a domestic relationship that was dysfunctional from the day she was born. Throughout her younger years, for example, she had to watch as Early liberally applied his horse training methods to the development and control of his life partner, her mother. As he grew more and more dissolute over the years, battering Mock became routine in their relationship . . . and poor Tiger grew up watching it happen.

Back in those days, people didn't question a husband's right to *discipline* his wife as he saw fit, especially if his wife had a reputation as suspect as Mock's. Early, therefore, felt free to *correct* her as needed, so that's what he often did, without much restraint or inhibition. Whenever she failed to obey his husbandly commands, he would, in his own words, proceed to "teach her pretty good." Because Mock had so few rights and because she knew there was nothing that could be done about it, she more or less accepted the right of her husband to treat her the way he did. Back then, a woman's rights and social prerogatives were not even close to what they are today, especially in a backwater Indian community such as theirs. She was up a creek without a paddle.

For years Mock stoically accepted her fate. All this changed one day in July of 1891, when she just up and disappeared. No one was ever able to say what became of her — whether, that is, she had simply "run off and left him," which is what Early told everyone had happened, or she had been killed or kidnapped or whatever. Knowing the couple as well as they did, people considered any one possibility as plausible as any other. In the end, though, there seems to have been no one around who considered it their business or responsibility to pursue the matter. Because Mock had no real protector, her absence elicited no concern on the part of anyone. She just disappeared, and she was never heard from again.

Their child, Bonnie, was eight years old. The only fatherly care Early ever gave her was whatever others shamed him into providing, and that was marginal at best.

As Tiger grew older, it came as no surprise to anyone when her father began to *train* his daughter the same way he had *trained* horses and all three of his wives before they left him. In those days sparing the rod was thought of as a sure way of spoiling a child, and this philosophy was one that gave Early all the license he needed to discipline his daughter in a deliberate and calculated way. He still resented having had to marry her mother, and he resented even more that he'd ended up with the sole responsibility for raising a child to adulthood, a child he still claimed may not even be his own.

He viewed his daughter in the same light as he had viewed

her mother before her — as a flighty sort of person, someone he constantly suspected of impropriety and promiscuity. His attitude was in all respect just as illogical and unfair as it sounds, but even during her childhood years he seems to have thought of her as a loose and immoral woman. He was determined to drive that kind of behavior out of her before it was too late. As a result, Tiger grew up terrified of her own father, as cowed by his presence as all the other creatures he'd trained before her. It was how he treated her, everyone said, that caused her to grow up as wild and as irresponsible as she was, especially after she grew old enough to begin having relationships with men.

NO ONE TO CARE

BONNIE TIGER LIVED UNDER her father's domineering thumb until he died on March 17, 1904, at the age of sixty-four. He ended up being viewed as just another hopeless, indolent Indian, a man who passed away too early due to having lived a drunken and dissolute life. He had been rejected by his family and friends, despised by his own three wives, and hated and feared by his own daughter. He left behind a dismal track record.

Upon her father's death, Tiger, who was twenty-one years old at the time, inherited and continued to inhabit the meager estate her father left behind. It consisted of a run-down and unpainted old frame house and some shoddy furniture, a couple of horses, a few cows and pigs and chickens, and little to no cash money to speak of. Her inheritance left her just what she had been before; an isolated and impoverished Indian, living off her garden and wild fish and game and whatever government assistance that was being doled out at the time. Her prospects seemed bleak indeed.

"WHAT A MISERABLE EXISTENCE they had," I said to Clarence after he finished describing what life was like for Etta (Burnham)

Tiger and her unfortunate daughter Bonnie while they lived with Early. "Under the control of a man like him, they didn't have a chance of enjoying a decent existence, and it sure seems to me that Bonnie got the worst of it."

Now that I knew how he had behaved, I no longer felt the least bit of sympathy for Early. At this point, I could hardly wait for Clarence to explain what happened to the two women.

"Well," he continued, "Mock and her daughter Bonnie's stories was just as interestin' to everbody in our area back then as they are to you today. People talked all the time about the trouble Etta herself got into, and nobody ever had much of anything good to say about her as a person or as a daughter. She lied to and disrespected her own momma and daddy, and she snubbed nearly everbody else. Them Burnhams was good people everbody thought well of, but the same couldn't be said for her, whose nickname, as I said, was *Mock*. Until she got herself in trouble, she didn't have no use for nobody. She always thought she was gonna leave town, so she didn't give a damn about whether she offended anybody or not. She never cared what anybody thought about anything. I wasn't there at the time, of course, but my dad told me all about her. Most of what I've told you about her up to this point, I got from him.

"That girl got into so damned much trouble, she ended up becoming a Sunday School example of what can happen when kids are disobedient and disrespectful to their parents. Her story became a local cautionary tale, somethin' that was brought up any time a set of parents had a point to make, especially them that was having' trouble keepin' their kids in line. Everybody referred to it as '*The Story of Mock's Bad Stomp*,' and there wasn't a person in our area who hadn't heard about it." (In later years, the story was published as a book entitled *Mock's Bad Stomp*.)

"Life turned out a lot different, though," he said, "for Early and Etta's daughter Bonnie when she grew up. Tiger, which was what everbody called her, managed to get into plenty of trouble too, but in an entirely different way. Back when her daddy died, she didn't know nothin' about what was goin' on in our part of the country. She had no idea the federal government was plannin' changes that would affect every Indian in the Territory. Her prospects was about to improve in ways she couldn't even imagine."

"That's great to know," I said. "In view of her dismal childhood, it's wonderful to hear that life got better for her."

"Whoa there," Clarence immediately replied. "Hold up just a minute. I didn't say Tiger *did better*, I just said that *her social standing and prospects changed*. They did, but that's what got her into a whole new kind of trouble. You ain't heard nothing' yet. Hold your water until I've told you about her father, Colonel George Jackson Caine, who was so notorious in our area back in the old days that he, too, ended up causin' all kinds of problems. My daddy's stories and all the rest I heard about his carrying' on when I was comin' up is why I know so much about him today. He really stirred the local pot while he was alive, that's for damned sure." (Clarence died without knowing that in later years a book entitled *The Disgrace of Colonel Caine* would be written to explain exactly how the infamous Colonel eventually met his end.)

12

GEORGE AND BONNIE (TIGER) CAINE

FROM THE DAY OF her birth, Early and Etta *Mock* (Burnham) Tiger's daughter Bonnie's life was beset by difficulties that would have tested the strength of even an emotionally stable and secure person, something she most certainly was not. On top of having had to deal with all the routine coming of age problems young people experience, Tiger grew up psychologically burdened by the unspeakable pain of growing up in a home where she was neither loved nor wanted. Clarence said it was well known within the community that for her, these challenges had been a heavy cross to bear.

Despite her fearsome sounding nickname and reputed toughness, Tiger was anything but a strong or discerning young woman, especially when it came to the management of her personal affairs. She grew up a wild and unruly child, living on the scantest of essentials — sporadic care that was grudgingly provided by her drunken and surly father, occasional government handouts of food and clothing, any small game she could trap, nuts and berries harvested out of the nearby Deep Fork River bottom, and fish caught in local creeks and ponds. In addition, she did odd jobs and various chores for neighbors from time to time, just to earn a little bit of spending money. Getting along by hook or by crook, she more or less raised herself, with her father Early seldom lifting a finger on her behalf.

It was not immediately evident to casual contacts that Tiger was a severely wounded person, but she most definitely was. The emotional damage she had suffered was as real as a heart attack.

Having been raised in woeful conditions, it wasn't a surprise to anyone that she grew up to be an insecure and unbalanced young woman. "What else," her neighbors must have wondered, just as I did after hearing about her childhood for the first time, "could have been expected?"

Her plight had been well known in the community, but she and her father were too stubborn and uncooperative to be helped or dealt with in traditional ways. When offered a chance to go live with a relative after she and her father were abandoned without a word by her mother, Tiger elected to go on living in the only home she had ever known. As uncaring as he was, she chose to remain with her father, probably because of her fear of the unknown and possibly due to fear of what he might do to her if she left him. After initially refusing an opportunity to attend a school established for Indian children in her area, a Creek Indian school in nearby Okmulgee, she relented, but then attended only for a while, dropping out for good a short time later.

Everyone in the community thought Tiger was being raised under home conditions deplorable enough for her own mother to abandon husband and child alike, but no effective social mechanisms acceptable to her and her father were in place to help deal with their situation. She had no choice, therefore, but to grow to maturity under the thumb of a man who was the object of local ridicule and disrespect, not only in the opinion of most of their Indian neighbors but in the eyes of local whites, civic and religious leaders, and other authorities as well. All of them considered it as predictable as changes in seasons that growing up in such circumstances would produce a young woman woefully unprepared for assuming the responsibilities of adult life.

Uncle Clarence made it clear that Tiger wasn't held in high esteem by her peers and neighbors, either. Most of them looked upon her as an exceptionally difficult person, not only because of her well-known record for general irresponsibility but also because she had a terribly negative attitude. Because most everyone had trouble getting along with her, she grew up living in the same way as her father — existing on the fringes of society as it was at the time, essentially alone, emotionally isolated, and getting by in her own private world. She was, in the opinion of most everyone, an accident ready to happen.

AS IF TIGER'S PERSONAL situation wasn't already dismal enough, she also had to deal with same gamut of realities that bedeviled all the Indians of her area during her time. As was the case for too many of her people, the forces of isolation, unworldliness, and poverty combined to make her a highly vulnerable human being, and her many personal problems had rendered her even more vulnerable still. All that had saved her in the past from being easy pickings for anyone with exploitation in mind was that nothing in her life was worthy of being exploited. She had no money or land or marketable skills, no wealth of any kind that would be of advantage to anyone. In this regard, she wasn't alone; a good many of the Indians of her area were in the same boat. In this sense, she was the equal of many of her peers, despite her marginal social status within the community.

Through further research, I learned that even though Tiger, like her father before her, had grown up in what still was the independent Creek Nation of the Oklahoma Indian Territory, she had come of age just as the social structure her people were accustomed to was going through a period of dramatic change that took place in the years just before Oklahoma became a state of the Union. She was caught up in several key events that forever changed the lives of the Indian people who lived there.

What happened was that the Creeks, even after being forcibly *removed* and *resettled* from their original homelands in the eastern United States to their new tribal location in the Oklahoma Territory, wound up living on land that white as well as black settlers and other interest groups soon began to covet. That the land had been assigned to the tribe by the federal government mattered only minimally to these groups, so they never stopped pushing their way further into the Territory. Basically, they just ignored all the treaties and Indian rights that supposedly existed at the time. Their trespassing was illegal, but it happened just the same. Powerful interest groups such as cattlemen and railroad companies continued to pressure the federal government to open any and all specifically unassigned land — and some that *was* assigned — in and around the Indian nations for homesteading and development.

For these and other reasons, the supposedly independent and self-governing Creek people were not able to escape all the scheming parties that were eager to get their hands on their land. Indian leaders clearly realized what the intrusion of white settlers would mean to their race and to their ownership of their land, but they lacked the political astuteness and power to change the course of events that were taking place. Numerous boundary and jurisdictional changes continued to occur in Oklahoma over the years, and all of them had the effect of pushing the Indians into an ever-decreasing amount of space.

The excuse the federal government needed to finally strip the Creek Indians of their last jointly owned tribal land was provided by the Civil War. What happened was that many of the Creeks, like many (but not all) of the Indian tribes, chose to side with the South against the Union. They sided with the Confederacy due to South's hostility to their common enemy, the federal government, and due to the belief of southern leaders in the concept of state's rights and regional autonomy. If the Southerners could win the war, some of the Creeks thought, they would be much more likely to sympathize with the Indians' desire for independence than the Union, which was dominated mainly by northern and eastern whites, who believed in a strong and centralized federal government.

The Creeks were already at internal odds with one another when this fateful decision was made. Most of the Indians had little use for whites of any political persuasion, but some of their main leaders thought the South had only the slimmest chance of winning the war and that siding with them, therefore, would only end in disaster for their people. What finally happened was a self-destructive internal split, one that led to one faction of the Creeks fighting for the South and another faction fighting for the North.

Creek soldiers on each side fought fierce and bloody battles against one another during the war.

When the South was finally defeated in the 1860s, the federal government had all the justification that was needed to, in effect, punish the Indians for siding against the Union. Retribution came in the form of insisting that the resettled tribes renegotiate their land treaties as compensation. The major motivation for renegotiating the treaties all along was that doing so would clear the way to open more land for white settlement and, at the same time, make room for freed black slaves, people that the government had promised to help after the end of the war.

The ensuing treaty renegotiations effectively dismantled not only the concept of Indian self-government, but also did away with a large part of the tribal ownership of land and the reservation system as well. The overall amount of land set aside for reservations was reduced by means of the new treaties, even as more Indian tribes from other parts of the country were resettled in the Indian Territory in the following years. What these changes meant for many of the Indians on a practical level was that they were eventually rendered even more vulnerable to exploitation by more sophisticated white speculators, developers, and settlers than they already were. Before the era was over, many of them ended up losing their shirts.

The specific legal framework employed by the Congress of the United States to free up more Indian Territory land for settlement was the Dawes Act of 1887. The Act was designed to deal with the special situation of the Indians that had been confined to reservations, and the effect of it was to bring an end to traditional tribal life and push more Indians into adopting white modes of living. The tribes themselves were dissolved under the provisions of the Act, and tribal ownership of lands was ended.

Individual land ownership, a concept that was still unfamiliar and suspect among the Indians of those times and therefore still not supported by many of them, became the law of the land. Each married Indian male was allotted one hundred sixty acres to a farm, while each adult single man or woman received eighty acres. Freed blacks were conveniently designated *adoptees* of the various tribes, thereby creating a legal justification for giving them allotment land as well. This gave the federal government a way of living up to promises of future assistance that were made to black freedmen during the civil war.

Once the Indian tribal land was broken down into identifiable parcels and deeded to individual Indian allottees, the new landowners (within certain limitations) were eventually freed to sell or lease or transfer their land rights as they so desired. At the same time, the Dawes Act also made it possible for non-Indians to claim and settle on any land that was not specifically allotted to individual Indians or blacks. The Creek Nation had been an isolated place that most whites didn't know much about, but that changed in a hurry after the new laws were implemented. Whenever any new tracts of Indian Territory were made available to outside settlers, white investors, speculators, and settlers immediately flocked in to take advantage of the opportunity.

TIGER'S FIRST SALVATION

TIGER'S FIRST SALVATION OCCURRED in 1904, when she was directly affected by the provisions of the Dawes Act. She became one of the Indians of her area who were on the receiving end of the federal government's land allotment program. She was given an eighty-acre allotment of her own due to having reached adulthood, and she also inherited the 160-acre allotment that had been deeded to her father before he passed away.

Becoming the owner of 240 acres of land was a major event in Tiger's life, one that left her feeling as high as a kite — totally elated by her new-found fortune. She knew the land was worth money, especially now that so many outsiders had become interested in settling thereabouts. Owning a block of land also conferred a certain amount of status that she hadn't had before. For these two reasons, she began to think that some of the greatest problems of her life either had been or were about to be solved.

Another federal government-initiated change that had an impact on her was that she was formally assigned a *full and proper* (meaning *white*) name when she received her land allotment. A middle name was given to her because the administrators of the program were required to record *full names* for anyone to whom government land was allotted, legal names having been deemed necessary for government census and record-keeping purposes.

Indians who had only partial or no formal or legal white names were simply assigned new ones, right on the spot, as allotments were awarded. With free land being doled out like manna from heaven, few Indians felt any great desire to question the practice. Not only did the assignment of new names seem fair and reasonable under the circumstances, but most of the Indians were also pleased to get them. It was in this way and for this reason that from that time forth Bonnie Tiger became legally known as Bonnie *Marie* Tiger.

For her, receiving a land allotment had been a great moment, a watershed event she fully expected to propel her to a new and better future. In the long run, though, that didn't happen; instead, receiving free land led to new challenges that she and many other Indians could not have anticipated.

My own take on Bonnie Tiger's situation, after all the background research I did, was that despite outward appearances, she ended up becoming one of the Indians who were effectively separated from their property by a white man, one of those who used means that ranged from the abuse of court appointed guardianships to outright fraud to get what he wanted. One of the ways some Indians lost control of their land was as simple — and as legal — as marriage, and it appeared to me that that's what happened to her.

Her many problems turned her into a plum ripe and ready for picking, and it was good fortune in the form of receiving allotment land that brought the fruit to market. What befell her wasn't a particularly unusual consequence of Indian land ownership in those days; similarly adverse outcomes befell a good number of others just like her, men and women and children alike. For too many Indians, in fact, placing an asset with a cash value in their hands was like pouring fuel on an open flame. Like Bonnie, many of them were not prepared to deal with the changes that came their way. In Tiger's case, the hammer fell in a way that would have predictable, had anyone been watching.

BONNIE TIGER WAS ONLY one of thousands of Indians who lived in a section of the Oklahoma Indian Territory that had become especially attractive to white developers, speculators, and settlers — aggressive people who saw great opportunity in these newly available areas of land. Immediately after the federal government made the land available, these folks started showing up in large numbers, each one of them looking to claim a piece of the pie as their own. The tactics these aggressive outsiders used to pursue their goals created a perplexing and threatening period of change for Indian people.

Tiger's immediate area was considered especially promising by many hopeful settlers, developers, and speculators, simply because it was fertile and still full of natural game as well as natural resources. Due to a high annual rainfall, it was an area that stayed green for most of the year, which meant that plenty of grass was available for grazing horses and cattle. In addition, there were large groves of commercially valuable hardwood timber — oak, hickory, black walnut, and pecan — in the bottomlands of local creeks and rivers. On top of all this, commercially accessible reserves of coal and oil had been discovered in the vicinity.

Tiger's back yard, it could be said, had moved to the front burner in terms of its readiness for economically viable commercial exploitation and development. In the past, her area had been too remote and rough to be easily accessible by land, but this problem was solved in 1905 when the Muskogee Union Railway (later called the Missouri, Oklahoma, and Gulf Railroad (the *MO&G*), announced plans for an extension into the area from nearby Muskogee.

At this point a group of wealthy investors, men by the names of Charles E. Davis, Ira E. Davis, Noah B. Davis, Elmer E. Schock, and J. H. Osborne, joined forces to form a company to develop the land around where Bonnie Marie Tiger lived. The investors hired two men, J. M. Kinyon and G. E. Carney, to launch their new venture and handle its day–to–day operations. They made the two men the exclusive land agents of the new business, which they named The Hoffman Townsite and Realty Company.

In January of 1905, a short time before the new railroad extension was completed, Kinyon and Carney identified a site for a new town site in the area they had been charged with developing. The new town was to be built within a plot of 160 acres they purchased from its original freedman allottee, a man by the name of George Hawkins. Tiger's own allotment land was only a short distance away.

As soon as the town site land was in their hands, the developers plotted it into residential and commercial lots that they put up for immediate sale. The lots were made available to buyers in August of 1905, just as the rail line to the town site was completed by the regional railway company. The town was named Hoffman in honor of William Hoffman, one of the vice presidents of the railroad company.

As soon as rail service was extended to the townsite, there was an immediate boom in the number of homestead claim filings and other forms of land purchasing and use. Speculators bought land in hopes of being able to resell it for immediate short-term profits, while others bought it for purposes of long-term investment.

Land churning was common in those days, and it was a perfectly legal practice. Investors and settlers alike were unabashedly interested in full and immediate exploitation of local natural resources such as timber, oil, and coal in order to make as much cash as possible, as quickly as possible. Land acquisition records for the years that followed indicate that many of the more astute developers were careful to buy up, whenever they could, mineral rights as well as raw land.

The town of Hoffman was officially incorporated on August 29, 1905, while the land it was on which it was located was still part of Oklahoma Indian Territory. It was launched from the beginning as a private commercial development, and the first lot at the townsite was sold the same day. The State of Oklahoma and, in turn,

McIntosh County, in which the town was located, did not come into being until several years later, in 1907. Then, in 1918, political jurisdiction over Hoffman was transferred to Okmulgee County.

FROM THE DAY HOFFMAN was incorporated, land investment opportunities in and around the town were aggressively promoted to all comers. Potential buyers were drawn in from many parts of the country, but most of them came in from nearby states such as Arkansas, Mississippi, and Missouri. Several of the men who were involved in the town site development company either already were or soon became among the first residents of the town, thus they had a vested self-interest in seeing it grow and prosper. Any land they didn't use for their own ventures was, of course, sold for their own personal profit. In turn, many of those who bought plots of land immediately marked them up for further speculative resale. Again, churning land for speculative purposes was a common practice in those days, and it was perfectly legal.

The developers were highly aggressive and expansive when it came to promoting their newly formed townsite. Touting the area in glowing terms, it was described in their promotional literature exactly as repeated below:

> *Hoffman, I.T., is at present a town of about 500 population, located on the M. O. & G. Railroad about 35 miles southwest of Muskogee and 12 miles east of Henryetta in the center of the Creek Nation, Indian Territory. It is surrounded by the most fertile and productive farm prairie and timberlands in the Territory, which is adapted to all the cereals of the North and also cotton, the king of crops in the South. It is located on a parallel west of Fort Smith, Arkansas, which gives us a climate that has neither extremes of heat or cold. This is demonstrated by the scenic effects produced by the profusion of which all flowers and shrubbery grow, and as a fruit country our soil is unsurpassed.*
>
> *With these surroundings we have a country we can well feel proud of, and as a location for a town Hoffman has many advantages that will attract the prospective homeseeker and*

speculator, as we have an ideal location for a tile and brick plant and a material that as a clay will stand the inspection of the most skeptical, and we are located accessible to the best coal fields in the Indian Territory. We are also accessible to the Deep Fork of the Canadian River, which would supply any demand for water for manufacturing purposes; and being well timbered with all the harder growths of marketable timber which would supply an unlimited demand for fuel for manufacturing purposes.

Since the time of opening, the town has grown beyond the expectation of all who reside here, and all who visit the place are very agreeably surprised at the marvelous growth of the town and the unsurpassed quality of the soil, that insures the town a good and permanent support. Any desiring a location of any kind or who is looking for a place of investment will receive the most courteous attention by visiting or addressing the Hoffman Townsite & Realty Company.

Somewhere along the line, a newspaper called *The Hoffman Herald* opened for business in Hoffman. The editor, a man by the name of O. E. O'Bleness, who, of course, also had vested interests of his own in the town, published a regular series of articles that further touted the many attractions of the new townsite, its people, and its many new buildings. Using his own words, on April 5, 1905, he wrote:

To begin at the beginning would be somewhat like writing the history before the historian were born, but even this would be possible where the land marks were so plain as they were when the writer of these lines first set his foot on the townsite of where Hoffman now stands. Our first visit to the town was in October of last year, and at that time it consisted only of a few trading places and a very few small dwellings, but after looking over the surrounding country, it took us only a short time to arrive at the conclusion that it was just such as would someday support a thriving city of several thousand people.

Whether it was by accident or otherwise, it matters not, but it is a fact that the townsite people could not have made a better selection for the location of a town than right here where Hoffman now stands. This land is rich, well-watered bottomland and capable of growing a profitable crop of almost anything in the vegetable, fruit or cereal line. To the north of the town lies hundreds, yes, thousands of acres of rolling, black sandy prairie land covered with a growth of bluestem grass from three to five feet high, which is only wanting the attention of the industrious farmer when it will produce crops that will return him a hundred fold for his efforts.

In fact, all the land surrounding the town is rich agricultural land, excepting a range of small hills to the south and west, and they are underlaid with heavy deposits of good coal and vast lakes of oil. In fact, only seven miles west on the M. O. & G Railway this coal deposit is now being successfully worked and it is only reasonable to presume that at no distant date a profitable coal and oil field will be opened almost within the town limits of Hoffman. Yes, we might go on and write columns regarding the country but the above is sufficient to show that the country around Hoffman when properly farmed is sufficient to support a city of several thousand.

If there was money to be made, the honorable Mr. O'Bleness, an objective journalist if there ever was one, clearly wanted to be in on the action.

Interested parties from neighboring states started making visits to inspect the townsite and the surrounding area, and some of them either made investments or stayed on in the hope of their own bite of the pie. At the time, purchasing land in places like Hoffman was considered a great opportunity for entrepreneurs and homesteaders of all kinds, from those interested in farming and ranching to those interested in starting small businesses or opening professional offices. The town had become, to use a common expression, a hot property, a place with a future that looked promising and bright.

The original residents of the Hoffman area — most of them Creek Indians and freed blacks or their descendants — were, of course, immediately and dramatically affected by all these changes. They were, in fact, more or less surrounded by newly arriving investors, speculators, and settlers, all of them eager to cash in on what the place had to offer. It was a heady time for everyone, natives and settlers alike.

New arrivals began to construct homes, create farms and

ranches, open new businesses, build banks and churches and other kinds of buildings, and to develop the basic government services needed to support local needs. Everyone was anxious to get about the business of making money in their new and exciting hometown.

Most of the town's new citizens came in as true settlers, people with dreams of owning their own land and cultivating farms, building up ranches, starting a small trade or craft business, or opening various kinds of retail stores or other commercial enterprises. By far the great majority of them were hard working people, individuals in search of an honest economic opportunity who had been drawn to the area by the spirit of adventure and the possibility of owning their own places. These were the dreams that combined to make the area something of a magnet, a lodestone that many were unable to pass up or resist.

At the same time, though, ample documentary evidence exists to prove that a good number of those who showed up in the area were far more opportunists and gamblers than true settlers or honest investors. Many of these people were interested only in finding a way make a quick buck, and they didn't have many scruples about how they went about doing it. Speculators, schemers, scam artists, and outright crooks descended upon the relatively naive and often illiterate native Indians and blacks who lived in and around Hoffman, all of them hoping to make a killing through any quasi-legal — and sometimes clearly illegal — means they could devise and still stay out of jail.

Researchers have documented through the examination of land transfer records for the early years of the townsite development period that some white trustees appointed by the courts to, for example, *help* minor or orphaned Indian and Negro land allottees actually either bought their land for a pittance or defrauded them of its true value through other legal but highly unethical means. In one way or another, many of the original Indian and Negro land allottees in the former Indian Territory were conned out of all or part of the value of their land. A good number of them ended up out on the street, literally as well as figuratively, without a dollar in their hands.

What made matters even worse for locals and new arrivals alike was that the banking and investment companies of those times were essentially unregulated. With little or no oversight or operating guidelines to restrict their activities, the public was not well protected from poor business practices, fraud, embezzlement, or overt criminal activity. Owners of banks, as an example, were among those who speculated freely and legally on local properties and business ventures in their own right, often unintentionally — and in some cases intentionally — subsuming the interests of their depositors to their own. Serious problems are far more likely to crop up when the assets of individuals and businesses become commingled with the personal assets of the owners of financial institutions. Problems of this kind were common during this tumultuous period of time.

Bonnie Marie Tiger's lot in life was greatly improved over what it had been only a few years before, now that she had become the proud owner of 240 acres of allotment land as well as the recipient of dependable government subsistence checks and regular rations of staples. It seemed to her that for the first time in her life, her Indian heritage was paying off in a tangible way.

Despite having become a property owner, though, her social status hadn't become any more elevated in the community; locals still looked down on her as a woman with an unsavory reputation. Worse still, she knew as well as anyone that Hoffman was a small farm town in which everybody knew just about everybody else, which meant that routine gossip would be the pipeline through which her reputation would become as well known to new settlers as it was to those who already lived in the area, whites and Indians alike.

Unfortunately for Tiger, the opinion everyone held of her was that she was an intemperate and unruly person. Folks considered it unwise to have anything more to do with her than was absolutely necessary, and, because she'd been raised under conditions that would have been a backbreaker for most anyone, no one thought of her as a good prospect for a solid marriage. Her many personal hang-ups and odd behavioral quirks, it was generally agreed, assured that there wasn't much chance of her being able to enter into and sustain a satisfying marital existence.

Sadly, her behavior as she grew to young womanhood only strengthened the widely held conviction that she was damaged and different. Having been whipped into blind and fearful obedience to a drunken father, she was forever resentful, once she was out from under his thumb, of any and all authority, whether it was rightful and legitimate or not. She was particularly suspicious and hostile toward men, especially Indian men — men, that is, like her own father. Residents of Hoffman were well aware of all this, and that's why it was so widely thought that things would continue to go badly for her.

Life was confusing for many Indian people at the time, but this must have been especially true for a single young woman like Bonnie, who had only a tenuous grip on her affairs in the first place. In those days, women everywhere still lived in a man's world, and this reality was even more highly pronounced out in her neck of the woods than it was everywhere else. At the time, it was a real problem for a woman to have a chip on her shoulder towards men.

Further, because she was a young woman who lived with a considerable amount of weight on her shoulders, Tiger was prone to grasping for simple solutions for difficult problems. What most everyone thought and said of her was "Like father, like daughter." People saw her as a woman with a ready-made reputation, and it didn't matter a whit to them whether she had come by it honestly or not.

TIGER'S SECOND SALVATION

BONNIE TIGER'S SECOND SALVATION occurred when she came into contact with a white settler by the name of George Jackson Caine, one of the many new arrivals who had shown up in the still relatively new Oklahoma Indian Territory town of Hoffman in search of opportunity, and the record indicates that she rather quickly grew to think of him as someone who had a good chance of moving up in their community. There's little doubt that she thought of him as a star to whom one's wagon could be profitably hitched. There is no record to describe how the two of them first got together, but their particular blending of red and white quickly led to a formal union. They were married on May 12, 1913, after a courtship of less than two months.

The majority of those who knew them considered their marriage to be fraught with potential problems, since it was widely believed that both partners had entered the relationship for all the wrong reasons. How could the future possibly go well for the couple, people reasoned, when the husband and wife alike came across as being obviously desirous of using one another only as a means to an end? He had married her, they thought, just to get at her land and regular income, while she had married him only because she was convinced that marriage to an Anglo would improve her social status in the community. As she saw it, his interest in her was one of the greatest benefits of having received allotment land and other allowances from the federal government.

Those who knew them weren't shy about predicting that their marriage had less than a snowball's chance in hell of standing up over the long haul. There's no way to prove what went on behind the closed doors of their marital relationship, but empirical evidence seems to show that it did indeed go downhill and that she wound up holding the short end of the stick. Even though I made an exhaustive effort to find out if there had been, there's nothing to prove that a real and lasting mutual attraction ever existed between them, despite their having produced a family. Instead, every word I uncovered seemed to confirm that Tiger, bless her heart, had gotten into a situation that was way above her head. For her, I'm convinced that marrying George Caine amounted to little more than bouncing out of the frying pan and right back into the fire.

THERE'S NO WAY TO prove beyond any doubt whether George Jackson Caine, or *The Colonel*, as he was called, and Bonnie Marie Tiger, or *Tiger*, as she was called, married for love or for money, but speculation about their motives was unceasing for as long as they were together. From the outside, it really did seem that she married him because she thought linking up with a white man would be a quick and easy way to take step up in life and that he married her to get at her assets.

It can be established without a doubt that for as long as the two of them were a couple, George Caine treated Tiger like a piece of chattel property rather than as a traditional wife. He seemed to have had no special respect for her — not much more, it appeared, than he had for any of the other Indians or blacks who lived around them at the time, and it was well known that that wasn't very much. In those days, out where they lived, there were a good number of whites who considered marriage outside their race beneath them. Marrying an Indian was considered less reputable than marrying within the race, and marrying a Negro was an illegal act.

Only after they were ensconced in a home of their own did the Colonel make his expectations of her perfectly clear. It would be her role, he said, to manage what went on inside their household, while it would be his role to manage what went on outside of it, and what went on outside of it, he took care to point out, included the management of their finances — *all* of their finances.

He expected her, he continued, to give their new home the best of care, to prepare good meals for them on a regular schedule, to make sure he always had cleaned and ironed clothing ready for wear, to be ready and willing whenever he wanted her, and to take care of any children they might have together. Handling these duties well, he explained, was what being a dutiful wife was all about.

Even though he promised to make a good living for them, he had absolutely no clue at that moment how he was going to do it. His thought was that, until he could figure how to make the fortune he was dead set on accumulating, they would be able to get by on savings he still had in hand, his earnings from the barbershop, and, if necessary, by leasing out or selling off additional portions of allotment land — land that had once been *hers* but now was *theirs* but, because he was the head of their household, was really *his*. He took for granted that his ship would come before long, and that he would find a way to earn enough to pay for the standard of living he thought he deserved.

When Tiger tried to bring up a few of her own ideas about what she hoped their marriage would be like, he shushed her up and said that she would have to happy with the many conveniences he would provide. "You'll have a nice home, great furniture and appliances, new clothing to wear, good food to eat, and enough ready money to do a great job of running our household," he said. "Why in the hell," he asked, "would any woman need more than that?"

Tiger was too inarticulate and far too caught off guard by his pronouncements to say much of anything in response, but she tried to get a word in edgewise, nevertheless. That, she learned in short order, was a mistake. Persistently trying to explain her own wishes with respect to the matters she understood to be *under discussion* caused her supposedly devoted husband to reveal his true self for the first time. When he did, she was so surprised that she could only stare at him in amazement. Up to that moment, he had never spoken to her in anything other than what she would have described as a loving tone.

Flush with anger and without mincing words, he told her to "shut the hell up and do what she was told." He was her husband, he said, and his wife was damned well going do what he wanted. In his household, he yelled in her face, the tail was never going to wag the dog. "You're going to run this home," he proclaimed, "the way I want it to be run. When I want your opinion," he said even more loudly, "I'll ask for it. Until then, you'll do what you've been told to do. That's how it's going to be for us, whether you like it or not, so you might as well start getting used to it."

When, a few days later, she tried to express her displeasure by bringing the matter up again, he flew off the handle even more. He wasn't used to anyone talking back to him, especially not a woman and even more so not the woman who had signed on to be his lawfully wedded wife. He slapped her around until she, as he put it, "finally came to her senses and stopped carrying on."

When she realized what her future was going to be like, Tiger's spirit sank like a rock.

Beyond the practical activities that were demanded of her, George went on to say that he expected nothing more than for her to do what she was told. How could she be the helpmate he needed, he explained, if he didn't explain what help he needed? That, he declared, was all he was trying to do. More than anything else, he told her, he would not brook any behavior that interfered with what he most wanted to do in life, which was to pursue his personal and business goals he had in mind. "I have to go all in to get where I want to be," he said, "and what that means for you is that I can't have anyone nipping at my heels over meaningless trivia while I'm out there trying to do my best. My gain," he continued, "will be your gain, so you'd better think about that before you try to question me again."

What it all came down to in the end was that George Caine had grander ambitions in mind than making Bonnie Tiger, his new Creek Indian wife, happy, and he clearly intended to carry on in pursuit of his goals as if the two of them had never married. He expected to go wherever he wanted, whenever he wanted, without offering a single word of explanation to her. "As long as I keep a solid roof over our heads and the heads of any kids we have together, and as long as I provide enough food for us to eat and decent clothing for us to wear," he loudly exclaimed, "that damned well ought to be enough."

To sum up the effect of their interaction as succinctly as possible, he scared the devil out of her, in the same way as her father had, back when she was younger.

So, at this early point in their marriage, she did the only thing she could do in the wake of her husband's having come down so hard on her: She caved in, gave up, and began to behave according to the script her husband set out for her. Because her new role was so much like her old one, she fell back into it easily. *This*, she bitterly concluded, *is the way men are, every damned, miserable one of them.*

After clarifying the sort of relationship he expected to have with her, George went on to resume his former lifestyle. He drank when and as much as he wanted, gambled when he felt like it, and chased after any woman who was available to be chased. Because he was handsome, ambitious, and free-spirited, he caught a lot of them, too. Besides that, he had more money to spend than an average man of his day, thanks again to Tiger, which was one more attraction he had to offer.

In all fairness, Tiger had had ulterior motives of her own before she took up with George Caine, reasons that went beyond the normal and natural human need for love and companionship, the need that had caused her to put herself on display. In her case, she was in search of ordinary social approval, due to having grown sick and tired of living as an outcast. She knew George had been drawn to her as much for money and property as for herself, but that had been okay with her. She had fallen head over heels for him, that's for sure; but, as true as that was, it was also true that she thought of him as a means to an end, a way of getting where she wanted to be.

Each of them had their own motives for getting married, and the only real difference between them was that George had a clear concept of what he was doing when he did it, while she really didn't know any better.

The most likely direction for a connection like theirs to go after a few years of living together was straight downhill, and that, to all outward appearances, was precisely what happened. He always stayed out front, while she was forced to stay behind the scenes, as if she were invisible. Much to everyone's surprise, they stayed together for the long haul and, even after getting off to a late start, went on to produce a family of six children — Walter, Carl, Ralph, Doyle, Norma, and Luther. Even with this lasting, tangible evidence of some form of bond between them, most of their acquaintances still doubted that Tiger and the Colonel had ever enjoyed a true union of hearts and minds.

WHAT TIGER STILL HAD to learn about George Caine was that the accumulation of wealth meant more to him than anything else in the world, *including her*. The possibility of getting rich had drawn him to the Indian Territory, and he made no apologies for being determined to do just that. He was willing to do whatever had to be done to make a buck, whether it was ethical or legal or not, and he was a person with a one-track mind. At the time of his marriage to Tiger, he still hadn't figured out *how* was going to do it; he just knew he *was* going to do it.

Wasting no time after the two of them were married, he leveraged her property as a means of setting them up with a good home that was well furnished and modern for their time and place. After bouncing from one job to another for a while, the security of knowing that access to *her* (now *his*) assets gave him enough confidence to move away from working for others to starting a business of his own.

After a few years, he wound up owning and operating a business called Caine's Barbershop and Card Room, which became a successful enterprise in and of itself. He eventually turned his main business into a shell for all kinds of off–the–record, illicit activities, from which he earned even more money. His primary business, though, the cardroom, remained his pride and joy, and it meant more to him than anything else. These legal and illegal activities were the way he built up the healthy personal estate he'd always wanted.

In reality, the success George Caine achieved at Hoffman townsite was due far more to pure blind luck than to foresight or any particular business-like insight on his part, in that he launched and expanded his offerings just as oil and coal deposits were discovered around Hoffman and their exploitation was getting into full swing. Because the population of the community and the surrounding area jumped from around five hundred to over two thousand during the years as oil drilling and coal mining boomed, it was a maximally opportune time to be where he happened to be. Timing and location, as always, are critical when it comes to successfully launching a small business, and it was in this way that the Colonel really got lucky.

Caine's Barber Shop and Card Room fairly quickly evolved into a popular and successful watering hole in town, a home away from home not only for oil and coal field workers but also for a large number of local men. It wasn't looked upon as an especially savory establishment, but it was well patronized. According to some of the old-timers I talked to, numerous arguments, fights, stabbings, and occasional killings took place there before it finally folded up. During the years of the big boom, lots of places just like it came and went out in the oil and coal belt regions of Oklahoma and Texas.

It was through aiding, abetting, and otherwise actively encouraging vices of all kinds while it was in operation that the Colonel built up his successful business operation in Hoffman. In the process, he built up a notorious personal reputation as well. For years, he remained the primary go-to guy in town for anyone who wanted a little high life or illicit action, regardless of what kind it happened to be. It also became well known that getting into an argument with him was not a wise thing to do, since he was apt to do just about anything if he got pushed out of shape over something.

None of his activities, of course, had salutatory effects on the respectable and hard-working citizens of the town, which was why few of them had much of anything good to say about him. They had no choice but to put up with the man, but to them George Caine was nothing more than a common boozer, gambler, bootlegger, schemer, and bully — a guy who was always on the lookout for ways of making a profit at somebody else's expense. His money-grubbing activities had made him financially well off for his time and place, but they sure as hell hadn't made him reputable.

The Colonel never gave Tiger any credit for his success in business, but the truth is that he probably wouldn't even have been able to take his first step if he hadn't been able to tap her personal assets. She never really had much, but she had a whole hell of lot more than he did, back when he was struggling to get a business started. Even so, he claimed full credit for every step of progress that was made during their marriage.

BONNIE MARIE (TIGER) CAINE died sooner than she should have on July 1, 1931, when she was only forty-eight years old. Because she was a woman who had young kids to raise, her death caught everyone flatfooted. It had never as much as occurred to anyone that such a thing could happen. The Colonel, for one, was especially upset by her demise, but not in a way that would have been described as proper for a grieving husband.

Because his various lines of business had begun to struggle due to economic decline in the area and he was up to his neck in combat with a major competitor, the Colonel's first thought on the day his long-suffering wife lost her worldly battle had to do with how damned aggravating it was that it had happened just when he needed her the most.

Officially, Tiger died of an unknown illness, but there was conjecture at the time that she might just have grown tired of living.

Not unexpectedly, the Colonel, having never been much of a husband, didn't turn out to be a decent single father either. He didn't *raise* his children in any commonly understood sense of the term; they more or less raised themselves, coming and going as they pleased and making their own decisions for as long as they lived at home. Lacking any effective parental supervision, all six kids ended up paying little to no attention to their schooling. Each one dropped out before finishing the eighth grade. Even those who stayed at it for a while longer than the others didn't receive a decent education, since they had no parental guidance and were therefore never serious about anything they studied.

Caine didn't take much interest in his kids, and his kids didn't pay any more attention to him than they were forced to. No appreciable amount of bonding took place, as it does in a normal household setting. The kids were never close to their father, nor were they ever close to one another. They hung around home only until they were old enough to go out on their own, and then they promptly flew the coop. One by one, as soon as they were old enough to do so, they moved away and from then on never had much of anything to do with their father, each other, or the town of Hoffman. That's why I hadn't been able to locate any more than a few of them, and it was why the few members I was able to locate (with the exception of one clearly reluctant cousin) hadn't hesitated to say that they had absolutely no interest in talking with me.

GEORGE AND BONNIE (TIGER) Caine's last child, Luther Jackson Caine, was born in Hoffman on March 29, 1923. Bonnie was Candy's paternal grandmother, and Luther grew up to become her father. What turned out to be so tragic for Luther, I discovered shortly after learning of his existence, was that his father's sins and shortcomings had been more than damaging enough to create enormous hurdles for him as grew to young manhood in their small town. The Colonel really stirred the pot while he lived there, and Luther's major misfortune was that the people of Hoffman never forgot the sins of his father. It is to Luther's own sorry story that this overview of Candy's family history now turns.

13

LUTHER AND PIRLEY (HICKS) CAINE

UNTIL I LEARNED ABOUT him through my own efforts, I had never heard of Luther Jackson Caine, my own wife's birth father. I had asked about her birth family many times, but my questions had always been evaded. At this point, I became more convinced than ever that the mystery surrounding her birth family had to be ended, once and for all — and the sooner, the better. Now that I had discovered Luther Caine's identity and actually looked at his photograph, I couldn't wait to find as much about him as I could.

It became evident rather quickly that there was a lot of information out there about the conditions of his childhood and youth — much more, in fact, than I had expected to be able to find. Sadly, though, I didn't find much of anything that anyone in his family — most notably his daughter Candy, my wife — would want to have repeated. He got off to an unfairly rocky start, I discovered, and then his life seemed to have never stopped spiraling downwards.

LUTHER WAS A PERSON who tended to provoke strong reactions on the part of people who got to know him. He didn't fit in to the happy middle; he was a guy who stood out among others, but for all the wrong reasons. It was much easier to gather facts about his life during the years before he married Candy's mother than it had been for other senior members on his side of her family, simply because there still were people around who recalled him quite well and most of them weren't the least bit hesitant about sharing their opinions.

I started off with the intent of learning more about the basic facts of his life, such as the conditions under which he grew up, how he did while he was a student, what he was like as a young man, and so on — all the fundamentals. After that, I intended to find out how he ended up earning a living as an adult. Finally, and most importantly, I wanted to find out how he came to meet and marry Pirley Mae Hicks, the woman who became Candy's mother. With all this information in hand, I expected it to be fairly easy to find out what happened after he and Pirley got together. Their relatives, I figured, would be able to fill me in on that. I knew from the outset that they hadn't lived happily ever after. If they had, Candy wouldn't have ended up an adopted child. But . . . Had they divorced? Been killed in a car accident? Something even worse? Or, were both of them still living, and, if so, were they still together? If they were still living, where were they? These were the kinds of questions that burned in my mind and drove my efforts.

More than anything else, I wanted to find out how Candy got separated from the Caines and ended up being adopted by the Wilsons. Why had they parted way with their child? Did they give her up, or had she been taken away? I already knew that she wasn't illegitimate, so what in the world had happened?

Moving forward under the assumption that the best way to learn what Luther was like in maturity would be to develop a better picture of what he was like as a young man, I gathered all the material that could be found about his early years in the town of Hoffman. Through many long hours of interviewing, library research, and related reading, I learned a great deal about his young life, his general circumstances, and the town he grew up in.

Overlapping my efforts in the library, I continued to write personal letters, make long distance telephone calls, and exchange email messages with anyone I thought might be able to help. Even though former residents and their heirs had scattered to different locations, by using one contact to ferret out others, I was able to identify enough of them to gather the facts I needed.

Documenting his childhood experience took quite a while,

but I was eventually able to put together a fairly good overview of how childhood and youth had gone for Candy's father Luther out in rural Oklahoma. Unfortunately, what I learned turned out to be so unpleasant that I've often wondered if it wouldn't have been better not to have looked into his life at all. As is often said, though, you can't un-ring a bell that has been rung.

All but hypnotized by what had been learned about him through those who would work with me, I got so immersed in his story that I once again temporarily lost track of that fact that I'd set out to document Candy's childhood experience, not her father's.

In the end, my efforts brought to light a slice of Americana that Norman Rockwell definitely would not have appreciated or wanted to paint. What I learned is that a lot of truth really does reside in the old sayings that the sins of the father are often visited upon the son and that the apple usually doesn't fall far from the tree. Candy's father grew up in his father's shade; there's no doubt about that.

FROM THE EARLIEST YEARS of his life, Luther had to contend with three major problems, any one of which would have been a handful for an average person to bear. Luther, though, wasn't an average person, and what this meant for him was that the combined weight of his problems made for an extraordinarily difficult childhood.

As has been noted, he was born and raised in the small and isolated farm town of Hoffman in the northeastern quarter of Oklahoma, where his father *Colonel* George Jackson Caine owned and operated a successful but disreputable business. He was the last of six children born to George and his Creek Indian wife Bonnie, who was called Tiger. The overriding tragedy of his childhood was that, after his mother died, he and his brothers and sister ended up having to take full charge of their own upbringing.

His mother and father, as has been mentioned but could have been surmised from the lifestyle they led and the circumstances of their marriage, were completely indifferent parents, two people who did as little as they could get by with in terms of caring for the six children they brought into the world. Worse still, after Tiger, their mother, died at a young age, the kids received essentially no further parental care from their father to speak of. The siblings, I learned, weren't of much help to one another, either. Each one grew up in his or her own way, then left home to live totally separate lives.

One by one, as soon as the kids grew old enough to do so, they left the family home and, as far as I could determine, never looked back. I couldn't even locate them. Even if I had, there wouldn't have been much about their young lives they would have wanted to remember. The only Caine I was able to contact was one distant cousin, who spoke to me grudgingly and sparingly.

I learned through Clarence and other old-timers who spoke with me that Luther and his siblings had endured miserable childhoods, for the most part due to circumstances over which they had no personal control. Luther, in particular, had a hard go of it, due to his having had some unusual personality quirks that tended to aggravate everyone he was around. "Their father," Clarence told me, "whipped the hell out of them kids on a regular basis, using his wide leather belt. He done it ever time word got back to him of their having gotten into some sort of trouble. It never did no good, though, especially not as far as Luther was concerned. He was more of a problem than them other kids."

First and foremost among the difficulties Luther had to contend with was simply that he was Early Tiger's grandson and George Caine's son, two distinctions of great disadvantage to him as well as his siblings in their smalltown environment. In rural towns like Hoffman, people tended to grow up fixed in their places. Everybody in town knew everybody else, and they also knew their fathers and mothers, brothers and sisters, aunts and uncles, cousins and in-laws as well — often for several generations back. In addition, they knew one another's preferences and foibles and shortcomings, along with every sin or transgression any one of them had ever committed. Mistakes and shortcomings of the kind Luther's father had made over the years were never forgotten, and the image they had of him was the first thing that came to mind when they thought of his kids. Worse still, once a person was labeled and placed in a box, it was next to impossible to get out of it. You were what you were in Hoffman, and that's all there was to it.

The second of Luther's major problems was that he was an absolutely incorrigible child, a kid who was difficult to deal with from an early age. "He's definitely his father's son," people said, and there's a record to confirm that he grew up behaving in accordance with their unspoken script. "As the twig is bent," locals were unhesitant about exclaiming, "so grows the leaf."

When he began to feel poorly treated at school, Luther refused to return. Because he preferred to hang around with other boys who had an attitude just like his own, he grew up totally uneducated and unskilled. Then, as a result of running around with local never–do–wells who routinely devoted much of their time experimenting with smoking, gambling, drinking, and foul-mouthed speech, he fell prey to each one of those vices. This pattern of behavior only worsened as he grew into his late teenage and early adult years.

On top of his other problems, Luther also evolved into a profoundly prejudiced and bigoted person. It isn't surprising that he ended up that way, I suppose, after growing up during a time when racial separation was the norm and in a town where overt segregation was deeply entrenched. Although the stable population of Hoffman was divided between whites, blacks, and Indians, blacks and to a lesser degree Indians were never considered the equals of whites in local society. Extreme racial prejudice was something young men of all races came by honestly in the environment that prevailed, usually early in life, and usually before they had any deep understanding of the consequences or ramifications of the stance they had adopted. It was like this in most rural farm towns in the South in those days, and, for that matter, throughout most of the country.

Segregation was not directly spoken of back then the way it is today, but the terms of racial interaction were understood by everyone in town. Whites and blacks and Indians readily mixed for commercial purposes — they traded at the same stores, sold their cotton at the same gin, and so on — but unspoken expectations and norms prevented the races, especially blacks and whites, from mixing on equal terms in schools, churches, restaurants, barbershops, transportation services, theaters, or other such places.

Whites lived mainly on the north side of town, while blacks, called *coloreds* or *the niggers*, as Clarence casually put it, lived on the south side, in what everyone routinely referred to as *Niggertown*. The blacks of those times, it should be noted, used equally offensive, thoughtless, and insulting terms to refer to members of the white community. The bigotry and ignorance that existed in those days — and there was a whole hell of a lot of it — was fairly equally distributed among the races.

Local Creek Indians had belittling expressions of their own for use in referring to their white and black neighbors, but, unlike the whites, they could and did mix much more openly with blacks than whites ever did. In those days, there were lots of instances of intermarriage between Indians and blacks and whites and Indians, but marriage between blacks and whites rarely happened. The latter, in fact, was actually against the law. As far as most whites were concerned, anyone with any discernable black heritage was, in fact, completely and forever black. Although it happened fairly often, many whites also frowned on intermarriage with Indians. Miscegenation, or race mixing, was not an accepted practice.

The purpose of mentioning all this is to clarify how and why Luther ended up becoming the irretrievably prejudiced and bigoted man he was. Racial prejudice was so deeply embedded in his psyche that he didn't know it existed and he never gave it any conscious thought.

The third and perhaps most over-arching major problem of Luther's youth was that he grew up under conditions of poverty extreme enough to adversely affect him for life, just as it did large numbers of other people who lived in his area. Because he was born just prior to the beginning of the Great Depression and Dust Bowl, his teenage and young adult years were lived out during a period of privation that was worse than even the poorest members of our society have to deal with today. There's no doubt that his thinking was warped by what he endured.

BECAUSE LUTHER'S ADULT BEHAVIOR and values and attitudes were so profoundly influenced by the poverty of his youth, I spent a great deal of time talking with staff of the Oklahoma Historical Society about the best way to get a better handle on the economic circumstances of his younger years. They directed me to studies and books that provided an excellent overview of the effects of the Depression on Oklahoma and, more specifically, the northeastern quarter of the state, where Hoffman, Luther's hometown, was located. In addition, various sources provided some haunting pictures and gloomily depressingly old newspaper articles and photographs to confirm how difficult those years turned out to be, and members of the Caine family would have been right in the center of it. The 1930s and 1940s were hard times for most everyone in Luther's area.

Economic conditions in his area eventually disintegrated so badly that tax revenues dropped too low to cover the cost of such basic public services as police and fire protection, and, after that happened, citizens voted to disincorporate their town. With this action, Hoffman ceased to exist as a functional municipality. It was a decision that accelerated the abandonment and deterioration of even more homes and businesses. In later years, many surviving buildings were destroyed by fires, tornados, and the inevitable salvaging and vandalization that occurs under such circumstances, until not a single commercial building and only a few homes were left standing in the town Luther grew up in. This, I discovered, was why nothing was left of the town when I made my trip up there to see it firsthand.

The foregoing overview is part of this story because it is impossible to understand why Luther turned out the way he did without knowing the fundamental circumstances of his childhood and youth. He grew up under conditions of grinding poverty, in an area where he observed personal, business, and institutional failure occurred on a wide scale. All around him he saw poverty, inequity, indebtedness, and hopelessness. He is sure to have noted that only a lucky few of his neighbors had the wherewithal to live an unworried life, while the great majority had barely enough to get by on. It had to have been a depressingly smothering environment in which to come of age.

GROWING UP DURING A time of such great want and deprivation seems to be one of the major reasons why Luther, in effect, spent the rest of his life emotionally railing against forces he could not describe. Over time, I believe, his bitterness morphed an unusual brand of subconscious resentment, an attitude of mind that handicapped him even more than he already was. Family members who tried to describe his behavior as a teenager said that he was not *deranged* as much as he was *unarranged.* He couldn't have been deranged, they said, because that implies that he once had a normal set of attitudes and values. All of his problems, I was assured, sprang from the way he was raised — or, rather, to the way he raised himself. Because he had no real parenting to speak, those who knew him considered it inevitable that he would have all kinds of problems as an adult, and they were right.

Nobody truly understood Luther's underlying condition, least of all Luther himself. Who knows, maybe some sort of then unknown and therefore never diagnosed problem or illness damaged him before he left his mother's womb — fetal alcohol poisoning, for example. It was known that both of his parents had been heavy drinkers, and end results like that do happen, probably even more often than most of us realize. Again, though, who knows?

The only thing people knew for sure about Luther was that whatever nurturing he did receive, it was too paltry to make a difference. Living a responsible and orderly life after growing up in an environment as arbitrary and chaotic as his would have been a major challenge for anyone, and it certainly turned out to be too great of a great challenge for him. Maybe, though, he wouldn't have been able to adjust to society under any set of circumstances, not even if his youth and childhood had been better guided and less poverty ridden. There are people like that, no matter what background they come out of.

FOR WHATEVER THE REASONS, Luther grew into young manhood beset by a whole raft of personal problems. There's no doubt, for example, that he believed everybody was out to take advantage of him. To the extent of nearly outright paranoia, he never trusted anyone. This problem created yet another great difficulty for him, in that it led to his having a hard time dealing with authority, even authority that was legitimately and reasonably exercised. He had a tough time getting along with teachers and administrators when he was young and in school, and he had an even tougher time cooperating with coworkers and supervisors later on, after he got out into the workplace. With the passage of time, this problem only increased in severity.

Another of Luther's unusual complexes was that he hated the fact that he had a mixed racial heritage. His mother was a Creek Indian full blood, but, because she hadn't been the least bit dutiful, he had been left to raise himself, more–or–less, in a white society. Eventually, he adopted the attitudes and values of his white buddies as his own. By the time he quit school, he had convinced himself that *Indian blood* was a major cause of his poor personal discipline, lax work ethic, destructive personal habits, and generally low station in life. He was so prejudiced that he lacked the basic sense of self-respect that ought to have been his as a birthright. Because he didn't like Indians, he disliked a part of himself.

Luther grew up brooding and searching for a better way of life, but he didn't have a clue how to go about building one. Always on the lookout for quick fixes and easy ways out, he never figured out that good outcomes have to be earned in a respectable way. All he seems to have understood is that others were enjoying the life he preferred to live, and he wasn't.

Following the examples of his father and his grandfather before him, at an early age he turned to hard drink as a way of anesthetizing himself to the difficulties of life. In those days, nothing prevented a young man from spending time in a bar if he wanted to, not as long as he had money and wanted to be there badly enough. Looking for escape and relief wherever he could find it, alcohol became his favorite refuge. That he took to it with such ease didn't surprise or upset his father, since he'd done the same thing himself. Long before Luther met Candy's mother, he had a well-established habit of hanging out in bars and coming home drunk on a regular basis.

LUTHER PORTRAYED AND LIKED to think of himself as a footloose and fancy-free man about town, a person without a care in the world, but the people I talked to, mostly his own relatives, made it clear that they saw him in an entirely different light. He wasn't fooling anybody, they said.

There's no way at this late date to be absolutely certain of all the factors that drove Luther to behave the way he did after he got married, but the people I talked to didn't mince any words when it came to describing how he behaved before the knot was tied. He wasn't just youthfully blithe and occasionally irresponsible, they said; he was off the wall irrational. As one of them put it, "That kid didn't have all of his oars in the water, that's for damned sure."

One of his relatives put forth perhaps the most concise and accurate description of his mental state offered by anyone: "He just thought," the man said, "that he was a no-count person, somebody who'd never amount to nothing, no matter what he done. He must've figured that if that was the way it was gonna be, then, hell, why not just go ahead and get on with it. He didn't see no further than right here and now, and that's all there was to it. For that boy, they wasn't no tomorrow that needed to be worried about."

At the risk of putting words in his mouth, I think what his relative meant was that he thought Luther had talked himself into believing that he had no hope of ever achieving success in life. The subconscious and distorted logic that guided his conduct seems to have been *when you know you're going to fail anyway, why bother striving for anything more than what you have?*

Because he felt there was nothing he could do to change either his fundamental self or the basic circumstances of his life, he simply lost the will to act positively on his own behalf. Thinking this way kept him on a downward spiral in life. Fatalism, a low self-image, and unspecified anxiety seem to have prevented him from trying to improve his own condition.

What was missing in Luther was not the *ability* but the *will* to act positively and proactively on his own behalf. Down deep inside, he seems to have felt that he *deserved* angst and misery in his day–to–day life. Even though it wasn't externally observable, on the inside he was an exceedingly troubled young man. It sometimes seemed that there wasn't any way for him to go but down.

LUTHER CAINE LINKS UP WITH PIRLEY HICKS

LUTHER CAINE WASN'T THE sort of man most young girls would want to hook up with and take home to meet Mom and Dad, and he most definitely wasn't the kind of man Mr. and Mrs. Dexter Hicks of McAlester, Oklahoma, had in mind as a partner for their attractive and talented daughter, Pirley Mae. The Hicks were a hard-working, staunchly conservative, and deeply religious couple, two people who were highly committed to and intensely involved in the affairs of their equally conservative fundamentalist church. From her youngest years, their daughter Pirley had been equally committed to congregational affairs, particularly when it came to participation in activities such as singing and choir practice. Singing was the activity their daughter most thoroughly enjoyed, and her parents took pride in her abilities and accomplishments in that area.

Pirley Mae was a tall, thin, outgoing small-town girl who grew up in a warm and caring family. She was talented and attractive enough to have had her choice of a number of suitors from among the young men of her congregation or the larger community — if, that is, she had stayed on the straight and narrow path, the one her parents started her out on when she was just a child. To her parents as well as to Pirley herself, she was a young woman who had excellent prospects.

Her most distinguishing attribute was that she was blessed with an excellent singing voice. It was good enough, in fact, to earn her a place in a gospel music quartet at her church as well as yet another quartet that was locally well known enough to perform each week on a gospel music segment of a half-hour live hometown country music program broadcasted by a radio station in McAlester. More than anything else in life, Pirley wanted to build on these experiences in order to move onward and upward to even better venues within the music industry.

Local notoriety made her something of a standout in her congregation as well as in her hometown, since any recognition of that kind was uncommon in those days. Her limited but inspiring contact with the music business had, in fact, left her more or less starstruck. She had decided that she wanted to become a professional singer, and she was convinced that she was good enough to earn real recognition as well as some hard money through her musical talent. According to her relatives, she became obsessed with the thought of becoming a recognized country music performer. In their opinion, her dream had become strong enough to be the driving force in her life.

According to her relatives, Pirley was bored to tears with the small town and highly conventional religious home life she lived with her parents. What she craved was an opportunity to escape from a routine she thought of as stifling and intolerably dull. Because time seemed to be slipping away, she became more and more willing to take a few chances to be sure that she got it.

Pirley's basic misfortune, I suppose, was that there just weren't enough good opportunities in those days for a respectable girl to be different in a small town like hers. Back then, acceptable behavior for a woman was quite a bit more circumscribed than it is today, especially for one in her social circle. It's not hard to imagine how she must have felt, especially if she really did have some genuine talent as a singer.

Her relatives all agreed that her downfall began shortly after she made her first trip to Tuley's Pavilion, a country music dance hall and bar located out on Highway 69 at the outskirts of town. Even today most parents in the area wouldn't welcome a beautiful young daughter's association with an outfit like Tuley's, but the feeling was doubly true back when the place was going strong. Pirley's highly religious and conservative parents, who are now deceased, liked it even less than most.

Back then, Tuley's was known as one of the most wide-open and uninhibited places in McAlester and, for that matter, the general area. One of Pirley's uncles told me that even those who went there regularly on weekends to drink and dance ran the place down. "It wasn't no damned honky-tonk," they joked. "Folks did get thrown out of there from time to time."

Most young single women in her circle wouldn't even have thought of going to Tuley's, and few respectable women in any social circle in those days would have gone there alone. Looking down and away and shaking their heads dejectedly as they spoke, family members made it clear that Pirley Mae had done both. From the point of view of her family and their social circle at that time, that was behavior beyond the pale.

Pirley gravitated toward Tuley's because it was the only place in town interested in hiring a *girl singer*, one that was needed by a country music band they sponsored for live entertainment at the dance hall. Ignoring her parents' unequivocal opposition and pointed warnings, she made up her mind that she was going to audition and that was all there was to it. "Stay away from that dump," her parents argued as forcefully as they could, "or you'll wind up in more trouble than you ever dreamed possible." Several family members readily recalled the friction that sprang up between daughter and parents in those trying times. Obviously, reasoning with a strong-willed young woman wasn't any easier back then than it is today.

Like a moth attracted to a flame, Pirley felt compelled to show up for a tryout, regardless of what her parents advised. From her perspective, Tuley's was nothing more than a stopping off place where she could get started in the music business, one that might lead to better opportunities further on down the road.

It really wasn't much of an accomplishment when she got the job, since a fresh and appealing female face in any of the groups that appeared on stage at Tuley's would have been a truly welcome sight. It was anything but the happy place that drew in crowds of fun-loving and cheerful patrons who enjoyed good country music that Pirley Mae wanted to think of it as. No, for her to become part of their overall operation was more of an instance of casting a pearl to a herd of swine than she realized.

Then, just as Pirley arrived at a peak of enthusiasm and got set to spread her wings for a while, the whole gambit at Tuley's fell apart. After only a few performances, two of the lead musicians decided that the gig wasn't paying enough to be worth their time. When the first two musicians gave up, the others saw that there was no choice but for them to take regular jobs themselves. The band folded up overnight, leaving Pirley high and dry, entirely on her own.

The disintegration of the group was a major disappointment for Pirley, since her greatest desire had been to continue as a singer with an active band. Her enthusiasm wasn't even close to being sated. Her short time in the limelight had been an honest to goodness thrill, and the last thing she wanted to do was to let go of her dream and return to a humdrum existence.

To everyone's dismay, what happened after the band folded was that Pirley became more or less a regular patron down at Tuley's, leaving her parents even more appalled. In the words of one of her relatives, "The more time she spent at that damned place, the more she done a complete turnaround. It wasn't long before she didn't do nothin' with the family or church anymore. She just wasn't the same girl no more. Neither her parents nor nobody else could figure out what got into her."

From a long-term perspective, it was indeed one of those times when Pirley would have been wise to have listened to her Mom and Dad. In her day and time and area, the term honky-tonk didn't have the same meaning that it does today. Today the term is used to conjure up images of colorful musicians and singers pumping out happy music in touristy places like New Orleans, Memphis, or St. Louis, places that offer music that's earthy and real. In her day, though, the people she had associated with in the past would have used the term to refer to describe a totally different level of establishments — low class, smoky beer bars, places they would have associated, often rightly, with boozing, dirty dancing, and reckless gambling such as poker playing or shooting dice. Most of the places they described as honky-tonks were cheap and disreputable dives, joints that often featured back-room hangouts used for one illicit purpose or another. "Pirley Mae," as several family members put it, "went off the deep end, that's for damned sure. Her parents was crazy with worry."

WHAT I'D HEARD LED my mind to imagine how on a hot Oklahoma summer night at Tuley's Bar and Dance Hall in McAlester, Oklahoma, Pirley Mae Hicks and Luther Jackson Caine met one another for the first time. It was just one of many such places Luther drifted into and out of in those days, joints he patronized to drink and party and otherwise escape from realities he was unable to handle in broad daylight. While Pirley may have started going to the place only because it offered a viable career opportunity, nearly overnight it seems to have become her regular place of retreat from what she probably thought of as a dull and monotonous existence. She and Luther alike must have seen the place as the only option their area had to offer as a substitute for the bright lights and cheerfulness of what they thought of as more enlightened cities.

From the evening of their first meeting, Luther and Pirley apparently hit it off quite famously. He was as trim and slim and good looking as he was free-wheeling and fun-loving. Being willing to say and do just about anything that strayed into his mind came across well to Pirley, who was in search for an opportunity to let loose and party. That they were kindred spirits seems quite certain. Neither one was of any mind to resist what the other had to offer.

"Luther," said several of Pirley's relatives, "just flat swept her off her feet, and from that point on, she wasn't nothin' but putty in his hands."

One of Luther's brothers, on the other hand, said, "If he hadn't of met that damned floozy, he might of growed out of it someday."

Their relationship seemed to be an encounter of equals from the outset. It is impossible to know how their first meeting came to pass, but, once it did, all that mattered from that point forward was that they satisfied one another's needs exceptionally well — so well, in fact, that they, too, just as his parents had in their day, immediately decided to tie the marital knot. It was in this simple and straightforward way that they made a decision that changed their lives forever.

Pirley's parents, who were already distraught over the path their beautiful and talented daughter had taken, were now truly at their wit's end. They thought she'd gone completely off her rocker, and they didn't make any secret of their opinion about Luther. According to her relatives, "Pirley Mae's mom and dad thought the guy was nothin' but trash, somebody that'd never hit a lick in his life. They done ever thing they could think of to get her to stay away from him, but once that girl got somethin' in her mind, there wasn't no way of getting' it back out. That's the way she always was, from when she was just a little ol' thing."

After a raucous New Year's Party, Luther and Pirley were married on January 2, 1941, before a local Justice of the Peace.

Whether anyone was present to witness the ceremony, none of their relatives seemed to know; they just knew that it hadn't been attended by any of them. All anyone in Pirley's family knew about Luther was that they could hardly stand him, and no one in his family had had — or ever cared to have — an opportunity to learn the least bit about hers. Then, after the marriage was a done deal, not a single relative on either side made any effort to learn anything further about them.

It really wasn't surprising that members of the two families hadn't gotten to know one another, because Luther and Pirley were barely acquainted with one another. How could that have been, when their decision to marry was made less than two months after a first chance meeting at Tuley's? If they had spent even a minimal amount of time getting to know one another before taking the plunge, it might have become apparent that both of them had more personal problems than could be enumerated.

All of my contacts agreed that the lives of Pirley Hicks and Luther Caine could not have intersected at a worse juncture for either of them. Theirs was an ill-fated coming together if there ever was one, right from the start of their relationship. Some human combinations, it seems, are so ill-considered and negative that no mutual support can be derived from them. Each partner quickly used up the shallow reserve of kindness, consideration, and love that the other had to offer, leaving behind only the bleakness of their individual lives on which to try to build a marriage. Predictably, it was a connection that turned out to be even more intolerably barren than the lives they'd lived before. Each one was in desperate need of the very type of emotional support that the other was totally incapable of giving.

IT WAS AT THIS point that Luther and Pirley left their respective families to start a household of their own. They rented a place in McAlester because Pirley was able to find a job there as a waitress at a truck stop out on Highway 69, not too far from Tuley's. They were truly fond of the town, mainly due to the good times they'd enjoyed there during the two months before they were married. They were looking forward to enjoying a lot more of the same good times in the immediate future.

Luther, too, located an entry-level job in McAlester, in his case at a local lumberyard. His new job didn't pay well, but, in view of the times, he was pleased just to have been able to find gainful employment. Job opportunities were scarce in those days, and wages were lousy all over. He was also pleased with the old house he'd been able to rent as their first home, not just because the monthly payment was low but also because it was located right next to the rental home of his own *Uncle* Clarence, who had been a friendly neighbor when he lived at Hoffman. The two of them really weren't what anyone would describe as *close*, but it *was* true that they did *talk*, at least from time to time.

As soon as the newlyweds got settled in their home and income started flowing in from their new jobs, they jumped head-first right back into the high life they'd lived before they were married. They had more money than at any time in their lives, just not nearly as much as they thought. Like so many young couples just starting out, they had no real understanding of how much it was going to cost to run a household of their own and pay all of their own bills. Their combined earnings gave them a false sense of security; in reality, they weren't bringing in much more than what was required to keep bread on their table and a roof over their heads. For a time, though, they were so oblivious of their real financial situation that they continued their revelries at Tuley's just as before, genuinely believing that they were going to live happily ever after.

It wasn't long, of course, before reality to intrude; in what seemed like no more than a wink, a whole lot of rain began to fall on their parade. And not just financial rain, either; other problems cropped up as well. Pirley, for example, had known since they first met that Luther was a heavy drinker and party hardy guy; it was this behavior, in fact, that had drawn her to him in the first place, since she liked to drink and party just as much as he did. Up to then, she had never had to deal with the way he tended to behave when parties were over. Mornings-after brought out a side of him she hadn't had much of an opportunity to see.

A typical evening for them would begin with both of them getting high and starting to feel happy, which was what Pirley liked for them to do. Luther, though, because he was a much heavier drinker than she was, would keep at it until he was stumble-down drunk or until their money was gone. Then, late in the night, after they got back home, he tended to become surly and angry over the least little thing. Many nights ended with Pirley on the receiving end of Luther's nasty temperament. He started slapping her around shortly after they were married, behaving as if he had every right to do just that.

Their relationship wasn't working out in the idealized way Pirley had hoped it would, but, as strange as it may seem, she was much more accepting of how Luther treated her than people today would imagine. She behaved as if she, too, believed that he had a right to treat her the way he did.

Luther's pattern of behavior was set during those early days of their marriage. He'd work when he had to, and then party whenever he could. Before long, he started stopping off for drinks right after his workdays ended. After having a few drinks to loosen up, he'd pick up Pirley at the end of her shift at the restaurant. Once they were together, the two of them would head out to enjoy more of the same. Pirley liked the night life just as much as Luther, so she was right there beside him whenever she could be.

After a time, though, what began to happen is that Luther would drink so much right after work that he'd either forget or just not want to bother going to the restaurant to pick up Pirley. She didn't drive, so she'd just be left sitting there, fuming over having been left behind. Sooner or later, she'd ask a co-worker or a friend to drop her off at home. Later, by the time Luther finally showed up, it would either be too late or he would be too drunk to go back out again. Whenever this happened, the two of them would fight and argue even worse than before.

According to Clarence, "Them two would screech and slam

stuff around like they was wanted to kill one another. It got to be the damnedest thing you ever heard. They carried on like they was crazy people. I tried to be good to that boy, but I sure as hell wished he and that nutty wife of his hadn't never moved anywhere close to me. All our neighbors felt the same damned way."

Whether Pirley was with him or not, Luther gradually lurched into a straightforward and predictable daily routine: He would drink until he got drunk or until his money ran out, and then go home to fall asleep. Booze quickly became the most readily available form of escape he could find, just like it had been for his father before him. At the same time, hatefulness continued to fester and grow in his heart.

Clarence said that the couple had many long and loud arguments, conflagrations that often culminated in physical abuse. Neighbors and a number of Hicks family members knew Luther slapped Pirley around on a fairly regular basis, often leaving her with ailments such as ringing in the ears, black eyes, a bloody nose, or bruises on various parts of her body. Her problem, though, was that she was so well known to be outspoken, smart-mouthed, and wild and irresponsible that many of them believed she was probably receiving more or less the brand of treatment that was deserved. Several members of her own family said that they'd "like to have kicked her butt, too, if they had a way of doin' it without gettin' throwed in jail."

A few members of each family, as well as their immediate neighbors, knew exactly what was going on in the Caine household, but in that part of the country in those days it was not considered appropriate or wise or healthy to interfere in family matters of this kind. It was up to Pirley and Luther to work affairs out in their own way. Because they were a young couple, others thought they would righten their own ship after a while.

No one fully appreciated how severe Luther's abuse of Pirley became over time. The two of them did not have fights in the way that we think of arguments today, as *differences of opinion* between two members of a dysfunctional couple. "No," said Clarence, "that ain't the way it was between them two. What actually happened," he said, "was that Luther beat the livin' hell out of her, not just once but again and again."

Predictably, home life started falling apart for the couple before they'd lived together for a single year. When Luther's hangovers got so bad that he started missing work, he got fired from his job at the lumberyard. Shortly after that happened, Pirley turned up pregnant. When she had to quit her job later on due to problems that arose prior to her delivery date, they found themselves in dire financial straits before they knew what hit them. After letting them get several months behind on their rent, their landlord decided he'd had enough and started pressing them to pay up. Their utility bills and car payments were overdue as well. Then, when Pirley's time came, they ran up yet another large bill, this time for medical services and a short stay at the public hospital in McAlester following the delivery of their first baby.

"There ain't no doubt about it," said Clarence, "they was in a pitiful mess, especially when they brung home that poor baby. They wasn't nothin' but kids havin' kids, even though they didn't have a pot to pee in themselves. I thought about tryin' to help 'em out, but, hell, I didn't have nothin' myself, not back then. Nobody did, times was so damned bad. I was still drinkin' a lot myself, too, back in them days.

"Then," he said, "one day I drove by their house sometime around May of 1942 and saw the front door standin' open and the shades of the windows slung back. I thought they'd finally been evicted, but they wasn't. Hell, no; they'd just loaded up an' skipped out, just to get outa payin' their bills. An old boy who lived close to us told me about it. Nobody know'd where they went; they just took off and left. Lemme tell you, they was plenty of times back then when I felt like doing the same damned thing myself. People don't understand how hard it was to get by back then."

FEW RELATIVES ON THE Hicks side of the family and next to none on the Caine side heard much of anything from Luther and

Pirley from that point on, and the only news they did hear came in bits and snatches. They'd pop up once in a while from out of the blue, then they'd disappear again, just as quickly as they'd shown up.

Not many years thereafter, the couple disappeared altogether, and they were rarely heard from after that. In all honesty, I heard no indication that any relative on the Hicks side lost much sleep over their absence, mainly because estrangements began taking place immediately after they were married. Some of Pirley's relatives weren't shy about saying that they thought their departure for points unknown was no great loss to anyone. Family members couldn't have done much about the couple's situation anyway, even if they had had any real concern about them; Luther and Pirley wouldn't have allowed them to. Nobody, I discovered, had any idea what became of them after they left town.

AGGRAVATINGLY, ANOTHER RESEARCH TRAIL that had offered high hopes of leading to paydirt evaporated completely. Not being able to learn anything else about the years Candy spent with her birth parents was the greatest of a series of frustrations that had bedeviled my efforts from the outset. When it came to learning more about that unknown period of time, I had bumped up against a barrier that could not be surmounted.

Even though I had been able to locate relatives on her side of their family who were willing to help, all of them responded the same way when I asked what became of Luther and Pirley after their marriage: They had lost contact with the couple altogether.

So, there I was, high and dry all over again. No matter how hard I tried, I couldn't find any more information about Candy's life with her birth family, which was what I wanted to know most of all. Any last thoughts I had of locating Candy's birth parents in secret simply floated off into the ether.

Because there were no other sources to turn to for more information, I gave up on the whole idea of secretly investigating my sweet wife's long-hidden past. Throwing in the towel in this way was anything but a graceful surrender; it was an aggravating and highly frustrating defeat. I was so damned angry I could hardly see straight.

14

JUDGE AND JURY MIKE

FEELING AT THE SAME time so aggravated about having reached a dead end in my research that I wanted to pull out large clumps of my own hair and yet so curious that I could hardly contain myself, I decided it was time to have it out with my unsuspecting wife: I intended to demand that she tell me the truth about her time with her birth family, no matter how sensitive the topic might be and regardless of any secrets she might be forced to reveal. For me, learning what happened during her childhood years had progressed beyond merely *wanting to know* to *absolutely having to know*.

So, one evening without prelude or warning, I asked Candy to sit down with me on our living room sofa, saying that I wanted to talk about something unique and special. Once she was seated, I announced that I had researched her family history, working secretly just as I had for my mom and dad's golden wedding anniversary. "Now," I said, "it's time to turn my findings over to you."

The fact that I had done such a project caught her totally off guard, just as I had hoped it would. "What I want to do," I said, without allowing time for her to collect her thoughts, "is give you a verbal overview of the information I've collected, then turn the project over to you for private and leisurely reading. After that," I continued, speaking softly and trying not to sound ominous or cryptic, "there are a few gaps I'd like to go over in more detail."

Blithely assuming that my project would surely become a treasured keepsake, I went on to explain that love for her had been my motivation for doing the project. "It's meant to be a gift from the heart," I said, "and I hope you'll accept it in that light." With that I showed her my history of her birth family as it stood at the time, even though it was not even close to being complete.

Candy was too taken aback to know what to say as an immediate response. With a prelude like the one I'd delivered, what else could she do but acquiesce for the moment? So, after dutifully offering up a quiet *thank you* and a very hesitant *okay*, she sat back to listen as she tried to collect herself. I knew very well that she hated the thought of getting into the subject I wanted to talk about, but I pressed ahead anyway.

MY OFFICIOUS PRESENTATION OF FINDINGS

THROUGH ONE-SIDED *CONVERSATIONS* that began that evening and continued for some time thereafter, I told her one by one about the elders of her birth family whose lives I had studied — Early Ray and Etta "Mock" (Burnham) Tiger, George "The Colonel" and Bonnie Marie "Tiger" (Tiger) Caine, and Luther Jackson and Pirley Mae (Hicks) Caine, always carefully avoiding any detailed references or questions about the latter as her birth parents. That topic, I had decided, would be brought up later, at just the right time.

Convinced that she would be as curious about my discoveries as I had been all along, the last thing I wanted was to rush the process. I went on to describe in great detail everything I'd learned about those of her relatives whose lives I'd studied, never failing, of course, to add my own opinions about how each of them must have thought and felt in their days and times.

I rattled on for hours on end, without ever mentioning her birth parents, Luther and Pirley Caine. That topic was held back so that it could be sprung on her after everything else had been covered. A demand for full disclosure would go over better, it seemed to me, if it was sugar-coated by my other findings. I thought she'd find it difficult to deflect or refuse to get into the highly personal questions I intended to ask, once she'd taken note of how much effort had been poured into my project.

My *overview*, as I had described it, continued off and on for a whole string of evenings and for several weekends as well. Whenever we had free time to engage in serious interaction, I tore right back into it. Seeing only what I wanted to see, I mistook outright shock for genuine amazement on her part. I was too caught up in pride of authorship and subject matter enthusiasm to take proper note of the effects my comments were having.

Slowly and systematically, I doled out the discoveries that had captivated me so completely to my silent, glassy-eyed partner. She listened in what I first took to be astonished silence, but it didn't take long for me to notice that the stories I had found so fascinating weren't coming across that way to her at all. No, indeed; they were coming across as depressing accounts of personal tragedies. She slumped a little further down into her seat after each sub-story I recounted.

To make the presentation visual as well as verbal, I embellished it with enlargements of the old photographs that various members of her birth family had allowed me to copy. They amounted to no more than a sketchy collection of ragged old pictures I had done my best to restore, but they had an enormous impact on her anyway — much more than I had imagined they could.

She listened so carefully and intently to each story that she seemed to *feel* as well as *hear* what her relatives must had felt in their day, back when they were caught up in their respective predicaments. She related so deeply to their misfortunes that she was truly taken aback, and the presence of the old photographs had the effect of deepening her empathy. She reacted to the shots, in fact, as if I'd dropped a handful of snakes in her lap rather than a collection of keepsake images. The people she saw in them were unmistakably her relatives, due to all of the recognizable features they had in common.

I couldn't help but notice that it wasn't the indignities or misfortunes or offenses her ancestors suffered that had the greatest effect; no, not by a long shot. That distinction went to how the men of her extended family had treated their wives and children. She was clearly more touched by those parts of my stories than by anything else.

Because I became even more animated when I recounted the more tragic of the events that happened to elders, the story, for example, of how Bonnie Marie (Tiger) Caine, Candy's paternal grandmother's life, ended so pathetically, tears welled up as one sad event after another was recounted, and, unfortunately, there were quite a few of them to cover, each one a little grimmer than the one that went before. At first her reaction seemed a lot syrupier than it really ought to have been, in view of the fact that she didn't know a single thing about any of the folks whose stories I was telling until I brought them up. I very quickly discovered, though, that that wasn't true at all; she was genuinely shaken by what happened to each and every person. Adding the old photographs had only made matters worse. Seeing them had the effect of filling her troubled mind with a whole batch of haunting visual images to go along with the highly distressing verbal accounts that had been delivered.

Up until then, the only effect the grimness of her relatives' lives had had on me had been to strengthen my resolve to learn as much more about them as I could. They'd lived through intriguing adventures and endured great hardships, after all, so I couldn't wait to uncover more of the gritty details. My interest in them had been more like that of an unwelcome rubbernecker at the scene of an accident rather than that of someone who had a right to be there in the first place. As sad as their lives had been, they had lived so long ago and in such a remote area that their tragedies were too far removed from the present to have had any lasting emotional impact on me. From my perspective, her elders were just historical figures whose lives I wanted to study.

Eventually, though, I picked up on how she was really feeling. Candy had related to the people whose stories I was telling as if each one of them were right there with us, as if they were very, very real, and as if their misfortunes had happened only recently, most likely because she was having so many problems of her own. Up till then, I'd never looked at them as the downers they actually were. To me, they'd been no more than what I described them to be — *stories*, accounts of distant events that had happened to long deceased people and that could have no impact on us in the here and now.

I was also very surprised by the fact that the information I presented turned out to be as much of a revelation for her as it had been for me, just a few months earlier. At first it was difficult to believe that she knew so little about her own lineage, but, as I was soon to discover, that's how it really was. She had only incidental and fragmentary knowledge of the Caine or the Hicks sides of her own birth family.

She'd overheard passing conversations between her parents about a few of their relatives, but not a single one of them had ever visited her family and her family had seldom visited any of them. If her folks had done any such visiting, she said, they must have done it without saying a word, since she couldn't recall having visited with any more than a few of them while she was a child. Luther and Pirley had talked about their parents, her grandparents, and a few others on occasion, almost always disparagingly. That, she said, was all she could remember. She didn't know a single thing about the fascinating lives of her own grandparents and great-grandparents. She didn't even know who they were, much less where or how they lived or what became of them in their later years. Their stories were just as new to her as they had been to me.

Well before I finished it had already become clear that my presentation wasn't going over the way I expected it to. My stories may have been fascinating, but they had truly upset her as well, at a time when she was already very troubled. After every story, Candy had become a little more distraught.

Even so, I plowed ahead until I finished as I had intended to all along, having determined in advance not to stop until the scene had been properly set for the questions I planned to spring on her. I intended to demand that she provide a full account of her life with her birth family, back before she was adopted by the Wilsons, whether she wanted to or not. That's where my secret research had come to a dead end, so that's where I intended to make her start filling in the blanks. The absence of this particular information had become glaringly apparent before my recitation ended, and I knew she knew it. There was a hole so wide in my presentation that a truck could have been driven through it. Clearing the air would seem only right, it seemed to me, once that she sized up what was missing. It would be time to bring an end to the keeping of secrets between us, and I knew she wasn't going to like it.

Candy remained quiet and subdued throughout my recitation——*most likely,* I thought, *because she'd been bowled by my having worked so long and hard to prepare a family history for her.* I thought she was genuinely amazed and pleased, even though she hadn't explicitly said so. At the same time, I knew she had also realized how aware I had become of the secrets she'd kept from me over the years. I knew, too, that she had sensed my unspoken annoyance, and that sooner or later I would try to make her delve into the time in her life she had so diligently endeavored to conceal. These were the thoughts, it seemed to me, that had caused her to be so pensive. *Serves you right,* I remember thinking to myself at the time. *Your day of reckoning has finally arrived. This is what you get for being so maddeningly secretive!*

AN UNEXPECTED REACTION

EVENTUALLY, THOUGH, EVEN I, as dense as was, saw that she really was way too rattled for me to go on any further, whereupon I became nearly as flustered as she was.

She'd shed a steady flow of tears when I showed those old photographs of her mother and father, shots that had been taken back when they were young and before they were married. She had never seen them, and, in fact, didn't even know they existed. She had fallen apart when I pressed her to tell me more about them.

It wasn't until her discomfort became so palpable that new crow's feet were forming at the corners of her eyes that even a dunce like me could see that it was time to stop.

My presentation had gone terribly wrong. Having thought of her as a highly interested but overly sensitive listener had been totally off the mark: she hadn't been *deeply moved* by my series of stories; she had been *traumatized* by them.

After drawing my comments to a painful close, I drew my presentation to a close by placing the *gift* I had worked on for so long in her trembling hands. It was really nothing more than a spiral-bound compilation of the stories, photographs, and other mementos we had just gone over. She tried to accept it in a positive manner, but the involuntary flinch that registered on her face as she accepted it gave away how she really felt. She would have been happier if I had handed her a red-hot poker.

She went on to respond pretty much as I thought she would after that. She said she had been bowled over by all the effort that had been lavished on my project, and then thanked me with hugs and kisses for having been so thoughtful. Although she said and did all the right things, a sense of dread had appeared on her face and her voice had noticeably begun to quiver.

"Take your time as you look it over," I said, in a tone that came across as more threatening and suggestive than I intended, "but after you've read it through at your own pace, I'd like to talk about parts of it more detail. I have a lot of questions to ask, and I'm really looking forward to hearing from you."

She knew, of course, that I wanted to talk about the one topic that hadn't been mentioned in my narrative, her time with her birth parents, which was conspicuous by its absence. That these thoughts passed between us in only a few seconds was a clearcut instance of how two people who've been married for thirty years can *talk* to one another without saying a word. She knew exactly what I wanted to know more about, just as I knew the thought of having to talk about that period of time had filled her mind with dread.

A FLAW OF CONCEPTION

I HAD EMBARKED ON my project thinking that Candy's family

would turn out to be made up of good and upstanding people, tainted on occasion by a bad apple or two. That's the way it is for most families, so there was no reason for me to think hers would be any different. What I actually discovered, though, turned out to be nothing of the kind. For three direct lineal generations back, the people who would have mattered most in terms of her own upbringing had grown up in environments mean enough to have made them truly miserable human beings. She didn't know a thing about these people until I told her about them, but she had most certainly felt their pain when I did.

I should have given up on my inquiries then and there, but, of course, that isn't what I did; instead, I pressed ahead further, behaving as dumbly as a brick. "I won't stand for any more secrecy," I finally ended up proclaiming. "We promised not to keep secrets from one another, but that's exactly what you've been doing all along. Who has any more right to know about your childhood years than your own husband?"

OUR INTERLUDE OF ARGUMENTATION

WHAT FOLLOWED THEREAFTER WAS the interlude of argumentation I had expected all along. Candy pleaded with me to drop the topic altogether; I insisted that she talk about it in depth. It's fair to say that during the weeks that followed, I did everything but pound a shoe on the table, just to make it clear that I meant business: It was time for her to come clean about her past.

She begged me not to be so insistent, saying that the past was over and done with, and that she didn't want it brought up again. "I just don't want to get back into *all of that.*"

"All of what?" I responded, disregarding her obvious distress and refusing to let up. "Why," I asked, "shouldn't I know as much about your side of our family as you know about mine? I've shared all there is to know about my own folks, so why aren't you willing to do the same?"

The more we argued, the more angry-sounding and

obstinate I became. During the weeks that followed, I didn't let up for a minute on demanding a detailed accounting of her pre-adoptive years. Carrying on as if I had lost control of myself, I loudly and righteously proclaimed I had a perfect right to know what she was keeping from me. "It's time to clear the slate," I shouted, "time to tell me all about your early years."

She resisted for as long as she could, but, in the end, I finally wore her down. The last thing she needed was for her husband to force her into re-living the miseries of her childhood, but I browbeat her until she consented to doing just that. She didn't give in willingly, though; she relented only after seeing that I would never let it go, and, even then, only reluctantly.

A PYRRHIC VICTORY

OTHERS WOULD HAVE THOUGHT it unbelievably callous of me to behave the way I did, but I didn't think it wrong of me at all. In my view, I was only asking for what I had a perfect right to know. I knew in my heart that there was literally nothing Candy could have experienced or done as a child that would change the way I felt about her, short of her having been a serial killer or a mass murderer or something like that, and it didn't even occur to me that talking about her early years could have any lasting impact on us in real time.

The truth of the matter, though, was that I confronted her as much out of blind curiosity than because she hadn't confided in me about her past. I was dying to know, for example, if she had been the innocent baby taken from the hospital to live in the clearly dysfunctional and financially destitute household Luther and Pirley Caine created for themselves. Had a financial collapse or a divorce caused them to put their baby up for adoption? Was that how Candy came to live with the Wilsons?

In all honesty, I had become so engrossed in what I was doing that I had fallen in love with my own project.

Once it became clear that Candy was the only one who could fill in the gaps in my history of her family, it became her turn to fall under the microscope. Allowing her to evade providing an explanation of what happened during the years between Luther and Parley's marriage and when she was adopted by the Wilsons had become unthinkable. The lack of information about this period of time was such a conspicuous gap in the narrative I had compiled to date that I had become dead set on seeing it filled.

Convinced that her long-standing practice of keeping secrets bottled up inside was the major cause of her own unhappiness, I decided that the best approach to reducing her inner turmoil was to insist that she put an end to it altogether, just as soon as possible. I talked myself into believing that forcing her answer every question I had would help clear the air between us and thereby minimize the anxiety against which she constantly struggled, but, lordy, was I ever wrong about that.

15

A MOST RELUCTANT CONFESSANT

SO, IT WAS IN the unforgiving way that has been described that I successfully badgered my fragile and clearly suffering wife into revealing the experience she had lived through as a child. More than that, I also insisted that only the most detailed and elaborate account of those early years would do, even though I had no idea at all where her story might lead. She had to "tell it from the beginning to the end," I exclaimed, "just as actually happened, sparing no details and leaving no stone unturned."

Based on the assumption that it would be good for her to "get it all out there," I pressed her into divulging every recollection she had. It would amount to an exorcism of sorts, I recall thinking at the time, a catharsis that ought to be helpful.

"That part of my life has always been too painful and upsetting even to *think about*," she said, "much less to *talk about* with anyone, especially my husband. My entire childhood," she said, "amounted to nothing more than a set of memories so pitiful that all I've ever wanted was to expunge them completely, just so I'd never have to think of them again."

But, doing just as I asked, she went on to describe her childhood experience as carefully and as methodically as she could. Over a period of weeks, she laid out in great detail everything she could recall about those years, ultimately delivering an explanation that brought me face to face for the first time with what conditions had been when she lived with her birth parents. Her reluctance to discuss that period of time, I soon discovered, hadn't only been because it would be painful for her to talk about, but because she knew how distressing it would be for me to hear.

In technicolor and in excruciatingly painful detail, she really got into it — in fact, once she started talking, the floodgates opened to the full, until her story began to pour forth like caustic acid out of a laboratory beaker.

Surprisingly, the more Candy revealed about her past, the more impossible it became for either one of us to stay detached and objective about it. Before long, I found myself as almost as emotionally torn over what had happened as she was, until it was all I could do to hold my emotions in check. Her sorrow quickly became my sorrow, until, by the time she talked herself out, we were equally distraught.

Even though I had forcefully demanded that she "tell it like it really was," I was truly taken aback when she did. It seemed impossible that someone with her strong values and obviously wonderful qualities could have been raised in the circumstances she described. Before long, it became crystal clear why she had never wanted to talk about those dismal years.

Demanding that she exhume a past as unhappy as hers turned out to be a serious misstep, one that could only be blamed on my own extreme naiveté when it came to contending with the kind of emotional anxiety she'd had to deal with since then.

No one, I had been thinking to myself as I listened to her comments, *could have come through a childhood like hers unmarked,* and it had become as clear as a bell before she finished speaking that she certainly hadn't; worse still, it couldn't have been any clearer why. Instead of alleviating any of the stress she'd been feeling, forcing her reveal her childhood secrets had only made it worse, and, from that point forward, our lives began to change in profoundly disturbing ways.

16

PAPPY WAS A PISTOL

CANDY BEGAN TELLING HER childhood story by confirming that her birth parents, Luther and Pirley Caine, had resolved their financial problems at McAlester, Oklahoma, in May of 1942 by skipping out of town late one night in a great hurry, leaving behind not only a landlord who had been dunning them for months of past-due rent but also a whole list of other angry creditors. Apparently, this was their first use of an approach to dealing with financial exigency they honed to perfection over time. There wasn't anything fancy about what they did, but it worked, and it worked time and time again. Candy wasn't born until long after this first abscondment; she knew about it only because she'd heard them laughing and joking about it on multiple occasions over the years.

After leaving McAlester, Luther landed his family about eighty-five miles away in the City of Tahlequah, arriving there with three mouths to feed, no place for them to live, and not a single dollar of income coming in. They were in a serious fix, of course, one bad enough to have upset anyone. Luther, though, being the resourceful guy he was, got his family out of immediate trouble by working out a rental deal on yet another old house, this time one in such bad condition that a desperate landlord allowed them to move in on terms of *rent due in a month.*

With terms like that, it's not difficult to imagine what the place had to have been like. "I'm sure it was a dump," said Candy, "just like all the other so-called *homes* we lived in while I was growing up."

Once their housing problem was solved, Luther's next challenge was to locate a job. He knew he had to get serious about it, since he and Pirley were nearly flat broke. While he went out in search of work, she stayed home to take care of their new baby, Johnny Ray Caine, the son born to them prior to their hasty departure from McAlester. This was when I learned for the first time that Luther and Pirley had had more than one child, and I recall having thought with some relief that the baby I wondered about had not been Candy after all.

WHEN THE RUBBER FIRST MET THE ROAD

WHAT WAS MOST SIGNIFICANT about their move to Tahlequah was that Luther, for the first time, had to face up to just how woefully unprepared he was to be a breadwinner even for himself, much less for several dependents. Now that had to get serious about locating a decent niche in the world of work, the rubber, so to speak, finally had to meet the road, and, just as acquaintances and members of his own family had warned, his problems in this arena began to create life-long difficulties for himself and his family.

His basic difficulty was that he really wasn't all there when it came to any interactions for any useful purpose — searching for, landing, and then holding down a meaningful job. Even before a serious discussion of his readiness to take on a job opening could get off the ground, he had an unfortunate proclivity for shooting himself in the foot. Conversations for a focused and objective purpose such as job interviewing tended to go downhill rather quickly, beginning just as soon as his negative attitude and unusual personality quirks started to become apparent.

Even the most reasonable questions about his past or habits or values could degenerate into a defensive or combative reaction, responses strong enough to make an interviewer hesitant about adding him to a work team. His body language and general tactlessness clearly indicated that he resented any questions about his habits or values and immediately documented his highly argumentative personality. Findings of this kind, as would be expected, led to lots of *thanks but no thanks* responses from interviewers.

That he was poorly educated and had no particular job skills was painfully obvious, and his physical appearance made matters even worse. He had been tall and skinny as a teenager, but he had grown up to be a husky, hulking man. Guzzling beer all the time brought that about, as it so often does. He was big enough to come across as intimidating and threatening when there was a scowl was on his face, and there was a scowl on his face most of the time. Basically, he *looked* combative, irritable, and angry because he *was* combative, irritable, and angry. It was hard not to notice.

When it came to finding meaningful employment, Luther's dilemma could be summarized in a few words: He was uneducated, untrained, argumentative, physically intimidating, and had an obvious attitude problem, all in the same package.

Even when he did get hired for an entry-level position, it typically didn't take long for him to create a whole raft of problems for his employer. It was a real challenge just to get him to show up on time, sober and ready to put in a full day of work. Even when he did show up in good condition, the chip he carried on his shoulders led to repeated clashes with co-workers and supervisors alike.

Whenever an exasperated supervisor took him to task in hope of correcting his troublesome ways, the many negative traits and values that burdened him would immediately come into play. Acting out his innate problems, he would respond defensively, then argumentatively, and then, finally, combatively. He would display every reaction under the sun, except the ones that are needed to sustain a smoothly functioning workplace — receptiveness to learning, amenability to correction, and ordinary cooperative behavior. Time and time again, his behavior led to so much lost productivity or conflict, or both, that he forced those who had given him a chance to have to say the dreaded words *we're sorry, but we're going to have to let you go.* Whenever this happened, he would burn his bridges by cussing out the bearer of bad tidings, and then move on in search of something else.

AUTHORITY ANXIETY OF THE HIGHEST ORDER

I NEVER ACTUALLY MET Candy's father but describing him as a phobic holds up exceptionally well, especially when his particular phobia is defined a fear or aversion to authority figures of all kinds. Throughout his life he was held back, it seems to me, by an irrational fear of being *controlled* or *told what to do* by anyone, in any way. His fear was unrealistic and irrational, and that's why I thought it ought to be characterized as a phobia.

As we move forward in life, we learn that some level of legitimate control over our actions is to be expected, most notably, of course, on the part of our employers. They pay us for our time, and we do what they want us to do with the time they've paid for. This is nothing more than the normal trade-off that must be made by those who want to hold down a meaningful job. Concessions of this kind have to be made, if we are to get along in the world; we have to *give*, in other words, in order to *get*.

Luther, it seemed to me, had never gotten this basic message. For him, even this level of control over his actions seems to have been a real problem, enough of a hang-up to prevent him from earning a decent living in a normal and honest way. Because he wouldn't follow directions, resisted all reproof or correction, and couldn't abide by a schedule, he was incapable of getting along in a typical work environment. This was the major (but not the only) reason why he was never able to make the grade as a breadwinner or head of household.

Psychologists say that a true phobia exists when a person has a persistent and irrational fear of a specific object or activity or situation in combination with a compelling desire to avoid that which is feared. Simply disliking something, even very intensely, doesn't make a person phobic. Furthermore, even when a phobia can be shown to exist, specialists don't consider it a true disorder unless it causes some sort of harmful disturbance in life. Only when an irrational or unreasonable fear impairs a person's ability to function well at normal tasks does an aversion to anything constitute a true phobia — a condition serious enough to be so diagnosed and to warrant formal treatment.

Phobics are separated from average people who suffer from various aversions or serious dislikes by the fact that they are totally unable to control their emotional response to the object of their fears. They will try to avoid what they fear at virtually any cost, even when costs are significant and truly consequential. This holds true no matter how unreasonable or unjustified their fear might be, and it is often pointed out by specialists that sufferers may be just as capable as anyone else of understanding that their fear is excessive or unrealistic.

I'm no psychologist or mental health specialist, but what I've concluded after quite a lot of study is that Luther's behavior fit the foregoing conditions like a glove. He acted like a phobic, talked like a phobic, and behaved like a phobic; so, as far as I'm concerned, it's fair to say that he suffered from a phobia. In any case, he was a troubled man, whether he was phobic or not. What was certain and indisputable is that his work life was a complete disaster, and that he and his family suffered a great deal as a result.

It wouldn't have mattered much if he had been formally diagnosed as a phobic, since, back in his day and time and place, it would have been next to impossible to have gotten counseling that would have helped him deal with his many problems, even if he had wanted it — and my guess is that he probably would not have wanted it.

DOOMED TO JUST GETTING BY

WHAT HIS EMPLOYMENT-RELATED problems meant for Luther and his family was that they were forced to live off substandard wages and endure long periods of unemployment for as long as they were together. Even when he was able to find decent work, he tended not to do well on the job, since he lacked any meaningful level of control over his behavior and emotions. He was, as has been pointed out, completely incapable of getting along with co-workers and supervisors alike — or, for that matter, anyone else. The impression I've formed is that he didn't like himself very much, and, for that reason, he didn't like anyone else, either.

As years passed by, Luther bounced from one low-paying job to another, never staying at any one place long enough to earn higher pay or to build up any seniority or vested rights. Most of what he did earn, he and Pirley spent on drinking and partying in the way they had enjoyed back when they first met. They had a lot of fun, but their lifestyle kept them in dire financial straits nearly all the time.

Whenever their financial problems got too far out of hand at one location, Luther and Pirley would move their family to a distant town and start the same process all over again. After only a few such moves, their relatives lost track of them altogether. Over time, dodging creditors and staying just a few steps ahead of the law became a normal aspect of their everyday lives. The family became lost to others only because Luther and Pirley wanted them to be lost. Then, because they feared the possibility of being tracked down through their own relatives, normal relationships could not be sustained by any member of the family, even for those members who would have liked to maintain them. This is how life goes for those who get by in life through building up debts and running away from bill collectors.

A DUBIOUS MEASURE OF SUCCESS

EVEN THOUGH THEY LIVED in poverty and their relationship was seriously dysfunctional, Luther and Pirley ended up staying married for quite a long time — over twenty years, in fact. One major consequence of being together for so long was that they became an effective couple in one highly notable way — the production of children. They brought a total of twelve of them into the world, an even dozen blessed events, a child every 1.7 years or so. Had her two miscarriages also carried to term, Pirley would have had fourteen mouths to feed. Large families were as common as dirt in their day and time and place, especially among poor people out of rural farm communities. Despite the lousy economic conditions that prevailed during those pre-family planning times, that's just how it was. Children were born to them at the county hospital nearest to wherever they happened to be living at a given time. They were never thrilled when a new child was brought into the world; they just accepted it as an uncontrollable, as *just the way it goes.*

Candy said that her father had had no preferences or involvement when it came to naming their children, so the selection of names had been her mother's province alone. It was a task Pirley relished, primarily because she had always hated the plainness of her own first and last names and she didn't want her daughters to have the same problem. It was for this reason that she gave each of her girls, as she put it, "French-sounding" first and middle names she considered to be "as cute and girlish as possible — Collette Lucille, Claudine Louise, and Candice Lee." (She didn't know the French spelling was *Lea* rather than *Lee.*) Then, for reasons that only she could have explained, she gave all her boys names that ended in the letter y — Johnny, Arley, Freddy, Jerry, Terry, Tommy, Billy, Bobby, and Ronny. Ronny, that is, was not a nickname for Ron or Ronald; it was an actual given name.

Candice, my Candy, was far from an only child; she was one of a dozen blessed events, and not, as I had originally thought, the first, but the fifth. She was born at the county hospital in Phoenix when her father had the family out there as he searched for work. She was born near the middle of Luther and Pirley's brood of twelve children. I was taken aback upon hearing about this, having never imagined that she came from such a large family. In her adoptive household with the Wilsons, I was told that she had been an only child.

Candy told me that her childhood years had passed by without any form of personal recognition or individualized treatment to make her feel like a unique and special human being, just as it did for each of her siblings. Their childhood years were spent as anonymous members of a nondescript pact of featureless, rag-tag children, all carried along by the current of life that surrounded them. She grew up feeling, as she put it, "more or less lost in the shuffle."

She was raised, that is, just like the rest of her brothers and sisters — without ever receiving any personal attention or specific guidance to speak of. Kids were so omnipresent in their household that her parents were oblivious to any of their personal or special needs. They were constantly seen and heard, but they were never really listened to or given any serious recognition or consideration as unique human beings.

FEAR AND LOATHING AT HOME

LUTHER AND PIRLEY CONTINUED to fight like cats and dogs as his drinking problem continued to worsen. Because she was expected to stay home and take care of all the children while he was supposedly out trying to earn a living for all of them, Pirley felt greatly shortchanged by the ever-increasing size of their family. She especially hated when Luther stopped off at a bar after work without coming home to pick her up first. Bitterly resenting being left home alone with a bunch of snotty-nosed kids, she complained loudly and at great length whenever it happened. Because her constant complaining aggravated Luther all to hell, it became another major cause of ongoing argumentation between them, ranking right up there with their financial problems.

If there was any going out to be done, Pirley's initial preference was for the whole family to do it together. Taking the kids along meant that they would be left outside in the car while she and Luther were inside a bar, drinking and laughing and generally having a good time. She considered it acceptable mothering to just check on them once in a while, delivering candy and cokes on occasion to keep them happy. If they got too whiny and irritable, she or Luther would whip their butts to get them quieted down. She knew this wasn't the ideal way to handle kids, but she thought of herself a more responsible parent if they were kept nearby as opposed to leaving them at home, alone.

She was truly pleased when, in later years, some of the kids grew old enough to be left in charge of the younger ones, allowing her to feel better about leaving them at home while she and Luther went out on the town. The many problems that can arise when kids are left to raise kids seemed to have been of no concern to either one of them.

Arguing and fighting became routine within their household, even as new babies were added over the years. Conflict became as normal for them as having oatmeal for breakfast in the morning, and their kids grew up right in the middle of it. Luther's drinking continued to worsen until he became a total alcoholic, whereupon his condition became a serious problem for every member of his household, including himself. Already a deranged and angry man, it made him even more dangerous to be around.

As so often happens when family life disintegrates in this way, Luther made conditions even worse within their household situation by becoming ever more prone to taking out his frustration on Pirley and the kids. They routinely wound up on the receiving end of his increasing drunken rages. When he wasn't emotionally or physically terrorizing them, he neglected them altogether. Demanding whatever he wanted whenever he wanted it, they all learned to jump at his commands, knowing that, if they didn't, they would suffer serious physical consequences. He believed in making liberal use of his belt, always justifying what he was doing as a requirement of maintaining what he considered to be an orderly household.

ENNUI THE WIND BLOWS

JUMPING AROUND FROM ONE lousy job to another turned out to be a miserably depressing and ego-deflating way for Luther to make a living. Economic conditions were tough all over in Oklahoma when his and Pirley's kids were young, but they were truly hard for unskilled and difficult-to-place men like him. With all his many problems, it didn't come as much of a surprise to anyone when he started taking his frustration out on his own family. His behavior wasn't unprecedented for men in his situation, due to how dismal the economy was in those days. It isn't difficult to imagine how much pressure he must have felt.

In the early forties when Luther and Pirley went out on their own, prospects for making a decent living in their area within the state of Oklahoma must have seemed hopelessly bleak, since only low-paid jobs were available to men who hopped from one small town to another the way he did. It would have been pointless to go back to his hometown to look for a spot, since there was no work to be found in Hoffman. Economic opportunity was so lacking there at the time that more than a few people were going to bed hungry every night.

Nor could he go back to towns such as McAlester or Tahlequah; he owed so much money in those towns that creditors would have been after him in a minute. Hopping from town to town to avoid creditors had to have been an exhausting way to live. Luther had to have been a very worried man, knowing that he might be tracked down and brought to justice at any time, regardless of where he lived at any given moment. He and Pirley existed on the financial razor's edge, so short of money that they didn't know from one day to the next how they were going to make ends meet.

Even for semi-skilled workers, jobs had never been plentiful in their neck of the woods, but for unemployed men like Luther, who, again, had no education or training or personal discipline or self-control to speak of, job prospects had to have been grim indeed. For people like him, there weren't many good ways of making a decent living. What made matters even worse was that his ill-kempt appearance, glaringly negative attitude, and the ever-present cigarette that dangled from his mouth made him all the more unemployable. His attributes and habits made him a virtual poster boy for the highly derogative but unfortunately all too commonly held stereotype of a shiftless, low-life Okie.

Like many of his contemporaries, Luther had combed the state of Oklahoma in search of work that could be done by an unskilled laborer. When no work of this kind could be found, he started doing the same thing many others like him were doing at the time — he joined the progression of people who began to travel out west to states such as Arizona or California in search of seasonal employment.

No one was surprised when men in Luther's situation began leaving Oklahoma in search of work in the forties. There were few jobs to be had where they were, so they had to do something. Western states such as Arizona and California became favored destinations for most of Luther's counterparts simply because they had heard rumors that jobs were to be found out there. Even field or orchard work, they figured, would be superior to what they could find near home, which was next to nothing.

Luther was just one of a great many men who began to travel back and forth between Oklahoma and states such as Arizona or California during those trying times, searching for any jobs that could be found. Like others, he made exploratory trips at first, leaving his family behind as he checked out prospects. He made the same journey again and again, most often to do agricultural work in or around Phoenix or in the San Joaquin Valley of California. He irrigated fields, picked, swamped, or packed fruit, hoed, picked cotton, and did many other agriculturally-related jobs.

When the work ran out in one town in Arizona or California, he moved on to another. In California, for example, he worked in towns large and small all up and down the San Joaquin Valley, including Arvin, Poplar, Porterville, Fresno, Visalia, Hanford, Bakersfield, and others. Moving about in this way was how he got to know his way around states other than Oklahoma.

As ragged as his life at home in Oklahoma had been, it had to have been a challenge for him to spend so much time away from familiar surroundings and faces, living in places where people like him weren't always wanted or made to feel welcome. Being forced to become a migratory farm worker isn't what anyone would call an uplifting experience, after all. Lots of men were so negatively affected by what they went through during this period of time that it showed for the rest of their lives, and it seemed fairly clear that Luther ended up becoming one of them. In his case, rough times seemed to have exaggerated his already highly negative mindset and then brought about an even greater sense of disorientation and anomie.

Back wherever Pirley happened to be living with the kids,

daily life involved just as much drudgery for her as it did for Luther. Whenever he went away in search of work, she was left alone to take care of an ever-growing number of kids who, because they had had no effective parenting or authority figures to answer to, became more mouthy, unruly, and obnoxious with every day that passed. She got herself and all of them by on small amounts of money he left behind or mailed home and through public handouts, fending for all of them as best she could. She and the children were ragged and hungry all the time, especially after his trips away started lasting longer and longer and she had no idea when he would return.

Every time Luther returned home after being away for a long while, Pirley, who became a little more unstable each time he departed, was about ready to jump out of her skin from cabin fever and from having to wrestle day after day with a wild and uncouth bunch of ill-behaved, yelling, hungry kids. Her life, just like Luther's, had to have been a soul-crushing challenge.

Now that some of their kids were old enough to be left in charge of the younger ones, she and Luther would get out of the house just as soon as they could make it happen. Leaving the brood in charge of the oldest and toughest boy or girl who happened to be at home at a given time, they'd head out for another night of drinking and partying. Whenever he returned home, they would fall back into the pattern of behavior that had made them happy when they were younger, just as quick as a wink.

ALWAYS ON THE GO

AFTER MAKING MANY TRIPS away alone in search of work, Luther and Pirley eventually began traveling together from one place to another, usually to do seasonal field work in one state or another. Whenever they did this, they'd pull their kids out of school, load as much as they could carry into whatever old car they owned at the time, and then head out — always with just enough cash on hand to get them wherever they were going.

Upon reaching their destination, they would camp under a bridge or just live out of their car, parking it as close as possible to the orchard or field in which they found work. When the work ran out in one town, they would move on to another, and, when work ran out for the season, they'd use whatever they had been able to save to head back to Oklahoma for the winter.

Their pattern of behavior remained the same for the family until the early fifties, when Luther and Pirley began to think about staying out west for good. This was only a fanciful notion, of course, due to the *build–up–as–much–debt–as–possible–and–then–skip–out* lifestyle they had adopted. If they had attempted to stay in any fixed location after being found out, they would have ended up in jail. For as long as they were together, therefore, they continued to bounce between towns in Oklahoma, Arizona, and California, staying at any one location only until they built up as much debt as possible and creditors started coming after them. When that happened, they would move on to wherever Luther thought was best.

Whenever they went to California to do seasonal agricultural work, they usually started out from a privately-owned farm labor camp located on the outskirts of the San Joaquin Valley town of Porterville, a business called Hood's Camp. They were used to the small development, so they'd stay there until local work ran out, then move up north to other towns in the San Joaquin Valley. When no further work could be found, they'd head back east, usually to Oklahoma but sometimes to Arizona.

Hood's Camp was nothing but a small cluster of ten-by-eighteen-foot wood frame cabins that had been designed as temporary housing for farm laborers. In addition to the cabins, within the camp was a small grocery store, a garage, a used car lot, and a communal restroom facility — featuring, by the way, the first shower and flush toilet to which the Caines had ever had access. The whole operation was owned and managed by a no-nonsense couple whose names were Hobert and Ortha Hood. The Caines knew them well, from having lived there before.

From the camp, Luther and Pirley and all their children would leave each day to do farm labor piecework such as picking or hoeing cotton, cutting lemons or oranges, or cleaning fields and orchards of weeds and pie melons. The kids, even the babies, went along with the rest of the family. Those members of the family who could work did work, including the children, who were put to it just as soon as they were physically able to do anything worthwhile.

It was an ongoing struggle for Caines to make a living this way; they were poorly paid and their work was never dependable. On many occasions during this period of time, Luther and Pirley must have longed for the good old days of their early married life back in rural Oklahoma.

Candy told me that one good memory of the years she spent with her birth parents was that her mother and two older sisters used to love to dress her up and style her hair. They'd cut and curl it in ways that were elaborate and unusual for a little girl of their time, then tie a bright scarf around her neck to make her look even prettier. It didn't take much effort to visualize her this way, since Candy was a beautiful child, anyway. In fact, all three of the sisters were charming little girls, and they all grew up to become beautiful young women.

For Candy, though, even the beauty treatments she so much enjoyed turned out to be a mixed blessing, in that it made something of an anomaly of her within her surroundings. In those days, an overly fancy hairdo and makeup on a girl of her age in a location like theirs really made her stand out. Even dressed in the ragged and poorly laundered hand-me-down clothing that were all she had to wear, being made up caused her to appear older than she really was. Then, because she *looked different*, people thought she really *was different*. The end result was that some boys and young men of the area didn't always know whether to treat her as a young woman or as a child.

Despite these concerns, Candy recalled being attractively made up as one of the few pleasant memories of the way her family lived back then, which was a time when not much else about her life could have been described using that particular adjective. For her, the way her mother and sisters dressed and made up had been a welcome temporary escape from the grim banalities of real life.

WANDERING AS A WAY OF LIFE

THE PATTERN OF WANDERING and drunkenness Luther got used to over the years became a pattern that lasted for the rest of his life, even if it became less necessary and irrespective of the adverse effect it had on his wife and children. It got to the point that there were times when he would take off for days or weeks or even months on end, without ever explaining where he was going, how long he would be gone, or what he intended to do when he got there. The fact that he was a married man with a whole batch of hungry children never seemed to have much of an impact on what he chose to do.

Initially, his absences were typically nothing more than drunken binges, from which he'd sooner or later return and begin spouting insincere apologies for being away so long. Pirley, inevitably, would begin to vent her rage, and the two of them would engage in yet another round of arguing and fighting. Later, after making up, they'd go back out for more drinking and partying. Then, with hardly a ripple, their past pattern of behavior would resume as if Luther had never been away.

For reasons he didn't have to explain to Pirley and never even thought about explaining to any of their children, from time–to–time Luther would return home inspired and excited about moving the family to yet another town. Whenever this happened, he and Pirley would pack up their meager belongings, load up all the kids, and head out for the new location — typically a place known only to him. On occasion, the new location was not even known to him, not until they arrived at the spot. Always falsely explaining that greener pastures and more fertile valleys would be found someplace else, he kept his whole family at loose ends and upset nearly all the time.

Their moves normally took place quite suddenly, often on a weekend or during a holiday, which is generally the best timing for moving by those who owe large amounts of back rent, utility bills, grocery bills, and so on. And, since they never knew where they were going to live until they arrived wherever he took them, it was not possible for any of the kids to leave a forwarding address for their personal friends, or even for members of their family. If he or Pirley wanted to get in touch with anyone after they got settled at a new location, they'd either send a letter with no return address or simply make a pay telephone call. Eventually, the kids gave up on trying to maintain contact with friends or family or anyone else, knowing that their parents really didn't want them to.

CONDITIONS CONTINUE TO WORSEN

PIRLEY CONTINUED TO LIVE in fear of Luther's irrational behavior, having learned early during their relationship that he could — *and most definitely would* — do any one of them serious harm when he was in one of his drunken rages. She never questioned Luther's decisions. In her case, she could be beaten whether she was pregnant or not, and she was pregnant most of the time. "He terrorized all of us," Candy said, "especially my mother. He beat her up whenever he was of a mind to, and, if one of us kids said or did anything to interfere, he'd pull off his leather belt and whip us too."

In open-mouthed amazement, I asked Candy, "Why on earth didn't somebody do something when this was going on? Wasn't it obvious that he was beating your mother and the kids, especially if there were times when she had to be taken to a hospital and treated by doctors and nurses?"

"Sure," Candy replied, "cops and other people — social workers, I guess — came out to see us time and time again, but nothing was ever done to stop it. They'd threaten and spit and fume, but whatever they did was helpful only for a little while. He was arrested and thrown into jail again and again, always on charges like domestic violence, drunken driving, public intoxication, or drunk and disorderly conduct. He'd serve out his time in the city or county jail wherever we were living at the time, but he'd always get out after a little while. When he did, he'd come back home and do the same thing all over again.

"The problem with getting him thrown into jail was that he'd be furious when he got back home. That's why Mom stopped calling for help or filing complaints about whatever he did. When he came home after being locked up, he'd start terrorizing us as soon as he walked through the door. Back then, there was little help to be had by a wife with a house full of ragged and unruly kids like us, especially a wife who was almost as undisciplined as her husband.

"If the authorities acted like they were going to take some sort of truly serious action, Dad would just pack all of us up and move on to another town. Mom had no money or work skills or support system whatever to fall back on, so she just gave up. She lived in so much fear of him that she stopped even thinking of pressing any charges. In fact, she acted as if nothing *ought* to be done about the way he was, as if he had a right to treat her the way he did, as if she somehow deserved it.

"You have to remember," she continued, as if reading my mind, "that in those days divorce wasn't the ready option it is today, most definitely not for a poor woman with a scraggly brood of children. There weren't any shelters or other support systems for battered, penniless women like her, at least not any she knew about. Even if she had wanted to get away, there would have been no place for her to go. I never saw any solid evidence that she ever really wanted to get out of their marriage, anyway."

This is only conjecture on my part, but what seemed to take place gradually over the years was that Pirley finally gave up on even thinking about trying to run a functional household or act like a normal mother. Eventually, she got to be more or less just like Luther, a person who took pleasure wherever and whenever she could find it. The fact that there was never much pleasure to be found in their dismal situation made her grasp ever more desperately at any opportunity for any chance to let loose for a while that came her way. Over time, she, too, just like Luther, became progressively more irresponsible, until she became a woman who routinely caroused, boozed, and carried on in ways that many would describe as being wanton and promiscuous. Whether she *actually was* wanton and promiscuous, only she could say.

As Pirley's increasingly dissolute behavior combined with her already irritable and argumentative personality, she enraged Luther all the more. Her own behavior convinced him that she deserved every stroke of *discipline* he meted out, and he didn't hesitate to mete out quite a lot of it. Then, as is so commonly the case, irresponsible behavior begat even more irresponsible behavior, until they became locked in a cycle of abuse so severe that they were incapable of finding any way of extricating themselves from it.

Did she conclude that it would be best to join in his behavior because she could not control him, or did she come to enjoy his lifestyle just as much as he did, maybe even to the extent of leading the way to their own further decline? Who knows? Asking that question now is like asking which came first, the chicken or the egg. The answer is that it really doesn't matter, since the end result will always be the same, regardless of which answer is selected. Misery, as they say, really is a lover of company.

"Luther wasn't no stupid man," said the cousin I spoke to back when I was researching Candy's family history. "He had some smarts, but he was way too far out in left field to make good use of it. Nobody ever figured out why."

Luther wasn't dumb; he was something much worse than that: He was an intelligent man whose mind had become irretrievably warped, first by the destructive influences of his own miserable childhood and secondly by his hopeless addiction to alcohol. When he was sober, he had to have been aware of the havoc his behavior was causing in his own life and in the lives of his wife and kids. How could he not have been aware of it, when it was so obvious a blind man could have seen it. I'd be willing to bet, in fact, that it was personal awareness of the destructiveness of his own behavior that made matters all the worse for his family. I think his own guilt depressed him so much that he drank all the more, just to escape the thought of it.

Yet another extremely hurtful consequence of his pervasive drunkenness was that he routinely lost most of the income he was able to earn on petty gambling at poker tables in the smalltown beer joints he frequented. Losing money this way, of course, left his wife and kids in increasingly desperate straits at home. Because they were being neglected by their father and their mother alike, more often than not the kids had way too little to eat, and what they did have usually was of the poorest quality and nutritional value. They were often, in fact, flat out hungry. This was a reality Candy remembered quite well.

At this juncture during her disturbing revelations, Candy digressed from her main line of thought to tell me three unforgettable side stories, memories that were followed up by a confession that was nearly unbearable to hear. Each of them — the three stories as well as the unintentionally and unknowingly-made confession — have been embedded in my mind ever since. The first story had to do with something relatively minor, given the enormity of all the other problems she and her siblings were up against at the time, but the other two were about incidents that had life-long, highly adverse effects.

A SLIP IN TIME

THE FIRST INCIDENT TOOK place in 1957 while the family was living in an old and run-down house in Glendale, Arizona, when Candy was eight years old. It had to do with an incident at school that upset the two younger girls, Candy and next oldest sister Claudine, so much that they came home crying their eyes out. Some kids on the playground had made a game of chasing them and looking up their dresses — which were really nothing more than light slip-over shifts with shoulder straps — to see the thin and stained panties that were all they had to wear underneath. "We never understood why they got it in their pea brains to do something like that," she said, "but that's what they did."

The kids, first some boys and then some girls, had started to laugh at and tease the girls because they wore no slips under their dresses. They started following them around the playground, mocking them with little rhymes they made up as they went. The girls had run away crying and embarrassed, now miserably aware of a new problem they hadn't even as much as thought of up until then.

When their older brother Arley noticed how distraught they were, he wouldn't let up until he made them tell him what happened. After hearing about what had taken place at school, he did all he could to console them. He told them that the other kids had been wrong to say what they'd said; that their classmates did not realize or truly intend the hurt they'd caused; that they should do their best to ignore taunts of that kind; and that the two girls should never do anything of the kind to other kids. Teenaged Arley behaved like a father that day, instinctively performing a role that ought to have been the province of one or the other of the girls' parents, Luther or Pirley.

Later that night after his two sisters went to bed, Arley snuck out of their house and walked into town. He prowled the streets until he found what he was looking for — a clothesline hung with a wash of men's clothing. Most everybody dried their clothes outside in those days, so a wash of the kind he was after wasn't hard to find. He stole two wife-beater style undershirts off the line, the kind with thin shoulder straps and large armholes that lots of men back then.

After staying up late that night to do some cutting and stitching, the next morning he gave the altered undershirts to his sisters. They were so long and loose after being resized that they fit the two girls like real slips. They were thrilled to death to have them, and, at school the next day, the teasing stopped.

God bless you, Arley, I remember thinking to myself as Candy told this simple story and I sat there silently listening, tears falling from her eyes as she spoke. Hearing her talk about this pathetic incident brought tears to my eyes as well, and I think I felt just as upset as Candy and her sister must have been at the time, back on the school grounds when the teasing actually occurred.

SLAPS THAT NEVER STOPPED STINGING

THE SECOND OF CANDY'S three stories was about an incident that occurred in 1959 when her family was living at a place called Linnell Camp, a farm labor housing development near the dusty central San Joaquin Valley towns of Tulare and Visalia. The camp was no more than a collection of drab labor housing units, but it was by no means the worst of the ragged old places the family had occupied in the past and it did offer access to outdoor spigots of running water as well as communal bathing and toilet facilities. Despite this, Linnell Camp became nothing more than a place of more bad memories for Candy and her siblings.

Because they were being left alone for longer and longer periods of time, the kids' situation became increasingly desperate. Now that the younger children could be cared for by their older siblings, their parents were spending more evenings and weekends than ever out drinking and partying with their fair-weather friends.

Times were so desperate that some of the children, including Candy, began to walk the local roadsides and scrounge through nearby dump sites in search of pop bottles or other abandoned items of value, anything that could be sold for cash to pay for candy or milk or whatever they and the younger kids could eat. They scavenged through garbage cans outside of stores and restaurants in search of anything edible, and, whenever they thought they could bring it off without getting caught, they stole whatever they could from any store or market they entered. The few grocers and retailers in the area knew quite well what the kids were doing, and it wasn't long before some of them complained to local law enforcement that something had to be done about "the damned ragamuffins who steal us blind every time we turn our backs."

Max and Ethel Blackwell, a couple that operated a small grocery store not far from the labor camp, were among the local merchants who had complained about the problem they were having with the kids. When law enforcement officers took no immediate action to put a stop to what was going on, they devised a plan to deal with their problem on their own. Basically, they decided to lay in wait to catch the kids in the act, knowing that their past behavior was certain to be repeated. They had planned in advance what they were going to say and do, once the kids were in their clutches.

The kids, of course, who remained just as hungry and as deprived as they'd as they always were, had no real options to exercise, so they fell right into the Blackwell's trap. The couple could have caught any one of them, but it just happened to be Candy and her brother Freddy who were caught stealing on that particular day at their store. Freddy, who was the older and larger of the two criminals and also a male, was grabbed by Mr. Blackwell, who took him outside and slammed him down hard on a bench at the entry of the market, just across from the gas pumps out front. Mr. Blackwell sat down right beside him, holding the culprit firmly in place until the police he'd called could get there to pick him up.

Frozen in fear at the sight of the large and angry store owner who was manhandling and loudly berating her brother, Candy said she tried to hide behind a row of racks on the other side of the store. She reacted, she said, just as she did when she was about to get another whipping from her father, by cowing and cringing in fear.

What happened then was that Mrs. Blackwell, who was just as angry and nearly as large as her husband, grabbed Candy by the hair of the head as she cowered before her, jerking her upright so that she could scream insults directly into her face. When Candy claimed she hadn't taken anything, Mrs. Blackwell slapped her hard. When she made the same claim again, she received yet another slap. Every time she denied having stolen anything, the woman slapped her again, each time a little harder, screaming at her all the while.

Candy was slapped again and again as she proclaimed her innocence, until she finally confessed and started begging the woman to stop. After pulling three or four items out of Candy's coat, Mrs. Blackwell half-dragged and half-pushed her captive around the store, holding her firmly by means of a fist full of hair and yelling at her every inch of the way, until every item she had attempted to steal was put back in place. After that, she marched Candy out of the store and over to the bench where her brother Freddy was being held, still pulling her along by the hair on her head. Needless to say, Candy was scared witless. "She hit me really hard," she said, crying quietly. "My ears rang and I felt dizzy for weeks afterwards."

Once outside, Mrs. Blackwell slammed her down hard on the bench, right beside her brother. As the two of them sat side by side, both adults continued to scream insults at the top of their lungs into their faces. The Blackwells were so mad they weren't about to let this become a forgive-and-forget situation. "This time around," they screamed, "by God, you damned kids are going to get the punishment you sure as hell deserve."

So, there they sat, the two neighborhood criminals, on a bench outside a rural grocery store, with two adults screaming in their faces and calling them thieves and white trash and any other foul name they could think of, listening to their stomachs growl as they waited for the police to arrive and take them off to juvenile hall. Freddy was eleven and Candy was ten, and they had stolen candy bars and canned food.

After a while, an officer finally showed up at the store to pick up the criminals and to take a report from the loudly indignant and highly self-righteous merchant couple, who continued to curse not only about the kids but about their worthless parents, the school system, society, and local law enforcement as well. "We told you so," yelled the Blackwells. "These damned kids have been stealing from us for months, and none of the damned people who are supposed to help us have been doing a damned thing about it."

The words that came out of the mouths of what the kids knew to be two highly powerful and authoritative adults rang in their ears for many years thereafter. They were still ringing, as a matter of fact, over forty years after the incident; when Candy told me what happened, she could still quote from memory much of what was said to her at the time. Their words have rung in my ears, too, since Candy repeated them to me that quiet evening in our own living room.

After writing up the Blackwell's complaint, the cop loaded the two sobbing kids into the back seat of his car and drove them away, intent not upon taking them to juvenile hall but upon delivering them to parents he expected to work with him to devise a punishment to fit the crime. He envisioned a meaningful discussion with a concerned couple, but what he saw when he got to the Caines' rundown old home was a bunch of kids that were even more ragged than his two hungry detainees.

He saw children who were far too young to have been left

without adult supervision, but there they were, just the same. The older kids, obviously still young and highly irresponsible themselves, had been left in charge of the younger ones, who began wailing the moment they saw that Candy and Freddy were in trouble with the police. When the cop asked to see their parents, none of the kids could say where they were at the time. When he asked how often they were left alone this way, the kids said: "All the time."

After looking around a while to better size up the situation, the cop called all the kids together before delivering a lecture to Candy and Freddy that stressed how they were likely to wind up in reform school if they stole anything else in the future. After that, he just drove off and left all the kids standing there. Nothing else came of the incident at the store that day, and, as far as any of the kids ever knew, their parents were never ever told what Candy and Freddy had done.

What really happened, though, unbeknownst to any of the kids, was that they had been delivered into the hands of an experienced, mature officer, a cop who had a lot of common sense as well as a kind heart. Taken aback by the squalid conditions that existed in their home, he knew there were bigger fish to be fried than two shoplifting children.

When he reported what he'd seen, a supervisory officer was dispatched from the sheriff's office to investigate the kids' situation in more detail. After only a brief visit, the senior man saw that their conditions were even more out of hand than the first officer had appreciated. At this point, he placed an urgent call to the Tulare County Department of Social Services, saying that that office ought to send out a Child Protective Service worker to conduct an even more detailed investigation.

The CPS investigator who visited the Caines' home was aghast when she grasped the plight of the kids, which was in all respects as desperate as the senior officer had described. The children were skinny and underweight for their ages, and they were clothed in rags and unsupervised in any way. In addition, all of them were dirty and hungry. Their conditions were so appalling that she didn't hesitate to take what she considered to be appropriate action.

When Luther and Pirley rolled in drunk and happy later that evening, they were welcomed by a social worker and a police officer. After being read the riot act, they were threatened with formal charges if they didn't improve the living conditions of their kids. Upon advising the Caines that they could be charged with serious crimes, the authorities departed after promising to return the following day with more help.

Luther and Pirley, as would be imagined, had taken their warning seriously, so they worked as fast as they could to deal with the problem that faced them, just not in the way the officials or anyone else would have expected. Instead of doing anything that might have improved the plight of their kids, they just packed up their old car with as many belongings as could be carried, loaded up all of their kids, and headed out for a new location.

When the authorities returned the next day, the whole family was gone. How they got the money for travel and where they took off to, there was no way to tell. At that point, there was nothing else they could do. Who knows, maybe their departure was just what the locals wanted to happen. Now that the Caines were out of their jurisdictional area, they had no responsibility for doing anything about them at all. In the end, no charges of child neglect were filed against the Caines, simply because they were nowhere to be found, and all that happened to Candy and Freddy was that they got a hurried and half-hearted slapping before the family departed, not for stealing, really, but for bringing the law down on their parents.

Luther had no idea where he would take his family after their departure from Linnell Camp in Tulare County out in the San Joaquin Valley, but he certainly wasn't in a state of panic when he drove away. It wasn't the first time he and Pirley had been threatened with dire consequences for not taking better care of their kids; they had, in fact, become used to it.

He didn't decide where he was going to take his family until they were safely on the road. Thinking as he drove that it would be quicker and easier to get back on his feet in a familiar location than in someplace entirely new, he decided to take the family back to

Glendale, Arizona, simply because he already knew the area. Then, once he got the family back to familiar surroundings, it didn't take long for him to find another dilapidated old house they could crash in. Much more easily than would be imagined, he and Pirley picked up on their former lifestyle as if nothing had ever happened.

What followed thereafter, as would be expected, was yet another period of extreme privation for their kids, even though their parents were able to carry on as usual. "I've never been able to forget the months that followed," Candy said to me as she dabbed her eyes, "due to what happened to me personally while we were there." At this point, she told me the third of her three memorable stories.

CANDY'S BRUSH WITH DEATH

CANDY'S THIRD STORY had to do with a bout of serious illness she had to endure when her family lived in Glendale, Arizona, one that happened in 1960, when she was eleven years old. It got started, she said, with what seemed to be nothing more than an ordinary sore throat, a condition that cropped up overnight due to being raised in unsanitary conditions and without any parental attention being paid to their basic physical or nutritional needs.

Struggling but neglected, her condition worsened as each day passed. What was at first thought to be only a minor throat problem soon progressed into an illness that was anything but minor or routine. As her temperature rose and she became progressively worse, she developed a high fever and started having serious shakes and chills. When nothing was done for her, her sore throat and fever worsened until she developed a serious case of strep throat. Even though she was coughing like a barking dog, her mother paid little attention it, assuming that she would get over it after a while.

Then her strep throat progressed into a case of scarlet fever. Scarlet fever can turn into rheumatic fever when it isn't properly treated, and that's what happened next. Candy said that if she had been taken to see a doctor when her fever first spiked, her strep infection would have been detected using cultures obtained using a cotton swab and a straightforward lab test. After that, it could have been cleared up using an antibiotic. Her condition would have been handled in this way for the specific purpose of preventing a strep infection from lapsing into something far more serious, such as the scarlet fever and then the rheumatic fever she eventually contracted. In her case, though, none of these steps were taken, and she ended up contracting the more serious complications.

From what she had learned since by talking with medical professionals, the initial symptoms of rheumatic fever had most likely appeared a week or two after her strep infection was left untreated. It is a condition, she said, that sometimes occurs as the result of an immune reaction to specific strains of strep bacteria. Rheumatic fever is more dangerous than strep because it is, in fact, a serious disease of the heart. Thankfully, it doesn't crop up often, and the great majority of strep throat infections do not lead to rheumatic fever.

Her own case of rheumatic fever resulted in inflammation in several of her internal organs. In addition, it affected the joints of her body with arthritic-like swelling, redness, and sensations of heat.

More often than not, doctors had told her, any heart inflammation that occurs in this way can be resolved with no permanent effects. Sometimes, though, healing takes place only after one or more of the valves is permanent scarred, which can result in obstruction of blood flow (called stenosis) or reversed (backward) flow of blood (called regurgitation or insufficiency). Sometimes, over a period of months or years, serious complications can develop and surgery may be required to repair or replace the damaged heart valve or valves.

The doctors Candy spoke to about all of this as an adult told her that when rheumatic fever is present, its symptoms can be detected through careful observation. With proper treatment using antibiotic drugs, her condition could have been contained and its risks greatly reduced. Basically, the approach that could have been taken was to administer antibiotics to eliminate any remaining strep organisms and large doses of aspirin and, sometimes, cortisone-like drugs to suppress the inflammatory process rheumatic fever causes. When cases of rheumatic fever do occur, they said, it is usually found in kids. Adults, she was told, would, of course, have either spoken up or gone to a doctor before their condition got that bad, but children usually don't know how to do this.

This was the progression of events that occurred in Candy's case. She came close to dying where she lay, nearly under her mother's nose, simply because no one was looking out for her.

Doctors Candy had spoken to told her that a child ought to be taken in any time a sore throat lasts more than twenty-four hours and is accompanied by a fever. In her own case, multiple signs and symptoms of a serious illness had been evident for many long days and nights. She had suffered from inflammation of the heart as well as weakness and shortness of breath, and for some time her heart had beaten abnormally as joint pain shifted from one part of her body to another. In addition, there had been twitching movements in her limbs and face, and her severe throat infection had been accompanied by a persistent fever. Even after all of this, her mother just let her lay there and suffer. If her mother been watching closely, she would have noticed that Candy's condition had gotten so bad, she could hardly breathe.

Once again, it was her older brother Arley who came to her assistance, in this situation by insisting to their mother that Candy was so sick that she might end up dying, just like their younger brother Terry had years before. Had she not been taken in, that's most likely what would have happened.

The *beds* the kids slept on in those days were nothing more than blankets spread on the floor, with a few more dirty blankets used as covers. Their pillows were anything that could be rolled up and placed under their heads, most commonly an article of clothing. Candy lay in misery in such a setting until her body became so racked with chills and fever that the blankets below her were soaked in sweat and the skin all over her body took on a yellowish color. Her joints — her ankles, knees, elbows, and wrists — had swollen to the size of grapefruits, and she became too weak to rise from her pallet to go the bathroom. All she could do was lie there, fitfully rolling in her own sweat and waste.

Her condition had to sink to this point before Pirley finally realized that her son Arley had been right to say what he'd said; if something was not done right away, Candy might actually die. Immediately falling into a state of near panic, Pirley suddenly realized that she had no car and no money, and, therefore, no way to get her suffering daughter to the Maricopa County Hospital emergency room for some sort of treatment. Luther couldn't help because he was in the Maricopa County Jail at the time, serving a sentence for drunken driving, and their car wasn't available because it had been impounded when he was arrested.

Pirley had no idea where her older kids were at the time, but if their car had been on hand, which it wasn't, she or Arley, who was fifteen years old, could have driven Candy to the hospital. (Well, actually, she did know where one of her boys was: He was serving time in the Maricopa County Juvenile Detention Center for slugging a teacher who attempted to split up a fight between himself and another kid at school.) In any case, the bottom line at that moment was that she had no way of getting Candy in to see a doctor.

Close to having an anxiety attack, Pirley got Candy in for treatment by having Arley help carry her down the dirt road that led from their place out to the main highway. After flagging down a truck, she pleaded with its driver to drop them off at the hospital emergency room on his way into Phoenix. The driver, who immediately saw what a fix they were in, agreed, then took them there as quickly as he could.

Upon their arrival at the hospital, emergency room staff rushed Candy in immediately. When the doctors on duty realized the seriousness of her condition, they berated Pirley for not bringing her in sooner. As bad off as she was, Candy was able to overhear them bawling out her mother, complaining that her child was so sick that she could easily die. That comment absolutely terrified her, of course, because she knew it meant that she might never get well.

Once admitted, she didn't leave the hospital for forty-six days. Her life literally hung in the balance for quite some time, until, with proper care, treatment, and nutrition, she finally began to recover. She has since learned that serious permanent internal damage was caused by this childhood ordeal. She has been officially diagnosed as having Chronic Obstructive Pulmonary Disease, or, as they call it, COPD. She has to take various medicines on a daily basis, just to keep the condition under control, and the fact that she still suffers from this illness as an adult is an ongoing worry for both of us. Her condition today is just one more example of the many ways she and her siblings were put at risk through parental neglect during their childhood years.

Candy told me before we were married that she had had rheumatic fever as a child, but it was not until she told me this story that I learned how it had been contracted. Having had rheumatic fever as a child is not something that can be ignored; we have to live with the consequences of it every day. What is so terribly tragic about childhood ordeal is that it was so completely unnecessary; simple forms of treatment could have stopped her problem from getting worse.

"Didn't your sorry parents give a damn about you kids?" I asked, in angry indignation. "Were they as dumb as bricks and completely unaware of the suffering they were forcing you kids to endure?"

"The truth," she replied, "was probably a little bit of both. Basically, they didn't see any problems because they never thought to look for anything that might be amiss. Our problem, in turn, was that neither one of them ever looked out for us, when that's what both of them ought to have been doing all along. I wasn't the only one of us kids to go through an ordeal like my illness. We were all in the same boat."

"Damn your parents anyway," I said, swearing bitterly. "There's no excuse for any parent being so oblivious of the condition of their kids. I wish I had been there when you were sick, so I could have knocked their heads together a few times, just to get their attention. That's what both of them deserved."

Candy also recollected that while she was in the hospital recovering from her illness, Pirley, as always, would leave her younger siblings in the care of any of the older ones who happened to be around so that she could to go into town for a visit with the members of her family who were, so to speak, *temporarily tied up*. In a small way, these visits were made somewhat more convenient than they ordinarily would have been, since, at the time, the three Maricopa County government agencies she needed to stop off at were situated not too far from one another. On the same day, therefore, she was able to visit her daughter Candy in the Maricopa County Hospital, one of her boys in the Maricopa County Juvenile Detention Center, and her husband Luther in the Maricopa County Jail. *Thank heaven,* I suppose she must have thought at the time, *for the smallest of favors*. Pirley was so down and near totally out of luck back then that she would have been thankful for any convenience that came her way.

When Candy's condition improved enough for her to be discharged from the hospital, she was released back into the *care* of her parents — but really only Pirley, since Luther, by that time, had been released from jail and was nowhere to be found. She and Pirley left the hospital carrying a list of prescriptions and directions for administering antibiotic treatments that were to have been continued for a full year to prevent any relapse or worsening of her condition. In addition, for several years after her initial recovery, she was supposed to have stayed on a schedule of various suppressive medications to prevent secondary problems.

What actually happened after her release was that she didn't receive a single dosage of follow-up medication or any additional treatment, not after the medicine sent home with her from the hospital was used up. The family had no medical insurance, nor did they have any spare money to spend on more medication. Her doctor's instructions, therefore, were simply ignored.

Before the end of her first evening back at home, her father showed up at home again, then became angry at Pirley or one of the kids for an offense of one kind or another, after which he chased all of them, even Candy in her weakened condition, outside and into a field with a belt raised in hand, poised to give anyone who could be caught a whipping. He behaved as if Candy had never been sick, as if neither he nor Candy had ever been away.

This episode happened, again, when Candy was just eleven years old, but today she still has to deal with the lasting health consequences of having contracted rheumatic fever as a child. Our dentist, for example, requires her to take an antibiotic before he'll provide treatment. In addition, she suffers from painful arthritis in her hands and other joints, and her weakened heart will continue to make her highly susceptibility to various respiratory ailments.

Candy's description of this appalling episode in her young life was so troubling that I went through a great deal of personal effort to find more about the possible long-term effects of her illness. I even contacted the Maricopa County Medical Center directly to ask for a copy of her case history, only to be told that her records were destroyed years before by a fire that had occurred at the hospital.

A NEARLY UNBEARABLE CONFESSION

CANDY CRIED SO HARD, her chest heaved as she relived these three dreadful incidents from childhood, and, once again, I cried right along with her. Her stories were upsetting enough to leave me feeling half sick, and it was easy to imagine how traumatic each incident must have been for her at the time. There is no way to adequately explain how poignant it was to hear my sweet wife describe the unspeakable neglect she had endure, crying as she spoke, over forty years after the fact. Both of us were generally mature and fairly sophisticated people, but the events she described were so moving that they have been disturbing to me ever since. Crying together as we sat holding hands in support of one another, all I could think was "Damn her miserable parents to hell and back; what they put their children through had most definitely warped them for life."

God bless her brother Arley, I've thought time and time again since we talked about her past, for what he did in the midst of their trials. He had tried his best to stand up like a man, like a real adult, by doing all he could do, even at the risk of significant physical punishment to himself.

My heart ached more every time I thought about the misery Candy and her brothers and sisters had to endure, but I found what she said shortly thereafter even harder to bear. She said she had tried to keep as much of this information away from my prying eyes as she could, thinking that my hearing about it might in some way affect the way I felt about her. Nothing, as far as I was concerned, could have been further from the truth, but the fact that she had made such a statement meant that she didn't feel confident that I would stand by her through thick and thin. For me, her wording amounted to a nearly unbearable confession.

To some extent, she even became something of an apologist for the inexcusably neglectful behavior of her parents, thinking that minimizing the impact of their failure to do what they ought to have done for their kids would make hearing about it somewhat less traumatic for me. "They didn't know what they were doing," she said. "They didn't know any better, and they were just too troubled to do what was right." Her tearful comments made me so angry I felt like punching a hole through the nearest wall.

It was easy to envision how her family's impoverished situation must have appeared to the professional people who tried to deal with them back the — the doctors, nurses, social workers, CPS workers, teachers, police, and so on. They had to have been just as appalled as I was.

Now that Candy had made abundantly clear how much harm Luther and Pirley had done to their children, I didn't feel the least bit of compassion for either one of them. Why should I, when my own precious and vulnerable wife had been on the receiving end of their outrageous neglect and she had suffered from it from that point forward? Because I was an aggrieved husband rather than a priest or social worker or defense attorney, I wished they had been thrown in jail for what they allowed to happen. As far as I was concerned, that's what they deserved.

LIFE IN A HOUSE OF CARDS

THE CAINE FAMILY WAS living in a financial house of cards, there was no doubt about that. Their situation continued to worsen as the years went by, until they finally reached the point of no return, the time when abject poverty totally overcame them. It was a god-send that bags of food and boxes of secondhand clothing had once again begun appearing on their doorstep; this was manna from heaven for the kids, who, although they may have known in the backs of their minds how these items came to be there, were too hungry and needy to look any gift horse that happened to trot by in the mouth. Whether the goods arrived there due to the pity of concerned neighbors or the action of a local charitable agency was the last thing they worried about; what mattered to them at the time was that help was, in fact, there, and that it kept them from doing without.

According to Candy, what the older kids — the ones who were left nominally in charge of the younger ones while their parents were away — said at the time was "What the hell is the point of asking a lot of questions or worrying about where the stuff comes from when not a one of us, even the littlest kids, has decent clothes or shoes to wear and there was nothing in the house to eat? Hell," they said, "if somebody out there is dumb enough to give away good stuff, why should we be too damned proud to accept it? In our situation, what sense would it make for us to start asking questions?"

That was wise of them, I thought upon hearing how the kids reacted, imagining that in their shoes I would have done the same thing. It would have been tough to refuse donated food, that's for sure. Just as a human heart can become a lonely hunter, the stomach can become a ravening lion.

When their parents were *out*, which was as often as Luther and Pirley could scrape together enough money to get through the door, the kids were still left at home alone to fend for themselves. Luther would often go off alone, but Pirley would tag along whenever she could. While they were away, the younger kids were cared for by the older ones, who were, of course, haphazard about it and left to set their own rules and standards of behavior.

Needless to say, at their age, the older kids were anything but enlightened caregivers in terms of providing good parenting or meeting the fundamental needs of their younger siblings. The smaller kids grew up on the receiving end of child rearing techniques that have been practiced since the beginning of time — shouts of threatened mayhem, whacks on any conveniently accessible part of the anatomy, and swift kicks in the butt.

Given their low-income level and poor living conditions, few photographs had been taken of the Caine family while they lived together under the same roof. Even when a camera and film were available, photography was a luxury that hardly registered on their scale of *need to do* activities. Besides that, Luther and Pirley and the kids were seldom in good enough condition for any decent photographs of them to be taken.

Candy produced a few long-hidden images at this point, shots that had been taken back when she lived at home with her birth family. They were poor in quality due to having been taken on the spur of the moment using poor film, a cheap camera, and then being poorly developed, but they captured the truth of her home situation quite well. As she explained the misery going on behind the scenes, we cried together as we looked at them, due to their having the unnerving effect of making a few of her memories seem even more painfully recent and real.

"Even if money had been available for taking photographs back then, not much went on in our place that any of us would have wanted to remember. Mom and Dad were hardly ever in what could have been considered a family-oriented frame of mind, not even on the best of days."

Candy was hard pressed to think of *any* positive family memories of her time with her birth parents. "Most of what I do recall," she said, "I'd like nothing more than to put out my mind forever, not just for my own peace of mind but also because I have always thought that your hearing about my young life would somehow make you think the less of me. Now that you've heard all about it," she asked, "can you cite one single thing about what I've told you that can lift us up in any way?"

"Nothing that happened to you as a child will ever diminish the way I feel about you today," I assured her over and over again. Our discussion had veered off in such a negative direction that I started feeling even more guilty than ever about having forced her to relive a childhood that had been miserable beyond words.

Her parents' despicable behavior — especially her father's — had had such a harmful effect that she had been damaged for a lifetime. What this meant, of course, was that her birth parents had had an enormously negative effect on my life as well, because, in a marriage as close as ours, when one spouse suffers, the other suffers right along with them, their lives are so inextricably intertwined.

LUTHER LOSES ALL CONTROL

CANDY WENT ON TO explain that conditions in their household had never stopped declining, until those nights that Luther came home late and nearly falling down drunk became fearful occasions for mother and the kids alike, whether Pirley had been out carousing with him or not. Returning to a ragged home and having to face a pack of hungry, cranky, needy, squalling kids brought out the worst in him.

Her father's condition eventually deteriorated, she said, to a point where he started losing all control over his drunken rages, and, whenever he got that way, he would react by venting his anger on any member of the family he could reach. He'd beat Pirley right in front of the kids, usually over some minor or meaningless provocation. Using either the front or back of his hand, it was not uncommon for him to blacken her eyes, bloody her nose, or create large bruises or swellings.

The kids stood by cowering and crying and watching on numerous occasions as their mother was hurt so badly that she could not get up. "Mom was hospitalized on multiple occasions after being beaten," said Candy, "but nothing was ever done to stop it from happening. She always lied about what had taken place and refused to press charges. Eventually, I think Mom just got too afraid even to think about making any more complaints. She knew what would happen after he returned home after whatever punishment he received."

If one of the older kids did or said anything to interfere with what he was doing, he would slap or hit or kick them around the house. He routinely whipped the kids with his belt for various kinds of offenses, and he verbally berated and criticized every one of them. He hit the older kids, especially the boys, with anything that happened to be reachable — a switch, a flyswatter, a broom handle, or a stick. It didn't seem to matter to him; one would do the job as well as another. He was a big, angry, irrational, drunken man, and he kept the whole family terrified all the time. Every one of them literally jumped at his commands.

There were times, Candy said, when some of the kids would be whipped even after they had already gone to bed. In a drunken stupor, for example, he might wake one of the girls — Candy or one of her sisters — from a sound sleep and order them to fix him something to eat, to do a household chore, or simply to give them hell for one thing or another. When an episode like this took place, it usually ended with verbal abuse or a physical whipping, or both.

The kids lived in such fear of winding up on the receiving end of one of their father's drunken rages that they learned to wake one another as soon as they heard him coming home late at night. Grabbing a blanket or a coat or something else to place on the ground as bedding, they'd run outside to sleep in the fields or brush until he stopped cursing and plundering around the house and finally fell asleep. Sometimes he would punish them the next day for having run out, but the kids had learned that punishments administered when he was sober were usually less severe than what could happen when he was drunk.

As conditions in the household continued to worsen, Candy said that it had been her two older brothers, Johnny and Arley, who bore the brunt of Luther's rages. When they tried to be a protector of their mother or one of the girls or younger kids by crying out or stepping in when his abuse became too much to bear, he would turn his attention to them instead. Both boys truly suffered at their father's hands, she said. "He didn't just whip them; he really beat the hell out of them, so badly he really ought to have been thrown in jail."

Eventually, the older boy, Johnny, was whipped and beaten so often that he broke down under the pressure. He just gave up, whereupon he became as much of a reprobate and bully as his father, not against members of his family but in terms of how he behaved in school and within society at large. He became a total juvenile delinquent, staying out until all hours, getting into trouble — drinking, stealing, bullying, and so on. Another way of putting this would be to say that he became a younger version of his father. Eventually, he became totally uncontrollable, by Luther or Pirley or anyone else. Shortly thereafter, he ended up in a reformatory, after which he dropped out of school for good. When this happened, he stopped trying to protect his mother, leaving that chore to the second oldest boy, Arley.

According to Candy, her brother Arley never stopped trying to protect their mother or the younger kids from being beaten. For a number of years, therefore, he became his father's prime target. "You're trying to turn my own damned kids against me," Luther would rail at Pirley as well as Arley, whenever Arley followed Johnny's example and tried to intercede on behalf of his mother or his siblings. All the kids, including Candy, were there to see the many whippings he received as he tried to keep Luther away from Pirley or one of them. Neither boy had been able to stop what was going on, but, to their great credit, they did the best they could.

Crying quietly, Candy said to me, "I'll always love my brother Arley for what he tried to do for my mom and us kids. He was just a boy himself, but he was the only one in the house who never stopped trying to act like a man, even when all the odds were stacked against him."

CONDITIONS CONTINUE TO DISINTEGRATE

LUTHER'S WANDERING, WHICH AT first had been to some degree

justifiable due to the fact that he usually left in search of work and that he often did bring home some of what he earned to help sustain his family, gradually evolved into becoming the way he lived for the remainder of his life. He moved his family from town to town all over the central San Joaquin Valley and even between states, usually after building up as much debt as possible and always without leaving behind a forwarding address. The *homes* Luther settled his family in became worse each time they moved, until he finally had them living in places that were little more than shacks. More often than not, in fact, they were no more than paint-bare, abandoned places, roofs they could squat under without being spotted by a property owner who cared enough to run them off.

Near the end of their time together, the Caines lived in places that had no access to electricity or running water. Instead, they used water out of storage barrels that Luther filled at night from anywhere he could find a spigot. They used a wood burning stove for heating and cooking, and their toilets were thrown-together outhouses he set up in fields or backyards outside of where they lived. They got clothing and furniture from second-hand stores, Salvation Army outlets, charitable drop-offs, or local dumps, and they lived off public relief and handouts in combination with whatever income Luther brought home from whatever full– or part–time work he could find.

The kids received medical care only when they got so dangerously sick that they had to be taken to the emergency room of whatever county hospital the family lived closest to at the moment. They were never taken to a dentist. Because their home had no facilities for bathing or heating or cooling, there was a sick child in the household almost all the time. The kids endured most of the normal childhood illnesses without medical intervention of any kind, and, with so many of them living in a confined setting, illnesses and conditions of multiple kinds were passed around and jointly endured.

Candy took great pains to describe many of the health problems that beleaguered the kids, and, as she did, I could not help but cringe and squirm in my seat as distasteful facts were poured out in vivid detail. "It seemed," she said, "that one or the other of us was sick all the time. We had skin problems, various kinds of infections, and coughs and croups and crud of all kinds. We lived in such drafty old dumps that runny noses and respiratory problems, for example, bothered us continuously. Even to this day I can hardly stand to be cold, because of how miserable I felt back then."

One of the more disgusting problems she told me about were the skin conditions that often afflicted the kids, especially the older boys. At the time the kids referred to their ailments as *risins*, but I could tell from her description that she was talking about boils — the infections that spring up when, for example, hair follicles around pimples get infected with bacteria. Theirs were most likely caused by nothing more than a lack of routine personal hygiene, but they could also have been caused or made worse by, as I soon learned, their poor diet, run-down physical condition, friction between skin and dirty clothing, skin problems like acne or dermatitis, or related problems. All this was truly unpleasant to think about, but I envisioned it very well.

The boils that plagued the kids seldom went away of their own accord; instead, they got large and red and became increasingly painful and itchy, until they turned into large sores filled with white or yellow pus. "Sometimes they'd burst," she said, "and then they'd drain until they healed. Too often, though, they'd come back, near the same place or on some other part of the body. They were really miserable to live with."

The only way the kids knew to get rid of the pain was to pick and squeeze the sores. Squeezing and lancing them under the conditions they lived in, as would be imagined, only served to spread the infection that caused them, as did their routine failure to properly wash and clean infected areas of drained matter from the *doctor's* or patient's bodies.

The *doctor*, of course, was never a parent; the job was done by an older brother or sister, using an old needle that was simply wiped off with a rag before and after, commonly without paying enough attention to cleanliness or to where the procedure took place. The process had to have been disgusting for the older and younger kids alike, and it could not have been a pleasant sight. My skin crawled, just listening to Candy talk about it.

As nauseating as this particular problem was, some of the other medical problems the kids had to deal with were even worse. "Sties," said Candy, "were another ongoing headache for us. Sties and what we called *pinkeye* were continual problems. It was routine for us kids to wake up in the morning with our eyelids so crusted over with matter that we could hardly see. We'd rub and wash them out as best we could, using rags soaked in the same pan of water. It was standing practice for us to spend a good amount of time each morning pulling out lashes along with whatever else was encrusted on our eyes. I don't know what all of it was; all I recall it that it was miserable to deal with."

I turned a little bit green, just from imagining what this had to have been like.

Probably the most potentially dangerous condition the kids had to deal with were the various kinds of respiratory problems they suffered from on a regular basis, all of them most likely caused by living in old houses that were drafty and dirty and poorly heated and cooled. Candy said that problems of this kind were made even worse by Luther and Pirley, who were chain smokers. "As soon as one cigarette was nearly done," she said, "they would use it to light up another. When they were awake, they were smoking. Every item in our house was saturated by cigarette smoke — clothes, furniture, blankets, curtains, and anything else that could be named. Even when they had no money to buy food for us kids, cigarettes were always available.

"Because we were raised in constant exposure to second-hand cigarette smoke," she said, "it was only natural that most of my brothers and sisters picked up the habit as well. By the time they were barely into their teens, all four of the older ones had already become serious smokers. They got addicted to tobacco long before they were old enough to give that decision any conscious thought; it was just another of the many disgusting habits they had the misfortunate of inheriting from our parents. I never got started doing in, thank God, but I easily could have."

During months of cold and damp weather, the kids suffered from all kinds of congestions and coughs, conditions that turned dangerous on more than one occasion. It was typical for bad colds, bronchitis, croup, and the flu to be passed around from child to child, and serious problems were routinely left untreated, leaving the kids to suffer miserably and needlessly.

One of the children, Terry, died of a chest ailment that was afterwards assessed as a case of the flu that had turned into pneumonia. It happened when he was just around eight months old. Luther and Pirley took him to an emergency room, but only after they had waited too long for his health to be restored. It was a pointless death, one that should never have happened.

Insect and vermin infestations were a persistent problem for them — roaches and rats and mice and various other kinds of bugs were common in the run-down old houses they grew up in. "Our home conditions caused us a lot of needless agony," she said, "especially when the weather was hot. Two kinds of bug infestations that made our lives miserable were head lice and scabies, mainly because we didn't find out what was wrong until we were told about it at school. Having problems like that was embarrassing for all of us, but it was especially mortifying to us girls."

Lice are nothing more than small insects that live *on* the skin, while scabies are mites that dig *under* the skin. "I'm convinced that we had them both," she said, "because we were miserable in both ways. They fed at night off blood in our skin, which is mainly when they do their digging. They'd pop up in surprising places — between our fingers, in our armpits, around our waists, or around the crotch. We were told that they weren't a serious problem, but the itching they caused really made us miserable."

Through reading I did after our discussion, I learned that this particular bug is spread by physical contact, mostly during daily activities such as sharing clothing or bedding down beside an infected person, which was standard practice for the Caine kids. The old blankets they had no choice but to sleep on were rarely cleaned. Worse still, mites and other pests can even be spread from dogs to humans, and the kids often went to sleep lying next to one or more dirty old stray dogs they had befriended and taken in as pets. When they were growing up, they regularly slept together on and under the same blankets and wore the same underwear for indefinite periods of time. The *beds* they slept in were not comprised of a box springs and mattress; they were nothing more than pallets spread out on the floor each night.

Head lice were a recurring problem for the kids, one that was always mortifying because it was another condition that usually wasn't detected by their parents (who rarely ever bothered to check them) but by their teachers. They show up most often, Candy explained, when personal hygiene is too poor to prevent them. They're nothing more than little yellow-gray bugs that live on the scalp or on the back of the neck or above the ears, but they can be a real headache to deal with. Their eggs, or nits, as they're called, attach themselves to hair shafts and follicles, and they, too, are easily spread by close contact, especially between school kids. Both the lice and the nits cause itching, and the itching leads to scratching that, in turn, leads to even more skin irritation. Once a head lice infestation pops up at a school, it can be a real pain to get rid of.

"I know all this now," she said, "but I sure didn't know it at the time. Our classmates and teachers alike considered us a plague on wheels, knowing that we brought problems like this kind to school again and again. We weren't the only ones, of course; but we were always thought of as being the most likely culprits."

"On repeated occasions," she continued, "one teacher or another would call one of us aside to ask why we didn't bathe more often and to suggest that we really ought to pay more attention to personal hygiene. Students had complained about us, teachers would explain as they handed over notes to take home to our parents."

Knowing how brutal kids can be to one another, I kicked myself for having forced Candy to open up what had amounted to be a Pandora's box of dismal memories. With every word Candy said, it became clearer why she had wanted to forget about those days altogether.

STAYING AHEAD OF LOCAL AUTHORITIES

CONDITIONS NEVER BECOME BETTER for members of the Caine family; instead, they got worse, especially for the kids. The combination of their parents' habit of repeatedly pulling up stakes and moving from place to place, their chaotic home conditions and poor nutrition, and the lack of the most fundamental level of normal guidance and nurturing all combined to have predictably negative effects on all of them. Their home situation had grown so obviously out of control that outsiders could not fail to notice. Their teachers, for example, were among the first to ring an alarm.

Having kids in school had always been something of a double-edged sword for Luther and Pirley, since it got them in hot water on more than one occasion. It was much easier to send the kids to school than to put up with them at home, but, whenever they did, attention was drawn to problems they really didn't want anyone else to know about. It was at school that their poor condition and ill treatment was most readily noticed, and it was noticed by people who took these conditions seriously and were ready and willing to raise a fuss about it. Whenever this happened, the Caines would find themselves in a whole bunch of trouble.

The Caines weren't concerned about whether or not their kids got a good education, but they were damned concerned about staying out of trouble with various kinds of childcare professionals — teachers, school administrators, truant officers, public health officials, welfare agencies, and local law enforcement authorities. They were forced to play the game, since there was no practical way of hiding the fact that they had a whole pack of kids. Besides, there was one feature of public schooling that the Caines as well their children greatly appreciated: the free lunch program that was available for eligible children. For all of them, the program was a God-send; the kids because they would have gone hungry most of the time without it, and the parents because it kept them from being accused of not feeding their children. As long as the kids were covered by this program, the kids had a minimum of one square meal per day. Wherever they lived, therefore, Luther and Pirley registered the kids for school and made them attend whenever they thought of it.

Despite their best efforts to avoid it, the Caines had been turned in repeatedly for various kinds of problems that stemmed from their obvious neglect of their children. Anyone who saw the condition of the kids could have turned in their parents, but more often than not it was done by one teacher or another.

"Why, then," I asked Candy, amazed that this problem had been allowed to go on for so long and in so many different locations, "hadn't their neglect of you kids ever gotten them into truly serious trouble?"

"It should have," Candy replied, "but it never did."

"Why not?" I asked.

"Well, like I've already said," she replied, "any time the situation got too hot for them to handle at one location, they'd just pull up stakes and move someplace else, without leaving a forwarding address and before any official investigation and serious charges could be brought. Beyond warnings and bitching and moaning, none of the *professionals* who were supposed to watch out for us were ever able to do a thing to correct them, not until our household fell apart for good, later on down the line."

THE COLLAPSE OF THE HOUSE OF CAINE

AT THIS POINT IN the kids' lives, Luther moved his family from whatever town they had been living in out of the San Joaquin Valley in California to the small and then out–of–the–way town of Gila Bend, Arizona. The town, as far as I could determine, had had a population at the time of less than 2,000 and was the home of approximately five hundred families. As the crow flies, Gila Bend is located about seventy miles from the city of Phoenix, the seat of Maricopa County.

"Why there, of all places?" I asked Candy. Gila Bend seemed such an unusual place to go, in view of the situation they were in at the time.

"My father," Candy replied, "moved us there, if I remember correctly, because he found a job at a service station garage on the highway that went past the town. When he was willing to work, according to my older brothers, he was a decent self-trained mechanic. On the other hand, though, he may have taken us there for no more reason other than that at some point in his travels he had spotted the old place we eventually squatted in without having to pay rent or because he thought the town would be a good place to hide out. There's no way to know today, any more than there was back then. We never had any choice but to do what he said; it didn't matter one iota to him whether we liked it or not."

She went on to explain that the hovel they moved into was indeed nothing more than an abandoned, dilapidated, weathered and unpainted old wood frame house out in the desert between Gila Bend and Phoenix, a *home* that her father, just as Candy speculated, had most likely spotted as he drove past it at some point during his past wandering. "He probably didn't have a clue how he was going to earn a living for us after we got settled," she said. "He was most likely much more concerned about keeping a low profile than anything else." Candy went on to say that her family was still living in this particular squatter home when their all too predictable household disintegration finally occurred.

Their new *residence* was nothing more than an abandoned house, but Luther and Pirley were pleased to have it, mostly because it was out of the way, free, and it got them out of the elements and away from the prying eyes of the law.

What worked out very well at their new location was that Luther was able to rig up illegal access to water and electricity. The house sat on an active farm that was tended by Mexican laborers, even though it was owned by an old couple who lived in town. The farm was irrigated using a series of electrically operated water pumps. Working at night, he tapped a wire for electricity and dug in a pipe to get running water out to the old place, then carefully buried both lines under sand and grass and weeds.

As a sink for cooking and washing, they used large pans of

water that were filled at the tap. Household heat came from a wood stove he bought at a second-hand store. For a toilet, he did what people have done since the beginning of time; he dug a pit behind the house, then built a simple outhouse over it.

After taking these simple steps, Luther and Pirley were home free and back in business again — at least until such time as they were noticed and kicked off the place by whoever owned it. They were, as mentioned earlier, nothing but squatters, but they figured the old house would do for the time being. It would do, so Luther reasoned, until he could get a good job and they could move to a better place somewhere in town.

They established a mailing address by flagging down the rural mail carrier and filling out a card. After that, Pirley registered the kids at the closest school, claiming that their paperwork would arrive *later.* The kids got to school each day by catching a bus that stopped at the entrance to the dirt road that led from the highway to the old house, which couldn't be seen well from the road.

What is so amazing is that they were able to get away with the whole caper, going about their business as if they had every right to be where they were. Maybe they seemed so pitiable to the absentee owner that, even if he had noticed them, he just didn't mind that they were there, since there was nothing of any real value at the old place that could be damaged. Or, maybe the owner just couldn't bring himself to put such an obviously impoverished and ragged family out on the street.

In any event, just as soon as the dust settled, the Caines resumed their former pattern of behavior, as if nothing had ever happened. Before long, Luther started disappearing all over again, always justifying his absences to Pirley by claiming that he was going out in search of work. Sometimes he was gone for days and weeks at a time, as had been the case in the past.

He did, in fact, find work on occasion, usually casual labor positions that put a little money in his hands from time to time. When he did well, he would buy bags of staples for the family and cigarettes and six-packs of beer for himself and Pirley and head home for a warm family greeting. Pirley and the kids were so hungry and needy that they were always glad to see him, regardless of how he had treated them in the past.

When he had the energy as well as a little money in his pockets, Luther would spend his evenings at the nearest beer joint, where he'd drink and smoke and gamble and otherwise carry on with anyone who happened to be there at the moment. Pirley would join him whenever they weren't arguing or otherwise on the outs, leaving the older kids in charge of the younger ones. Life, in short, went on for them just as it had in the past, as if their routine had never been interrupted.

The final collapse of the Caine household occurred when Luther's bitterness, discontent, and misdirected self-hatred continued to grow unabated, until he sunk into a state of dejectedness so mystifying that no one could get along with him under any set of circumstances. He evolved into a hopeless alcoholic, to the extent of regularly coming home besotted enough to strike or beat up his wife or kids at the slightest provocation. Alcoholism destroyed any self-control he had left, until he got to be just as much of a danger to himself as he was to everyone else.

The member or members of his family who happened to get slapped around depended solely upon who came in range of him when he was angry and drunk, and he was angry and drunk most of the time.

The kids' long-standing practice of running out of the house and into the fields to get away from him when he was in a rage continued, just as before. When he finally went to sleep or passed out for the evening, they'd quietly come back home, just as they had in the past. By this time, though, Luther's mental acuity had declined to the extent that, when he woke up, he barely remembered or cared what had happened the previous day.

The kids were still being left to fend for themselves while he or he and Pirley were out drinking and partying, and older ones were still being left to write their own rules and discipline the younger ones as they saw fit. That, though, was where the similarity between the past and the present ended; their overall situation had become even worse than it used to be.

When their father started disappearing for longer and longer periods of time, Pirley became even more disconnected from reality than ever. As her condition continued to decline, she became of even less help in terms of caring for the kids or their household. This, of course, made getting by even tougher for the children, who were already in desperate straits. Even though bags of food and items of hand–me–down clothing once again started appearing out of nowhere, seldom was there enough to meet the family's growing needs.

It was never clear who turned the family in this last time around, but, one day in April of 1962, two caseworkers from the Maricopa County Department of Social Services arrived at the family's doorstep to present their legal authorization to investigate the conditions that existed within the household.

Once again, no more than a brief on-site examination was required for the investigators to reach an immediate conclusion, which was that something had to be done for the kids, just as quickly as possible. There would be no running away from the problem this time, either, because Luther wasn't on hand to haul all of them away.

It would have been obvious to the CPS investigators that they had before them a beaten down wife and mother with a house full of ragged and hungry kids to feed, kids who were being inexcusably neglected as well as physically abused. There was no food in the home, there wasn't a dime on hand to buy any, and the kids were openly begging their mother to make them something to eat. For as long as they could recall, the kids said, they had been going to bed hungry.

The fact that the children were dressed in rags and clearly malnourished was evidence aplenty of extreme child neglect. There was little to no food to be found in the house — which, investigators soon discovered, the family had no permission to occupy in the first place. Not much detective work was required to substantiate various other findings, since the children, when they were pressed, admitted it was true they had, for example, been routinely rummaging through trash bins behind the lunchroom of their school and at grocery stores and restaurants in search of edible items and that they had been stealing food out of local stores.

Whether or not any of the kids suffered from outright malnutrition or rickets was never officially determined, but they exhibited some of the classic symptoms of those dreadful conditions, including weakness and tenderness of the joints, shakiness, scrawniness, and extended stomachs, and, when they were lifted, they were as light as feathers. There are records to show that, after the kids were removed from the household and fed decent food for a while, many of these deficiencies quickly disappeared.

Candy said that while she and her siblings were growing up, they rarely had milk to drink, and that no attention had ever been paid to the overall quality of their diet. Worrying about dietary balance, she said, wasn't a matter anyone in their household ever thought about; their focus had always been about whether they would have anything to eat at all.

The investigators would have noted that living conditions within the home were clearly deplorable, but they would have had no immediate way of knowing that it was no better or worse than any of the other places the kids had lived in in the past. The place was infested with vermin such as cockroaches and mice, and the floors were littered with dirty clothes, trash, and dog feces. The blankets and night clothes in use were stained by spills and spoils of various kinds, including urine left behind by younger children, who had severe rashes due to wearing soiled or poorly washed cloth diapers. The kids were an absolute mess; they were dirty, their hair was matted, and their clothing was ragged and filthy.

In addition to child neglect, the investigators would also have seen clear-cut evidence that outright physical abuse had been taking place as well. First, several of the older kids were bruised, marked by whippings their father had administered using a doubled belt or a switch. Secondly, they would have learned from the younger kids that their mother had just stood by when the older kids were being whipped. Finally, they would have noticed that Pirley, too, showed clear evidence of having been battered and beaten, and that she was openly afraid of what her husband would do if he found out that she had been talking to them.

Investigators had no choice but to take full control of their situation. Pirley was told — and, as appalled and scared as she was, she had blankly agreed — that the kids would be picked up the following morning, which was the earliest time by which clearances could be obtained and arrangements could be made to transport them into town in a county vehicle and placed in some form of suitable housing. Having arrived at an understanding with Pirley, the investigators departed for the purpose of preparing their statement and making all the physical and legal arrangements that were required for removing and placing the children elsewhere.

At that point, the officers and CPS workers left Pirley to prepare for what was to take place the next day and to deliver the bad news to Luther, if and when he happened to show up. Luther didn't learn about what happened until he got home much later that night, staggering in drunk as usual. He was greeted with the bad news by his distraught wife and a few of their older children.

Luther saw right away that he and Pirley were about to be accused of crimes that they themselves considered abhorrent, but that he also felt absolutely innocent of having committed — child neglect as well as outright child abuse. As unbelievable as it may sound, they thought they were being unfairly persecuted, simply because they were too poor to take better care of their children.

Even as they railed to one another against the injustices of society, they knew they were singing to the choir in terms of defending themselves; they knew that nothing they might said would resonate with the CPS workers who were going to come back that morning to shut down their household, take away their kids, and press charges against both of them.

THE ULTIMATE BETRAYAL

AUTHORITIES EXPECTED LUTHER AND Pirley to be present to face the music the following morning when they showed up to do what had to be done. Instead, Luther panicked after the two of them talked their situation over late in the night. Because he was unwilling to contend with the potential consequences of charges as serious as they were certain to be accused of, he headed out the front door just as soon as Pirley nodded off to sleep. He simply walked down the dirt road that led from their place out to the main highway, then thumbed a ride from the first driver who was willing to pick him up, leaving Pirley to hold the bag alone.

Luther had been in jail until only recently, and he was tired of it. He couldn't bear the thought of being hauled back in again, this time for offenses of a kind that might lead to an even longer sentence. What was different about this departure was not just that he had once again left Pirley and the kids behind, but that he left with no intention of ever coming back. Enough, he had decided, was enough.

Pirley, as would be expected, was beside herself when she woke up in the morning to discover that Luther had skipped out, leaving her to face the music by herself. Fearing that she might be held solely responsible for the condition of their household, their situation suddenly became way too hot for her to handle, in the same way that it had for Luther. She was at her wit's end already, but at this point she totally panicked, having reached the end of her own personal tether.

For Pirley, abandonment by Luther became the straw that broke the camel's back. The facts of her situation were obvious enough for anyone to grasp: Her husband had left her alone again, this time, she felt certain, with no intention of ever coming back; she had no money and no prospects of getting any; and her kids had, in fact, been going to bed hungry for a long time. These indisputable facts were more than enough to cause her to collapse under the strain.

When the older kids woke up the next morning, they found their mother lying in bed, writhing around and moaning rather than sleeping. She was semi-conscious, but they couldn't wake her up, no matter how they tried. Then, when one of them noticed a half empty bottle of rat poison on the windowsill aside her bed, it didn't take much imagination to figure out what she had done.

One of the older boys, Freddy, immediately ran out of the house and sprinted about two miles down the main highway to find a rural neighbor who would call an ambulance. Candy recalled that Freddy had to ask the neighbor to explain how to get to where they were living, since he was unable to give directions to their home. He didn't even know the name of the owner of the abandoned place his own family was living in as squatters.

The neighbor, who didn't want to have anything more than he absolutely had to with the affairs of a family as wild and as ragged as he knew the Caines to be, didn't offer to help Freddy in any other way, not even to drive the breathless and panicked boy back home after an ambulance was called. He simply closed the door and walked back inside, leaving the boy to run two more miles back up the road to where his mother, for all he knew, lay dying.

Eventually, an ambulance showed up to transport Pirley to the emergency room at the hospital, where her stomach was pumped and other kinds of treatment were provided. They had been called just in the nick of time to save her from an agonizing death.

It had been a dangerously close call, but Pirley did, in fact, survive to worry another day. Even after recovering from her poisoning, she remained in a desperate state of mind. No matter what her attendants said or did, she wouldn't stop wailing about how she wanted to die. Overcome by mental anguish and delusional nightmares, she raved and carried on inconsolably. Continual sedation was required to keep her quiet and manageable.

It was obvious to the medical staff that Pirley was suffering from severe mental exhaustion, and that there was no way that she could be safely released at that time. They knew that for the foreseeable future she would be incapable of taking care of herself, much less having anything to do with caring for her unusually large brood of highly needy children. So, after she improved physically, she was transferred to a mental care facility for emotional recovery under ongoing observation and continual long-term care.

As it turned out, Pirley needn't have gotten as upset as she did; in the end, the only charges that were filed against her and Luther had to do with child neglect rather than outright child abuse. Luther and Pirley might have lost their kids, but they most likely wouldn't have been brought up on any charges for which criminal penalties applied. What would be the point, local authorities probably would have concluded, when the main perpetrator was nowhere to be found and his wife was so helpless and struggling that pressing serious charges would have been utterly useless?

From the beginning of their operation, the major concern of the local powers had been on getting the kids out of their failed household and out from under the thumbs of their irresponsible parents, and they now had all the legal authority necessary to do just that.

The most positive consequence of Luther's unforgivably irresponsible abscondment was that it confirmed to CPS workers that what they were about to do was right and proper. In their view, only a totally unfit husband and father would have taken flight in the midst of the mess his family was in, leaving a bedraggled wife and a whole household fully of equally bedraggled kids, right in the big middle of a dire emergency.

Luther's hasty departure was helpful in the sense that it made the agency's terribly difficult job just a little bit easier than it would have been otherwise. From that point forward, the kids became wards of the Maricopa County Department of Social Services and the state of Arizona, in accordance with the court order that had been obtained to provide the necessary legal authority to remove them from their home and place them in a safer environment.

It was at this point that Candy floored me yet again, when she emphasized yet again two more unexpected revelations, the first of which was that her parents really never believed themselves to be guilty of any of the many accusations that had been leveled against them, and the second was that she and her siblings had initially agreed with them. Luther and Pirley had convinced themselves that their family was being unfairly persecuted, and their kids had picked up that lead.

My thought was that the kids would have been delighted to be taken out of their miserable circumstances, but that doesn't even come close to describing the way they initially reacted. Instead, Candy said, "We all wailed and screamed and carried on as if we were being carried off to be tortured."

Situations of the kind Candy and her siblings had to go through, I quickly realized, were way beyond my range of experience. Through reading I've done since Candy told me how her family was broken up and the kids became wards of the state, I've learned how naive I was about what actually takes place during situations like these. Uninformed, detached observers do not understand even the most basic facts about what can happen when these procedures are conducted, and, clearly, I was one of them.

Children living in squalid and neglectful circumstances, for example, often aren't the least bit appreciative when outsiders show up to *protect* them, and they don't always react the way we think they ought to. Even though they have been living in a highly dysfunctional home, they don't automatically welcome being pulled out of familiar surroundings. Typically, they don't know much of anything beyond what they have personally experienced, thus they often cling in great desperation to the very parents who have neglected and abused them, screaming and begging to be left alone. No matter how badly they need relief, it is not uncommon for kids to want to stay in familiar circumstances and to bitterly resent the interference of any outside *saviors*.

The dynamics that may come into play when a household is shut down by outsiders can be difficult to anticipate, which means that the whole process can be difficult and highly troubling for everyone involved — even for the experienced child welfare professionals who are in charge. A kid taken out of an abusive environment sometimes behaves like a dog that has been beaten and kept half-starved by a master who condescends to stroke him once in a while. Because it knows nothing else, it remains more responsive to its abuser than to anyone who tries to give it a helping hand. Any change in its way of life may be viewed as a dangerous threat, and they can be ferocious against anyone who dares to offend their master.

This was just what happened, Candy said, when the Caine household was shut down.

"Miserable," Candy cried. "That's the only suitable adjective to use to describe what happened the day our family home was dissolved. It was a miserable experience for each of us, and it had to have been equally miserable for the professionals who carried it out. There's no way it could have anything other than a heart-rending ordeal for them, just like it was for us."

AFTER THE DUST SETTLED

HER MOTHER, CANDY SAID, had followed Luther's example and simply taken off to go her own way after she recovered enough to be discharged from the mental hospital. She never tried to get back with any of her kids, thus she never functioned as the *mother* of her children ever again.

Candy learned later through the few members of her birth family with whom she did have occasional contact that she didn't divorce Luther until years after their family disintegrated. Candy had no way of knowing if any her siblings had reestablished contact with their parents, since she seldom heard from any of them, with only one exception. She heard years later that her mother had remarried, but that her second husband died at a relatively young age. After that, she heard nothing more about either one of her birth parents, until she received word of her father's death years later.

Even though Luther abandoned his family, Candy learned in later years that he had shown up on occasion at the homes of a few relatives. He would appear for a while when and where he wanted, usually to ask for a handout and always while he was either drinking or drunk. He'd leave just as unexpectedly, often never to be heard from again. The family members he'd linked up with, she said, had considered it just as well.

Where Luther went and what he did with himself in the years following the dissolution of his family is uncertain, but what happened at the end of his life is well known by the few members of his extended family as well as by Candy and her adoptive parents, the Wilsons. Those who made up this small group knew exactly how he ended up, because the last time they saw him was at his hastily arranged funeral on October 21, 1970, in Visalia, California. They found out about his death only because authorities used scraps of information found in his wallet to notify a few of them, and they, in turn, had notified others, including the Wilsons. The Wilsons left it up to Candy to decide whether or not she wanted to attend, and she decided that she did.

From those who were present for the service, it was learned that over the years, Luther's alcoholism had worsened to the point that his brain and internal organs were damaged beyond repair. He reached what can only be described as a *lose–all–control–and–fall–down–dead–drunk–and–forget–about–everything level of alcoholism.* His death occurred in the company of a motley, forlorn group of other drunks, down and out men just like him who lived in a derelict communal flophouse in the San Joaquin Valley town of Ivanhoe, when, during a final drunken stupor, he choked to death on his own vomit. After one of his counterparts called the cops, they all took off, leaving him dead where he lay.

"Can a grown man really check out that way?" I asked when Candy told me this. "Can they really choke to death like that?"

"Yes," she calmly replied, "they can and they do, and that's what happened to my birth father. You wanted to know all about him, so now you do. Are you pleased," she said, "to know what you have learned?"

Noting that I was too bowled over to respond, she simply went on to describe what else had happened at the funeral as I continued to listen, now, though, with my mouth and eyes much more widely open. What she said was so appalling that I didn't know what to say.

Not a single friend and just a few dutiful members of his family were present for Luther Caine's service. Not a single person from Pirley's side of the family was on hand. Only one of his twelve children was there, but she really wasn't there to mourn his passing. At age twenty-one, Candy, accompanied by her adoptive parents, was his only child in attendance. Those who were present had had little to no contact with the deceased over the years, much less a meaningful relationship. Those who viewed him in his casket were truly taken aback by his appearance, after noting that he looked more like a worn-out man in his late sixties than the forty-seven-year-old man he actually was.

The funeral took place less than three months after Candy and I were married, and she and the Wilsons had attended without mentioning it to me. It was just one more of the many facts they never wanted me to learn about her birth family. They had always taken great pains to make sure nothing about her birth parents would ever be discussed with anyone, not just me. All three of them had wanted the same thing, which was to make a total break with the past, thinking that that would be best for her. Only then, the three of them believed, would she be able to keep her past out of mind.

Candy said she didn't cry on the day of her father's service, since she had cried so much in her younger years that she didn't want to waste any more emotional energy on him. In fact, she said, bitterness toward him had been her only reason for attending the funeral; she wanted to be there, she said, with tears in her eyes, to make certain it was really him.

"It's just not possible," she said to me, "to forget all the misery he put me and my mother and brothers and sisters through, back when all of us were still together." She had never forgotten the hunger, sickness, isolation, humiliation and brutality they had endured at his hands.

Candy may not have cried at her father's funeral, but many a tear flowed down her cheeks when she told me about his pitiful passing. Hearing her describe her father's death and funeral was so upsetting that I lost my composure as well. So, once again, there we sat, crying together on our own living room sofa.

As it became increasingly clear to me how much pain I was putting her through, I finally came to my senses. My incessant probing wasn't going to help her; it was only going to make her more miserable, which was the last thing she needed at the time. I had gone where I had no right to go, and now she was more upset and disoriented than ever. This, it was plain to see, had been the high price of my own prideful intrusiveness.

How, I wondered in amazement, *could someone who had been as caring and sensitive and kind as she had been over the years have gone through such a life-altering experience and still remained whole?* Learning that my beautiful wife had lived such a nightmarish childhood was shocking in and of itself; realizing that she had managed to keep it a secret for as long as we had been married was even more astounding.

Even though she noted how stunning her revelations had been for me, she went on with them anyway. She stayed at it until all her cards, so to speak, had been placed on the table, and she had nothing left to say. Having acquiesced to my demand to leave no part of her childhood story untold, she wanted to get it all out there, once and for all.

Lord, I remember thinking to myself as she told me her story; *how could she have withstood that much misery without being irretrievably scarred?*

Then, like a bolt out of the blue, a whole new explanation of the demons she had been struggling against for as long as we had been together suddenly popped into mind, even though I ought to have thought of it much sooner, since it had been apparent for quite some time. Candy *hadn't* been able to keep her balance after the ordeal of her childhood years, I finally realized; she had been traumatized by it. At this point, even a dolt like me could see that she had been struggling to do exactly that for as long as we'd been married, and this, I finally realized, had been a major cause if not *the* major cause of her misery over the years.

It became clear for the first time why she had behaved throughout our married life as if she were two different people, one happy and ebullient and the other morose and depressed.

"What on earth became of each of you after your family was broken up?" I asked.

Incredibly, when I thought I had heard worst of what had happened during her childhood and that the siblings' situation couldn't possibly have gone any further downhill from there, it turned out, according to Candy, that that's exactly what had taken place. Unbelievably, conditions for too many of the kids became even more traumatic *after* they were taken out of their home by Child Protection Services and made wards of the state.

17

THE DIASPORA OF THE CAINES

THE COMBINATION OF THEIR father's abandonment of his family and their mother's attempted suicide was a life-changing calamity for Candy and her siblings as well as a major problem for the case workers of the Maricopa County Department of Social Services who handled their situation. As I listened to my dear wife's explanation of how her family's dissolution was handled, it was easy to imagine the thoughts that would have echoed through the CPS workers' minds on that dismal day back in 1962, when the Caine household was legally dismantled.

What in holy hell, the case workers had to have been thinking, just as I did while Candy was retelling the story, *are we going to do about one distraught and suicidal mother and eleven young people all still living out of the same destitute and totally broken home, most of them kids, but ranging in age from three to twenty-one, for whom past parental care has been nearly non-existent and for whom there are absolutely no material resources to be brought to bear or no extended family members on hand to pitch in and help out?*

With their alcoholic father nowhere to be found and their suicidal mother confined to a mental hospital, the kids' predicament was grim indeed. Even if Luther or Pirley or both of them had been on hand, the agency would never have returned the kids to a parent or set of parents so obviously unfit for the task of caregiving.

Several aspects of the Caine family's situation would have stood out as the agents prepared to deal with the dissolution. It would have become obvious right away, for example, that the kids were notably deficient in terms of such fundamental social skills as civility of language, reasonably courteous behavior, and conducting themselves in an orderly manner, and that these problems would make them exceedingly difficult to place.

What would have stood out as being even more unusual to the agents was the Caines' older kids — aged twenty-one, nineteen, and seventeen — were still living under their parents' dysfunctional roof when they really didn't have to. *Why on earth*, they surely would have wondered, *were the older kids still there, if their parents had been neglectful and abusive for as long as they had lived at home?*

It wouldn't have taken much investigation to learn that the older kids hung around home only because they had begun to use the family's fairly roomy old house as a free crash pad, a place they could sleep at night whenever there were pauses in their directionless revelries. Because they were backwards, unacculturated, and aimless young people, they had no solid ideas about what they wanted to do with themselves. For years, their lives had consisted of nothing more than bouncing from one occasional job to another, drinking, partying, carousing, and having good old times whenever and wherever they could, often getting into all kinds of trouble in the process. They'd never done anything that was truly constructive; instead, they had lived their lives by mimicking the feckless behavior of their own aimless parents.

Having a free place to sleep was best for them, they had always figured, until they could get something better going, which, unfortunately for them, as far as case workers could determine, hadn't ever happened and didn't appear likely to happen any time soon.

The number of children involved in the Caine family dissolution and the fact that no parent or relatives were on hand to help meant that there was little hope of keeping any of the kids together. It would have been apparent to the workers that as soon as their immediate needs were met, they would have to be split up and sent to separate locations. Short- and long-term arrangements would have to be made for every child that needed them — foster homes, adoptions, places in group homes or orphanages, or whatever.

THE CASE WORKERS MOVED forward by first arranging temporary care for each child — short-term foster care homes for the younger ones and temporary housing at the local juvenile hall for those who were older. After that, they began searching for more permanent living arrangements — temporary or permanent placements with any family members able and willing to help, longer-termed foster homes, orphanages, or, especially for some of the younger ones, adoptive parents.

Using the legal and administrative capabilities at their disposal, the agency was able to locate and establish contact with a number of relatives on the Caine and Hicks sides of Candy's family. Some of the family members who might have been persuaded to take in a child lived in the Phoenix area, but others lived far from there, in some cases even in other states.

As it turned out, though, most of their relatives refused to become embroiled in any of Luther or Pirley's problems, even after hearing about the plight of the kids. In their view, the kids' parents would come back sooner or later, and that, they believed, would be when their troubles would begin.

So, I thought as Candy told me how her relatives had felt, *this was why some members of her extended family hadn't been more forthcoming and others wouldn't even talk with me when I contacted them during my research.* When the chips were down, they had turned their backs on members of their own family. This was bad enough, but Candy went on to explain that even those members of her extended family members who had been either persuaded or were shamed into taking in one of the kids had eventually made their situations even worse. Because she had been taken in by a relative herself, she understood this phenomenon very well.

During pauses in our conversation as I mulled over what had happened, I asked myself if it was really so surprising that family members reacted the way they did. First, they barely knew Luther or Pirley, and they didn't know a single thing about any of their children, so why would they have been eager to take one of them in? Luther and Pirley had spent little to no time with any of their relatives, and any time they had spent with them had culminated in nothing more than a batch of unpleasant memories. Secondly, many of the relatives who were located lived outside the state of Arizona, which meant that they felt totally remote from the problem. Third, some of them were too old or to infirm even to consider taking in a child. Fourth, others said they couldn't afford to take on any additional financial responsibility. Finally, some didn't hesitate to openly say to case workers, "It's their problem or yours, not ours, and we just don't want to get involved."

In all fairness, most of the reasons family members gave for not taking in one of the children were readily understandable. In the end, only a few relatives, all on the Hicks side of the family, were found who could be either persuaded or shamed into providing homes for any of the kids. At one time or another, the two youngest girls, Claudine and Candy, and Freddy, one of the boys, lived for a while in such a setting. The five youngest boys — Jerry, Tommy, Billy, Bobby, and Ronny — were sent to temporary foster homes, since it was thought that their chances of being formally adopted were reasonably good. (One boy, Terry, as mentioned earlier, died of pneumonia before the family was broken up.) For the sake of companionship and continuity, the agency had hoped to keep the boys together in pairs during their placements, but, when that approach turned out to be unworkable, they were separated and sent to different foster homes.

Out of what they surely would have seen as stark necessity, the three oldest kids — Johnny, Collette, and Arley — saw that they had no choice but to accept the disintegration of the family as the beginning of their independent lives. Their immediate problem, though, was that while they were old enough in terms of chronological age to get by as adults, they were emotionally and socially backwards, and they had next to nothing in terms of material resources. Their change of circumstances had come about so suddenly that they weren't prepared to deal with it, but they had to bite the bullet anyway.

Candy said that she had been too upset and disoriented even to ask where the three older kids intended to go, much less to ask where any of the younger kids would be sent. "Even if I had asked my three oldest siblings what they intended to do," she said, "they wouldn't have been able to tell me. How could they when they didn't know themselves?" All the older kids knew at that moment was that they had been slumming around for years anyway, doing whatever they wanted to do, whenever they wanted to do it, without any parental input or guidance.

What happened to the three older kids after they were forced out in the cold world was that they quickly discovered how license is not the same thing as preparedness. In effect, they didn't know what to do with themselves. As dysfunctional as their home had been, they had at least had a roof over their heads, a place to crash whenever they needed to, whereas, afterwards, they had no place to hang their hats at all. Getting by on their own proved to be a lot tougher than they expected.

The younger kids had a tough time too, in that they ended up being bounced from one temporary foster home to another for varying periods of time, until longer-termed arrangements of one kind or another could be found for each of them. As it turned out, though, some of these placements didn't last long or work out well from the outset. In some cases, the placements that were found weren't the least bit suitable; they were just the best that could be located under the circumstances. Time and resources were as limited back then as they are today.

Some of the boys were placed in homes that weren't even remotely sound, and that's describing their placements in the most benevolent of terms. Not until years after the fact was it discovered that some of these homes had turned out to be outright evil. Again, though, there was no way to know this at the time; CPS workers just did the best they could.

There's little doubt that the harried and much overburdened child protection service workers who were involved in handling the Caine family dissolution would have breathed a collective sigh of relief when all the children, in one way or another, were finally placed. Candy and I could readily imagine how they might have felt pleased with themselves before they moved on to the next in the never-ending series of family crises they had to deal with. *God bless them,* I thought, knowing that they regularly had to contend with situations that the faint of heart — people like me, for example — would never have been able to handle, not on an ongoing basis.

From this point forward, the welfare of all the kids but Johnny, Colette, and Arley, the three older kids who had voluntarily gone out on their own, depended on the charity of strangers and periodic follow-up visits made by the child welfare case workers who were assigned to monitor their status. Years passed before Candy learned much of anything about what became of her siblings. When bits and snatches of news did reach her while she was growing older, it was nearly always profoundly upsetting. Legally splitting up a family, even a clearly dysfunctional one, doesn't automatically bring about immediate relief for the children.

CANDY, MY OWN DEAR wife, God bless her precious soul, reminded me that she had fared much better than most of the kids, not initially but over the long haul. "My initial placement," she said, "was a holding cell at juvenile hall, simply because no appropriate foster home was open at the moment and no one on either side of my family was immediately available to take me in.

"Eventually," she continued, "one of my relatives had a change of heart, whereupon CPS immediately and unceremoniously shipped me out to stay with them. Of course, I didn't know one thing about the family. Then, finally, after being bounced around for a while longer, I ended up with my wonderful adoptive parents, the Wilsons."

"Wait just a minute," I said. "It seems to me that what happened to you couldn't have been as simple or as painless as you've made it sound. Matters clearly didn't go well after you were placed with a member of your birth family; if they had, CPS would have left you there. What I want to know is *why* that didn't happen. You said you'd stop holding back," I reminded her, "so tell me how and why you wound up being placed with the Wilsons."

So, with a sigh and after more incessant badgering that she didn't have enough strength to resist, she did just as I asked: She went on to explain in full the real story of how she wound up living with her adoptive parents, Ernest and Jewel Wilson. Her response, I regret to have to say, upset both of us so much by the time she completed it that I very much regretted having asked the question at all.

AS IT HAPPENED, THE uncle and aunt on her mother's side who took Candy in were strangers who had dishonorable motives. If they ever had any real feelings of love or concern for her, they never bothered to show it, even though they did willingly volunteer to take her in. The problem was that they had agreed to take on the role of caregiver only after it occurred to them that worthwhile benefits could be derived from allowing Candy to live with them, not to mention that they would receive a state stipend for doing so. Neither of these motives became apparent until after she lived with them for a while.

Once she was placed with the couple, it became evident right away that their intention was to capitalize on the Caine family's calamity by using Candy as a maid and household laborer, simply because they made no pretense of doing anything other than precisely that. After laying out a strict and elaborate set of behavioral expectations, her aunt outlined a long list of chores she wanted done on a daily basis. Candy, they had determined, was going to work for her keep, and that's all there was to it. She was put to work as soon as they had her behind closed doors.

From that point on, her aunt and uncle forcefully made their displeasure known if their home was not cleaned as expected, their own kids weren't properly attended to, dishes and clothes were not washed and put away, or other chores weren't completed as instructed. As long as Candy was in their household, they intended to do as little domestic duty as they could get by with.

Her aunt and uncle weren't overly concerned about whether or not Candy went to school each day, but there was always hell to pay if she didn't do the chores that were assigned to her in the way they expected them to be done. Their demands went far beyond any reasonable expectations that she ought to *pitch in to help,* Candy said, in the same way that the punishments they administered when she failed to do as she was told were far in excess of what was right or proper.

This went on for quite a while, until Candy finally worked up enough courage to complain about the way she was being used. Because her relatives believed that she ought to have been thankful without limits for having been willing to take her into their home, the little rapport they had left have went downhill rapidly from that point forward. Once Candy started to complain, the couple's first reaction was to begin to punish her all the more severely.

For a while, case workers didn't realize that anything improper was taking place within the household, since they took for granted that her new accommodations had to be a great improvement over the grubby conditions she had lived in in the past. Her social workers and hosts alike were surprised that she had rebelled against the way she was being treated.

Not long thereafter, the couple concluded that it was going to be too much of a hassle to turn Candy into a maid and servant who would work without complaint at their beck and call. Keeping her around, they decided, was going to be more trouble than it was worth. As quick as a wink after that, they told the agency that Candy would have to be placed with some other family member, one, they said, that would be willing to put with, as they put it, *her behavioral problems. Put her with anyone*, they essentially said, *other than us*.

What this meant for Candy was that she would be sent to live with yet another family totally new to her, and that she would have to start all over again. Despite this, she said, she wasn't sorry to leave the first household, because being there had emotionally worn her out.

Her next placement didn't work out well either, this time because an entirely new problem came to the fore — one that the social worker assigned to check on her from time to time could not ignore, not even for a little while. When Candy whispered during a follow-up visit that more and more with each day that passed the man of the house, who had apparently noticed that she was a beautiful little girl about to turn into an even more beautiful young woman, was becoming ever more insistent on giving her a hand getting dressed and ready for school in the morning and ready for bed at night. It was he, not his wife, who constantly tried to be affectionate toward her, who regularly tried to get physically closer in any way he could. "It doesn't seem right," she complained, "and I really hate it." When the social worker heard about all of that, another placement was arranged in a hurry.

Candy's next placement was with yet another set of relatives, cousins on her mother's side, this time a couple who didn't ask much of her but who didn't give much, either. Because they really weren't too well off themselves, it wasn't long before they began to think her upkeep was too much of a financial burden and more disruptive of their routine than they were willing to accept. Basically, they decided to get rid of her because they just didn't want to deal with any extra responsibility. Why they allowed her into their home in the first place was never clear. "It may have been," she conjectured, "because they thought the state stipend for keeping me would make more of a difference than it actually did; I really don't know." From what she told me, though, it sounded like her suspicion was right on the money.

"The woman of the household," she said, "was not as much

of a problem as her husband, who decided early on that he had been mistaken to go along with whole idea of taking me in. Before long, he decided that he just didn't want to put up with me any longer, but, rather than telling me so directly, he made his feelings known by treating me curtly and rudely, even though he should have behaved like a mature adult because I was still a child. He didn't, though; he criticized me freely and often, as if he blamed me personally for what had happened to my family.

"He hurt my feelings by belittling me," said Candy, "and he was so harsh about it that his words have rung in my ears ever since. Without justification, he accused me of being promiscuous among the boys of the neighborhood, boys I had to ride to school with on the bus and that I had to be around all the time. He did it right in front of them at our bus stop as well as within the neighborhood, embarrassing me so much I wanted to die.

"When I asked why he was doing it, we had an argument that ended with my calling him a liar and him whipping me. This may sound like a trifle now, but it wasn't at the time and it still isn't today; it was so humiliating that I've never be able to forget it. He was cruel to me when there was no reason for him to be, when I hadn't done a single thing to deserve it.

"Eventually," she continued, "they found a simple but immediately effective way of pushing me off on somebody else, an approach that was even more hurtful and callous than the way my other relatives had gotten rid of me; they dumped me — literally drove off and left me — at the home of an elderly widowed great aunt, a kind and well-meaning lady in her early eighties who was in ill health and living off social security in a retirement home.

"Claiming that they had to deal with an emergency out of town, they asked the older lady to watch me 'for a few days' while they were away. She generously agreed to do so, of course, but then the couple never came back, and after a while it became clear that they were never going to. Instead, they called the agency and complained that I had become too boy-crazy and troublesome for them to handle and that I had gone to stay with my great aunt for a while.

"The older lady was truly concerned about my welfare," Candy said, "but she wasn't able to take care of me. As much as she would have liked to, she just couldn't handle it, physically or financially. Even if she had been able to take me in, children weren't allowed to stay for any longer than a short visit in her tiny place for seniors. Being left with a child on her hands caused the elderly woman to become teary-eyed and upset, and this, in turn, caused me to become even more distressed than I already was.

"I felt like nobody wanted me," Candy said, with tears glistening in her eyes as she spoke, and it nearly broke my heart to hear her say it.

Her great aunt, who was upset and nearly at wit's end over having such a huge responsibility unexpectedly dropped in her lap, called the county welfare office to explain what had happened and ask for help. The only solution the agency could come up with, short of placing Candy in a group facility, was to launch a search for a new foster home, since no other relatives could be found who were willing to step in and help. As soon as a new foster home could be found, they promised, Candy would be provided yet another *fresh start.*

Candy said that when she heard what was in store for her, the news made her physically ill. That she would have to go live with yet another household of strangers was the last thing she was wanted to hear, since her nerves were already so frayed that she was having horrible dreams at night. She felt more secure and cared for in her elderly great aunt's home than at any place she'd ever been, but now she was going to lose that, too. By this point, she said, she had become nearly as distraught as her elderly great aunt, to the extent that both of them were beside themselves with worry. *God,* I thought as she continued to explain this episode, *is there no damned end to her miserable childhood story?*

18

THE KINDNESS OF STRANGERS

“THEN,” CANDY CONTINUED, “JUST when I was feeling so low that I wanted to take some of mom’s rat poison myself, something happened that changed my life forever. I guess you’d have to say that I found myself on the receiving end of an extraordinarily stroke of luck, a turn of events I surely didn’t expect. This was when I was taken in by Ernest and Jewel Wilson, which happened, it seemed to me, by sheer chance.”

“Wait a minute,” I said. “Nobody adopts a child ‘by *pure chance’*. When people do something like that, they do it only after long and careful personal consideration and an equally deliberative legal process. Something as big as an adoption isn’t spontaneous, like buying a new outfit or taking a weekend vacation. We’re talking about a lifetime commitment here, not an impulsive act. You can’t be serious about your adoption being *by chance*.”

“Well,” she said, “I can’t tell you exactly what went through their minds at the time, but the whole thing sure seemed spontaneous to me. I got a phone call from the Wilsons one day, and not too long after that I was living with them. They didn’t adopt me until later. Regardless of how it happened, ending up with them was the single best thing that had ~~ever~~ happened in my life.”

“I can see why you felt that way,” I said, “but there had to have been a lot more to it than that. Before I can get all this out of my head, I’ve got to hear their side of what happened. All three of you owe that to me,” I said, “after having kept this story from me for so long.”

“No,” she immediately objected, “I don’t want you to talk

with them at all about this. It would just get them more upset than they already are, knowing how much trouble I've been having lately. Dredging up the past the way you've made me do has only made it worse. I didn't want to talk about any of this, and I definitely don't want to go over all of it again with them. Wanting to know more about those miserable years is your hang-up, not theirs or mine."

"Yes," I insisted, "we most definitely *are* going to talk with them, and, what's more, we're going to do it *in person*. The three of you had no right to right to keep any of your background from me, and now that I've heard part of what happened, I refuse to be kept in the dark any longer. Once and for all, we're going to get the whole story out in the open, and we're going to do it face to face.

"Call them," I demanded. "Tell them we want to come for a weekend visit, just to get away for a while, but don't tell them what's up. Once we're there and sitting down together," I said, "I'll be the one to bring it up. Don't argue with me about it any longer," I yelled. "I've had enough of your secrecy and evasiveness. Just do it."

In all honesty, what I really wanted was to avoid giving Candy or the Wilsons an opportunity to come up with some new way of evading the issue.

So, she did what I demanded of her, but only because I left her no choice; she booked two round-trip tickets for a three-day weekend trip from Granbury, Texas, to Visalia, California, out of the Dallas–Fort Worth Airport. We flew into Bakersfield, where we rented a car and then drove north a few hours up the San Joaquin Valley to reach the Wilsons' home. Few words passed between us during the trip. I was upset with her, and she was angry with me. More accurately, I really ought to say that she seemed more spaced out than anything else, like she'd been stunned into silence, as if she could hardly believe what I had pushed her into doing.

THE WILSONS, OF COURSE, knew something important was afoot from the minute Candy called to set up our sudden visit. Like most loving parents, they had X-ray vision and extra-sensory perception when it came to picking up on their child's moods and emotions, and Candy's call had been no exception. Even before we arrived, they sensed that this would not be a typical visit, even though they really didn't know what to expect. I'm convinced, though, that they had a fairly good idea.

After exchanging greetings and hugging one another in the way we always did at the beginning of a visit, we all sat down at their kitchen table, just as I wanted us to. I didn't waste a minute before getting down to the matter to be discussed. Once we were face to face, I brought Ernest and Jewel up to date on what had transpired between Candy and me up to that point.

To their credit, they saw right away that the time had come to place all of their cards on the table, so they followed my lead and proceeded to do what they thought *we — but, really, only I* — wanted them to do. Because Candy looked away with an unhappy, spacey expression on her face, they realized that I already knew most of her story, and that from that day forward, there would be no further evasion. Paraphrasing the words of the principals themselves, they went on to explain how the three of them had come together.

DECENCY PERSONIFIED

ON SEVERAL OF THEIR stays in the San Joaquin Valley to do work in the fields, Luther and Pirley had lived in a tin cabin at Linnell Camp, a farm labor housing development located a few miles away from the nearby towns of Tulare and Visalia. They and any of the kids who didn't have to or want to go to school would leave from the camp in the morning to do farm labor jobs such as chopping or picking cotton, picking peaches, or packing fruit.

On occasion while they lived at the camp, Luther and Pirley would take his family with him to one of the few of his relatives they ever visited, a cousin who also used to make seasonal trips from Oklahoma to the Tulare area to work in the fields but had finally rented a home there. Whenever they got together, the cousin would invite a few of his neighbors to join them, and his neighbors, in turn, would bring along a few of their own personal friends along with them. Among those who turned up in this way were Ernest and Jewel Wilson, who had gotten to know one of Luther's cousin's neighbors when he visited their church in nearby Visalia, and a friendship had sprouted from that interaction.

It was during one of these visits that Ernest and Jewel first got acquainted with Candy and her next older sister, Claudine. Candy didn't learn until many years later that the Wilsons had been deeply touched by the ragged condition of all the Caine kids, but they were especially taken with the two stringy-haired young girls. Skinny and poorly dressed, the girls were starved for ordinary affection, even though they were so notably shy in the midst of what they clearly thought of as a group of affluent strangers that they hardly dared to make a peep. It was also obvious to the Wilsons that the kids and their mother alike were fearful of saying or doing anything that might upset the girls' father, who clearly was an obnoxious human being as well as a heavy drinker.

The Wilsons, a childless couple, went out of their way to befriend the two girls, mainly by speaking to them kindly and through offering them small gifts. In simple ways like these, they and the girls built up enough trust to form a relationship of sorts. Once their bond was established, it lasted from those days forward.

From then on, the Wilsons made it their business to wrangle an invitation to any future gatherings at which they expected the two girls to be present. Supposedly, they came to visit with their friends, but what they looked forward to most of all was seeing the two girls, Claudine and Candice.

Before long, the girls and the Wilsons began eagerly looking forward to any visits that could be arranged. Now that a firm friendship had taken hold, the Wilsons took advantage of any and every occasion they could think of — birthday parties, holidays, picnics, and so on — as reasons to invite the girls to visit them at their home in nearby Visalia. They'd pick them up at the camp, then take them back home afterwards. Luther and Pirley had no qualms or reservations about any of this; in fact, they didn't monitor what any of their kids were doing on a day–to–day basis. They were too focused on themselves to take that much notice.

Soon, a warm and rewarding relationship came into being between the girls and the Wilsons, and, before long, they became regular guests at the Wilsons' home, for short visits at first, and then for occasional overnight stays. Their fondness for one another grew in this way, but, at the time, none of them expected anything more to come of it than that.

Some months later, the girls' relationship with the Wilsons, just like every other good thing they had ever known in their lives, was torn away from them as well. It happened one day when Luther, for reasons known only to him, suddenly decided it was time to uproot his family once again, on this occasion for unspecified *better work at higher pay* out in Arizona. He took them away overnight, as was his practice, and without telling anyone where they were going and, of course, without leaving behind a forwarding address.

When the Wilsons learned after the fact that the Caines had moved away without saying a word about where they were going, they were deeply upset. Because they had grown to love the two little girls, they knew they'd miss them terribly. The Caines' overnight move was as much of a traumatic experience for them it was for the girls.

They had no way of knowing that the family's sudden departure was in no way extraordinary for Luther and Pirley — or, of course, for any of their kids. They'd have been even more upset if they had known that the family had skipped out because they were only a day or two ahead of being confronted by child welfare workers and a number of angry creditors.

As fate would have it, though, it was at their new location at Gila Bend, Arizona, where the Caine family fell apart for good.

The Wilsons heard about what happened a short while later, and only then by the sheerest of coincidences. The news got to them indirectly, through friends who had heard about it and, in turn, happened to mention it to the neighbors of Luther's cousin who had once lived in Tulare but who, by this time, had moved on himself.

As the Wilsons told me about all of this in their own words, I realized that the dissolution had been as troubling for them as it had been for Candy and her siblings. That the family had suddenly moved away truly upset them, but, when they heard why the move had taken place, they became even more troubled still. They were so worried, in fact, that they had trouble sleeping at night. They were concerned about all the kids, but they were especially troubled about the welfare of the two gangly and fragile young girls, Claudine and Candice. Beside themselves with worry, the Wilsons hardly knew which way to turn.

Eventually, though, through collecting bits and snatches of information during the days that followed, they were able to piece together a fairly accurate account of what was going on in the kids' lives. Their situation, the Wilsons discovered, had been as much of a nightmare as they feared it might have been. They learned, for example, that Candy had been bounced from one relative or foster home to another, and that she really hadn't been wanted anywhere she was placed. After that, they learned that she was temporarily living with her elderly great aunt, but that arrangements were being made to transfer her to yet another new foster home and that move was to take place as soon as a suitable placement could be found. Claudine, they were told, had already been placed in a new foster home and, as far as anyone could say at that moment, she was doing as well as could be expected.

The news was too much for the Wilsons to passively bear. Already emotionally strung out over hearing of the dislocation and misery the kids had been living through, they couldn't get *their* bright-eyed and ragged little girl out of their minds. They were so concerned that they felt compelled to make telephone inquiries to find out how Candy was holding up. It was through talking with the cousin who had made it clear that he really didn't want her living with his family any longer by unceremoniously dumping her at the home of a great aunt that they learned where she was at the time.

Because there was a listed telephone number for the older lady in the Phoenix telephone directory, the Wilsons were able to call Candy from their home in California, just to ask, as they put it at the time, "how things were goin'." Even though she was living in absolute dread of her pending placement in yet another foster home with absolute strangers as she sat beside her elderly relative and talked with Wilsons, she answered shakily but bravely, not wanting to worry them, by saying, "Just fine."

It hadn't been hard, though, for the Wilsons to, as they put it, "hear the tears between the lines. It was," they said, "all we could do to keep from crying as we talked with her, knowing that she was struggling to sound positive and strong so we wouldn't be troubled on her account."

Finally, they said, upon hearing Candy quietly sobbing over the phone, they could no longer conceal the fact that they were in tears as well, even though they knew that their crying would upset her all the more.

Ernest Wilson went on to describe how he had spontaneously asked, "Why don't you just come stay with us, gal? We've got plenty of room."

He then went on to describe how Candy had paused for a while and then quietly responded, "I'd really like to, if it would be okay."

Ernest's reply had been, "You bet it'll be okay; let's get you out here right now."

It touched me deeply to contemplate the relief my sweet wife must have felt when the Wilsons' loving invitation was extended to her during this spirit-crushing interlude in her young life. Their telephone call was totally unexpected, and I could well imagine how enormously uplifting it must have been. It felt that way to me, too, as we sat there in the Wilsons' pleasant home, seated at the same small kitchen table from which their heart-rending call had been made, the same table at which we had enjoyed many wonderful dinners together, back when Candy and I were courting as well as after we were married.

In only a moment, I was crying like a baby. Hearing what transpired between the three of them that day was more than I could handle without losing my composure.

Candy and the Wilsons didn't have to ask why I had become so emotional; they knew without even looking up. Before long, all four of us were crying together and holding hands across the table, reliving what had happened to their beautiful daughter, my sweet and loving wife, our Candy, back when she was an innocent and defenseless child. In front of all of them, I cried as freely and as openly as I ever had in my adult life. We all did; what happened had been so unbearably sweet but sad.

As we sat there together and quietly talked about her past, it was easy to appreciate how the Wilsons' modest home promised such comfort to Candy. At a time when she was so helpless and apprehensive that she was beside herself with worry, their call had been a Godsend, not just because they had promised her a place where she would have food and shelter but because she instinctively knew that she would be going into a home where she would be loved and valued as a precious human being. The three of them did not directly speak or allude to this during our exchange, but we all knew that love had sealed their agreement from that day forward, just as sure as there's a God in heaven.

I find it difficult to express how touched I was by their explanation of how she came to live in the Wilson home. It had taken place on the heels of an ordeal that would have been terribly difficult for any child to bear, much less for a troubled young girl to deal with alone. What happened to Candy had been a nightmare for all three of them.

Their story enraged me as well, so deeply that I nearly hit the ceiling when I thought about what her parents had allowed to happen. If Luther or Pirley had walked through the door as we were talking, they would have had a real problem with me. All I felt for her father at that moment, to be totally honest about it, was so damned much disgust over his failure to properly look after Candy and her hapless brothers and sisters I wished I could have bashed him over the head with a club, just to get his attention.

Even after their meeting of minds was reached over the telephone, Candy's torment still wasn't over. She and the Wilsons still had to convince her great aunt to allow her niece to go stay with people she didn't even know, which required a great leap of faith on her part. Unlike her birth parents, the elderly lady was actually conscientious with respect to her responsibility for doing right by Candy and therefore justifiably concerned about what might go wrong with such an arrangement.

After receiving assurances from the cousin who once lived in California as well as others who vouched for the Wilsons and upon talking with them at length by telephone, the kind and caring lady finally went with her instincts and bowed to what Candy begged and pleaded for her to do. In her heart, I thought, her great aunt must have somehow sensed that it was the right thing to do under the circumstances, even if it wasn't strictly legal. Earnest and Jewel Wilson were decency personified, and I think, somehow, the caring older woman sensed it.

At that point, all that stood in the way of culminating the arrangement was to find a way to get Candy from Phoenix, Arizona, to Visalia, California, where the Wilsons lived. Because they were unable to get time off work to go get Candy themselves, they sent enough money to her aunt to cover the cost of a one-way Greyhound bus ticket from Phoenix to Goshen, California, the bus station in the center of the San Joaquin Valley nearest to their home in nearby Visalia. After that, her aunt arranged for a neighbor to drive Candy to a Greyhound station in Phoenix for the journey from Arizona to California.

Candy said the trip was a nerve-wracking and exhausting experience for her, partially due to being emotionally wrung out before she ever got on the bus but also because she had never traveled anywhere by herself. The trip, she said, seemed to take forever, mainly because much of it took place at night and the bus stopped at so many small towns along the way. She said she wasn't used to being totally alone, much less on a huge bus on a long cross-country trip in the company of what seemed to be a whole load of rough-looking passengers, people who seemed to be staring at her every time she looked up.

She was afraid because she was a young girl traveling alone, and she was convinced that all the other passengers knew it. She was so fearful that she could hardly work up enough courage to go to the bathroom when the bus stopped, and she didn't until she was nearly desperate. She said she couldn't fall asleep, either, not until she became too exhausted to stave it off.

She was afraid the whole time she was in transit, to the extent that she hardly uttered a peep to anyone. "It was scary," she said, "partly, like I said, because I had never traveled by myself, partly because I had had no idea of much more than the direction we were going, and partly because of the way some people looked at me. A group of rowdy young guys in military uniforms made me especially nervous. I spent the whole trip cringing behind the bus driver, afraid even to get off at stops unless and until he got off as well. Until the trip was over, I followed the driver wherever he went, never letting him out of my sight unless I was forced to."

At the time of Candy's journey, the Greyhound station at Goshen was nothing more than a drab, run-down, quick in–and–out stopping point off Highway 99, the state highway that ran down the center of the San Joaquin Valley. It was a dismal looking little place just off the road, right out in the midst of the fields in which most of her fellow riders either had been or were going to be employed. Because the building was covered by a thick coating of dust blown in off the plowed fields that surrounded it, it normally wasn't patronized for anything other than utilitarian purposes; most of those who arrived at or departed from there did so only because they had to get from one place to another, just to make a living.

It was on a cold, dusty, windswept day of business as usual in the San Joaquin Valley that the bus pulled in at the Goshen Greyhound station on December 21 of 1963, but Candy said it was a day she would remember for the rest of her life, for there, standing where he knew the door would open when the vehicle pulled to a halt, was Ernest Wilson, with a huge smile beaming on his face. Jewel had stayed home to prepare for the arrival of the new member of their household.

Seeing Ernest's kind smile after being trapped for so long in what had seemed to be a never-ending series of strange and intimidating faces was such a relief that she immediately burst into tears. When she ran to throw her arms around his neck, her normally crusty savior immediately broke out in tears as well.

Jewel was waiting with open arms when Ernest and Candy pulled into the driveway of the Wilson home. Soon, the three of them were crying together, this time, though, thank God, not out of sadness or tragedy, but out of joy over being reunited. In their hearts, they said, they knew they were at the beginning of the way life was meant to be for them.

Ernest's words to me at this point were: "We felt so sorry for the poor little thing. She was really beaten down. All she had in the world was in a ragged little bag, and all she had in the bag was an extra thin cotton dress, a few underthings, and a comb. There wasn't no toothbrush or toiletries or no other personal stuff. Even put together, what she had wasn't worth no more than a few dollars, if that much."

Candy had just turned fourteen and I was in the middle of my senior year of high school when she spent her first night as a member of the Wilsons' household on Saturday, December 21, 1963, a day they celebrated from that point forward as their *anniversary*. She said she had felt a huge sense of relief combined with a strange sense of numbness as she was getting adjusted to living with them, largely because she was too wrung out and emotionally exhausted to think clearly about much of anything. She had no idea how their arrangement was going to work out from that point forward, but she somehow knew that it was going to be the first day of the rest of her life.

"WHY DIDN'T YOU TELL me about all of this before?" I asked, still astonished, even after they filled me in on what had happened. "Didn't you know I would find out about it sooner or later?"

"Well," Ernest and Jewel replied in the same voice, "we did it because it was what the three of us thought would be best. We thought that secrecy was what Candy needed. She needed to put her memories of the past behind, to try to forget the privations she had had to deal with, just so she could move on to something better. It seemed to us that what happened had been bad enough that never talking about it again would be our best option. That's what she said she wanted, and we most definitely agreed. That's why all three of us pledged never to say another word about it, nowhere, not at any time. We stuck by it too, until now, until you forced it back out into the open. We didn't withhold information just for the sake of keeping secrets from you or from anyone else; we did it for her sake. You weren't even on the scene, if you will recall, back when our decision was made. We agreed to do what we did because we thought it would be the best way to protect her."

Glancing at the three of them — Candy and Ernest and Jewel — sitting there at their kitchen table on the day we all talked about all of this, so obviously full of love for one another, it was easy to appreciate why Candy felt the way she did about her adoptive parents. Whether they knew it or not, I learned a great deal from the three of them that day: I learned, for example, that while tragedy can devastate people for a short while, those who truly love one another will find a way to build themselves back up for the longer haul. When their hearts are in the right place, people who have suffered together can build bonds that make them stronger than they've ever been before. I felt honored and proud, just to be there with those two good people. *God bless Ernest and Jewel Wilson*, I thought as we talked, *now and forever.* I loved them even before that point, but since then I have looked at them through new eyes altogether.

OUR WEEKEND WITH THE Wilsons was over in an instant, and soon it was time for us to load up our rental car and head to the airport so that I could get back to work on Monday morning. Still half dazed by what I'd learned, I ended up even more so after Ernest took me aside for a moment just before we said our goodbyes.

"I hope you realize what a can of worms you've reopened," he cautioned, with a worried look on his face. "Our main problem has always been that even though we were able to get the girl out her misery, we were never fully able to get all of the misery out of the girl. We did as much as we knew how to do, but we know we got only part of the way there. I'm sure you know what I mean, after having lived with her for so long. All I can say is that you ought to be extremely thoughtful about whatever you say and do from this point forward."

Jewel, too, tried to keep up a good front as we departed, but I could see that she was just as worried as Ernest. Candy, I couldn't help but notice, seemed as vacant and as distant as she had been throughout our trip, except while we were in the presence of the Wilsons. While we were with them, she had tried her best not to break down in front of them.

As we were on our way and after we got back home, I still couldn't muster enough good sense to leave the matter alone. What I'd been told was just too big, too momentous to let go of. I insisted that she pick up where the Wilsons left off. "How did it go," I wanted to know, "once you were living with them? I've always thought that all went well after your adoption, but did it? Did things really go well for you from that point on, and, if not, why not?"

I knew for a fact that her time with them had *not* always gone well, and I wanted her to tell me *why*. I felt compelled to *make her tell me why*, in fact. What I really wanted to know was *what in the hell bothered her all the time? Why was she always so damned troubled? Don't I,* I said to myself, *have every right to know? How can I be of help to her,* I wondered, *if I don't know what*

I'm dealing with?

AFTER HEAVING YET ANOTHER great sigh of resignation in reaction to my dogged persistence, Candy went on to say that the room the Wilsons had ready for her had seemed like the most wonderful thing in the world, although, in truth, it was just a small second bedroom in a modest but neat-as-a-pin wood-framed home. For her, though, the little room became a welcome port in what had been a dreadfully stormy sea, a safe haven that would have warmed the heart of any weary mariner.

For her it was a new experience to go to sleep at night off the floor and alone in a bed of her own, especially in a room that had decorative pictures on the walls, lacy curtains on the windows, and an old-fashioned bead-fringed lamp on a nightstand for her to read by. It was a scene she remembered and treasured for the rest of her life. For Candy, a living arrangement that involved privacy, quietness, orderliness, cleanliness, and, most of all, warm and ongoing love, all co-existing within a place where she was truly welcome, was about as rare as finding a stack of money lying out on the street: Up until that point, nothing that had ever happened in her life could have been described as an incidence of good fortune.

Ernest and Jewel Wilson were polar opposites of her birth parents. Where they had been loud and demanding and threatening, the Wilsons were quiet and yielding and encouraging; where they had been oblivious and inconsiderate of her needs, the Wilsons were observant and attentive; and where they had taken no specific notice of her, she was now the center of attention for two caring adults. Only the day before, all she had were two thin cotton shifts to alternate between for daily wear; now she had a small wardrobe of new and clean outfits from which to choose.

It came as no surprise to hear Candy say that getting adjusted to her new surroundings turned out to be something of a challenge. Shy and timid about more or less everything, for a while she was bowled over by all of the changes that were taking place in her life. As delightful and positive as her new surroundings were, the changes were still a lot to absorb.

"We noticed during the first week she was with us that she didn't eat much when we had meals together," Ernest remembered as we spoke, "and that seemed unusual for a growing young girl. When we asked why she ate so little, she said she thought if she didn't eat too much, we'd be more willing to let her stay. That," said Ernest, "was something I never forgot. No kid should ever have been made to feel the way she did at the time."

"It all seemed too good to be true," Candy added, "and I was worried that someone was going to show up and take it away. That's what had always happened in the past, so why wouldn't it happen again in the future? Remember, too, that no one ever told the social service people in Arizona I was leaving, and I was still a ward of the court."

Jewel Wilson, as it turned out, proved to be a sensible and reasonable woman who took great care in terms of how she dealt with her new daughter. Her approach was to contend with one problem at a time, and she was thoughtful and insightful enough to anticipate many of the problems Candy was having. She told me that she had had complete faith that God would provide all the guidance she and Ernest and Candy would need to be able to find the right way forward.

Without pushing or cajoling or even raising her voice, Jewel patiently and unobtrusively helped Candy adjust to her new surroundings. Ernest Wilson's only comment about this period was that "I was never worried about a thing; Candy was always a pleasure to be around, and we felt lucky to have her."

By now it had become abundantly clear why Candy loved Jewel Wilson as much as she did: It was because Jewel had thought from the beginning that all Candy needed to find the right way in life was love, patience, and kindness. Because Jewel was a person who truly believed that all things are possible through love, she was convinced that Candy would be able to make all the adjustments and choices required to do quite well for herself. She knew the process would begin slowly and then accelerate, but only after Candy was persuaded that she was loved for what she was rather than for misguided concepts of what she wasn't.

There's no way Jewel Wilson could have known what was going on in my mind as I listened to her describe how she had overseen Candy's transition to their home, but she'd have been surprised if she had. I wanted to throw my arms around her and hug her for all she'd done, even though I hadn't been able to find the words to say so while we were together. I had just sat there, stunned, when what I really wanted to do was throw my head in her lap and bawl like a baby, just to thank her for all the help she had given to the needy young person who had grown up to become my sweet and lovely wife. Jewel had always had a special place in my heart, but now I loved her more than ever. For the first time, I fully understood what wonderful care she had lavished on our dear girl.

Candy loved Ernest and Jewel even before her adoption could be arranged, but it wasn't until she had been with them for a good while that she grew to appreciate just how unique they truly were. They were quiet, modest, unassuming people, but they were resolutely dedicated to the one thing that was at the center of their lives: their faith. Christianity was not just a concept to which they paid lip service by routinely attending church; instead, it was a guiding light for everything they said or did. Their belief was not superficial, bounded, or transitory; it was real, unlimited, and substantial. They did their best to be actual *practitioners* of their religion, not just *churchgoers*.

In short order, Candy also discovered that Ernest Wilson was unique in several other specific and notable ways as well. After serving as a Navy gunner during World War II and as a cop for a while after that, he eventually became a self-employed general contractor who did home remodeling and cement work on his own clock. While he was a quiet and modest man, he was also as stubborn as a mule and as tough as a board, especially when it came to the way he thought life ought to go on inside his home. His belief system was centered on the doctrines of his church, love for his family, and his own common sense.

As a straightforward man of simple tastes, he didn't talk a lot. He believed only in what he could see with his own eyes and appreciate with his own good sense. While he was not formally educated or eloquent, he had one great strength that everyone he knew sooner or later came to appreciate; he was a man of his word and a hard worker, a person who could be counted on to get a job done when he said he would. He did a lot of jobs, too, and not just to make a living. He did a lot of them on behalf of his church and to help people who fell within its gravitational pull.

Basically, he wasn't a voluble philosophizer; he was a *reliable doer*, someone who could always be counted on to do his share, and then a little extra. His peers had learned that he would always be there in a pinch, and that he worked with a positive and infectious sense of purpose. He didn't just work hard; he worked hard for the right reasons, and people knew it; that's why so many came to care for him as much as they did, why he had so many respectful friends. What Candy grew to appreciate most about him was how he was always there for his friends, which indicated that he would be there for her as well — always, and without fail.

Having clear-cut priorities, Ernest firmly believed, was the key to living a life of quality and meaning. His priorities were as clear to him as a pathway paved with gold; they were God, family, and country, and he had no doubts about any plank in his platform. To his way of thinking, the most important thing in life was simple to understand: You either believe or you don't believe, and all the rest flows downhill from there. Candy said that she knew without ever having to be told after arriving in his home that from that point on, her life was going to be conducted in only one of two ways — his way or the highway, and that his way was going to be God's way, as best as he could understand it.

In this sense, therefore, matters were either black or white for Ernest, right or wrong, godly or ungodly. He had no use for abstract modes of thinking or any of the various *alternative lifestyles* that were blathered about in the media, concepts outside the realm of his beliefs and personal experience. You wouldn't discuss with him, for example, your great interest in the creative or performing arts or your fondness for a recent work of fiction, but you could talk with him at length about an addition to the church building, how to help out a new member who had some problems in his personal life, or about helping a troubled family get back on track in the community. Hands-on projects of that kind were right up his alley.

Ernest was the antithesis of a man who has ready answers for all the ills of the world but who, for one reason or another, can't get along with his next-door neighbors. For him, the only sure way to heaven was the way spelled out by his church. Beyond that, his home was his haven, and his wife Jewel and new daughter Candice were at the center of his worldly existence. He had few interests that extended beyond the affairs of his own household and of the congregation to which he and his wife had dedicated their lives. He was not a man to apologize for believing the way he did, and it suited him just fine that others had no doubts about where he stood.

A senior man of his church, a man whose views he highly respected, once summed up the way of thinking that guided Ernest's day–to–day conduct with a simple saying: "If not, why not?" If, the older brother was in effect asking, beliefs other than those upon which their Church was founded could be thought of as being of equal weight and value, then why would it not be perfectly acceptable for any one of the brethren to abide by those views as steadily as their own? This, the elder brother had implied, was a way of thinking that could never be right or proper, and Ernest had agreed with him wholeheartedly.

As Christian fundamentalists, the Wilsons were conservatives to the core. What they believed was what they believed, and there were no two ways about it. For them, the only way to stay on the straight and narrow path was to avoid the confusion of contrary thought, and the best way to deal with other points of view was to stay away from them altogether. All of their time and attention, therefore, was focused on the affairs of their church, they fellowshipped only with members of their church, and they maintained only casual relationships with anyone who did not live the same way they did.

The Wilsons were God-fearing people who expressed their straightforward faith through the way their lived their lives. They would knock themselves out to help those who were down and out, and they would give of their time and effort until it hurt. They were Christians in the only way they knew how to be, even if they weren't overly tolerant of beliefs and ways of life that were not essentially the same as their own. They were *do as I do* kinds of people, not the *do as I say* kinds of adults Candy had been under the thumb of for her entire life. The way the Wilsons lived their lives and what they had done for her was all the evidence she needed to judge the quality of their hearts.

Jewel knew better than anyone when she and Ernest took in Candice that she would be dealing with a troubled child, but she also knew that God would be there to help as long as they asked Him to be. That, she told me, was where she had kept her focus all along — on making sure that her new daughter wanted Him to be there for her, too, just as much as she did. Having the right priorities, as far as Jewel was concerned, was the key to creating a better future, not just for Candy, but for anyone.

She said she had dealt with Candy's periodic lapses into silence by giving her plenty of time and space. Her occasional retreats to the bedroom to hide under the covers as a means of escaping pressure was handled the same way, and when she was awakened by a nightmare, either Jewel or Ernest would sit by her side until she worked her way out of it, holding her hand until she got back to sleep. Afterwards, when she was back on level ground, Jewel would sit down with her and calmly and quietly discuss what had happened and talk about how she might deal with similar episodes in the future.

Jewel knew that Candy had a lot to *learn*, but that shc had a lot to *unlearn* as well. The brand of therapy she practiced didn't require any special training or specific expertise, but it was labor intensive, physically tiring, and emotionally trying. In terms of practical results, though, her approach was as effective as most any other form of support that might have been delivered. Her treatment was nothing more than a Christian mother's love, but it was exactly what her daughter was most in need of at the time.

In summary, the Wilsons offered just what a child who had gone through an experience like Candy's is usually starved for — affection, structure, faith, predictability, and a complete lack of ambivalence when it comes to standards and values and matters of right and wrong. Given the total absence of personal guidance in her former environment, the Wilsons were, again, nothing short of a Godsend. Ernest became the father figure Candy needed, and Jewel became the mother who was always there for her. In tandem, what they provided was solid ground on which to stand, sincerity of heart, clarity of purpose, and a positive frame of mind; the foundational building blocks that were required to restore Candy's hope of a new beginning, a belief that a good future might lay ahead for her after all.

"As far as I was concerned," Candy said, "the day my formal adoption papers were completed was when Candice Lee Caine died and Candice Lee Wilson was born. In more ways than one, I knew that a whole new life had begun for me, one that was going to be infinitely superior to anything I'd known in the past, and I swore to myself that I was going to make the most of it." She said that she had never *intentionally* looked back from that day forward, and that she had always tried her best to take full advantage of the unexpected opportunity that had been placed in her hands.

Living with the Wilsons not only brought about wonderfully positive changes in Candy's life; it turned out to be a tremendous blessing for the Wilsons well. They probably didn't even think it at the time, but by taking in Candy, they had taken out the best insurance policy any couple can ever have — the full support and commitment of a dutiful, principled daughter.

IN THE WHOLESOME AND positive environment of the Wilsons'

home, Candy grew from a child into a young woman. For the first time in her life, she began to believe that the future really could work out well for her. Her initial feelings of shyness and uncertainty were slowly but surely replaced by uplifting feelings of confidence with regard to the future. Because she wasn't a fool, once she had a genuine opportunity to make something of herself, she did her best to make sure it happened.

Little by little, unwanted recollections of her earlier life, even though they were never fully eliminated, were brought under control. Bit by bit, the timidity and fearfulness that once defined her were replaced by a more outgoing and assertive personality, one that reflected the mood and outlook of her new surroundings. Better still, the many positive changes taking place inside of her began to register in her demeanor as well. Inner happiness placed a beautiful smile on her face and added a warm glow to her cheeks, until she started to look, as the saying goes, *like a million dollars*, which was a perfect description for how she truly felt.

Candy prospered in her new environment beyond what anyone expected, even to the extent of developing a whole new outlook on life. Having never been taught or guided in any but the most negative of ways, she became an open vessel into which new content could be poured. She was profoundly changed as a result of her guidance by the Wilsons, especially by Jewel, who, without being the least bit insistent or obtrusive, carefully and lovingly helped her find her own way. Smart as well as highly observant, Candy's own faith and values were defined during this period of time.

She told me that she made a number of heartfelt personal resolutions while she was with the Wilsons, promises to herself that she has tried to live by ever since. First and foremost, she resolved that, in the future, her own life was going to be lived in accordance with the same high standards that guided thc Wilsons, since she recognized, even as young and vulnerable as she still was, that what they believed in was worth all the money or status or other rewards the world had to offer. The calculus she applied was short and simple: *The Wilsons' faith had made them the way they were, and the way they were was the way she wanted to be. They were more than worthy of emulation, so emulate them she would, not just while she was physically with them, but for as long as she lived.*

She also resolved that if and when she had a husband of her own, she would work as diligently as she could to make sure their relationship was as loving as the one that existed between the Wilsons — the kind, she believed, that every family had a right to enjoy. *Her marital relationship*, she pledged, *was never going to be like that of her birth parents, nor would her children, if and when she had any, ever have to go through the misery she had had to endure as a child. Her husband and children would be loved, and they would be told that they were loved. Come hell or high water,* she pledged to herself, *she was going to become an exemplary daughter, wife, and mother. She would do whatever was required for her husband and children to be successful in life, no matter how much personal sacrifice or effort might be required.*

She further resolved that in any home she might be lucky enough to have one day would be nothing like *the miserable circumstances of her childhood and youth.* She swore she would *wear herself out keeping it clean and orderly and making sure no drinking, smoking, or foul language would ever be allowed there.* She'd been around so much brutish behavior, derisive criticism, and excessive punishment that she couldn't stand the thought of ever being around it again. Her home would be *a place of comfort for all of its occupants, a loving refuge where positive support, common courtesy, and attentiveness would be the only acceptable form of behavior. It would be*, that is to say, *a home just like that of Ernest and Jewel Wilson.*

Above and beyond all else, Candy swore to herself that *she would love and honor Ernest and Jewel Wilson for the rest of her life.* Because they were good and kind, she wanted to be equally good and kind; because they were generous and giving, she wanted to become even more generous and giving; and, since God had enabled them to become what they were, she wanted to demonstrate the highest level of Christian behavior, just so she could be more like them. She knew quite well that the Wilsons weren't perfect people, but she also knew they had been her personal salvation, and that basic fact outweighed all other considerations. For these reasons, she adopted their beliefs, values, and way of life as her own, wholly and completely.

Candy's pledges were anything but shallow or immature girlish fantasies; they were earnest resolutions — promises she has held to through thick and thin. As her husband, I knew this better than anyone else, due to having been the main beneficiary of her many uplifting commitments. Without a doubt, she has done what she said she was going to do — that and, in fact, much more, despite having had to contend with nightmarish emotional problems throughout her life.

YOUNG PEOPLE CAN BLOSSOM beyond all expectations under the right conditions. Like the delicate flowers that sometimes rise up seemingly out of nowhere on flat and desolate prairies when heat and rain and soil conditions are just right, she grew up to become a uniquely special person — a bright, cheerful, dutiful, ethical human being, someone others took great pleasure in being around. She evolved into a greater blessing than the Wilsons themselves could have imagined, back when they took her in.

Enjoying a good life, Candy had discovered through living with her mentors, was far more a matter of living by faith and principle than of being rich or poor, and this was a message that became music to her ears. Her own life, she had decided, was going to change, and it was going to change in a hurry. Because she had already had a clear understanding of how the other half lived, she wanted nothing further to do with it.

She didn't just pick up a few pointers while she was living with the Wilsons; she was literally imprinted by what she saw and felt. Because they were there for her when nobody else was, she accepted their lifestyle and beliefs and values as completely and irrevocably as they had accepted her. What they did, she did; what they believed, she believed. She turned her heart over to them, totally convinced they were worthy of her full dedication — that and, in fact, much, much more.

The Wilsons had proven themselves worthy of every ounce of love and trust Candy vested in them, based on how they behaved for as long as the three of them lived together. Their commitment to her was demonstrated in the old-fashioned way — through working for it on a daily basis, through being parents who richly deserved her full respect. Once they made their bond with Candy, they didn't veer from it for an instant. For her, they became what all parents are supposed to be, that and a great deal more.

Yet another inner pledge Candy made during this period of time was that the Wilsons' love for her would be returned a thousand times over, and, from what I've observed, it's clear that she has always tried to be there for them. The way she dealt with them was living evidence of the truth residing in the old saying that *a daughter's a daughter for the rest of her life*. Candy willed herself to become a daughter who was just as upright as her adoptive parents, one who relished the thought of being there for them when they got older. Because she was a firm believer in giving credit where credit was due and in paying her debts, she knew she would be their ace in the hole during their senior years.

Every spring out on the Texas plains near where we lived in Granbury, bluebonnets burst into view in such a display of beauty that people in our general area were willing to travel great distances just to look at them. This same phenomenon, it seems to me, occurred as Candy grew into young womanhood, in the sense that her demeanor and thoughts and values became so evident that they made others want to be around her. Her attributes provided living proof of the power of love and solid values to produce wonderful changes in the heart of a human being. She evolved into what most of us only aspire to be — a truly good person, a person with an inner glow that appealed to most everyone she was around.

Throughout her life, people in general, not just infatuated

young guys like me, had been impressed by her friendly and considerate ways. Not only was she valued as a friend among her peers and acquaintances, adult members and elders of the Wilsons' congregation became admirers of her as well. It couldn't have been any clearer that she would become a loving and dutiful partner for a lucky guy one day. On several occasions, I had heard Jewel describe her by noting that "*she can sure brighten up a room, and she never meets a stranger.*" I couldn't have agreed more.

Candy, in short, blossomed into the bright-eyed and beautiful young woman who rang my bell at the church conference back when we first met, the occasion that turned out to be so fateful for both of us. She attracted the admiring attention of other single guys for the same reason she attracted mine, but why I was the one she chose has never been clear. All I know is that I couldn't be happier that she did; a rose is a rose wherever you find one, and I knew all along that I had found one in her.

CYNICS AND OTHERS WHO think of themselves as *realists*, those who know the basics about the incident we got caught up in later on in life, may ridicule all the many positive comments I've made about Candy, but it won't bother me in the slightest if they do. My description of her worthy qualities is, if anything, understated rather than overstated, and I don't need affirmation from anyone to know that every word I've said about her is absolutely true. I know that all of us fall short of becoming what we are capable of being in life, but I also know it couldn't be any truer that she is exactly what I have described her to be — *a truly good person.*

Yes, there really is such a thing as *a truly good person* — not, of course, in an absolute sense, but in relative terms. At one time I used to agree with those who say that the whole idea of referring to any one individual as being *more worthy* than any other is a ridiculous notion, but some people really do deserve a great deal of credit for the exemplary ways in which they conduct their lives. To be a bit more pointed about this, only in the most abstract and philosophical of ways would Charlie Manson ever be placed at the same level of worthiness as Mother Teresa.

If a scale of measurement could be devised to measure kinds of qualities to which I have alluded, Candy would score higher on it than many of us — higher than me, for example. People have described her as, for example, "an unusually kind young woman" or "the best friend I have ever had," and "a person I just love." Others have said that they truly value her friendship, and many of them have not hesitated to seek out her advice on one thing or another. They haven't hesitated to let me know it, either. By way of contrast, hardly anyone, I'm sorry to say, has ever made comments of that kind about me.

Candy, of course, is no saint, but her attributes most definitely fall far more on the debit than the credit side of the ledger. She's a giver, not a taker; and, just like the Wilsons, a doer rather than a talker. She is one of those people who always add a little more to the kitty than they ever take away.

Candy's behavior and attitude of mind are clear byproducts of, first of all, having had to endure childhood conditions that were abysmal enough to make most of the daily challenges of life seem manageable by comparison and, secondarily, of effectively having been remade through living with Ernest and Jewel Wilson. Their great faith and kindness had the effect of magnifying the inner strengths that have been mentioned, and the results have shown up like a bright light on a cloudy day.

Candy's exceptionally strong convictions have been our secret weapon over the years, in the same way that they ended up becoming an absolute blessing in the aftermath of the tragedy that came close to derailing us forever. What happened to us was the worst ordeal we had ever had to endure, much more painful, for example, than misfortunes such as the deaths of friends or relatives before their time or the tragic divorces of people we admired and respected. Her strength is what got us through.

Many a marriage has fallen apart over less than what we had to deal with, especially now that divorce has become such an easy out that many have come to accept it as a fairly normal part of life. Once again, though, Candy's commitment to our relationship never wavered, not even in the face of the absolute mortification that *we — but mostly she* — had to put up with during our darkest days.

19

I HOPE YOU'RE FINALLY SATISFIED

PRYING LOOSE THE SECRETS of Candy's past turned out to be anything but the emotional release for her I expected it to be. Her childhood story was too utterly heartbreaking for anything that benevolent to happen. The fact that I had given her no choice but to recall in great detail the miserable events of her younger years had the effect of aggravating the worrisome emotional problems she was already having at home. She was becoming a little more troubled as each day passed. It was agonizing to watch what was happening, and I couldn't stop cursing myself for having accelerated her downhill slide.

Speechless and emotionally drained, I felt as limp as a rag, knowing that I was powerless to be of any real support. We were too disheveled and stressed out to have any extra weight placed on our shoulders, but I had unwittingly done just that. Because I was too troubled to think clearly about anything, all of our problems seemed to cave in on me at once, and Candy, as I was soon to discover, was feeling much the same way.

During the weeks that followed, all I did was wander around our house, constantly berating myself for having been so callously insistent on making her do what she clearly didn't want to do. *Why had I come on as hard as I did? Why had I been so insensitive?*

In short order, it became apparent that my behavior had to be attributed to my having become so deeply immersed in finding out all there was to know about Candy's past that I had given little to no thought to the possibility that what I was doing might any adverse effects on us in the here and now. For me, any thought of backing off had become unthinkable; I had demanded to know what I wanted to know, and I had gotten it.

WHEN SHE FINALLY FINISHED telling everything she could think of to tell and had answered every question I could think of to ask, the only response I could muster was to stare at her with my eyes wide open and my mouth agape. Basically, I had discovered that an old soul lived in my beautiful wife's relatively young body, and that there would never be any other option but for us but to learn to deal with the realities of her past. The memories that haunted her could never be dismissed. As William Faulkner once observed, "Our pasts are never really dead and, in fact, they are really never even past."

"Well," Candy said, summing up our situation quite well by looking right into my eyes and saying, "you insisted on knowing how I came to be adopted by the Wilsons, and now you do. Are you satisfied? Do you feel better? Are you — *are we* — better off now than we were before? All I can say is that I hope you're finally satisfied!"

20

SOMETHING HAD TO HAPPEN

AFTER CANDY ANSWERED EVERY question I asked about her childhood, an awkward and uncomfortable silence settled within our home, a silence that was accompanied by an enormous sense of unease. *This is what happens*, I thought, *when people dig up memories that never should have been exhumed.*

It seemed as though the weight of the world descended on our formerly happy home. In the atmosphere of defeat that followed her revelations, a side of her surfaced that I had never seen. I discovered, for example, that my dear wife was not in all instances the genteel and forgiving person she had always appeared to be; in fact, where her birth parents were concerned, she didn't seem to be forgiving at all. Her anger and bitterness toward them, I soon discovered, was far too chillingly negative to be anything but unhealthy.

"No one," she said to me all of sudden one evening a few days later as we were sitting in our living room, "would believe the neglect and abuse we suffered at our parents' hands, my brothers and sisters and me. What they put us through — what they allowed to happen to us, especially to my younger brothers — was totally inexcusable, and I'll never forgive them as long as I live."

For her to have made such a harsh and unforgiving statement was totally out of character, something she had never done before. Her comment was bad enough in and of itself, but it was uttered in a bitter, hateful tone that caused me to cringe as I heard it.

Up to this point in our lives, Candy had always been a

remarkably warm and loving person to be around. Because she rarely used harsh words or uttered a negative thought about anyone, hearing bitterness come out of her mouth was highly upsetting. But I didn't question it at the time. Why? Well, I suppose it was because I fully related to how she felt, and, in fact, actually agreed with her, now that I knew how her parents had treated their kids.

From that point forward, her demeanor began to change even more dramatically, especially if I said anything further about her birth parents. Reviving her past had not only made her sad; it had also made her angry.

After inadvertently blundering into the subject a few more times, I stopped making any further references to her past. In fact, I dropped the subject like a hot potato, and deeply regretted having brought it up in the first place. It was too late, though; once the cat was out of the bag, it seemed clear that we might never be able to get it back in again.

SEEMINGLY OVERNIGHT, BOTH OF us began to lose control of ourselves at roughly the same time, she as a result of having been forced to relive her dismal childhood and me for being overcome with guilt for having made her do it. Worse still, our decline began to accelerate while I was still trying to prove myself at work and when we were right in the middle of one of our busiest times of the year. My nerves had been shot to pieces, and her condition was even shakier.

The fact that I lost my composure had been highly upsetting for Candy, since the possibility of my doing just that was what she had tried to avoid for as long as we had been married. We had been together so long that she didn't have to say a word for me to understand what was running through her mind at this juncture. *Now*, I knew she was thinking, *it's bad enough that my miserable parents took away my childhood; now it looks like they're going to destroy my marriage as well.*

I sensed, too, that she blamed herself for having acquiesced to my demands to tell her childhood story, which had upset both of us. Her reasoning, I knew without asking, would be that *if she had not caved in and let it out, neither of us would be as shaken as we were.* It was her nature to assume responsibility for every problem that affected us, whether she caused it or not. That's just how she was.

What on earth have I done? was the refrain I repeated to myself so often during the following weeks that it became something of a mantra. *Why had I forced her to relive her torment in the first place, and why in the world had I done it at the worst possible time — when she was already highly upset and my capabilities at work were still being tested?*

I was about as discombobulated as a man can be and still appear outwardly normal and functional, and she was becoming more distraught with every day that passed. Her condition was so shaky that attempting to talk with her about the challenges I was having at work was unthinkable. She couldn't have handled it. Adding another pressing concern to her already full plate of worries might have driven her right over the edge.

Under normal circumstances, she would have been as much help to me as I would have been for her during a stressful period, but, in the aftermath of our discussion, she couldn't help me and I wasn't able to help her. We were too consumed by our own separate worries.

Candy had had a premonition that if I ever learned about her past, I would either be unable to deal with it or that I would for one reason or another hold it against her. Her childhood had been so painful that she feared it might somehow have an equally damaging effect on our own marriage and home. I knew that wasn't even remotely likely, of course, but she mostly definitely didn't. Our cups were literally running over with worry. Neither of us could sleep well at night, and it was abundantly clear that we were in imminent danger of falling off a cliff of my own making.

DURING THE DAYS THAT followed, it would be fair to say that Candy slowly drifted away and that I lost even more self-control, both at home and on the job.

Candy began retreating into longer and longer periods of withdrawal, episodes of silence that I chose to continue thinking of as intense immersion in quiet concentration. It got so bad that she stayed preoccupied much of the time, so much so that she appeared to be on the verge of disappearing into her own inner space. She'd gone through episodes of this kind for as long as we'd been married, but now they were becoming more prolonged and severe. On occasions she would bounce back to her normal self for a while, but then she'd lapse right back into another funk.

Soon, even odder things began to happen. One evening, for example, as we sat in our living room quietly reading, she said to me out of the clear blue sky in utmost seriousness, "It seems to me that the people in my family you told me about reacted just like the Jews did during the Nazi period in Germany; they were crushed without ever fighting back. That'll never happen to me again, I can promise you that. I'll have to be beaten to the ground — even to death — before I'll put up with the kind of abuse and disrespect those people suffered, the ones you always read about. Nobody should have to put up with treatment of that kind and it will never happen to me again." Then, without another word, she returned to her reading.

I didn't know how to react. I simply listened, and then, afterwards, went on with what I was doing, in the same way that she had. It hadn't appeared that she wanted or expected any response from me, so I had just listened without saying anything in response. Nevertheless, her flare-up left me feeling disturbed and uneasy, and warning bells began to go off in my head. *What was it*, I wondered, *that had made what she said so troubling?*

Days later, during a quiet moment, it suddenly dawned on me why Candy's comments had been so disconcerting. There were two points, really; *the way she spoke* and the *specific terms she'd used.* First, what stood out so clearly was the intensity with which her thoughts were uttered; I knew her well enough to realize that she meant exactly what she said. Secondly, the verb tense she'd chosen was troubling because it indicated that a subconscious shift had taken place in her thinking. Instead of saying, "*I wouldn't want it to happen to me,*" she had said "*It's never going to happen to me again, you can take my word on that.*"

DURING THE WEEKS THAT followed, we continued to float through one of the strangest periods in our married life.

Overtaken by a guilt-induced malaise, we were too burdened to make any decisions that would have helped get us on top of our problems. Both of us assumed sole responsibility for jeopardizing the relationship that had been our solid foundation for over thirty years, but neither one of us could get a solid handle on what to do about having sunk so low.

Intense emotional anguish began to overtake Candy, to the extent that changes in her conduct became painful to observe. It seemed to me that she was about to go to pieces, right before my eyes. Watching her made me feel guiltier than ever and hastened my own decline, until, before long, I became just as depressed as she was.

ON ANOTHER DAY AND at yet another unexpected moment, she said to me one evening in a somber, deadly serious tone, "You know, I was robbed of my childhood — we all were, my brothers and sisters and me. It wasn't fair, and it wasn't right. We didn't deserve it because we didn't do anything wrong. We were just kids, but our lives were wrecked before we even knew what was happening to us, before we had a chance to live. Where were the adults when we were growing up, the people who should have known better than to let us be treated that way? Why wasn't anyone there to help us? We weren't old enough to watch out for ourselves, so why didn't someone protect us? They really hurt me.

They hurt all of us. For my brothers and sisters and me, what they allowed to happen damaged our entire lives."

Because I knew exactly what she meant, I did not disagree: She and her brothers and sisters really had been failed across the board. But the angry way she used the collective *they* left me feeling especially uneasy. The personality changes it suggested were more than worrisome; they were downright scary, since they meant that she might have become irrational.

When I tried to reason with her, she would begin to rail against the injustices she and her brothers and sisters had suffered at the hands of their parents. Her cart was clearly going off the tracks, but I still made no effort to set up the professional help she so obviously needed. Instead, I kept trying to solve her problems in the same was I was trying to solve mine — entirely on my own, without outside help of any kind.

As would be imagined, my paltry efforts to help her were all to no avail. Her emotional health continued to decline, until one evening not long before the horrific incident that took place shortly thereafter, she walked into our bedroom so immersed in intense concentration that she was muttering out loud. Under a furrowed brow and lost in deep thought, she didn't seem to know what she was saying. I recall hearing her repeat over and over, "No wonder. No wonder," but what she meant by repeating those same words, I had no clue. All I knew was that her behavior was becoming stranger by the day, and that she was becoming too nervous and apprehensive to sleep for more than a few hours at a time.

YOU COULD ALMOST WATCH Candy's resentfulness morphing into outrage and then into outright anger. A palpable sense of her wishing that she had a way of evening the score, a way of striking back against those who abused her, seemed to linger in the air. There was no doubt that she was highly frustrated, probably because there was no longer any one around for her to strike back against, not for mistreatment that had occurred over 40 years earlier.

What made her wrath especially worrisome was that it wasn't aimed at any specific target or in any discernable direction; it was just unspecified anger. There didn't seem be anything I could do about it, even though her reactions were clearly pointless and dangerous. So, that became her status quo: Undirected anger was lodged in her mind, and there it sat, festering like an open wound.

What a shame it is, I thought, *that there weren't more angry people around years ago, back when she was suffering as a child; if there had been, maybe her parents would have gotten more of the help they had so sorely needed.*

At times Candy ranted and raved as she stormed around our house, behaving as if she were about ready to explode, but at other times she behaved as if she might be coming out of it. There was no way to tell how or if or when her anger would be acted out. I had a sinking feeling, though, that if she ever were to go off the deep end, she might end up saying or doing something she would regret for a very long time.

The truth, though, was that Candy's emotional wounds had been so aggravated by what she'd learned about her family through listening to my stories that her emotional condition never stopped deteriorating. She seemed to have absorbed the pain of her elders, then added it to her own. After that, inner frustration left her seething with subconscious anger. It couldn't have been any more obvious that a slow mental unwinding was taking place, and that even more advanced mental instability was clearly possible.

There got to be times when she would suddenly and unexpectedly recall a particularly distressing event that had taken place during her younger years, then start talking about it right on the spot, regardless of where we were or what we happened to be doing at the moment. We had agreed during times of greater lucidity that public discussion of these topics was not to be done, but, whenever a truly bad memory resurfaced, she would flare up anyway. Then, after carrying on for a while until she could be calmed down, she would sometimes descend into yet another period of abject gloom.

HOPING TO DIVERT HER attention from all the negatives that were taking place in our lives, one day I suggested that we get away for a while by flying out for a visit with my brother Rick and his wife Belinda at their home on the outskirts of Templeton, California. Templeton is a small town out in the foothills just north of San Luis Obispo, about an hour inland from the Pacific Ocean. They have a house on eight acres, situated on the top of a low hill, about eight miles northeast of town. Because they had a comfortable home in a scenic location, I thought a visit with them would get Candy's mind off her worries for a while.

Because he's a frugal sort of guy, my brother made a practice of doing everything he could to save money by keep living costs low. His goal at the time was to retire at the earliest possible date, mainly because he was aggravated in equal measure with his job as well as with some of his coworkers and supervisors. Whenever he spoke about his place of employment, he'd do it using language that was direct and to the point. He told anybody who was willing to listen that he intended "to get the hell out of that damned place as soon as humanly possible." He wasn't the least bit subtle about saying what he thought, that's for sure.

Anyway, one of the ways Rick cut living costs was by heating his home using a combination of a fireplace and a large potbellied stove, a stove that looked like those that were common many years ago, even though it really wasn't. He and Belinda were also very proud of an antique kitchen stove they used on a regular basis. Even though their place was equipped with a central heating and air conditioning system, they used wood for fuel as much as they could.

Their wood-burning stove was set up in an attractive way, and it was extremely cozy to be around when it was in use. During the cold, damp days that are fairly common inland from the Pacific coast, it was great to sit beside it after coming in from the outside.

One day during our visit, as Rick and I were outside feeding his horses and dogs and llama and other pets and Belinda and Candy were in the kitchen preparing our dinner, Belinda asked if Candy would mind putting a little more wood in the stove, and Candy, of course, had done as Belinda requested. She was in the process of closing the stove door just as Rick and I walked back into their living room from outside. Candy glanced up to say "Hi, guys" as we walked by, then quickly turned her back to us and pretended to be stoking the stove.

Rick didn't notice anything amiss as he headed down the hall to wash up for supper, but I immediately picked up on something being off. After walking over to the stove to warm up after being out in the cold, only a brief glance was required to see that Candy's eyes were welled up with tears and that she was visibly upset. Whispering, I asked what in the world had happened. Had something gone wrong between her and Belinda? All four of us had been in great moods just a few minutes before, and I had no idea what could have upset her enough to start crying in that short period of time.

She put me off by whispering, "Don't say anything; I'll explain it to you later," whereupon I spent the rest of the evening worried that she and my sister–in–law had gotten into a tiff of some sort while my brother and I were out cutting wood, even though something of that kind would have been totally out of character for either one of them.

The change in Candy's demeanor put a damper on our entire evening, and I'm sure Rick and Belinda thought some sort of problem was taking place between us. They had no idea what was going on, but, without their ever saying so, I felt sure they'd known from the moment of our arrival that we were under a lot of stress.

As soon as we were alone in our room later that night, I began whispering complaints about how she had wrecked our evening for no apparent reason. Just as I was getting wound up, she suddenly threw herself down on the guest room bed and began sobbing uncontrollably, trying her best to be quiet enough that my brother and his wife could not overhear her.

Lying on the bed with her face down in the covers, she cried so hard I knew something had to be seriously wrong. Shaken by seeing her so distraught, the first thought that came to mind was that my having complained about her behavior had brought it all on. I pleaded with her to forgive me, saying that any small problem she and Belinda might have had couldn't be all that bad and that we could straighten it all out in the morning.

When she finally regained enough control to begin talking with me, she rolled over on her side, put one arm up under her head, and explained that no one had said or done anything to cause her to become upset. "All that happened," she said, "was that I suddenly recalled an incident that occurred during my childhood, one that flashed so vividly through my mind that I started to shake and cry before I could control it."

She told me that when she was six years old, her family lived in an old home that was poorly heated by a tall wood-burning stove similar to the updated version Rick and Belinda had in their living room. In her family's case, it was the only heat source for their drafty old place, which meant that in cold weather every member of the family headed straight for it when they got out of bed in the morning. Because her folks liked the room to be warm and ready when they got up, they had assigned the task of stoking the coals and putting in new sticks of wood every morning to their older kids.

One morning, though, Candy woke up early and arrived at the stove before her older brothers and sisters. Their mother was still in bed, but on this particular morning her dad had arisen early and gone outside to bring in an armload of wood. Candy arrived at the stove before she realized her father was already up.

Because it had been a cold night, the coals had burned down so low that Candy was afraid she might not be able to get the stove heated up before everyone else got up. If that were to happen, she knew her parents would not be pleased. She attempted to rekindle the fire by throwing in a few folds of some newspaper advertising pages that were laying on top of a small table located not far from the stove. What she failed to notice was that three one-dollar bills had been placed between an advertising cutout and the top folds of the paper. She didn't see the currency, so she had no idea it was there.

When her father returned with an armload of wood, he immediately started placing sticks of it in the fire. Upon seeing the burning bills in the stove and realizing what Candy had done, he lost his temper completely. After slapping her back and forth across the face, he grabbed her by the arm and pulled her over toward the stove. Forcing her skinny little arm inside the open door, he demanded that she retrieve the burning money. It was too late to save any of the bills, but he pressed her arm against the entry opening for a second anyway, just long enough for him to believe that he'd taught her a valuable lesson.

She said she'd avoided having her knuckles and fingers forced against the coals by pressing her clinched fist against the side of one of the sticks of new wood he'd just placed in the fire, but that he held her arm against the hot side of the open side of the door long enough make sure that she was burned. Her screams awakened the rest of the family, who came running into the room. Her father, she said, had simply glared at her before saying to the others, "Your stupid sister just burned herself on the stove." His look alone were warning enough that she was not to say a word about what had really happened. Instead, she simply held her arm and continued to cry out in pain.

When Luther told Pirley what Candy had done, she smacked the crying girl across the top of the head. Neither of them, her parents both said, could believe that one of their kids would be dumb enough to burn money, not when they barely afford to buy food for the family. Neither one of them made any effort to dress or otherwise attend to what turned out to be a severe burn on Candy's arm. That, they clearly believed, was something she deserved to have to deal with on her own.

Her older sister Collette, who was just a kid herself, helped by covering the burn with lard and then wrapping it with a rag. It hurt and remained red and festering for quite some time before it finally healed, leaving behind a scar on her arm that remained visible for the rest of her life.

The burn eventually healed, but the emotional damage that had been caused by this unforgivably cruel incident was never forgotten. The mere act of stoking my brother's stove earlier in the day rekindled her memory of what had happened forty-three years earlier, to the extent that she had been moved to sudden tears.

The raised scar on her arm had been obvious for as long as I'd known her, but when I asked how she got it she said only that she had accidentally burned herself on a stove when she was a child. It wasn't until that night that she told me the real truth about how it got there. She showed where the scar had been located after the incident, then went on to explain that it had, as she put it, "traveled up her arm" as she grew older. I had never heard of a *traveling scar*, but I've since learned that this does happen on occasion.

Candy's father had been unspeakably cruel that day, but her story became even more appalling after she explained why he — and then, later, her mother — had become so angry over what she'd done. Their reaction would have been marginally understandable if they had become upset over losing what little cash they had at the time, but nothing even remotely that laudable had gotten them riled up. What angered them was that Candy had not only burned their cash but also a discount coupon they had set aside to buy cigarettes, which had been an unpardonable sin from the standpoint of her nicotine-addicted parents. Her father had cruelly punished his six–year–old daughter by pressing her arm against a hot stove, solely because she had innocently burned a few dollars and a discount coupon that had been set aside to buy smokes.

After Candy calmed down and finally fell to sleep, I lay there beside her, wide awake with my eyes full of tears, unable to stop thinking about what I had been told. Thinking about it made me feel sick at heart. *Do such awful things really happen?* I exclaimed to myself. *Are there parents out there so monstrous that they could punish a little girl in such a cruel way for making a trivial and innocent mistake?* Yes, I realized, there really are parents who do things that bad, and parents of that kind had been the cause of my own precious wife's troubled mind.

Rick and Belinda surely had to have been highly puzzled as we left their place the next day, wondering what on earth was going on with us. They didn't say anything, though, probably because they thought we were having some sort of argument. They just wished us well, then invited us to come back any time we liked.

NOT LONG AFTER WE got home from our vacation out west, I had a disturbing nightmare of my own, one much like the ones that Candy had been having for as long as we'd been married.

My nightmare was about a large and hateful older man who was whipping a young girl with a broad belt. Holding her steady by gripping her tiny upper left arm like a vise with his huge left hand, he swung a belt held in his right hand as hard as he could. The lashes he meted out were not gentle; he was giving her a brutal whipping, delivering it with grim determination while his face was contorted in rage. I heard every slap of the belt against her frail little back, buttocks, and legs through the thin cotton dress she was wearing, and each stroke landed with stinging, sickening effect.

The little girl didn't cry out, nor did she try to avoid the blows in any way. She just stood there, stoically bearing the pain, knowing she was utterly powerless to prevent what was happening. The beating seemed to go on forever.

Watching from a close distance as it went on, I squirmed and twisted in anger from where I was partially hidden, vicariously experiencing the sting of every blow. The man and girl seemed not to notice me, even though I was looking right at both of them. As I looked on, the single thought that rang through my mind was that *some things that happen in our lives can never be forgotten.*

I woke up a little while later, tingly and shaken, after having one of my worst nightmares ever. It was so bad that from time to time I still think about it today. I recall it well enough to accurately describe the faces of the man and girl, even though I don't know who they were and I don't recall ever having seen either one of them. The little girl was not Candy, and the large man was not her father.

After this ghastly dream, any lingering thoughts I had about making further inquiries into Candy's past came to a screeching halt. I couldn't bear the thought of stoking any more of the bad dreams she had had in the past, nightmares like the one I'd just had. I was upset even before I had it, but afterwards I became more of a basket case than ever. Thinking that my own nightmare had been an example of the kind that Candy had been experiencing over the years (and I sincerely suspected it was), there was no way in hell I wanted to be responsible for any more of that.

MY FIRST UNMISTAKABLE WARNING that Candy was becoming sufficiently mentally unbalanced to be of danger to herself or to others occurred in the wake of yet another incident that happened without warning, an event that came about so unexpectedly as to leave me reeling. I didn't appreciate the full significance of it until after I regained my composure, which is the only reason I have to offer for not reacting as I should have at the time.

It happened during yet another excursion away from Texas, this time for a short visit with my parents at their home in Stockton, California. The highlight of our trip was to be a personal reunion between Candy and her younger brother Tommy, who she'd told me about but with whom she had had no contact since their family was broken up. A few months earlier, Tommy had somehow managed to get in touch with her. Because he happened to live only a few hours away from Stockton, the two of them decided that Stockton would be a convenient place for them to meet up.

They eagerly anticipated their reunion, and, I have to admit, I was excited about it as well.

Candy relished the thought of getting reacquainted with Tommy, but she was a bit apprehensive because it was impossible to anticipate how their visit would go or where it might lead. They hadn't seen each other since they were young kids. They had, though, exchanged pictures and talked on several occasions by telephone in preparation for their two-person get-together.

Tommy well remembered how they had been neglected by their parents, but his worst problems really hadn't begun until after their family was broken up and he became a ward of the court. After being placed in the foster care system, he was bounced from home to home for years. He was profoundly damaged by how he was treated in one of those households, and he said he had never fully recovered from the experience. That this was true had come through loud and clear during telephone calls and through photographs he and Candy had exchanged. He'd had hard time of it. Every shot showed that he was a wounded and struggling human being.

We stayed in my folks' spare bedroom the Friday evening we arrived in Stockton, and then slept in on Saturday morning because we had gotten in so late. Earlier in the morning, my folks had quietly gotten up and gone shopping in preparation for the barbecue dinner they'd planned for the evening. Tommy arrived early, just after my folks left but before I got out of the shower. He was greeted at the door by Candy, the older sister he hadn't seen for many long years.

Surprisingly, Tommy showed up shaken and upset, trembling in the wake of an incident that had occurred only a few minutes earlier. He was so clearly out of sorts that Candy immediately took notice and asked him what on earth had happened. His response was "Nothing, not a thing," followed by a plea for her just to forget about it so that they could enjoy the little time they would have together. "I'll be fine," he said, "if you'll just give me a minute."

Candy, though, wasn't having any of it. The two of them

barely had enough time to exchange a decent greeting before she was able to pry the basic facts out of him. Even though she really didn't understand *exactly* what had happened to him a few minutes earlier, she had heard enough. She wasn't about to let another member of her family be traumatized or another instance of abuse go unpunished, especially when it came to a kid like Tommy, upon whom the ill effects of having endured a traumatic childhood glared out like a beacon through his mannerisms, demeanor, and everything he said or did.

Tommy told her that he had had a run-in with "two guys in an old gray primer-coated pickup truck" at a nearby shopping center he'd stopped at on his way to their meeting. It happened because he moved out of the parking lot in his old car a little too slowly to satisfy the two men behind him in the gray truck. To show their irritation, they bumped his car from behind, just to deliver the message that he was getting on their nerves. When he felt the bump, Tommy stopped and got out of his car to go talk with them, thinking that an accident had occurred.

There was no real damage to either of the two old vehicles, but the two men tore into Tommy just as soon as they got out of their truck. Upon noting that he was a diminutive, timid, hesitant sort of guy, they decided to bully and intimidate him for a while before going on their way.

Although he apologized and tried his best to get them to leave him alone, they shoved him around, called him vile names, and challenged him to fight. After daring him to report the incident, they kicked a dent in the rear side panel of his car and then both of them hacked and spit on it before they drove off. They drove out of the parking lot laughing and jeering, leaving Tommy quaking in his boots.

Because he was too shaken to know what else to do, Tommy had just driven on over to my parents' home for his reunion with Candy. He arrived still quaking and highly upset, but he didn't intend to say a word about what had happened. What he didn't count on, though, was the forcefulness of his older sister. Candy was persuasive enough to pry out of him that he'd stopped at the shopping center to buy a bouquet of flowers for his long-lost sibling just before the incident happened.

Wounds of the kind Tommy suffered as a child are never fully forgotten, and Candy knew in an instant that he hadn't been able to stand up for himself. The neglect he had endured may not have been the direct cause of what took place a few minutes before, but his reaction definitely was; it was as obvious as a huge neon sign.

Candy flew into an absolute rage as she listened to Tommy's explanation of what happened, and that's describing her reaction mildly. Tommy, who was sitting shaken on my parents' living room couch, was as rattled by his sister's reaction as he had been by the incident itself.

"They did what?" she yelled. "Who in the hell do they think they are!" She was so loud I could hear her yelling from down the hall and inside the shower stall.

Tommy started shouting, too, in his case to do what he could to get her calmed down. "Sis," he yelled, "don't worry about it; it's all over now. Those hoodlums don't matter a bit to me, and they aren't worth any more trouble. I'm here to see you, not to worry about them."

When I stepped out of the shower dripping wet and stuck my head out of the bathroom door to ask what in the devil was going on, I saw Candy raging around the house, rummaging through dresser drawers and looking in closets. At first I thought she was just being irrational, until suddenly it dawned on me that she was looking for my father's gun, the small pistol he carried for protection when he and Mom traveled across the country in their motor home. Dad had shown it to us during an earlier visit.

"You and Tommy would let them get away with running over us like that, the cowards, but I sure won't!" she raged, not really addressing either of us in particular. "Nobody is ever going to do that to me again!"

Yelling at her from the bathroom door, I said, "Candy, would you please calm down until I can get dressed?"

I heard Tommy exclaiming yet again as well, this time

saying, "Those guys are nothing but a couple of nobodies, punks who get their kicks by bullying other people. They were just showing off, and they're not worth any more trouble, so let's just forget about it."

When she couldn't find my dad's gun, Candy grabbed a fireplace poker instead, gripping it so tightly her knuckles were white while her face was red and contorted with rage. Before I could get dressed to reach her, she had run out of the house and jumped in our car. Holding the poker in one hand and the steering wheel in the other, she squealed out of the driveway, locked in a black rage and hot in pursuit of two unknown and, according to Tommy, large and burly men in an old primer gray pickup truck down at the market.

My last view as I ran half-naked and dripping wet with only a towel around me into my mom and dad's living room was of her in our car, skidding around the corner and past the stop sign at the end of the street as she gunned for all it was worth. All I could think of is what might if happen if Candy, who weighed about 120 pounds soaking wet, happened to find the two men, knowing that thugs like them might knock her in the head or do something even worse if they were challenged. By this time, I was just as shaken as Tommy.

She had torn away in such a rage that I was scared witless. I knew what she'd been going through at home, but I had never seen her behave as wildly as she did that morning. As quickly as I could, I threw on my clothes so Tommy and I could jump in his old car and go after her. We tried our best to catch her before she could get to the market, but by the time we got on the main street, she had already disappeared.

We drove straight back to the store parking lot where the run-in had occurred, then up and down nearby streets in hopes of spotting our car or the primer grey truck. After thirty minutes that seemed like two hours, we simultaneously realized that we might never find her doing what we were doing. At that point, we rushed back to my parents' home to call for help from the police.

Just before the cops showed up at my parents' home,

Candy suddenly screeched back onto their driveway, still shaking and in an absolute rage. After accusing both of us — Tommy and me — of being too cowardly to go after the two guys, she demanded that we immediately call the police. Just as I was explaining that they had already been called, two officers stopped at the front of the house and were in the process of stepping out of their patrol car.

As soon as she saw the cops, Candy ran back out the front door and headed directly towards them, proceeding — even before they had a chance to get out of the vehicle — to scream out an angry and basically incoherent version of what had happened that morning. It was the first and only time I'd ever seen her like that, totally irate and completely unhinged. It scared the hell out of me, just like it did Tommy. It had to have been a real shock for her already shaken brother to see her unfolding in that way, all of a sudden and right in front of the cops. He had to have been thinking his long-lost sister was a real psycho, so much so that he probably regretted having looked her up.

Candy angrily demanded that the cops immediately head out in pursuit of the two men who had accosted Tommy, practically ordering them to charge into action. Knowing that they would have little to no chance of finding the perpetrators without a full description as well as the exact location where the incident took place, the officers' first reaction was to insist on collecting information before they would take another step. To do that, their first order of business had to be getting her calmed down enough to be explicit about what had taken place. As simple and as reasonable as this may sound, it wasn't easy to do under the circumstances.

Because the officers' lack of urgency made her even angrier, Candy immediately accused them of cowardice, just as she had Tommy and me. She was absolutely beside herself with anger. Despite her insults, the two cops wouldn't do anything until the information they needed was collected. Then, once they had it in hand, they said they'd drive around to see if the two men could be located.

The officers calmed her down a bit by promising to get back immediately if they spotted the primer gray truck. It couldn't have been much more obvious that they thought their complainant was overwrought as well as just a little bit eccentric, if not outright crazy. After pointedly cautioning the three of us, especially her, not to try to enforce the law on our own, they left to cruise around in search of the truck Tommy had described.

Even then, though, Candy still didn't calm down. She continued to storm around the house, as mad as hell over what the two men had done to her brother. For some time, she stayed too worked up and agitated to deal with the incident rationally, but, after a while, I was able to persuade her to take a sleeping pill to calm her nerves and relax for a few hours. After some additional consolation from Tommy and a little time for the medicine to take effect, she finally calmed enough to get some rest.

Even though Candy had finally settled down, Tommy remained too upset to know how to deal with the situation. Poor guy; he'd come to see us in hope of an emotional lift from his older sister, but now he was worse off than ever. When I suggested that it might be best to hold off until our next visit with my parents, he didn't disagree. Even so, the mystified and troubled expression I saw on his face as he drove away left me feeling sick at heart.

There was no doubt in my mind that he had driven away blaming himself for what had happened. On an occasion when he ought to have been uplifted by enjoying a little quality time with a loving sister, he'd been knocked down yet again. *Lord,* I thought, *doesn't anything ever go right for these kids?*

That Candy had avoided a serious car accident or getting a speeding ticket or being beaten senseless by two thugs that crazy day has to be chalked up as pure blind luck, because any one of those outcomes could easily have happened.

When my parents returned home from their own trip to the market, they were mystified to hear that the happy occasion they expected to take part in had gone awry. I just told them Candy wasn't feeling well, then said that she'd decided to nap for an hour or so. Tommy, I said, had called to say that he'd gotten hung up, and would have to reschedule his visit for some other time. My folks had no clue what had really happened. Filling them in would only have made them as upset as we were, and that wouldn't have helped anyone.

Candy was better by late that evening, but she remained as angry as ever about what had happened. In an uncertain and clumsy effort to put the whole thing behind us, I did my best to make light of it by teasing her about having tried to take on two full grown men with a fireplace poker. Her reaction had been so off the deep end and totally out of character for her that I didn't know what else to do.

She was a little sheepish and apologetic about some of what she'd said, but it was clear that she hadn't forgotten what happened and that she hadn't stopped thinking about those two nameless guys, not even for an instant. What would have happened, I couldn't help but wonder, if she had found my father's gun and then located the two guys?

Even though my parents sensed that some sort of tug–of–war or silent argument was going on between us, they didn't push the issue. Like my brother Rick and his wife Belinda, they suspected that trouble was afoot, but thought it would be best not to intrude.

We left for home the next day shaken and scared. We knew that something totally off the wall could have happened if Candy had been able to find the two guys; they might have knocked her in the head and dumped her body in an alley, for example, or she might have shot both of them, and either outcome would have been disastrous.

FROM THE DATE OF our visit with my parents, my time at home with Candy became a matter of living on pins and needles.

I woke up one night thinking about what Candy had said after her brother's run-in with the guys in the old gray truck. What popped into mind was not just the fact that she'd gotten so angry, but the wording she'd used after Tommy told her what happened: "Nobody," she had said, "is ever going to do that *to me* again." Why, I wondered, had she said *to me* rather than *to him*, when it was Tommy who'd been roughed up?

There wasn't a doubt in my mind that she had personalized the incident in a way that made her just as much of a victim as her brother. Her desire to even the score by striking back had been motivated as much by her own need to defend herself as by wanting to defend him. These two needs, I realized, had been inextricably intertwined.

We needed help, and we needed it fast. But to my everlasting shame, I was too deeply locked in denial and so nearly overcome by problems of my own that I didn't do a single thing to get her the help she so very clearly needed.

IT WAS WRENCHING BEYOND description to be at the side of the woman upon whom all my hopes and dreams were centered when she started losing control over her thoughts and actions, when her descent into irrationality — what most people would refer to as a nervous breakdown — became so clearly observable as to be unmistakable.

Our efforts were focused on doing whatever we could think of to keep ourselves on track. We tried to conceal our worries from one another, hoping against hope that we would somehow be able to heal ourselves and thereby get back to normal. I feared for her what I feared for myself — a complete emotional collapse, one that would tear me down so completely that we might never fit together again.

OVERCOME BY A PROFOUND sense of foreboding, I began to wonder *when*, not *if*, our lives were going to fall apart. It may come across as indefensible for me to admit to it now, but, strangely, I felt as if something of great import *ought* to happen to us. Through some sort of misguided and explainable sense of empathy, I think I felt much like what Candy was feeling at the time — outraged over the injustices that had been committed against her, her siblings, and other members of her extended family. I knew she felt like lashing out, mainly because I felt the same way myself.

Although it was abundantly clear that Candy might not be able to work herself out of the condition she was in, I still didn't make a move to set up the professional help she needed. In hindsight, it seems incredible that I hesitated to seek out some sort of intervention before her mental torment became too severe for a fragile person to handle on her own. I didn't, though, I just kept on keeping on, in the same way I had in the past. I lived my day–to–day life as if I were caught in that brief instant between when it becomes clear that a car wreck is about to occur but just before it actually does, mesmerized and frozen in place yet powerless to stave off the inevitable.

21

NIGHTMARE AT PECAN

THE PEOPLE WHO LIVED at Pecan Plantation were no different from those who lived anywhere else, but there were a few residents whose behavior really stood out. As a case in point, one gentleman — a surgeon, I think — was always so intent on avoiding even the most routine kinds of interaction with his neighbors that on occasion his behavior came across not only as eccentric but also as a little bit bizarre. Each morning as he went out for a run as a means of exercising himself and his dog, he would literally turn around and temporarily walk or jog backwards, just to avoid making eye contact with anyone who happened to pass him on the street. He tried to disguise what he was doing, but it couldn't have been any clearer that he just didn't want to be bothered with exchanging friendly waves or nods with anyone who wanted to greet him. He didn't discriminate; he behaved the same towards everyone, for no apparent reason other than that he just didn't want to socialize with his neighbors. Admittedly, he was an odd duck, but other residents of the development had some equally noticeable proclivities.

More than a few of the male residents, for example, were so pleased with themselves for having become highly successful retirees that they felt a subconscious need to make sure others knew it as well. Through loud and boisterous bonhomie out on the golf course or in settings such as the clubhouse lounge or dining room, they acted out in ways that made sure their less fortunate neighbors (guys like me, that is) knew how well they'd done. Others had no choice but to listen, whether they wanted to or not.

In a different but related way, there were female retirees (often the spouses of the aforementioned male residents) who tended to be highly ostentatious in terms of dress, coiffure, accents, jewelry, and other bling in which they bedecked themselves. For some of them, even the vehicles they drove a few miles to various functions at the clubhouse had been chosen for the express purpose of making a nonverbal statement.

Crowing over accomplishments, in other words, was not an uncommon phenomenon at Pecan, usually not in the form of outright self-laudatory comments (although there was some of that, too) but in terms of behavior. Another way of putting this would be to say that there were those who, if they had been wise or lucky enough to have accumulated a lot, felt a compelling need to let everyone else know all about it. Because people who behave in this way can be found in any communal environment, most of us learn that the best way to deal with folks of this kind is to ignore them whenever we can. Turning the other check is *almost* always preferable to confrontation of any form. There are times, though, when those who have bump up against those who don't in ways that are impossible to ignore, times when taking the high road just doesn't seem like the right thing to do. On occasions of this kind, unpleasant things can happen in even the most pleasant of settings.

A WEEKEND UNLIKE ANY OTHER

THE MORNING OF SATURDAY, April 13, 2002, began in the same way as many others just like it — weekends on which I had to put in extra hours to stay on top of a job that had become exceedingly busy on a fairly regular basis. We were barely hanging on at home, but I was still in the process of proving myself at work. I had never worked just to get by; I had always endeavored to excel; and the way in which I approached my duties had not changed. I knew Candy shouldn't be left alone in her condition, but, because I was determined to do my best on the job, I went in anyway.

What we had intended to do that morning was what we normally did on Saturdays when work or other commitments did not prevent it: sleep in for an hour or so and then go to the club dining room for a leisurely breakfast followed by a cover–to–cover reading of the *Fort Worth Star–Telegram* and our local newspaper, the *Hood County News*. Going to the clubhouse Saturday morning had become something of a ritual for us; it was a welcome respite from the unspoken pressure that characterized our daily lives.

When our weekends were disrupted by my having to work, Candy usually went to the club later in the morning to meet up with me for lunch. I would skip breakfast to get to the college early, hoping to finish whatever had to be done as quickly as possible to rejoin her. Handling it that way typically left us with a long afternoon and evening to do with as we pleased. On that particular Saturday, we had agreed to meet back at the club for lunch, knowing that I would come in hungry after having eaten nothing at all.

BREAD AND BUTTER RUDENESS

AFTER I LEFT FOR work that morning, Candy went to the dining room at the club to have something light as she waited for me, just as she said she would. Upon arrival, she was seated at a table adjacent to one occupied by two other guests — a retired couple about ten years senior to us in age. The three of them were the only guests in the dining room at the time.

Candy told me after the fact that she had found it impossible not to notice that the two people were frowning and extremely annoyed, and she, of course, couldn't help but wonder why they were so upset. It was finding out what had gotten them so riled up that put in motion an imbroglio that sprang up out of nowhere only a few minutes thereafter.

The couple were upset because the quality of service they had received that morning in the dining room had been very poor. They had had to wait too long for their breakfast to be served, and, when it finally arrived, it had been sitting for so long that their food was cold. They had watched as their young waiter, Derrick

Cole, whom Candy and I had gotten to know during many previous morning visits to the club, laughed and joked with his equally young co-workers while their meal cooled on the service counter. They were also annoyed by the fact that the appalling slow service they'd received was likely to make them late for their reserved tee time on the golf course.

When Derrick returned to their table, the couple wasted no time in taking him to task for ruining what should have been a good breakfast and for possibly making them late for what they had expected to be an enjoyable round of golf on a perfectly beautiful day. They had the kid dead to rights, so they proceeded to work him over like a rag mop. They didn't hesitate, for example, to point out how they had watched as he and his co-workers became so caught up in horseplay that they didn't even notice that a customer's food was ready.

Derrick knew he'd dropped the ball, so he just stood there with a hang-dog expression and apologized profusely as he tried to take his punishment like a man. "There was no question that they had a legitimate complaint," Candy said later on, "but what those pompous so-called *adults* did to the kid from that point on made them even guiltier of inappropriate behavior than the kid himself."

Many of the waiters at the club were just young people from the local area, often students out of Granbury who took jobs at the club to pay their ways through college. Some of them, though, were sons or daughters of people who lived right there in our development, people who thought their kids ought to work for whatever they got. Young people were generally delighted to land a job at the club, in equal parts because the work environment was exceptionally pleasant and customers tended to be quite friendly. In addition, they occasionally were given generous but unauthorized tips. By club rule, they weren't allowed to accept gratuities, but some customers chose to give them anyway. Some of them, in fact — people like us, for example — absolutely insisted that they be accepted. Because their base salary wasn't particularly high, any tips they received were, of course, welcomed as supplementary income.

While most patrons thought highly of the club wait staff, it was well known that they got carried away on occasion — joking and laughing and indulging in lively and boisterousness behavior, especially when they weren't closely supervised. Because they were young people, it wasn't uncommon for them to act out once in a while. This particular day, unfortunately, had turned out to be one of those occasions.

Derrick, the waiter who was being grilled that morning, happened to be a young guy Candy had gotten to know fairly well during our many previous trips to the club. She had befriended him, she said, because he had reminded her so much of a boy she once dated in high school. She enjoyed talking with him so much that we always asked to be seated in his section if he was on duty. My kidding her about trying to relive her high school days through bantering with Derrick had become one more reason why we enjoyed dining at the club as much as we did.

Most adults accept the fact that dealing with young people can require a little extra patience on their part, and most of us are willing to allow them a fairly long leash; in fact, we tend to forgive behavior on the part of youngsters that we wouldn't tolerate from individuals our own age. Human nature being what it is, however, there are some adults in every environment who are not the least bit tolerant of mistakes made by anyone, young or old. There are people who want — and, in fact, even expect — their own mistakes and shortcomings to be forgiven, but who rarely bother to be equally gracious toward others. Pecan Plantation, unfortunately, had as great a share of folks like this as any other place.

It was the way in which the supposedly mature couple sitting aside her railed against their young waiter that Candy found too upsetting to tolerate. Their reaction went far beyond the level of scolding the young guy clearly deserved. She ought to have dismissed their behavior as nothing more than the snobbishness and rudeness it really was, but Candy's terrible frame of mind caused her to blow what they were doing totally out of proportion.

Because they'd worked themselves into a cranky and

condescending sort of mood, the couple proceeded to tear into Derrick in an unnecessarily nasty way. Loudly criticizing not only his service but also his manners, they tried their best to embarrass him as much as they could. On top of that, they threatened to report him to his immediate supervisor as well as to Mark Bradley, the overall manager of the Pecan Plantation Country Club. Derrick was trying his best to do to apologize to them, but it wasn't enough; they clearly *wanted* to pull his chain, so they kept on turning the screw.

From where she was seated adjacent to the couple, Candy had overheard their interaction from beginning to end. She said she tried to keep quiet and stay out of it, but the behavior of the couple seemed so unreasonable and unnecessarily mean that she wasn't able to hold her tongue. She said she just stood up in place without even thinking about it, saying spontaneously and before she even knew what she was doing: "Okay, okay; you've made your point. You're right, and he knows it. Why don't you leave him alone now? Haven't you belittled him enough? You're the adults here, you know."

The two people, who were already worked up and irritated, promptly told Candy to "mind her own damned business" and became angrier than ever. Then, clearly because they had become angrier, they ordered Derrick to go get Mark, the club manager. Derrick, who by this point was completely mortified and totally convinced that he would be fired for sure if the club manager were to be brought out to deal with a brouhaha he had created, tried even harder to mollify them by groveling even more and apologizing more profusely. He practically kowtowed before them, but by now the couple had decided to rub the kid's nose in it as much as they could, if for no other reason than just to spite Candy.

"When those two obnoxious people sent Derrick to get Mark," said Candy, "that was the last straw. I got so mad I couldn't see straight, because I knew that they were really angrier about what I said than they were with Derrick. Instead of helping him, I had only made matters worse. It was obvious that that hateful pair had decided to teach both of us a lesson at the same time."

When the two adult patrons, who were now red-faced in anger, demanded that he get his supervisor, Derrick had practically run out of the room to do as he was told. "From the hangdog expression on his face as he left," Candy said, "it was clear he thought he was doomed."

Their interaction really got out of hand after Derrick left the room, when all three of the supposed *adults* stood up and began exchanging insults and screaming at one another. Once they started going nose to nose, the angrier each of them became, until the gloves came off for real.

WRONG PLACE, WRONG TIME

"WHEN THOSE TWO POMPOUS, snotty people raised their voices and started shouting so close to my face that I could feel spittle hitting me," said Candy, "I lost all sense of where I was or what I was doing. The man, in particular, was bigger and angrier and more intimidating than he knew. When he yelled at me, he stayed right up in my face, clearly taking for granted that he would be able to intimidate me. His wife did the same thing, and I just couldn't stand it. In my mind, all I could think of was that bullying couple in the store who came down on us when Freddy and I were caught stealing food as kids. I screamed at them because I thought they were going to pull my hair and slap my face, just like they did back then." She said she even remembered calling the waiter *Freddy*, and that she thought for a moment he really *was* Freddy.

In her confused state of mind, she said she thought she was coming to the defense of her brother. As she saw the situation, the owners of the store were belittling an innocent young person in the same way she and Freddy had been belittled as hungry children. "It felt," she said, "like we were being bullied all over again, and it made me feel worthless and small the same way it did when we were kids. It just didn't seem right."

When Candy refused to back off and instead continued to press the argument with the two now exceedingly angry people, that's when a full-fledged spitting match really got under way. The waiter, who understandably felt largely responsible for their argument, had tried to cool them down before he left, but his clumsy efforts had done nothing but add more fuel to the fire.

Immediately after Derrick literally bounded out of the room to go get our club manager, Candy said that she finally lost all control. She grabbed the nearest thing she could get her hands on — a glass of water that was on her table — and threw it right in the man's face. She said she had decided long ago that she was never going to stand for that sort of treatment again, not without fighting back.

When that happened, the man's wife immediately jumped to his defense. "My husband couldn't hit a woman," she said later on during our trial, "but I sure as hell could. That crazy bitch started it by throwing water on Carl, and we had every damned right to defend ourselves." Candy said that when the woman stepped forward and slapped her hard across the face, that was absolutely the last straw.

"That hateful witch couldn't have done anything worse to me," she said, "because that's the same thing that was done to me back when my brother and I were hungry kids." No one was on hand to witness what happened next, but Candy said that the whole situation went black for her after she was slapped. The woman said at trial that Candy went after her immediately, scratching and slapping and cursing and screaming as if she'd lost her mind — which, in fact, she actually had.

When her husband jumped between the two women to prevent them from scratching each other's eyes out, he got a little more physical than he intended. "He didn't actually hit me," Candy said. "He just shoved or pushed me really hard, much harder than he realized. He was so big and angry looking, I knew I was helpless against him, but I made up my mind then and there that the two of them weren't going to do this to me again."

In the couple's own words, "She screamed and cussed us like a raving lunatic, claiming that she 'didn't steal anything,' that 'they'd better keep their damned hands off of Freddy,' and that 'they'd better not pull my hair again.' She was," they said, "obviously out of her mind, a real nut case." The man said, "If she had come at Emily again, I'd have knocked her flat on her ass. She was really out of it, practically berserk. Neither one of us had ever seen anything like it."

Candy, seeing that it was hopeless to try to fight back against two people who were physically so much larger and stronger, suddenly turned around and ran out of the club, screaming, "You're not going to get away with it again!"

The couple by this time were fully convinced that they had come into contact with an insane person. They yelled back insults and curses of their own as she rushed out of the dining room, obviously thinking that their point had been made and that they had won the battle by having run Candy out of the place in tears, totally disheveled and distraught.

Most of these events took place when there was no one in the dining room but the three participants. Candy ran out of the restaurant just as Derrick returned with his boss, hoping to get their argument calmed down. They passed Candy in the doorway as she rushed out in a rage, but she said that she didn't even notice them.

The couple, to their credit, I found out much later on, snapped back to their senses soon after Candy departed, probably because they finally realized how ridiculous they would have looked if any of their friends had walked in while the two women were engaged in a physical catfight of the sort they associated with the lower orders. Once it finally registered how embarrassed they would be if such a thing were to happen, they cooled down rather quickly. Having regained a modicum of their customary composure, they wanted nothing more than to, as they put it later on, "get their butts out of the clubhouse as quickly as possible and get on with their damned round of golf."

"We're going to report this whole affair through proper channels," they swore as they passed Derrick and Mark, "and we're going to do whatever we can to do to find out who that crazy bitch is and make sure she gets kicked out of Pecan."

All poor Derrick and his supervisor Mark had been able to do after they rushed back into the dining room was stand there with their mouths wide open, completely taken aback and utterly at a loss in terms of figuring out what had just happened, much less deciding what ought to be done about it.

The couple's greatest concern at that moment had switched from the argument to considerations of a more immediate personal nature; all they wanted for the moment was to make sure that none of their friends or acquaintances or other members of the club had a chance to see them flustered and red-faced and embarrassed while their hair was messed and their clothing was in disarray. Their final words to the mortified waiter and his confused manager as they gathered up their personal items and marched out of the dining room were "You're sure as hell going to hear from us later on, but for right now, the two of you should just get on back to your work." The final settling of accounts, the couple had decided, would have to take place later.

MADNESS IN THE MIDST OF PLENTY

CANDY, THOUGH, FOLLOWING HER unintelligible screaming match with the two people in the dining room, had not forgotten their argument for a moment; even though she had charged out of the building in tears, she was still in a blind rage. Unbeknownst to the couple, who, it should be pointed out, after having temporarily lost their cool in response to what they considered to be insultingly bad behavior, would most likely have eventually passed her off as a nut case and gone on about their business — if, that is, Candy hadn't left the club for the express purpose of retrieving the handgun we had hidden away at home. It was at this point that the unsuspecting couple became two very unfortunate people indeed.

There was no way they could have known that slapping Candy and screaming in her face was the worst possible thing they could have done to her. Their treatment of her was so reminiscent of past injustices that it drove her right over the edge.

I've been asked many times after the shooting why we kept a handgun in our home when we lived in a gated development that was widely considered to be as safe and secure as any community in our state, but, as reasonable as the question appears to be, I've resented it since the first it was put to me. Asking it implied that there might have been some level of advanced intent or pre-planning to do harm on our part when there had been no premeditation of any kind at all.

The gun was in our house for the most innocent of reasons — because the elderly woman who owned the home before us had left it there. She and husband had purchased it for their own protection after his retirement and their move to Pecan, back before they got used to living out in the country. By the time they figured out that they were living in the safest place they had ever lived, they had forgotten all about the gun. Even after her husband passed away, the widow had felt no fear in the night; the development was that calm. When her heirs sold her belongings at auction and then put her home up for sale, they overlooked the gun. I found it buried in insulation between rafters in the attic when I was remodeling and restoring the place.

It was a single-action 22 caliber handgun, still in the holster that came with it upon purchase. It was inside a plastic bag and wrapped up in what had once been oiled cloth but that had long since dried out. It had been in its hiding between rafters for so many years that there were rust spots on the barrel and the hammer was stiff to cock and the trigger mechanism could not be easily pulled. Until the day Candy fired it, it hadn't been used for years, not by us, anyway, and, maybe, for all we knew, not even by anyone.

Candy and I couldn't decide what to do with the gun after we found it, but we eventually concluded that it would be a good idea to keep it on hand, *just in case.* In case of what? Well, we really didn't know. As I've already mentioned, we lived in a development where there was hardly any danger of home intrusion or burglary, much less a personal assault. We kept it, I suppose, only because it was already there, not because we really thought it might be needed.

After we decided to keep the gun, we were very careful and deliberate when it came to hiding it in our house. Like everybody else, we had heard stories about freak accidents associated with keeping a weapon in a home. On top of that, we were well aware of Candy's emotional condition and the fact that she had done some sleepwalking in the past. To deal with these concerns, we separated the bullets from the gun as a safety measure. We made it her assignment to hide the bullets and mine to hide the gun itself. Our thought was that if we ever brought it out of hiding, it would have to be the result of a conscious mutual decision. Being cautious people, we wanted to avoid any chance of anything untoward happening.

What I did not know was that Candy had accidentally discovered my hiding place for the gun one day while she was cleaning at home, and that she had just not thought to say anything to me about it. She knew, therefore, where both the gun and the bullets were located. Before she raged away from the club that day, she knew where she was going and exactly what she intended to do when she got there. She left in blind anger, intent on getting even with the people who had slapped her face and screamed at her.

After leaving the club, she ran as quickly as she could out to where our car was parked at the front of the building. Still in a fury over what had happened, she started it up and stomped on the accelerator as hard as she dared. Screeching around corners and running through several stop signs, she made a beeline trip back to our house to get what she was after.

Our house was less than five minutes away from the club and, like many other residents at Pecan Plantation, we never bothered to lock our doors. Our gun was in her hands only a minute after she got home. After loading it as quickly as she could while shaking with anger, she was back at the club in less than ten minutes.

Stomping on the brakes and skidding to a halt at the curb

in front of the clubhouse, she left the engine running and flung open the door. Upon jumping out of her car, she ran up the front steps just as fast as she could. With the gun in hand and blood in her eye, she ran through the front door and back into the empty foyer.

Once inside the building, she ran across the foyer and back to the dining room in search of the couple who had offended her. Normally, a receptionist is on duty whenever the club is open, but there was no one at the desk at that particular moment; the desk clerk had gone back to the kitchen for a few minutes, hoping to talk with kitchen staff about the strange commotion that had taken place a little while earlier. It was unusual for any form of physical altercation to happen at Pecan, which meant that the one that had taken place earlier that morning drew quite a lot of attention — a whole lot more, in fact, than the offended couple wanted it to.

Having straightened their clothing and combed their hair and calmed down a little bit after leaving the dining room, the couple had gone to the dressing room to put on cleated golfing shoes and pick up their clubs. They were in the process of leaving the clubhouse to play their round when Candy charged in to confront them for a second time.

Without a moment of hesitation or uttering a single word of warning, Candy ran right up into the faces of the two startled people and started yelling. "Who the hell do you people think you are?" she said. "You're not going to get away with it this time!" After that, she aimed our old-west styled gun at them from only a few feet away. The couple recoiled in horror at the sight of the screaming banshee of a woman holding a gun, but they had no chance to protect themselves. Before they could grasp what was happening, Candy started shooting.

At point blank range, she shot the man twice, grazing his cheek with one shot and hitting the outside of his upper right leg with the other. She shot at but missed the man's wife, too, who had been a step or two behind her husband as they walked into the hall. Instinctively, both of them had raised their hands and arms to protect themselves, but it was too late. If Candy's aim had been just a little bit better, there's no doubt that she would have shot both of them dead center. As it was, though, both of the man's wounds were superficial. Even so, the shooting had to have terrified them, especially since it had taken place in only an instant and without a word of warning.

When the poor man, who had already been wounded twice, finally realized that Candy was trying her best to shoot him again and that he was still in mortal danger, he bolted right past his wife and out of the dining room. It was an instinctive reaction that took place without any regard for the welfare of his partner, who simply followed his lead and ran out of the room behind him. Candy, who was determined not to let them get away, ran out right behind them, struggling all the while to re-cock the rusty hammer of the old gun so that she could get off yet another shot.

With my ranting and raving wife right on their heels, the terrified couple stumbled across the foyer and down a twenty-five-foot hallway to the door of the stairwell that led from the main floor of the club up one level to the guest rooms and library and then back down again one level at the other end of the hall to the pro shop and snack bar below. After running down the flight of stairs and coming out in the pro shop on the bottom floor of the building, they wound up just below the dining room where they had had breakfast earlier.

CHAOS ON THE GREENS

SCATTERING GOLF CLOTHES and clubs and other items of merchandise behind them, the couple ran across the pro shop and headed for the double glass doors that opened onto the putting green about ten yards outside the door. With Candy close behind them, they burst out of the building, crossed the putting green, and ran onto the beautifully manicured green of the golf course at the same time, screaming at the top of their lungs. The couple screamed for someone to save them from Candy, while Candy's screams were all about how she was going to teach them a lesson they'd never forget.

Golfers already on the greens ran away in shock. No one had any idea what was happening. All anyone knew was that two of the three people who burst out of the pro shop were visibly bleeding from wounds. The man, in particular, looked hideously wounded, since the bullet to his face had scraped across his cheek and through part of his scalp. Visible red blood had drained and splattered down the front of his white Nike Men's Victory Solid Golf Polo Shirt and closely matching PGA Tour double pleated white shorts. Panting, sweating, shaking, and bloody, he was an absolute mess. His wife's attractive white golfing blouse and skirt were smeared with blood, in her case from having brushed up against her husband as she tried to help him. Both of them appeared to be bleeding profusely, when only one of them actually was. The third person in the group, Candy, had no blood on her at all, but she had a gun and was clearly just as agitated as the people she was chasing.

When the three of them suddenly charged out onto the green in a state of blind panic and looking terrified, those who saw them instinctively drew back and ran for cover. In the memorable words of one man who testified at trial later on, *"They scared the hell out of everybody out there. They looked like a bunch of crazy people, you know, especially after we saw all that blood on those white clothes and that one of those three screaming idiots had a gun in her hand. We got the hell away from them just as quickly as we could."*

So, instead of springing to the aid of the desperate couple, golfers on the green ran away from them. When someone yelled that an argument of some kind was going on, some who were present — specifically those who did not see the gun in Candy's hand — immediately jumped to the conclusion that a domestic blowout of some kind was taking place between the first two people, something that had gotten out of hand and then turned bloody. Later on during the trial, it was determined that this was why some of those who had run away from the couple had ignored Candy altogether. Their first impression had been that she was trying to put a stop to the argument, not that she was involved in it herself.

Golfers further out on the main course also noticed the commotion, but none of them had heard the shots that had been fired inside the club. Some of these folks started running back up toward the building to check out what was happening, thinking that an accident had taken place and that they might be able to help. Because some golfers were running toward the club while others were running away, the situation seemed as chaotic as hell.

Something of a chain reaction had occurred, with most people thinking that they'd been caught up in some sort of dangerous domestic blowout. "Nowadays," one man said later on, "you just can't tell when or where you're going to run into a real nut. We just ran to get away from whatever the hell was going on, following one another's lead without really thinking about it."

When several people yelled, "She's got a gun!", they panicked all the more.

Golfers scattered every which way, some running down the fairway and others down the street that led away from the circle driveway at the front of the clubhouse. Most of them were totally confused, not knowing for sure what they were in the middle of — a robbery, a shooting by a disgruntled employee, a blowout between estranged spouses or lovers, a terrorist attack, or whatever. For a little while, all scenarios seemed equally plausible. Only a few observers truly realized that two of their fellow club members were being chased down by an armed woman, a woman who was berserk enough to shoot them on the spot.

When the desk clerk and members of the kitchen staff ran out of the building to see what the commotion was about, they couldn't understand what was happening either. All they knew was that something serious was taking place, so they immediately called the Granbury police and urged the dispatcher to, in their own words, "Get some cops and an ambulance out here in a hurry because a shooting of some kind is going on right now. Hurry, please!"

Candy finally caught up with the two people when they stumbled and fell on the fairway, both alive but streaked with blood and still cringing in absolute terror. A hair piece and the scarf the woman had been wearing were hanging off the side of her head, and she was beside herself with fear. Her husband was yelling too, but now he was begging Candy not to shoot them again.

In full view of everyone, Candy hovered over them with the gun in her hand, pointing it directly at them and trying her best to get it to fire again. When it would not fire after three or four more clicks of the trigger, she just stood there shouting down at them, screaming the vilest curses she knew how to string together. It was only after she realized that she had no means of doing the couple any further harm, some conjectured after the fact, that she turned around and headed back toward the clubhouse.

No one was foolhardy enough to try to overtake her, since she still had the gun in her hand and there was no sure way of knowing whether it could be fired again or not. All anyone knew for sure was that the gun was still firmly in her control, and that was more than enough information to keep everyone at bay. No one dared approach her.

After reentering the pro shop, she walked back up the stairs to the first floor of the club. After reaching the wide entryway foyer, she walked over to one of the side couches and sat down, the gun still dangling from her hand.

Peering from around the corner of the hallway and into the foyer, some of the bolder golfers watched her, trying to figure out what she was going to do next. Noticing that she appeared to have a dazed look on her face and that she had gone into something of a trance, several of them slowly started edging over toward where she was sitting, golf clubs raised and ready to crack her over the head if she made a wrong move.

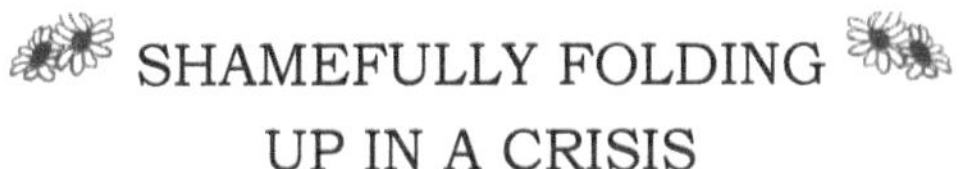

SHAMEFULLY FOLDING UP IN A CRISIS

TODAY, I KNOW EVERY detail of what happened that day by

heart, not only because I heard it explained in excruciating detail at least a thousand times during the painstaking investigation and the seemingly never-ending trial that took place many months later. Worse still, I had become a firsthand witness to the end part of what had taken place. By the time it was all over, not one iota of what had happened was unknown to me.

None of this was known to me, though, when I got back to the clubhouse that day. After leaving my car in the parking lot and heading toward the dining room to join Candy for lunch as planned, it became obvious that something unusual had just taken place. Because there were so many people outside and such a large commotion was in progress at the front door of the building, my immediate reaction was to skirt whatever was happening. Assuming that whatever it was would prove to be nothing more than a tempest in a teapot, I wasn't the least bit curious to learn any more about it. All I wanted at that moment was to resume the weekend with my wife and have a good lunch.

Not even bothering to ask anyone what the ruckus was about, I tried to avoid the whole affair by going around to a side hallway entrance, intent on reaching the dining room by entering the clubhouse in a roundabout way. This required walking up a hall stairway to the second floor, heading down the hallway to reach the library, crossing through it to reach the stairway that led back down to the first floor, and walking across the foyer to reach the doorway through which the dining room was entered.

From the library, a beautiful and ornate curved wooden interior stairway led back down to the foyer on the first floor. The entrance to the dining room was located a few steps away from the stairway landing, which was diagonally across the foyer from the front entry into the clubhouse. For me, as a frequent user of the library and dining room alike, it was a familiar path.

Curiosity didn't get the better of me until after I reached the second floor and headed through the library, where I stopped at the railing above the foyer side of the room. From this vantage point it was easy to check out whatever was going on below, since all I had to do was to look down into the foyer before heading on downstairs to the dining room. The open railing that bordered one side of the library directly overlooked the foyer and, therefore, provided an excellent view of whatever was happening below.

Just as I stepped up to the railing to see what was going on, Candy glanced up from where she was sitting across the room on the couch aside the far wall. She wasn't crying or distraught, but her face was so pale and her eyes were so blank it was impossible to tell whether she recognized me or not. When I saw that she was holding our gun in her hand, my mouth fell wide open and I froze in place right where I stood, unable to move a muscle.

After a few seconds, her glance shifted downward and over in the direction of the hallway that led to the pro shop on the floor below. Because it seemed that she was about to make a move, I saw a few guys raising golf clubs upright in their hands, watching her warily and edging toward her location. *That's strange,* I thought. *They're holding their clubs like weapons.* I watched as they slowly moved over to where Candy was sitting, looking as if they were going to beat her over the head at any moment.

After a few seconds, Candy's eyelids fluttered and her head slowly tilted downward. The gun dropped from her hand onto the lushly carpeted floor, and then, without a word, she fainted dead away, collapsing on the floor right beside the weapon.

What in holy hell is going on? was the only thought I was able to manage.

FROZEN IN SHOCK

AT THAT POINT, THE men lifted her up and held her securely by the arms so she couldn't do any more damage. They weren't hurting her in any way, but I still should have immediately rushed down to help. I didn't, though; I just stood right where I was, with my stomach at my feet, feeling like I'd been cemented to the floor.

All that registered in my awestruck mind was that she'd had our gun in her hand, a gun that was supposedly safely hidden away at home — a gun that no one else but her would have known anything about. I knew right away that it was ours because it was an easily recognizable old-fashioned western-style revolver. It suddenly looked incredibly sinister and wicked, lying there where it was, near the oriental-themed area rugs and the ornamental plants that decorated the clubhouse foyer. It seemed so out of place that I mentally recoiled, just from *thinking* about what its presence implied.

My head began to swim as I watched what was taking place below, and I really started to tremble when I noticed what appeared to be spots of blood on the highly waxed and otherwise spotless hallway floor, still red and fresh and shiny looking. Without even asking, I knew in an instant that Candy had done something unspeakable, that she had committed the sort of atrocious act I had been fearful of for a long time. I had no way of knowing it at the moment, but she had fainted only a short distance away from the dining room where the argument had taken place and the first shots had been fired that morning, just a few minutes prior to my arrival at the club.

I stood there, rooted in place and watching in abject fascination as events continued to unfold below me, my mouth still wide open and my feet and legs still unable to function.

Even though Candy was clearly woozy, the guys who had rushed forward held her securely. Before they raised her up, one had kneeled over her legs and others were securing her torso while others held her arms and hands. After lifting her back up to a sitting position on the couch, they finally had her firmly under control. After that, other people cautiously entered the foyer, every one of them staring intently at Candy and wondering if it was really safe to be there.

More golfers came into the room a few minutes later, this time supporting two bloodied and terribly upset people. The man they were steadying looked truly awful. Holding his mouth and jaw with both hands, he was bleeding profusely, and the front of his white golf shirt was covered with blood. The woman brought in with him was crying hysterically and there was blood all over the front of her outfit as well. Dressed in white clothing, they looked like they were about to bleed to death.

Dear God, I thought as I watched, *what on earth has she done?*

LOCAL AUTHORITIES ARRIVE

WHEN WORD FINALLY GOT around that it was safe to go back inside the club, people started flowing into the foyer from all directions. Everybody wanted to find out what had happened. Golfers came up from the pro shop, the putting green, and the fairway proper; guests came down from their rooms; and residents from the homes that clustered around the clubhouse either walked up or drove over in their cars.

Within a matter of minutes, the foyer became an even more crowded and confusing place, a room full of uncertain and tentative people. Everyone was trying to figure out what had happened, and why. The room literally buzzed with excited conversation, unfounded speculation, and agitated chatter, much of it focused on calming down the two unfortunates who appeared to have been shot.

Candy was sitting on the couch, still in a half-swoon, securely in the grip of four grim and determined older men. On another couch diagonally across the foyer sat the two bloodied victims, each one being comforted and supported by folks who had taken up positions around them. The victims and the perpetrator were separated by no more than thirty feet, but, at that moment, they didn't seem to be aware of one another's presence.

"Don't touch the gun and don't step in the blood," someone yelled out. "The cops will want to see the crime scene just as it is. They'll do whatever needs to be done when they get here."

Soon, three patrol cars and an ambulance skidded to a stop outside the building. Granbury police officers and an emergency medical team from the local hospital rushed into the room at the same time. While the EMTs tended to the two injured and bleeding people, responding officers were quickly surrounded by people who wanted to tell what they had seen. Everyone tried to describe what had happened at the same time, until, in only a few seconds, the room got so loud I could hardly make out a word.

Two people I immediately recognized appeared at the club as well, a man and a woman I knew to be reporters for our local newspaper, *The Hood County News*. Having learned by monitoring law enforcement radio that something newsworthy had happened at Pecan, they were on the scene right on the heels of the cops. As they exhaustively photographed and videotaped what they saw, they interviewed anyone who was willing to talk. Most of their effort, of course, was focused on Candy and the two bloodied people, before the three of them were taken away. After that, they turned their attention to the official investigators, presumed witnesses, and any bystander who was willing to talk.

It was impossible from where I stood to tell how seriously the two people had been hurt, but they looked for all the world like they were about to expire. The blood on their white clothing made their injuries look truly dreadful. They were taken away by ambulance only a few minutes later, strapped on stretchers and fitted with oxygen masks and the wires and tubes of emergency monitoring devices. Watching the ambulance tear away from the front of the club with its siren screaming made my knees go even more wobbly.

Soon, another police car arrived at the front of the club, it too with its siren blaring. Pulling in just as the ambulance departed, it carried two detectives who had been sent there to conduct a formal investigation. Before the detectives had a chance to enter the club, yet another vehicle pulled in beside them and skidded to a stop, this time Pecan Plantation's own ambulance and crew of four volunteers. It had taken them a while to get there, but there they were, ready to help as called for. They weren't needed, though, because the other ambulance crew had beaten them to the punch.

The two officers who arrived on the scene first were clearly relieved when the experienced detectives showed up to take charge of the investigation. As patrol officers, they weren't used to handling situations as complex as the one they'd suddenly walked into; it was beyond their level of training and expertise, and they knew it. The crime scene was totally confusing and, besides that, probably had already been irretrievably compromised.

The experienced detectives immediately restored order by directing everyone to take a seat in the dining room until they could be called out one at a time to provide statements. Along with members of the clubhouse staff, the patrol officers were directed to clear everyone out of the area until the crime scene was secure and the investigation could be completed. Once the foyer, dining room, hallway, stairwell, pro shop, and putting green were cleared of people, they posted signs and strung put perimeter tape to keep anyone else from entering those areas.

THE INVESTIGATION BEGINS

THE CROWD IN THE dining room buzzed with excited speculation as the investigators began calling witnesses out to the foyer one at a time to take down whatever they had to say. To preserve my perch on the second floor of the building, I stepped inside a utility closet that had a lock on the door but really wasn't locked and therefore could be opened at will. Like a fly on the wall, I was able to listen from upstairs without being seen to everything that went on in the lobby below. To anyone who had seen me coming in, I was no more than one more onlooker who had arrived at the site.

From my vantage point, I clearly overhead witnesses giving different versions of what had taken place. Several said with absolute certainty that there had been a marital dispute, that the wounded man and wife had shot one another, and that Candy had been nothing more than an innocent bystander who fainted when she saw what had happened. Another man said he thought the clubhouse dining room cash register had been robbed, and that thieves had shot two club members as they tried to flee the building. The more positive and credible of the interviewees, however, pointed directly to Candy, loudly and emphatically saying, "Hell no, she's the one behind the whole damned thing. She had the gun, and she did all the shooting." One witness after another pointed to Candy, glaring at her as they spoke.

Initially skeptical of comments made by the guys who were holding her down, the detectives quickly realized that, as unlikely as it seemed to them at first, the stunned, harmless looking woman they saw before them was, in fact, solely responsible for the melee that had taken place. They clearly had a hard time believing that an attractive, well-groomed, intelligent looking, middle-aged woman like her would have done such a thing, and most certainly not without some sort of provocation. They knew something highly unusual had taken place that day; their faces showed it plainly.

Others, too, were initially skeptical about Candy having played the key role in the incident, but I certainly wasn't. They had no clear understanding what had caused the incident, but I most certainly did. Even then, long before the police investigation was even close to being completed, I was already blaming myself for what had happened.

As soon as the detectives got a handle on what had taken place, they started shooting glances over to where Candy was sitting on the couch. I wasn't able to hear what they said, but I could see that it hadn't taken long for them to ascertain that she and she alone could explain what had happened that morning. After collecting all the statements and other information they needed, they moved on over to the couch, intent upon getting down to business with Candy.

With one detective sitting in front of her and the other at her side, they calmly and quietly tried to ask her a few questions. At that point they didn't know who she was since she had no identification with her at the time. She'd left her purse in our car, which was still parked just outside at the curb with the engine running; they hadn't identified it yet, either.

Candy was so deep in shock it was impossible to communicate with her. When she responded with nothing more than a blank stare, they realized that questioning would have to be put off until later. She was too disoriented and wobbly to get much of anything out of her; even I could see that from as far away as where I stood up on balcony.

Soon, one detective, after placing handcuffs on her wrists, made a half-hearted comment to the other about Miranda rights. "What's the point?" his partner replied. With that, I watched as they led her across the foyer and out the front entrance toward the car they'd left parked at the curb, one of them on each arm. Every eye in the room followed as they made their way out of the building, down the front steps, and over to their unmarked vehicle. Outside, people stepped back and watched in silence as Candy was seated and buckled down in the back seat. No flashing red lights or blaring sirens were used when they left the club; they just started up and quietly drove away, headed for a holding cell at the Hood County Public Safety Building in downtown Granbury.

From my elevated perch at the banister on the second floor overlooking the foyer, I had a better view of what was happening than anyone else in the building. In fact, by first looking out through the propped wide-open front doors of the clubhouse and the high windows above them, I was able to watch as they moved from the inside to the outside of the clubhouse, taking down a little more information as they went. In stupefied amazement, I had observed each step of this phase of their initial investigation, from the moment she was taken into custody until they placed her in a car and drove away.

SPECULATION AFTER THE FACT

AFTER SHE WAS TAKEN away, the crowd once again began to buzz with nervous chatter. "Who the hell *is* she?" I heard someone say. "What the devil made her do it?" said another. "I had just parked my cart and was walking up the front steps to go to the dining room when I heard three funny-sounding bangs," said Jack Davis, an avid golfer and longtime resident of Pecan that I happened to recognize. "There was a funny sound and at first I wasn't sure what it was, but I had a feeling that something was wrong. Then, when I walked through the front door and stepped into the foyer, the first thing I saw was her, the one that did it, the one that was sittin' on the couch. When I first saw her, though, she was runnin' down the hall and headin' toward the stairwell down toward the pro shop, screaming who knows what. You couldn't tell what she was sayin'. I didn't know what the hell was goin' on."

Isadore Martinez, a clubhouse cook, had also heard the same popping sounds and people yelling. He ran into the foyer to see what was happening. He had just walked out of the coffee shop and bar next to the dining room and was on his way back to the kitchen when he saw them. "It sounded like bullets to me, man," I heard him say, "but I wasn't sure. Bam! Bam! Bam! Whatever, man! It was not like what we hear at this place. People are really nice out here. Loud talkin' and laughin', sure, but it's mostly quiet, this place!"

As I continued to stand there in bewildered stupefaction, I overhead the two cops who had been at the scene all along talking beneath the balcony on the main floor below, thinking they could not be overheard. "What do you think, Sergeant; did she really do it all on her own?" the junior officer said to his more experienced partner.

"There ain't no question she done it, Junior," the senior man replied. "All of them people who were there by her on the couch, the guys who held her arms, they were right here all the time. She done it alright. The only question is why the hell she done it, the silly bitch. She's got more goin' for her than most people even think about havin', and what does she do but pull some dumb ass stunt like this. Don't that just take the cake?"

"Yeah, it does for sure," responded the younger officer, "but I wonder if she planned it? It ain't no big-time crime if it ain't premeditated. She didn't look in no condition to plan much of anything."

"Damn," responded the senior cop, "you're gettin' to sound just like all these damned rich people out here. That's the kind of bull stuff some shrink or lawyer's gonna say to get her off scot-free. What I hate about a situation like this is that bitch has probably never hit a lick in her life, but I'll bet she's got so damned much money she'll be lawyered-up before her bunk is warmed up down at the jail. You and me'd never get out of prison if we done somethin' like this, but you can bet your ass she will."

WANDERING IN CIRCLES

JOLTED BY WHAT THE two cops said, I abruptly stood up and began wandering aimlessly around the second floor of the clubhouse. After a while, I sat down for a few minutes in the same chair I usually sat it when I visited the library, lost in fervent prayer that what I had seen and heard had been nothing more than yet another bad dream.

Then, suddenly, I bolted upright again, this time with a start, unable to comprehend why I was listening to the unbearably offensive chanter of a crowd of even more unbearably offensive people, all milling around aimlessly as they maligned my own precious wife. Moving forward on rubbery legs, I stumbled over to one of the hallways off of which the clubhouse guest rooms were located. There were two such hallways, one on each side of the centrally located library and sitting area. Keeping one hand flat against the wall to brace myself, I stumbled down to the end of one of the hallways.

The hallway ran in a more or less in an east-west direction from one end of the second floor to the other, and, as I walked along, any guest room door I came to I tried to open, as I blindly searched for an exit from the building. I would have walked into any room that was open, whether it was occupied or not. Luckily, all of them happened to be locked.

After trying every door on the way to the end of the hallway, I finally found one that would open. It was the door to the exit stairwell, a stairwell that can be entered from each floor of the building. I walked down every turn of stairs, until I would up in the basement of the building. When I realized there was no exterior exit from the basement, I returned to the stairwell and began walking back up toward the top floor. It was the only obvious way to go, but it led right back to where I had been on the second floor. When it dawned on me that I was right back where I started, I turned around and headed downstairs yet again. I was so upset I had literally been walking in circles.

When yet another door I tried happened to be unlocked, I walked out of the stairwell onto the first floor, where small groups of excited and agitated people remained gathered, talking about the shooting. After staring at them for a while, I walked past them and left through the front door of the building. No one recognized me; no one, in fact, paid any more direct attention to me than they did to anyone else. As far as they were concerned, I was just another member of the crowd — one of them, so to speak. After that, I simply walked on out to my car, got in, and drove home. It didn't take long to get there, since our place was only a few minutes away from the club. Too numb to comprehend what I had just seen, after I got home I walked straight into our bedroom, undressed, and went to bed, even though the sun was still high in the sky.

INFORMING THE POOR, UNSUSPECTING HUSBAND

WHEN OUR DOORBELL RANG a few minutes later, I got out of bed and walked to the door. Dressed only in boxer shorts and a t-shirt even though it was midday, I opened the door wide and blankly stared out at our callers, looking as disheveled as I would have if I had been awakened out of a sound sleep. Because I was still dazed and reeling from having witnessed the aftermath of what happened at the clubhouse, the officer at our doorway had to have been taken aback by how weirdly I looked and acted.

As numb as I was, I couldn't help but notice the young cop flinch as I opened the door and stared at him through glazed-over, red-lidded eyes, his thoughts nearly audible as he took note of my grubbed-out condition. Reflexively stepping back a bit, he shot a quick glance toward his partner, who was standing on our sidewalk just behind him and just a bit to his right. *Jesus!* his reaction eloquently exclaimed. *What kind of screwball family are we dealing with here, and what kind of whacked-out character is this guy?*

He matches his crazy wife spot on, that's for damned sure.

After collecting himself, he said in officialese, "Sir, there's been a serious incident, one that involves your wife. We're still trying to sort out the specifics, but there's been a shooting incident in which some people were hurt. The other people were hurt, that is, not your wife. We think you'll want to come along with us to check on her while she's with our detectives, because it looks like she could be in serious trouble. You might even want to start thinking about contacting a lawyer."

All this, of course, was much more than the young officer really ought to have said, but he said it anyway, because he was nervous.

After looking at the two of them blankly for a few seconds, I mumbled an okay and headed out the door. When they suggested it would be best for me to get dressed before leaving, I turned around and walked back toward our bedroom to do as they advised. As I pulled on my clothes, I remember thinking, *Everyone's already mad enough to want to throw us in prison, so don't do anything to antagonize these guys. Just do what they say.*

As I watched them exchanging glances, it was obvious that they knew something was off-the-wall about my behavior. At that point, though, they had no way of knowing what it was. They didn't know, for example, that I had just come from the crime scene, that I knew what their visit was about, and that I already knew a lot more about the crime that had been committed than they did; I even knew, for example, who had committed it. For the time being, though, I decided it would be best to keep all these facts to myself.

The approximately twelve-mile, fifteen-minute drive from our home in Pecan to their station in Granbury was completed without my asking a single question or my appearing to be shaken in any way, and that, in and of itself, was regarded as highly unusual. In reality, I had been shocked into stunned silence. There's no doubt, though, that my reaction would have come across as strange and inappropriate to the two cops, who knew that most people in such a situation would have asked all kinds of questions and been highly upset.

Upon my arrival at the jail, I found that Candy had been placed in an observation cell until a psychiatric specialist could be called in by the Hood County District Attorney's office to examine here. After determining that she was in shock but otherwise uninjured, a doctor had administered a sedative to put her to sleep. It would be some time, he advised, before she would be able to communicate with anyone, not just because of the sedative but due to the nature of her condition. He said he would arrange to transfer her to a mental care custodial facility the following day, a place located only a few miles away.

It was obvious to everyone that Candy needed psychiatric care and that any further questioning would have to be put off until her condition was stabilized. Obtaining a statement at the time was impossible. She hadn't said a word since the time of the incident. When they allowed me to visit her so that I could confirm she was physically okay, I was no more successful in getting through to her than the detectives or the doctor who had tried to do so earlier.

Candy, the doctor explained, was in *a catatonic state*, a condition I'd heard of many times but had never seen close up. I knew what it was, but nothing like it had ever happened to anyone I knew, nor had I ever observed it firsthand. Seeing her this way scared the devil out of me. She was out of it and distant enough to make me fear that she might never be herself again.

Even so, once she was tended to, the investigation continued, at this point with a whole new focus. By this time the detectives had obtained statements from the two victims, who were recuperating at the same hospital Candy was taken to after the incident; for a while, in fact, all three of them were there at the same time. The investigators had also taken statements from those who had witnessed the incident at the club. Now, it was my turn; they were ready and waiting to question me.

Having been informed by the cops who had driven me back and forth from Pecan that how I had behaved indicated that I knew more than I'd said about what set Candy off, the investigating detectives listened carefully as I attempted to tell them what I could. I did my best, given my condition, but my contribution to their investigation amounted to little more than incoherent babble interspersed between bouts of self-flagellation over my own complicity. No one would have described what I said to them that day as a convincingly coherent statement. Basically, I blamed myself for everything that had happened, saying that the shooting wouldn't have taken place if it had not been for what I had done or failed to do. The investigators surely must have thought both of us were as crazy as loons, and, in a way, I guess they were right.

After talking with the detectives for what seemed like a whole day, I was released and told that I was free to check on Candy again. Advising that they needed me to come back to the station the following day to continue my statement, they mentioned that we had a right to obtain legal counsel before our case went any further and that I also might want to consider making some kind of psychiatric care arrangements for Candy. With that, they called in the same two uniformed officers who brought me in earlier to ferry me back to our home in Pecan.

As soon as the two officers dropped me off at our doorway, I rushed in to pack an overnight bag. After that, I jumped in our car and headed right back into town. Beside myself with worry, I returned to the hospital to sit with Candy. When I saw that she was still out like a light, I walked out into to the lobby to begin the long wait for the next shoe to fall, and, as it turned out, it didn't take long for serious fallout to begin.

THE END OF LIFE AS WE KNEW IT

TELEVISION IS OMNIPRESENT IN all institutional setting nowadays, and one was on in the hospital visitors' area. Sitting there among a gaggle of people waiting for word from doctors about their own loved ones, I watched and listened as our story was covered on the evening news. No one paid any attention to me until a reporter explained that the woman who had done the shooting had been taken to the hospital we were sitting in at that moment.

After the details of our story were presented, several people perked up and began looking around the room. Doing a double take as my picture was displayed on television, sets of inquisitive eyes began to dart back and forth from the screen to me. It was clear that several of those present realized that the husband of the shooter in the story they'd just watched was sitting right there beside them, wide-mouthed and with a stunned look on his face.

When the story ended and a commercial appeared on the screen, an older man who was sitting caddy-corned across the room to my right said to me, "Buddy, it sounds like you folks have a big enough problem to make me glad all my family has to worry about is a case of appendicitis."

Nobody else said a word; they just stared at me, until, finally, I stood up and walked out of the waiting area.

Some of the initial interviewees in the televised coverage had said they thought there had been an accident; others said they thought a domestic dispute had gotten out of hand; and others said there had been an argument and a fight. One fellow said he thought there had been a robbery at the club. Since no verifiable explanation of the incident was immediately available, the early coverage of the incident ended with reporters promising to *get to the bottom of the story* and *return to viewers as soon as more details became available.*

The shooting was a lead story on the evening editions of local television stations that served the Dallas–Fort Worth Metroplex, with each report trumpeting the incident as dramatically as it could be told. Replete with video obtained through interviewing witnesses, clubhouse staffers, and passers-by, news anchors breathlessly told the world what had happened that day at the *posh Pecan Plantation Country Club* out in the *resort town of Granbury*. Describing the incident as *an unprovoked and inexplicable instance of attempted murder*, two white-clad people covered in blood were shown being wheeled out of the clubhouse on gurneys and placed in an ambulance. Worried looking spectators were shown parting from one another to create a path, looking on in alarm as the victims and emergency workers trundled them out to a waiting ambulance.

Bylines in big bold letters exclaiming that "*MYSTERIOUS ATTEMPTED MURDERS AT PECAN PLANTATION*" had taken place were followed up by footage of Candy being led out in handcuffs as reporters were explaining all they knew about the details. As I watched, I was stunned into silence all over again. The shooting seemed too surreal to have actually happened.

The broadcasted coverage showed her close up and in great detail, first sitting in silence on the couch at the club and later on being led out the door for transportation to the Hood County Jail. Too little had been learned about us as a couple at the time of the first reports for anything to be said about who we were or what we did for a living, but it didn't take long for those facts to be gathered and for more detailed follow-up coverage to be aired. Before long, my own picture started appearing on screen, right beside Candy's. The first time I saw us together this way, my knees wobbled and I started to tremble like a leaf.

What made the shooting so inexplicably notorious was that it had happened at the well-known Pecan Plantation Country Club, a place where such things just did not happen. News anchors were quick to ask the question everyone had in mind: *What on earth had driven a privileged, intelligent, and attractive person like Candice Holder, the attractive wife of a local college administrator, to commit such a mystifying act in their beautiful setting?*

As I drove home time after time to change clothes and shower, all I could think about was that our world had come to an absolute end. Candy had been confined to a mental hospital, my career as an administrator at a public institution was surely destroyed, and both of us had become the butt of vulgar speculation throughout our community. I wanted to crawl into a hole and pull the ground in over me. If I had been given a choice between what had happened and being beaten with a club, I'd happily have chosen the latter. Our lives would be forever changed by what had taken place that day at the clubhouse.

22

LIFE'S LABOR'S LOST

I FULLY EXPECTED TO SEE an article about the shooting when I picked up the Sunday paper from our front step that first morning after I returned home to shower and change clothes after sitting all night at the hospital with Candy, but when I saw the first headlines, my hands shook and my heart began to flutter all over again. Because the shooting was one of the most unusual events that had occurred at Granbury in years, the Hood County News ran it under a huge headline that blared *"LOCAL WOMAN INVOLVED IN UNEXPLAINED SHOOTING AT PECAN PLANTATION!"*

Several of our neighbors had been interviewed, as had some of my co-workers at Weatherford College. People who lived all around us, it suddenly occurred to me, were opening their own morning papers to read the same story I was reading. I felt weak in the knees. In truth, I felt a lot worse than that; I felt like gouging out my eyes and jumping off a cliff.

The story appeared with photographs of Candy and me and our home prominently displayed in the coverage, and my name had become an integral part of what was being said — with particular emphasis on the fact that I was employed as an administrator at Weatherford College. Anything that would have been more negative for me from a professional standpoint would have to have been designed by the devil himself. Without stepping a foot back on campus, I knew my career at the college and in academic administration was over.

I drove back into town to sit with Candy at the hospital she'd been transferred to for psychiatric observation and care. She was still too drugged out and blank to know when I got there, but

I stayed with her anyway. It was in this simple way that the first day of the routine I held to for as long as she was hospitalized began. I sat with her every day, all day, and for as long into the evenings as the facility would allow. After being assured by her nurses that they would let me know by telephone if her condition changed in any way, I returned home each night to sleep a bit, shower, and change clothes.

I was interrupted early on my first Sunday morning at home by a phone call from one of the detectives, who said that he and his partner needed to talk with me some more about what they now routinely referred to as *our case*. After a quick visit to the hospital check on Candy, I went to meet with them. She was semi-awake but still far too groggy and distraught to communicate with me anyway. Her glassy-eyed expression and medicine-induced stupor made it clear that she wouldn't be ready to talk for a while. Her doctor had left instructions to keep her quiet and at rest so that she could gradually recover.

I spent the rest of the morning with the detectives, who questioned and probed and prodded until they finally ran out of questions to ask. Before I was released to return to her side, they reminded me once again that I ought to talk with a doctor of my own choosing about setting up some sort of ongoing psychiatric treatment. In addition, they once again advised that I ought to contact an attorney. By this time, it had become clear that I ought to pay closer attention to their advice.

In-depth coverage of the shooting appeared in a few consecutive editions of big city papers such as the *Fort Worth Star–Telegram* and *Dallas Morning News*, but it remained a lead item for months thereafter in the smalltown newspapers that served our general area. Now that local reporters knew where we lived, they began calling in search of personal comments by anyone who would talk with them.

Even before the first sketchy story about the shooting appeared in the local media, the whole of the Pecan Plantation and the town of Granbury became rumor mills of the first order. Once the scandalous expression *attempted murder* was used for the first time, all any listener remembered was the word *murder.* Then, when their misunderstanding of what had taken place was passed on, the buzz quickly became that several people *can you believe it!* had been murdered at Pecan.

This version of the shooting ended up being repeated again and again, even after later and more accurate accounts began to appear in the media. For a time, all many people *knew* about the incident was that *a crazy woman had murdered several people out in Pecan.* As badly distorted as this version of the event was, yet another bit of incorrect information was added to make the story sound even more inexplicable and strange. *And, can you believe it,* went the buzz, *her husband is an administrator out at the college. Isn't that the most irresponsible thing you've ever heard? Don't they do any screening when they hire people out there?* Many listeners accepted — and, of course, frequently repeated — this embellished version of the event, as if it were the gospel truth.

In only a matter of days, everyone in Granbury had heard multiple versions of the shooting, none of which were correct. The fact that lots of these folks had friends or relatives in Weatherford meant that everyone I worked with had heard it too. It became a lead story for every television and radio station in our area, and the local newspapers beat it to death for many weeks thereafter.

THE FIRST FALL OF THE AXE

THE FIRST AND MOST SIGNIFICANT in a series of changes that occurred after the shooting began with a cell phone call from my immediate supervisor at Weatherford College, Vice President for Academic Affairs Dr. Nelson Soder. The shooting took place on Saturday morning; Nelson called me on Sunday morning, well before I was able to muster enough presence of mind to call in myself and long before I had a chance to think through what it would have been like if I had appeared at work on Monday morning. At that point, coherent thought hadn't yet become possible.

The intent of his call, Nelson stated, was to express his

regrets, to check on how I was doing, and, of course, to spare me from having to worry about my responsibilities at the college at a time when I had so much to deal with at home. "Under the circumstances," he said, "take off as much time you need to attend to the situation and get your affairs back in order. Once all those considerations have been taken care of, we'll talk about where to go from there. Keep us posted on your progress. I'll call again shortly, after you have had time to settled down a bit. All of us are sorry to hear about your loss." He knew only too well what a commotion would have arisen if I, for some crazy reason, had gotten it into my head to show up at the college for work on the coming Monday morning.

"Thanks," I said, without attempting to offer any sort of explanation. "I appreciate your thoughtfulness. Tell everyone I said thanks." Then, feeling sick in the stomach, I hung up the phone.

Publicly funded institutions have to be even more sensitive to bad publicity than private businesses, and Weatherford College was certainly no exception in that regard. A small school located in a small pond can't afford to allow goings-on in the life of an individual employee to diminish its image in the minds of local taxpayers who provide the wherewithal for its existence. Even though I knew this was so, I was amazed as well as aggravated by how quickly the reality of it came into play. I still am.

If I had been able to think clearly at the time, I would have expected a call like his to take place. As it was, though, I didn't expect it to take place so quickly. Nelson's call, I learned later on, had been prompted more by several private discussions he'd had had with his own superiors rather than by any genuine concern for our immediate welfare.

Ultimate responsibility for the governance of colleges like ours is vested by state statute in local district boards of trustees, and the chair of our seven-member board at the time of the incident was a man by the name of Hamilton "*Cap*" Grizzard. Cap was a no-nonsense public servant from Springtown, one of the college's nearby feeder communities. I don't know how he earned or was awarded his nickname; all I knew was that it fit him like a glove.

What had happened behind the scene was that Cap, upon learning what the wife of one of *his* college administrators had done by watching the coverage of the incident on evening television and through telephone calls he'd received from various constituents, hadn't wasted a second before blasting off a hurried telephone call of his own to Dr. J. Henry Knowles, the president of Weatherford College, for the express purpose of discussing the adverse publicity that was certain to be created by what had happened in the personal life of a member of his administrative team, namely me. Cap has always been a take charge guy, which, I'm sure, was why his peers elected him chair of our college board.

He advised our president in clear and unequivocal terms that right then would be an excellent time to exercise the executive responsibility delegated to the chief administrative officer of the college for carrying out the various edicts and policies of the board of trustees to do whatever had to be done to lower my profile at the college, and the sooner, the better. Immediately after Cap's call, Dr. Knowles had contacted Dr. Soder, who was his academic vice president and, as has been mentioned, my immediate supervisor, who had then contacted me. That's how I came to receive that first *call of concern* as quickly as I did.

On Wednesday of the next week — after, I'm sure, a series of internal crisis management meetings — I received a second call from Nelson, this time about a personal appointment that had been set up for me one week later, not with my own supervisor but with Dr. Knowles himself. "It can be rescheduled, of course, if you need it to be," he said, "but we thought you'd like to talk with 'the college' as soon as possible now that you've had a bit of time to think about your situation."

"No, that'll be just fine," I replied, my heart sinking like a rock as I contemplated what was sure to happen at the meeting. *Without a doubt*, I thought, *meeting with Knowles could only mean more bad news.*

Our president was a man who often proudly — and many of us thought much too loudly — touted his great fair-mindedness by maintaining an *open-door policy* for employees of the college, but most of his subordinates considered the policy to be little more than window dressing for staff relations purposes. The reality of being an employee of the college was that few classified staff members, faculty, or administrators ever walked through his door unless they were invited to do so in advance, and, whenever employees actually were invited into the inner sanctum, it was usually for one of two reasons — when *he wanted something done*, or when *he wanted something not to be done*. Oh, various senior and, of course, tenured spear-carrying faculty leaders did go in on occasion to vent about one thing or another, but only a few unwary instructors or classified staff members ever used it in the way that was intended.

With thoughts of this kind flying around in my head, I showed up at Dr. Knowles' office one week later at the appointed hour. Feeling as wrung out and disheveled as a stack of dirty laundry, I knew I looked like hell. I was braced for what would surely be yet another blow to the midsection. Because the meeting had to do with how I made a living, I walked in with thousands of butterflies fluttering around in my stomach.

After a courteous welcome and a heart-felt expression of condolences, the locally well-known and generally highly thought of Dr. Knowles, in his most dignified and authoritarian voice, offered me an opportunity to *voluntarily resign* my position in order to spare the college any more adverse publicity than had already been generated. "As you well know," he said, "even the appearance of impropriety on the part of our faculty and staff can undermine local support for a community-based institution such as our own. Under the circumstances," he patiently continued, "I know that you, with your solid professional values, will want to submit a voluntary letter of resignation, one that will allow you to leave the college with a clean slate. I know," he said, "you'll understand why this particular step is appropriate."

He was every bit as considerate, understanding, and sympathetic as you would expect a fellow professional and person in a position of authority to be. Thoughtfully, he had even drafted an example of a letter that contained the wording he had in mind, one that "required only a signature and date but that I could take with me to read over and revise if I felt a need to do so."

"The college," I was told, "is not insensitive to the needs and special problems of its employees, since everyone knows how easily unexpected and *unwanted situations* can occur in our lives. For that reason, you will, of course, remain in paid status until the expiration of your current contract, at which time you will be free to pursue other interests."

Floored upon being informed that I would not be rehired for the following year even though I expected to hear just that, I thanked Dr. Knowles profusely for the great consideration that was being extended on my behalf. I was a company man of the highest order, it should be noted, even if a problem of my own making had swallowed me up at that particular moment in time. Meekly, I signed the letter of resignation and handed it back to him. After a few more words of encouragement and a hearty farewell, he walked me out of his office and back home I went. Our whole interaction had taken less than fifteen minutes.

What all the happy talk meant for me was that I had been released from any further active duty at the college and placed on administrative leave *so that I could deal with my personal problems at home,* and that my contract would continue until the end of the current academic year but that it would not be renewed after that. I had just three months and seventeen days of prorated pay coming before my annual contract expired on July 31. After that date, I would be out in the world on my own. Although I had *voluntarily* submitted my resignation, I had been, in effect, forced into accepting less than one semester of paid leave and an early sunset into what would be a greatly reduced level of retirement income.

Even though I was still foggy headed, it had been quite clear to me, just as it had been to Dr. Knowles, what this turn of events meant in terms of long-term professional consequences. We both knew that my situation was far worse than he made it out to be. Given what had happened, my administrative career in public education had come to an end. What I faced, therefore, was not just the loss of my job, but the loss of my career as well. Employment in public education being what it is, no college would want to hire an educational administrator with the kind negative baggage I would have to declare.

Departure from a place of employment for reasons such as a quest for higher pay, professional differences of opinion, or even a bad evaluation can be overcome. Usually, any one position can be replaced by another one someplace else; I, of all people, given my history, knew that as well as anyone. But, when landing a new job within one's field of specialization becomes impossible, losing a job takes on a whole new meaning.

What all this came down to for me was that now, on top of all of our other problems, I had to face the reality of my career of over twenty-five years in public education being effectively over. Once again, my head began to ache and my legs went wobbly, just from thinking about what had taken place. The thought of losing not just my immediate job but my entire career was more than enough to leave me dumbfounded and reeling.

My professional brethren — fellow educational administrators — often proudly but falsely proclaimed to be open-minded and evenhanded in the midst of difficult situations, but their behavior in a real crisis was sometimes anything but that. When the going gets tough, the first impulse of many of them was to cover their own butts, just like it was for the lower-level employees to whom they don't give enough credit. Public administrators like to think of themselves as being more open-minded and liberal than the average person, but most of them are actually far more conservative and judgmental than they would ever admit. Standing on principle really isn't as big among them as they like to imagine. I hadn't done a single thing wrong, intentionally or otherwise, yet there I was, hung out to dry, and not a one of them had said a word on my behalf.

The chips, so to speak, had never been down for any of my administrative colleagues in the way they were for me at that moment. I had become too tainted for any of them to want to want to keep me in the fold, the relatively cloistered and much smaller than outsiders would ever imagine world of college administration. Ours was an environment in which everybody knows everybody and the professional grapevine is such that one mistake — including unintentional involvement in a set of negative circumstances over which one has no control — can ruin a conscientious and dedicated person's career.

My future, I realized, would include a search for a work in the business world my colleagues and I had dealt with through the years in the form of advisory groups, focus groups, and task forces, but in which we had little recent work experience. It would either be that, I realized, or early retirement on a much-reduced pension. At this point, the stark differences between employment in the artificial world of college administration and the realities of having to make it on the outside became more than a matter of casual discussion.

ANOTHER FALL OF THE AXE

SHORTLY AFTER THE LOSS of my job, we were hit by yet another devastating blow, in this case one I would have anticipated if I had been thinking just a little bit more clearly. Because I was too mixed up and mentally strung out to see it coming, I wasn't ready for it when it did. It's just as well, I suppose; even if I had thought about it in advance, I don't think there's any way I could have emotionally prepared myself for the message that was delivered.

It turned out that Candy's two victims, the people she shot or shot at, Carl and Emily Stackhouse, were not only long-term residents of Pecan but also long-established members of the country club, people who had a large number of close friends and many social acquaintances in the development. Any passing feelings of concern residents of the development might have had for Candy or me — if, indeed, they had ever had any such concerns — paled in comparison to the outpouring of compassion that were lavished upon their grievously wronged and wounded clubmates. Because we were relatively new and hadn't been socially active or active as golfers, we weren't close to a single person in their crowd.

Many of these folks immediately joined a good number of other residents of Pecan, including some of our immediate neighbors, in making it crystal clear to members of the Board of Directors of the Pecan Plantation Property Owners Association that they wanted us out of their midst, and the sooner the better. Working busily behind the scenes, they drove their point home by stressing the long-term adverse impact Candy actions could have on Pecan Plantation as a real estate development, stressing considerations such as the assurance of public safety, the maintenance of a positive community image, and, of course, the protection of property values.

An event as dramatic and as threatening as a shooting near their homes was more than these folks were willing to accept, no matter what circumstances had caused it to occur. Quite simply, they wanted no further association with us. Through stares, glares, avoidance, condescending remarks, and, in some cases, outright hostility or criticism whenever they had passing contact with me, they loudly and clearly delivered the message that continuing to live at Pecan was untenable.

Late one afternoon, the Manager of Operations for the development, Bud Smith, a fine gentleman and one of many residents of the development who had been exceptionally friendly to us in the past, stopped by our home unannounced, just to, as he put it, *have a little chat.* I was at home for a while between my many trips back and forth into Granbury to be with Candy at the hospital, so I welcomed him into our living room.

After expressing his own condolences as well as sincere regrets on behalf of the membership of the property owners' association for what he referred to as *our unfortunate family incident*, he launched into a circuitous explanation of the deep concern among the membership with respect to the potentially negative effects our incident could have on the development. "It would be a double tragedy," he said, "if it adversely impacted the value of current properties by deterring prospective homebuyers from choosing the development as a place to live. Our older residents," he confided, "are particularly troubled by what happened; in fact, some of them are downright scared."

Without mincing words any further, he said that "it would probably be best for us to start making plans to move out of the development. Under the circumstances," he said, "we know you will understand that residents will continue to feel uncomfortable living near us, knowing about your wife's condition and her propensity for unprovoked, violent behavior." Packaging his message in a pragmatic investment–protecting–and–public–safety–oriented wrapping made it sound more righteous than it actually was and therefore made it much easier to deliver than it would have been otherwise. What he really wanted to communicate, of course, was that past acquaintances are one thing but that property values are another, and that it should be apparent what we ought to do under the circumstances.

My immediate gut reaction was to order the damned guy to get the hell out of our house, but that wasn't what I actually did. Instead, while he was sitting there and still in mid-sentence, I just picked up the phone and called a realtor I knew who lived not far from us in the development and asked him to come over and write up our listing. I knew we were of no danger to anyone, but in only an instant I realized that I had to get us away from this man and everyone else who thought like he did, just as quickly as I could.

While the immediacy of my action made Smith flush bright red, there was no mistaking the look that registered on his face shortly after I made that call. He may have felt awkward and embarrassed for a moment, but he was clearly relieved that a thorny problem had been so immediately and decisively taken off his plate. Once his problem was resolved, he thanked me and was up and out of our living room in only a matter of minutes. It was a pleasure to see him go.

FROM PECAN PLANTATION INTO GRANBURY PROPER

I SIGNED A MULTIPLE listing agreement with the realtor the

following day, even though I hadn't given a moment of thought to where we would live after our home was sold. My only plan of action was to get us out of Pecan as quickly as I could make it happen, then let anything else that might happen proceed from there. I agreed to the first selling price the realtor suggested, telling him to get the house on the market as soon as it could be arranged and that I would be flexible when it came to the acceptance of offers. If the residents of Pecan wanted nothing more to do with us, I sure as hell didn't want anything more to do with any of them. They'd condemned us before hearing our side of the story, and that was all I needed to know.

It came as no surprise when offers began to roll in not long thereafter. Our home was so beautifully restored and such a lovely place that the first three couples that came through the door wanted to buy it. They jumped at the chance to take advantage of the bargain basement price at which I'd listed it, just because I wanted to get out of Pecan as quickly as possible. The older couple who ultimately bought it as a retirement home could hardly believe the great bargain they'd gotten, for no reason other than that they'd shown up at the right place at the right time. They were as elated by their good fortune as I was downcast by our great loss.

Giving up our beautiful home was only one in a series of bitter pills we had to swallow in the wake of the shooting, but it was more difficult to handle than most of the others. Having put so much sweat equity into the place, leaving it was a truly painful experience. We had hoped never to move again, to stay put until the end of our earthly journey. Under the circumstance, though, I knew there was no choice but let it go; after what had happened, living at Pecan would never have been the same.

After our home was sold, I rented a small apartment in Granbury proper, not only to get away from Pecan Plantation but also to be close to the hospital in which Candy was being treated and to the courthouse where her case would eventually be tried. An apartment would do just fine, I figured, until we knew what would become of us. Holding out only those items that were necessary to set up a sparsely furnished and nearly undecorated but still functional short-term place to live, I arranged to have all the rest of our household property placed in storage.

THINGS FALL APART

WE WERE RUINED; THAT'S all that was clear to me for the moment.

It would have been a toss-up to say who was worse off at the time, Candy or me. I was too depressed to do anything that was remotely worthwhile. As embarrassing as it was to have to admit to it after the fact, my initial reaction to what Candy did that day at the club had been to go so deeply into shock that I wasn't able to be of any help to her at all.

A shooting, for God's sake, had been the only reaction I could muster; *How on earth could she have done something that far beyond the pale?*

Let me wake up, my mind screamed, *and find that the whole incident had been nothing but a freakish nightmare that would be forgotten with the light of day. Some sort of reprieve has to be due us because how on earth could anything so ruinous have happened to a couple who had spent their whole adult lives working hard and trying their best to stay on a straight and narrow path?*

Surely, I remember thinking, *there has to be some logical explanation for what had taken place. Had she been defending herself*, for example, I wondered, *after having been attacked in some way? Something must have set her off*, I reasoned, *or she would never have committed such an inexplicable crime.*

Then, tortured by thoughts of deprivation and mistreatment Candy had suffered as a child, my emotions would swing in a much more ominous direction. Black anger would flood into mind when I thought of all the misery that had already been heaped upon her. It seemed incredibly unfair that she might be held criminally liable accountable for what happened, but I realized that that was exactly what could take place for her.

Enough is enough, I thought, whereupon I would begin to fantasize about the vicious ways I would go about doing in anyone who attacked her and swearing that *anyone who hurt her in the future was going to have to pay a price.* Cursing like a storm trooper, every thought I had was in earnest. Anyone who had in the past or might in the future cause her any more pain would be my mortal enemy, and I intended to do anything within my power to fight back on her behalf.

Then, realizing that I was wallowing in unworthily hateful thoughts of my own, my mood would abruptly change and I would head off in an entirely different direction. *Would it be best,* I'd ask myself, *if we were to fall at the feet of those she'd injured, just to plead for a chance to right the inexcusable wrong that had been done to them that awful day?* Worried that any explanation of Candy's behavior we might come up with would be dismissed out of hand or laughed at, our situation seemed hopelessly bleak.

More disturbing at this time than anything else was how suddenly my mood could change. Dealing with my uncontrollable vacillations was maddening, but I was powerless to make them stop. We had always worked diligently to improve our lot in life, yet, there we were, up to our necks in a mess of our own making. Everything we'd earned during nearly thirty years of hard work as upright, responsible people had been lost in a single morning, and our lives had been turned upside down.

Feeling too devastated to know which way to turn, I had all kinds of trouble eating and sleeping, until nervousness caused me to break out in hives. Up till then, I had never fully appreciated what that actually involved, even though I'd heard it spoken of on many occasions. Now, I knew; it's one of the many afflictions that can happen to a person who has been so emotionally drained and exhausted on the inside that his feelings begin to show up on the outside.

From my perspective, I was solely responsible for what she'd done that day at the club. I had driven her to the edge of desperation, then made no effort to keep her from going over the line when she got there. I hadn't been the supportive husband I fancied myself as being; instead, I'd been a guy who failed to step forward when the relationship he should have been trying with all his might to protect was in danger of being destroyed.

I was sick with worry over what was going to become of us now that my career in education was effectively over. *How would I make a living for us,* I wondered, *when I had no career to go back to?* At a time when my entire focus should have been on her, I worried about my career instead. After reflecting on my own thoughts for a while, I began to wonder if there were any limits to my self-centeredness.

Even though my past behavior hadn't been born of bad intentions, the consequences of the lifestyle I had chosen had become so negative that it may as well have been. So much had been given up in pursuit of my professional goals that I had damaged the love of my life. Clearly, I had pushed myself too hard, for far too long, and for all the wrong reasons, and my career machinations had failed to produce the happiness everyone expects out of life. My own activities had brought about the state of mind that had eventually torn her down.

With my mind filled with thoughts of this kind, I sank like a rock. I became too limp-wristed and listless to do anything that would be the least bit helpful in terms of improving our situation in any way. All I could do was feel sorry for us, and for myself. Basically, I turned into an absolute drone. I knew I needed to snap out of it and start taking some positive steps, but I just couldn't manage to make myself do it. Depression rolled over me like a fog, whereupon I unraveled until I became nearly as helpless as Candy.

During the months after the incident while Candy was in the hospital, merciless press coverage turned the community against us and destroyed our reputations throughout the area. Basically, the shooting had come across as so incomprehensible that it was considered inexcusable, and this seemed to have had the effect of making the media feel free to engage in even more speculative coverage than would have taken place under normal circumstances. Once the gloves were off, so to speak, media outlets began to follow one another's practices in terms of embellishing the inexplicability of the incident. Faster than would be thought possible, stories about the shooting were sensationalized beyond recognition.

Reporters and commentators began to behave as if they had been given *carte blanche* to tear into us with a vengeance. They did just that, too; they had a field day at our expense, in fact, describing Candy and me in terms we couldn't even recognize and making comments about us that were so far off the mark that at first all we were able to do was read or listen to them in angry astonishment. Only those who have been on the receiving end of such an assault can appreciate what it was like.

Some comments shook me to the core, especially those that described us as "affluent residents of the posh Pecan Plantation Country Club," thereby implying that we lived some sort of privileged and therefore decadent or indecent lifestyle. When we were referred to as being people who lived "silver spoon existences," it came across as an assault to our ears, and, among the many aspersions that were thrown at us, this particular criticism was one that always made me boil with anger. Once they heard Candice's nickname for the first time, reporters and commentators used it from then on in every story that was put out about the incident, as if she had no given first name. They referred to her as *Candy* as often as they could, implying salaciousness at every opportunity. When her maiden name became equally well known, they stopped using my name with hers altogether. From that point forward, every article appeared with *THE CANDY CAINE SHOOTINGS* as a byline. Once this expression took hold, commentators began to run over us like wild horses, more often than not by portraying us as depraved sybarites. It was used at will by every misinformed *newsperson* who wanted to draw a little extra additional attention to a story.

Those who read these highly sensationalized reports, most notably our former neighbors and my co-workers, quickly accepted them as being exactly what must have happened. *Where there's smoke, there's fire* seemed to be the way everyone looked at what was being said of us. Because we weren't composed enough to defend ourselves, we ended up being roundly condemned by just about everyone.

We didn't really *live* during this period; we just *existed*, always praying that we would be able to find some way to get out of what had happened to us. During the months that followed, morning after morning began with our marriage vows ringing in my ears, especially our pledges to be there for one another come what may, in sickness and in health and for richer or poorer. In the joy of the moment, it had been easy to make promises of that kind, but I had never even dreamt of being caught up in a situation like the one that was before us at the time. I had expected to have to contend with the normal challenges of married life — making a living, raising a family, or helping my partner get along in old age, hopefully after having enjoyed a lifetime of happiness together — but I had never imagined the possibility of being tested in the way that lay before us. Criminal charges, for example, were beyond the realm of anything I had ever envisioned having to deal with.

Both of us were still too shaken and stunned to do much more than put one foot in front of another, just to get from here to there. Having come face to face with the sobering reality of life not always playing out in a storybook way, we had no idea what we ought to do. For even the most loving of couples, there are times when events run over them like a truck, and, for us, this was one of those times.

I knew only too well that our case would eventually wind up in the hands of Hood County District Attorney Preston Walker, a man known throughout our area for being a model of the hard-nosed public defender Texans like to see in that particular office. He was also known for being exceptionally well prepared and highly aggressive in court, and he had a reputation for winning most every case he brought to trial. Knowing that Candy was clearly guilty kept me lying awake every night, fearfully wondering how she would be punished. No other outcome, I had convinced myself, was even remotely possible.

23

GIRDING FOR BATTLE

FOR QUITE SOME TIME, the future target of Hood County District Attorney Preston Walker's wrath remained too disoriented to communicate in the room at the mental care facility into which she had been moved after the shooting. "What Mrs. Holder needs," the doctor told those who were responsible for assessing her readiness to face charges, "is treatment with tranquilizers and lots of rest in a peaceful and quiet setting. Until she recovers," he said, "the next step will have to wait."

I was as anxious as the district attorney to see her get better, but, of course, for totally different reasons: He wanted to file criminal charges against her, while all I wanted was to get her back home with me. In reality, though, I shouldn't have been in a hurry for her recovery, knowing how utterly unprepared I was to take the next step, whatever that step might be. What she'd done was quite a lot to take in, and I still hadn't fully come to grips with it.

Even though I stayed with her every day, I was in no better shape than her, emotionally speaking. I sat with her as long as the facility would allow, constantly worrying about the dark and troubled nights she was having to endure. It would only get worse, I knew, once she became fully aware of the enormity of what she'd done; when that happened, she would need all the comforting she could get.

I had known all along that Candy *was fragile*; I just didn't know *how fragile*. I really hadn't given any serious though to the possibility of the findings I'd presented as being harmful to us in the here and now, but they had been as explosive as dynamite.

To me, my project was nothing more than a collection of fascinating stories about events that had taken place in the lives of people so removed from our own time and place it was as if they had happened to historical figures. Because my discoveries captivated me, I took for granted that they would be equally captivating to others — Candy and the Wilsons, to be specific. The stories I strung together exacerbated memories that had haunted Candy for a lifetime, and they upset her in ways I had not foreseen.

For as long as I live, I'll never forget the vacant look on Candy's face that morning in the foyer of the clubhouse as I stared down at her from my vantage point on the second floor. She gazed upwards and directly into my eyes for a moment as I stood frozen in place, but, if she recognized me, it was only in a subliminal sort of way. In a split second, I saw that she had no idea what she'd done, and in yet another split second I fell as deeply into shock as she was.

The near fatal disaster she caused and the subsequent misery she had to endure were not accidents; they were direct consequences of my having ignored her right to a reasonable level of privacy, for a minimal amount of respect for her own needs and wishes. Secretly gathering facts about her past and then plopping them onto her lap as a complete surprise at a time when she was too vulnerable to handle it crossed a line that no one had a right to cross, not even a loving husband.

What Candy did that day at the club may not have been the direct result of an intentional act on my part, but it was most definitely an indirect consequence of how I had conducted myself over the years. I handled her family research project in the same way I handled my professional activities — without due and proper regard for her personal needs and interests. Through my own egocentricity, I had damaged the love of my life, the person who ought to have been my center of attention all along. Pushing myself so hard for so long and for all the wrong reasons did not produce the happiness I intended for us; instead, it brought about the state of mind that had driven her to despair.

As my personal failures became increasingly apparent, my

spirit continued to sink like a rock, until I became more feckless than ever. I stumbled along day after day, doing nothing more than criticizing myself and feeling sorry for the both of us. Too depressed to get my act together, I remained unable to do a single thing that would be helpful to us.

Lumbering back and forth to the hospital to sit with her was the best I could do. There got to be days when I became so preoccupied with worry that I would space out during routine conversations, no matter who I was talking to. One evening, for example, I choked up during a telephone call to my own parents, who, as would be imagined, were already worried sick about us. My loss of control left them more feeling more upset that ever. Because both of them were in their eighties, I felt as guilty as hell — and, of course, even more worried than I had been before I made the call.

One day, I happened to pass by two scruffy and surly teenaged boys who were standing near the doorway of a quick stop market I stopped at to gas up my car. Ignoring everyone around them, they were arguing about some meaninglessly forgettable affront one had committed against the other, until the bigger of the two boys suddenly slugged the smaller one on the upper arm with his closed fist. It wasn't a love tap; he hit him as hard as he could, and it clearly hurt a lot. Yelling out in pain, the younger boy started cursing at the top of his lungs, screaming that he would get back at the older boy, in one way or another.

I walked on by, got in my car, and drove off, leaving them there, still bellowing at one another. There wasn't anything I could have done about the argument between the two boys, so I had just gone on about my business, ignoring them as best I could. Their behavior was probably close to normal for the two budding hoodlums, who, I'd be willing to bet, actually thought of one another as friends. Be that as it may, my immediate reaction when the bigger boy hit the smaller one had been to wish to high heaven that I could have whacked him right back, hard enough to make his ears ring for a week. *Damned punk*, I remember thinking. *It would have served him right, and it would have felt great to set him straight.*

Then, almost immediately, I realized how wrong it was of me to react in the way I had: There are better ways, it goes without saying, to get a point across than by answering violence with more violence. The next thought that popped into my head was how my own first impulse upon watching two boys might be the most likely explanation for Candy's outrageous behavior that day at the club. Maybe she'd fallen prey to same reaction I'd had, and, due to her ongoing mental problems, she hadn't been able to hold back on repaying violence with more violence.

WHEN CANDY FINALLY CAME around at the hospital, she was in too much of a stupor to communicate in a meaningful way. We were still too rattled to be able to do much more than stare at one another. She knew she'd done something terribly wrong, but her memory of it was vague and incomplete. It was as if she had somehow mentally disconnected herself from her own actions. She hadn't even begun to come to grips with how truly dreadful her behavior had been, nor had she been able to give any thought to what a devastating impact it had had on our lives.

Eventually, though, Candy responded well enough to her prescribed treatment of medication combined with a long period of quiet rest for her condition to be stabilized. As soon as it became clear that she was getting better, I started leaving the hospital for short periods of time to do just what the authorities in Granbury had suggested: locate a psychiatrist and lawyer to help us contend with her medical and legal problems.

AS IT TURNED OUT, locating professional guidance was much easier than I expected it to be, simply because every mental health and legal specialist in the Dallas–Fort Worth Metroplex had read about what happened to us and many of them were ready and willing to take on our case.

I retained an attorney out of our own hometown, a guy by the name of Harry Foley I'd read about from time to time in the Hood County News and who was well known throughout our area. When we met, I liked him right away, mainly because he seemed to be an exceptionally good listener. I liked that about him more than anything else, in fact, since many of the lawyers I had interacted with in the past had struck me as being people who enjoyed hearing themselves talk much more than they liked to listen attentively to what others had to say. Too many of them had come across as being more inclined to engage in argumentation than to doing down and dirty trench work, and I wanted to hire a worker instead of a talker. As it turned out, I got just that when I retained Foley.

His first comment after taking us on was that neither one of us should say another word to anyone about our case except through him. His advice was so obvious that hearing him say it made me feel apologetic and stupid, since I had all but given speeches about us when I talked with detectives and others in the past. It worried me that I might have somehow weakened Candy's case, even before he had chance to put together a defense.

Foley's second bit of advice was that we needed to retain our own psychiatrist as soon as possible. He recommended a man by the name of Walter Koch (pronounced *Coke*), a person he'd worked with before and whose competence he highly respected. I accepted his suggestion, but my guess is that Dr. Koch, after my first meeting with him to confirm that we could work together, probably thought he needed to ply his trade on me before he ever directly spoke to his prospective client, my wife Candice.

Our interaction had quickly disintegrated into a scattered and blubbery affair, due to my being so worried and upset. It didn't seem to bother him, though, probably because he was used to working with unhinged people like me. In any case, whatever he thought of me or about our overall situation, I liked him right away, just as much as I liked Foley. He was cool, calm, collected, poised, insightful, and exceptionally personable — all adjectives that definitely couldn't have been applied to me at the time, since I was nearly as discombobulated as Candy. Thankfully, once Koch made his commitment, he stayed with us until our case was fully settled.

HIRING HARRY FOLEY AND Walter Koch was immeasurably helpful in terms of reviving my sagging spirits. Before they started advising us, I hadn't been able to do much more than wander about in a fog, cursing the darkness but not doing anything that was actually helpful. Once these two highly experienced professionals started working on our behalf, I felt better than I had in a long time.

Basically, after Foley and Koch got to work, I stopped talking with the cops and switched to having regular meetings with them. In the beginning, of course, they didn't know any more about our situation than what they'd picked up through the media, and they knew better than to place much stock in all of that. They knew without asking what had to be done to get down to the meat and potatoes of our situation and bring themselves up to snuff. Again, it was a great relief to have them on our side. Working solo most definitely isn't the way to go for anyone who has been accused of a serious and therefore highly troubling crime.

Because Foley and Koch were observant, intelligent, and considerate human beings in addition to being highly competent professionals, I was convinced that, once they really got to know Candy, they would become true believers in our cause as opposed to being nothing more than hired specialists brought in to get us out of a jam. I didn't want to work with anyone who would go through the motions on our behalf whether they believed in us or not; I wanted advocates who would be as strongly supportive of her as I was. It was critical to me that this would be the case. Judges and juries, I believed, have a way of sensing the relationship that exists between defendants and their representatives, and I wanted our team to be as solid at it could possibly be.

Before Candy was pronounced fit to be discharged from the hospital and returned to legal custody, Foley appealed for and successfully secured her release on bond. Serious charges had been filed against her, but she had no criminal record and was not considered a flight risk. On those grounds, she was instructed not to leave the area until her case was adjudicated, and then allowed to return home.

We were only in the initial throes of getting a handle on the emotional or legal problems hanging over us, but it was wonderful to have Candy back with me again. Even though the housing we returned to was nothing more than a sparsely furnished temporary apartment in Granbury rather than our beautifully restored home at Pecan Plantation, I felt better than I had at any time since the incident. It was of enormous relief for both of us to be back together again.

It would be necessary to wait until Candy was fully stabilized, Koch advised, before we could begin to deal with her psychiatric problems and the legal charges that had been filed against her. "We need the time anyway," he said, and when he spoke, I listened; after what had happened, I no longer doubted that Candy's mental problems had to be taken seriously. Koch made it clear that even with the best of care and under the most favorable of circumstances, recovery from a condition like hers can take a considerable amount of time. Because she was still fragile, the possibility of her having additional difficulties or relapsing rather that improving was ever present and frighteningly real.

FROM THAT POINT FORWARD, getting Candy back on her feet and prepared for trial became our mission in life — Koch's, Foley's, and mine. Whenever I was not with her, I was either talking with or gathering information for one of them. Her emotional recovery was our first priority, but we also moved forward on the legal front as we waited. We expected her case to be scheduled for trial as soon as she was back on solid ground. When that day came, we wanted to be ready with the best defense that could be mustered.

Koch's analysis of Candy continued throughout the months that followed, while Foley focused on preparing her defense for trial. All I did during this period of time was remain at their beck and call, trying to be of as much support to Candy as I could. Because my old life as a college administrator was over, I found that I had plenty of time to do so.

Day after day flew by as the three of us worked together on Candy's behalf, all the way up until her case finally went to trial. Our expenses mounted at an appalling rate as Foley and Koch's continued their work, but what could I do about it? A legal defense had to be prepared, and, at the same time, she needed ongoing psychiatric care.

Working with experts of Koch and Foley's caliber costs a fortune, but, without their level of expertise, I feared we would be torn apart at trial. To me, expert guidance was worth any price, since, without mounting a strong defense, I didn't think there was much hope of mitigating any sentence she might receive or reducing any damages that might result from a civil action. She was guilty; there was no way around that.

Our obvious problem was that with only a few months of paid administrative leave left coming from the college, real financial problems lay in store for us. Now that my career had been destroyed, worrying about how I was going to get us by financially became yet another worry that kept me feeling half sick most of the time. We had a fair amount of savings as well as some profit from the sale of our home to draw upon, but it was going fast. There was no way to know how long it would take to resolve our legal situation, nor was there any way of knowing how much we'd be liable for in the end.

Whether we liked it or not, we had come face-to-face with the sad reality of life not always playing out in the story book way we hope and pray it will. Even for couples whose marriages are built on mature love and rock-solid commitments, there are times when circumstances roll over them like a truck.

CANDY'S EARLY DAYS OF recovery were pathetic to watch. The process began with her bouncing back and forth between dim awareness and panicked bewilderment for weeks, with each fluctuation interspersed between long periods of the grogginess that follows medicated sleep. Whenever she recovered long enough for someone to begin talking with her, she got upset all over again as she remembered bits and snatches of what had happened. Then, after getting upset again, she'd go right back into yet another hysterical crying jag and end up having to be given more medication to get calmed down. At times she would return to the netherworld and refuse to talk. She could hardly bear to think about what she'd done that tragic day at the clubhouse, much less discuss it openly.

Eventually, though, the vicious shooter did begin to recover, and, yes, what has been said about the process is really true; a step–by–step explanation of the crime had to be provided to the perpetrator before she could fully comprehend what she'd done. Early on, in fact, Candy couldn't remember much more about her activities that day than the rest of us — the police, the detectives, the media, the clubhouse staff, members of the club, or, of course, me. Everyone's recollections had to be pieced together to construct a single, detailed sequence of the events that had taken place on the day of the shooting.

So, Foley and Koch and I worked together to do just that in preparation for her defense, using every scrap of information that could be gathered from any source. The district attorney, of course, was working just as hard and heavy to do the same thing, only for a different purpose: He wanted to convict her of a crime, while we wanted to construct a comprehensive and articulate explanation that could be used to exonerate her — or, at the least, mitigate any punishment that might be meted out. Both sides poured over every detail that could be collected, with the intent of reconstructing every single step Candy took that fateful day.

We all knew *what she'd done*, but not a one of us could

convincingly explain *why she'd done it.* That explanation was what was missing. Why in the world, all of us wanted to know, would such an unlikely person do something so completely out of character in a setting as tranquil as the Pecan Plantation Country Club? Until her story was put together for presentation at trial, the full explanation remained a mystery.

It took a long time to piece together a detailed reconstruction of *what* that took place that day, but it took even more time and much more intensive digging to figure out *why*. Candy and I had no interest in delaying or hampering the investigation in any way, so we did anything that was asked of us to aid and abet the investigative process, regardless of what might happen at trial. For us, it was a matter of personal honor to explain why she behaved the way she did. Just as much as the authorities, we wanted to figure out what caused her to go off the deep end that day. We, too, wanted to get to the truth, regardless of the consequences.

AS SOON AS SHE became more like her former self, Candy began to work all the more intensively with Foley and Koch to get down to the essentials of what had taken place that morning at the clubhouse dining room. As soon as Candy fully and clearly understood and was able to pause and reflect on what had transpired that morning at the club, she was as shocked by what she'd done as anyone else. Like the rest of us, she could hardly believe that she'd done it. As strange as it may sound, she was amazed that such a bloody incident could have taken place in a safe and wonderful setting like Pecan. The fact that she was the one who had done the shooting, well, that was more than she could stand to think about. To prepare her defense, though, that was exactly what she had to do.

The problem, though, was that every time one of us tried to talk about what happened in a serious way, she'd become distraught and despondent all over again. Weeks passed before she could remain calm enough to talk in any detail about the events of the morning in a rational way, and, even then, continual reassurance from Dr. Koch and me was required to keep her from going off the deep end all over again.

Her reaction was even worse when for the first time she saw police reports and newspaper accounts that included graphic photographs that had been taken at the scene. When the photographs were enlarged and vividly displayed, they had the damning effect on Candy that the prosecuting attorney would want them to have later on, when they were presented in court. Their effect on her was a likely mirror image of the impact they'd have on a jury of her peers; they appalled her to the absolute maximum. Foley and Koch and I saw in an instant how she would react and how she would come across when the same pictures were displayed in court; her guilt, we all knew, would be apparent as a billboard. We all knew what she had done, but we certainly didn't want to trumpet it in an open courtroom.

Now that Candy had grown strong enough to function under her own power, it became apparent that her view of the situation was quite different from that of her defenders. We were focused on figuring out how to convince a jury that she wasn't responsible for her actions, but she had no interest in making excuses for what she'd done. All she was able to think about was the pain she'd brought into the lives of others — the two innocent people she'd shot or shot at, employees of the club, me, our parents, our relatives, my coworkers on the job, and so on. The more she thought about it, the more insistent she became on accepting full responsibility for what had taken place that day. She was guilty, she figured, so why waste time trying to prepare an elaborate defense?

Of greatest concern to her was the status of the two people she had hurt. She wanted to know all there was to know about them — who they were, how seriously they'd been wounded, how they were doing, whether the shooting had impacted their ability to make a living or ruined their health, and anything else she could think of to ask. If she was worried about the possibility of having to spend some long years prison or how we were going to earn our daily bread from that point forward, she certainly didn't say much about it.

In her mind, she was guilty, and that's all there was to it. Once she fully understood the gravity of what she'd done, she said she wanted to make a full confession and then accept without question or argument any punishment authorities might decide to impose. She had committed an inexcusable crime, and, as far as she was concerned, severe punishment was richly deserved.

FOR CANDY TO THINK as she did was out of the question to every member of our team, but it was especially appalling to me. Throwing an absolute fit, I told her why I thought her attitude was ridiculous. "The last thing we should do," I exclaimed, "is throw in the towel before making our best effort to explain why you did what you did that day. If you'd been in your right mind, you'd never have done anything ~~so~~ that extreme. Isn't that obvious? Your reaction that day was clearly unpremeditated and spontaneous, not something that was planned in advance. There has to be a reason for it; can't you see that?"

"What we need to focus on right now," I said, far too loudly in view of her shaky condition, "is defending you with all the strength we can muster. Yes, you've done a terrible thing, but what earthly good will it do for you to sit in jail for years? What sense would it make to punish you for something you did when you were temporarily out of your mind?"

Koch and Foley echoed every word I had to say.

"It's true," they added. "What we ought to focus on is putting together a full and detailed explanation of the cause or causes of your outburst at the clubhouse. That," they confirmed, "is what any judge and jury will want to know. If we don't come up with a cogent explanation, one every juror can understand and take to heart, you just might end up in jail. You may, anyway," they pointed out, "regardless of the defense we put together. You never know what a jury is going to decide."

Because I knew in my heart that Candy wasn't knowingly responsible for what happened, any thought of her being held criminally liable seemed so unjust as to be unthinkable, and, as far as I was concerned, it just wasn't going to happen. She hadn't been herself that day; she'd been mentally ill.

I had dropped the ball when it came to protecting her in the past, but I wasn't about to do that happen again. "You're going to explain it all," I told her, "even if I have to squeeze the facts out of you myself."

Eventually, with Koch and Foley's patient assistance, Candy was brought around to our way of thinking, and, once that happened, we finally got down to the nitty-gritty of preparing an exhaustively detailed explanation of what caused her to behave the way she did that day at the clubhouse. We knew her defense would have to be complete and thorough enough for a judge and jury to understand that what she did was totally unplanned, an aberration rather than a deliberate act.

Day after day for months, Candy and I worked in close consultation with Foley and Koch to get to the bottom of what happened that horrific day in the dining room of the Pecan Plantation Country Club. Carefully and methodically, Koch and Foley helped Candy recollect every single thing she said and did on the day of the shooting, skillfully bringing out small events and comments that at first couldn't be remembered. Every bit of minutia she recalled led to additional recollections, until a detailed account of her every thought and word and action that day was brought to light and placed in print. Then, using additional information that had been uncovered through their exhaustively detailed investigation of Candy's past, the two men put together a detailed and articulate explanation of every thought and emotion that had driven her behavior during what we now all routinely referred to as *the incident.*

In the end, what became crystal clear was that Candy's strange reaction that day could be attributed to one thing and one thing only — the horrors she lived through as a child. It always came back to that, no matter what topic was discussed during all of her long hours of psychoanalysis or any of the other investigative processes that went on during the preparation of her defense.

WHEN THE LEGAL REQUIREMENTS for scheduling a court proceeding were met and Candy was finally summoned for arraignment, the series of criminal accusations filed against her included two counts of assault with a deadly weapon, two counts of assault with intent to kill, one count of carrying a concealed weapon, one count of possession of an unregistered firearm, and a few related charges. It truly rattled our cages to hear them for the first time, but, now that the charges were out there, our day of reckoning was at hand.

The charges had been brought, as expected, by Preston Walker, the Hood County District Attorney, on behalf of complainants Carl and Emily Stackhouse, two prominent local citizens who, although they had recovered physically, were still enraged over the ordeal that Candy had put them through. Worse still for us, residents of Granbury in general and of Pecan Plantation in particular had rallied behind them. Because there was no doubt that Candy had committed the crime, the prevailing public sentiment was that she damned well ought to be held to account. Everyone wanted her to be properly punished, regardless of why the shooting had been committed.

Foley briefed us on what to expect before we appeared at the old but beautifully restored Hood County Courthouse for her arraignment, but it was still extremely upsetting to hear charges of such gravity leveled against her in a public setting. Our fear of having to answer to them was plain for all to see, since Candy quickly lost her composure and I was just as clearly shaken. Everyone knew she'd done what she was accused of doing, and public sentiment was obviously against any trial outcome other than that she was *guilty as charged.* We departed in a fog, dazed and shaken up all over again.

Because so much time had elapsed since the incident, our trial date was set for Monday, April 14, 2003. Even though we'd been at work on her defense for months, once the date was set, our day of reckoning seemed so threateningly close that Candy and I started to panic all over again. Foley reassured us by promising that our defense would be fully prepared by the appointed hour, then said that it wouldn't hurt for each of us to pick up our pace a bit, just the same. "There's no such thing," he said, "as being too prepared, not as far as I'm concerned," and we couldn't have been more pleased to hear him say it.

Foley reassured us by adding that he and Koch thought we had a truly viable defense, but Candy and I weren't nearly as confident as they seemed to be. The thought of having to face a criminal proceeding was so intimidating that it was hard for us to think straight. This was a road Candy and I had never traveled down, and we sure didn't like the feel of it.

Even though I had always recoiled from the idea of psychiatric treatment for Candy, the period of intensive analysis she went through in preparation for her defense turned out to be an exceeding worthwhile undertaking for both of us. Simply because he was looking and asking the right questions, Dr. Koch was able to bring to light, clearly describe, and then suggest logical methods of dealing with problems Candy had been struggling against for her entire life, problems that no one else had been able to understand, much less clearly articulate. In so doing, he was able to help us come to grips with some of most dysfunctional aspects of our relationship. There's no two ways about it; working with this remarkably insightful man was enormously helpful in terms of getting both of us mentally and emotionally back on track and in control of our lives again.

Candy had finally received the level of intensive analysis and counseling by trained and insightful professionals that I should have gotten for her long ago, even as far back as when we were first married. Preparing her defense accomplished much more than simply helping us deal with our legal situation; it helped us get back on track as human beings and as a married couple.

It is impossible to say forcefully enough how thankful we are that Koch and Foley were able help us understand why Candy behaved the way she did that baffling day out at Pecan Plantation. Simply put, our two advocates put into words a legal argument that neither of us would ever have been able to draw out and articulate on our own. They did it in the nick of time, too, since our day in court was before us.

24

THE TRIAL OF HER LIFETIME

IN MY OPINION, OUR trial had to have been one of the strangest in the history of trials. It was adjudicated in a way that would have been considered unusual in most jurisdictions, but it was most definitely unusual within a highly conservative area like ours. I don't recall and therefore can't say much about any of the legal maneuvering that took place as it was conducted, but I do recall the essence of what happened in the courtroom. The overarching observation I would make is that it most definitely wound to a close in a way no one in our area would have bet on at the outset.

Candy's defense was fully organized and ready to be heard by the time our court date came up, just as Foley and Koch had promised. Foley had been as diligent as it is possible for a defense attorney to be, and Koch had been equally meticulous within his own area of expertise. In terms of being ready, willing, and able to explain how a person as unlikely as Candy could have behaved so strangely on that tragic day at the country club, not a single stone had been left unturned.

Our side believed just as strongly as the plaintiffs that Candy's victims and the public at large deserved a full and complete explanation of her behavior, and that's what Foley and Koch intended to deliver. It was impossible, of course, to know in advance how their defense would be received, but we knew they were ready to put forth an exhaustively researched, minutely detailed, and absolutely truthful explanation of why she behaved as she did on that fateful day. After that, our fate would be in the hands of a jury, the group of peers who would render a final judgment.

THE FIRST DAY OF ADJUDICATION

CANDY AND I WERE unnerved and shaky when we walked into the courtroom for the first time, knowing that we would have to face not only Hood County District Attorney Preston Walker and a judge and jury, but also victims Carl and Emily Stackhouse, their many friends and supporters, and a large number of observers from Pecan Plantation, Granbury, and Weatherford. Many wanted to follow the proceedings, and the courtroom was open to the public. Foley had warned in advance that we ought to expect a room full of spectators as well as a large number of reporters, since local interest in our case had never waned.

Other than Foley and Koch and ourselves, we expected only Ernest and Jewel Wilson to be present on our side, even though they were at an age where a prolonged stay away from home wasn't easy for them. My own parents' health was too poor for them to travel, and we had discouraged other members of our family from attending, knowing that they lived out of state and had jobs and families of their own to attend to. No one from Candy's birth family would be there, either, since the majority of them either didn't want to get involved or didn't care one way or the other about the outcome of our trial. Even if some had wanted to attend, they probably couldn't have, since they, too, lived out of state and had jobs and responsibilities of their own to worry about.

Sitting in the courtroom as the trial got under way, it was apparent from the beginning that everyone but our own little party was there for the specific purpose of seeing us found guilty and duly punished. Many sets of eyes shifted back and forth from her to me, the rabid shooter and her irresponsible husband. She was on trial, not me, but it appeared that they considered both of us equally guilty. With the plaintiffs, their many family members and friends, and other supporters glaring at us as if we'd killed and eaten some of their children, we felt like guppies in a bowl, defenseless captives unable to do anything more than await whatever fate they thought we ought to suffer.

District Attorney Walker began the proceedings by restating the charges against Candy, then went to present the mountain of evidence he had compiled against her. Every point he made was backed up either by the sworn testimony of a long string of eyewitnesses, large numbers of highly graphic photographs, diagrams of the crime scene, or other concrete evidence. As our side had expected all along, he left no stone unturned.

Walker was every bit as thorough and effective as he was known for being. Not only did he prove beyond a shadow of a doubt that Candy had done what she was accused of doing, he also explained that it would be a travesty of justice for the court to allow her to evade punishment by claiming mental incompetence at the time of the shooting, which, of course, was to be the heart of her defense. His case against Candy seemed so solid that we felt doomed, and all the initial confidence we had in our own defense immediately dwindled down to nothing.

Candy, who looked disarmingly contrite throughout Walker's presentation, had cried quietly from the beginning, but she was absolutely distraught by the time it was over. As early as when he restated the charges against her, she teared up; as each witness was called up to comment, she began to cry; when police and detectives delivered their statements, she cried even more; when enlarged photographs were introduced as evidence, she cried more deeply; and when the plaintiffs, still enraged over how they had been terrorized and made to look like fools, were called up to testify, she began to sob uncontrollably.

Despite continued efforts to keep her calm, it was impossible to conceal her obvious contrition. It was excruciatingly disturbing to observe her suffering, not just for me but for the Wilsons as well. By the time Walker summed up and concluded his case against her, we were just as upset as Candy. All three of us felt like we'd been beaten up and dumped in an alley. Walker's presentation had been so excruciatingly painful that it seemed to go on forever.

FOLEY DEMONSTRATES HIS GREAT WORTH

EVENTUALLY, THOUGH, THE TIME to present our response finally rolled around, and, when it did, Harry Foley, who was a lot less disturbed by District Attorney Walker's comments than we were, was more than ready to present a wholly different version of what had taken place that morning at the country club. He literally bolted into action, in fact, even to the extent of making himself looked more like a racehorse charging out of a chute than a defense attorney whose back was up against a wall. It was obvious that he had a lot to say, and that he was ready, willing, and eager to get on with saying it. His manner of speaking and body language were arresting enough to make everyone in the courtroom *want* to hear what was on his mind.

Without engaging in unnecessary theatrics or ever denying that Candy had done what she was accused of doing, Foley went directly to the heart of the matter before the court. "If you truly want to know what happened," he said, "you'll have to hear her story in full. That's the only way you'll ever be able to understand why Candice Lee 'Candy' (Caine) (Wilson) Holder behaved in such an appalling way that morning at the country club."

All but ignoring the massive amount of hard evidence and extensive witness testimony the District Attorney Walker chalked up against her, Foley immediately tore into what everyone had been waiting for all along — our side's explanation of why in the world Candy had behaved in such a crazy way that day at the clubhouse. Without making any excuses for what had to be done and without sparing any details, he went on to lambast everyone who had any part to speak of in terms of creating her state of mind that fateful day. By the time he completed her defense, he'd ripped to shreds nearly every person who had had a significant influence on her life — her birth parents, teachers, school administrators, representatives of social service agencies, her adoptive parents, and, of course, me, her feckless husband.

It's embarrassing to have to admit to it, but he tore harder into me than anyone else. Using language that was direct and unsparing, he made it abundantly clear to the court how badly others — *especially her husband* — had failed her over the years.

Everyone in the courtroom reacted as if they were spellbound by his simple statements. It was not just that his comments commanded attention, I noticed; it was the way he said them. He came across as if he had answers to secrets everyone in the courtroom desperately needed to know. As mentioned earlier, he had a nearly hypnotic way of drawing attention. When he had an important point to make, others tended to listen, even if they didn't agree with him. He came across as a person without pretension, someone who didn't fool around and who really deserved to be heard. His impact on those who were present was truly fascinating to watch.

From that point on and for the remainder of his time on defense, Foley spoke of his client as *this girl*, even though Candy was fifty-four years old at the time. It sounded odd when he first referred to her in this way, but long before he stopped talking, it had become clear that everyone in the courtroom had begun to think of her that way as well. They came around to seeing Candy in just the way he wanted them to, which was the same way he did — not just as the grown woman they saw before them but also as the wounded girl she had been since childhood.

Basically, what he presented as Candy's defense was her own life story, going as far back as the circumstances of her birth to indigent parents at the county hospital in Phoenix, Arizona. After calling up and establishing Walter Koch's impressive credentials within his area of professional expertise, he guided the doctor through a presentation of the findings the two of them had amassed. As each significant milestone of her childhood was discussed, he and Koch worked in tandem to explain how they thought her psyche had been impacted.

What made their presentation unusual and so surprisingly

compelling was that much of it was accompanied by enlarged photographs of people, places, documents, and, in some cases, actual events that spoke more eloquently and movingly than any words they might have employed. Their presentation provided ongoing confirmation of how a truly dreadful series of events had shaped my sweet wife's life.

Foley and Koch provided the court with a painstakingly detailed and excruciatingly graphic case study of just how badly parents, schools, and social institutions sometimes fail to safeguard the well-being of children, the weakest and most innocent members of our society. They went on to describe how neglect and abuse of the Caine children had gone on not just for a while but for years on end, until, finally, one by one, most of them came to disheartening ends. Candice, they pointed out, was unique only in that her mental exhaustion had occurred on a delayed basis.

They told how her father often left his wife and kids for weeks and sometimes even months at a time, forcing them to fend for themselves without any source of income beyond private and public charity; how schools and local social service agencies had not been sufficiently diligent in terms of detecting the plight of the children and coming up with workable solutions before it was too late to save the family; how, when the family finally did fall apart, their father had deserted the kids and their mother had attempted suicide; how many of the placements that had be found for the kids turned out so poorly that they were traumatized even worse *after* they were taken out of their home than while they were in it; and how most of the children, including Candice, the woman who was sitting right before them in court, had suffered for the rest of their lives from the ill effects of their childhood torment.

These events and others that had been equally damaging were explained to the court in great detail, to the extent that it wasn't long before everyone in attendance began to look at Candy in an entirely different light. Foley and Koch's presentation was powerful and convincing because, again, most of the events they described were documented by public records, medical and legal reports, sworn testimony, and, most effective of all, by photographs sad enough to touch the hearts of everyone who saw them. Not too much reading between the lines was required for those who were in the courtroom to comprehend that the Caine children had suffered inexcusable harm at the hands of their parents and that they had somehow fallen through the cracks in every social safety net program that was supposed to protect them.

Theirs was such a painful story that many in the courtroom were moved to tears before Foley and Koch finished telling it, just as I was when Candy told it to me for the first time. The kids endured agonies that shouldn't take place in a society as rich as ours, but they damned well did. Even though I'd heard her story many times as we worked on her defense, it upset me all over again as it was it presented in open court. It was like having our own dirty linen shown in public, and it felt like hell to have to laid out before a room full of strangers.

On top of the plethora of other documentary evidence they'd been able to obtain through legal or medical channels for use in court, Koch and Foley made highly effective use of the incomplete history of Candy's birth family I had endeavored for so long in secret to prepare. The photographs, in particular, turned out to be worth a thousand words when it came to defending her, as did the short stories I included. The most powerful of the pictures were, of course, those of the children and of several of the so-called *homes* they'd lived in before their family fell apart, back before they became wards of Maricopa County. Candy and I had cried when we first looked at them together, and they had the same effect on the jury. On repeated occasions, in fact, there was hardly a dry eye in the courtroom.

It was pleasing to see that some of my stories and photographs were helpful in terms of defending Candy, since the damned material had nearly destroyed us when it was placed in her hands for the first time. Until the day it was of help to her in court, my most fervent wish had been that instead of showing it to her, I had shredded all of it into fragments so tiny they'd never be seen again. It pleased me to no end to know my work had served a useful purpose after all.

Foley and Koch went on to explain that after the dissolution of her birth family, feelings of betrayal, hurt, and anger had lain buried in Candy's mind for the rest of her life. In Dr. Koch's own words, "These feelings were always in her, but they could never be outwardly expressed or asserted."

Why not? was the question you could almost hear the jurors and visitors alike asking. I knew that was what they wanted to know, simply because I had asked the same question myself, back when she first told me the truth about her young life.

"Well," Foley answered for Koch, "because since the day this girl was born, she was effectively forced to lock those kinds of emotions in. She never had enough power or freedom to get anything off her chest, to purge her mind of the sense of frustrated entrapment that had burdened her since childhood. Repression became the name of her game. Living with a load like that on her back was like always being hungry, without ever being able to get enough to eat. I can understand," he said, "just how she felt, and I think I would have felt the same way myself."

"It was impossible for her to speak up about anything when she was with her birth parents; they'd have beaten her down, literally, if she had dared to challenge anything they did. Any act of spontaneity or openness or self-expression that popped up in their household had been quickly and unceremoniously crushed, always by the allied forces of ignorance, neglect, abuse, drunkenness, and the grinding poverty that ruled this girl's daily existence. She was not alone, of course; all of her brothers and sisters suffered along with her. The kids tried to be of support to one another, but what power do children have in conditions as abysmal as theirs?"

"All the kids could do was what they had done; they simply endured, getting by as best they could. The older children stayed at home only until they could find a way to leave, but the ones in the middle and those that were even younger had no choice but to keep on keeping on. Not even when their birth family was torn apart and when all contact with brothers and sisters they loved had been, as far as they knew at the time, lost forever, did any of the kids, including Candice, have a proper chance to mourn their loss, to express their feelings of hurt and anger."

"Unfortunately," Foley added at this point, "even after an involuntary way out of their miserable situation was finally provided by Maricopa County in the State of Arizona, conditions did not get any better for most of the children; they actually got even worse. Removing kids from a dysfunctional home, as most of the siblings would eventually discover, is not automatically synonymous with supplying them with a better one. In too many of their cases, changing their places of residence amounted to little more than instances of moving them from one wretched situation and placing them in another. Candice, for example, ended up being bounced from a short stay in a juvenile hall to a series of short-term foster homes with strangers or relatives who really didn't know her and who, for the most part, just didn't want to get involved in helping her out of her desperate fix.

"Even after she was adopted by two people who were as kind and as worthy as any that could have been found — the Wilsons, whom you'll meet shortly, Candice still found herself living in an environment in which there was no outlet or means of ridding herself of ambiguous and confusing emotions that she couldn't have explained even if she had tried. As kind and as supportive as her adoptive parents had turned out to be, she felt through her senses rather than through her intellect that something she desperately needed was missing as she grew older.

"For two key reasons," said Dr. Koch, "Candice never could talk about what she was really feeling. First, she wouldn't have known at her age how to broach the topic, even if she had decided to try; secondly, anything that might in any way have hinted of ingratitude toward the Wilsons, whom she loved with all her heart, had been all but unthinkable.

"It couldn't be clearer why in this sense she felt smothered in her birth home," Koch continued, "but it is more difficult to understand how a similar kind of pressure could have existed in her adoptive home as well. That," he explained, "is a much more complicated matter, one that involved psychological pressure Candice placed on herself and that she was just was too young to make sense of at the time. By the time she matured, these problems had been internalized to the extent of their becoming a permanent facet of her unique psychological makeup."

"What she experienced in her adoptive home was the diametric opposite of how she had been smothered as a child, but her new surroundings put pressure on her anyway, just not in the same way. This was a new fact of life for her, a force that in some ways inhibited what would have been the natural growth of her own personality. All this was completely unintentional, of course; no one, not even Candice herself, recognized it at the time."

"Her new setting," Dr. Koch explained, "was light years better than the free-wheeling ways of the home in which she had gotten started in life. Her new circumstances were as safe and as supportive and as comforting as her earlier existence had been threatening and destabilizing and so consistently upsetting."

"Despite all this," said Koch, "her new environment, as wonderful as it was, was still confining, just in a whole new and unusual way, one that neither Candice herself nor her adoptive parents could possibly have understood at the time. Despite everyone's best intentions, Candice had landed in a new notch that she had to make herself fit into. How could it have been otherwise? As happy as she was to have an opportunity to make such an adjustment, her new setting did not provide the one opportunity she so desperately needed at the time.

"There was nothing wrong with the opportunity she had been given, it was just that she needed therapy as well. Candice was suffering from some truly hard-core problems, even though neither she nor anyone around her understood it at the time. Much more than most young people, she was in dire need of the sort of internal *bringing out*, if you will, that all kids need to become fully independent, whole adults. At a time when primal scream therapy was what she really needed, every ounce of her effort was being devoted — *willingly, I might add* — to fitting into her wholesome new environment.

"Most everyone seems to have expected that Candice, as a consequence of having had a rocky start in life, would focus all of her attention on preparing for a good marriage, maintaining a proper home, and raising happy and wholesome children. What she really needed at the time, though, was intensive therapy of a kind that no one in her circle envisioned, due to her problems being too deep-seated and cleverly concealed.

"No path through life was ever forbidden or even explicitly discouraged for her, and the Wilsons most certainly would have been supportive of whatever direction she might have chosen to pursue in the future. But, again, what she needed most was something that neither she nor the Wilsons could envision at the time. It's readily understandable that they couldn't help her in the way that she needed, but it's a real shame that she didn't get the help she needed. Her context was such that she couldn't participate in the normal self-examination young people need to engage in to learn how to make it on their own. Give and take outside the home would have helped bring her problems out into the open so they could be confronted head on, but that didn't happen for this girl. Instead, what did happen was that her frustrations and inhibitions were left to fester and to grow. No one was as fault for this, of course; it was just what happened.

"The end result was a way thinking that was too narrow and confining, one that constrained rather than fostered opportunities for the deep introspection and self-exploration she needed to work out solutions on her own. Candice," said Dr. Koch, "grew up to be an outwardly beautiful, impressive, and socially admirable young woman, a model of what everyone in her circle expected her to be, but, on the inside, she remained a troubled human being, one who was about as repressed as it was possible to be without her condition becoming obvious to the people she was around. The adjustment and behavioral problems she did manifest seemed rather mild and not too unusual for a young girl in the process of becoming an adult, but they all too effectively masked much more serious problems."

At this point, Foley called to the stand Ernest and Jewel

Wilson, the adoptive parents he had introduced and that he had been talking about for some time. While they were on the stand, all he did was guide them, one after the other, through statements of their own, statements during which they described to the court what their daughter had been like when she lived at home with them. Because he'd spent a good deal of time talking with the Wilsons to explain Dr. Koch's views about the downside of Candy's time in their home, Foley thought he had a good idea what effect their live testimony would have on the jury. He was right, too; people reacted to them just as he expected.

What came through loud and clear as everyone listened to Ernest and Jewel Wilsons' testimony was that they were being addressed by two humble but proud and admirable people, a man and a woman they would have been pleased to know under any set of circumstances. As they testified, everyone in the courtroom, including the jurors, could see that the Wilsons didn't give a hoot in hell what anyone thought of them or of their conservative religious lifestyle. All they wanted was to try to help their daughter, just as they had from the time their initial bond was formed. It couldn't have been any more obvious that they found it hard to believe that Candy had actually done what she was accused of doing, or that they were clearly terrified by what might happen to her in the future.

They unabashedly blamed themselves for Candy's actions, tearfully declaring that they had always tried to do their best for her but that they had never fully appreciated what she was going through. "Candy," they said, "had been a perfect daughter, a dream of a child. She was our constant ray of sunshine," they said, "more than we would have thought to ask for."

For me, watching the three of them in court that day felt like having my guts run through a wringer, knowing that I was more responsible than anyone else for the anguish they were suffering at that moment. It was plain to see that the Wilsons would have walked through fire for Candy if it would have helped, and, glancing over at her as she cried in her chair, it was clear that she would have done the same for them.

It was obvious to everyone in the courtroom that the Wilsons were parents that any child would have been fortunate to have, and that the relationship they had with their daughter was one any parent would respect. By the time they left the stand, once again there wasn't a dry eye in the courtroom. Foley had gotten to know the Wilsons before he put them on the stand, and he knew how they would come across. *Good people are good people,* I'm sure he thought, just as I did, *and it's wonderful when you have them on your side.*

MY TURN UNDER THE MICROSCOPE

"THEN, FINALLY," SAID FOLEY, "there was Candice's husband, a man who was so blindly devoted to his wife that he could not bring himself to admit that she might actually have personal problems of her own. It was his perspective on their marriage," Foley said after he called me up, "that led to a whole new source of pressure being placed on her fragile back. She knew her husband loved her so much that he didn't want to admit that she had any faults. This made her all the more determined to conceal what was going on inside her. Instead of relieving some of the pressure she felt, the intensity of their relationship actually made it worse.

"Because her husband had made a living for them by holding down a series of ever more responsible and visible positions in publicly funded institutions," Foley pointed out, "over the years she struggled continuously against her own inner demons to avoid disappointing him. Her intention was to become whatever she thought he wanted her to be, even if trying to do so kept moving her closer to the deep end of the pool. What she wanted was for their lives to be perfect for him, not for herself.

"Her problem, though," Foley continued, "was that the expectations she set for herself were impossibly high, given the enormous trauma of her childhood years. She was the most devoted of wives, but moving around so much, being away from her touchstones, the Wilsons, and worrying about the problems her husband was having in his career . . . well, it all combined in such a way as to push her ever more precariously toward to an emotional breaking point. As the years passed by, she inched closer and closer to becoming emotionally overwrought, then finally reaching a point where she just couldn't take it anymore, without ever knowing why."

By this point in Foley's presentation, it had become painfully clear to everyone in the courtroom that the way I conducted my career and how I minimized and otherwise neglected Candy's obvious problems had been terribly hurtful. It was too significant as a causal factor to be ignored, so Foley didn't hesitate to point out in open court how harmful my behavior had been. He had no choice but to point this out, but that didn't lessen how mortifying it was to have my inexcusably negligent behavior described in great detail before a roomful of highly attentive, wide-eyed listeners.

Every time a juror's eyes shifted from Foley to me as he spoke, I felt like digging a hole and crawling into it, and, judging from expressions I saw on various faces, it seemed clear that some of them would have been quite happy to throw shovels full of dirt in over me. What else can I say except that it was unforgettably painful as well as highly embarrassing to be excoriated for my failures before a whole room full of rapt listeners? If I could have taken back everything I had done — my moving and, therefore, all our years of separation from her parents, my lack of attentiveness to her, and so on — I would have done it in a heartbeat. It was too late for that. Instead, it became my great misfortune to have to live the rest of my life with thoughts of all the many ways I failed her permanently implanted in my brain.

OUR ADVOCATES' INSIGHTFULNESS ON FULL DISPLAY

"NONE OF THE PRESSURE her husband placed on her," Foley pointed out, "was inflicted by design or with any malign intent; that should go without saying. Nevertheless, " he said, "the cumulative effect it had on her psyche was the same as if it had been. I'm sure you've heard, haven't you, that *the road to hell is paved with good intentions*, and that *as fallible human beings, we tend to hurt the ones we love?* Well, those old adages are repeated so often because they happen to be true, and they provide a perfect description of what happened to this girl.

"To say all this in a different way, she was literally smashed down when she was with her birth family; ignored and devalued when she was placed with relatives who tried to use her as a laborer; unintentionally and uncomprehendingly confined when she was with her adoptive parents; and, finally, repressed even after she married a man who loved her dearly. Unfortunately, that's the way matters stayed for her, right up until the day she reached her personal boiling point, the moment where she had taken as much as she could stand. When that point was reached, she cracked," said Foley, "and I probably would have done the same if I had been in her shoes for all those years.

"What happened to this girl at every phase of her life," he continued, "is that her greatest personal needs and most troubling inner feelings were either ignored or allowed to fester. Neither expressed nor explored, she simply subdued and pushed her own needs ever more deeply into her subconscious mind. Left with no apparent outlet, the end result was that the dangerously strong feelings of hurt and fear and anger she harbored never went away.

"Because she never felt free to confront her problems head on, a decent person who had been severely wounded as an innocent child learned to get along through devising coping methods that concealed her angst and inner anger. This happened without her or anyone else ever realizing what was going on, and it took place as she dealt with the challenging process of getting along in the world day after day.

"One of the coping techniques she mastered, for example, was lapsing into periods of silence when she became upset or distressed, in the same way ostriches are said to bury their heads in the sand when they're threatened. The more difficult the problem, the longer the period of time this behavior would go on. But," said

Foley, "when people are truly troubled, silence most definitely is not golden.

"Another coping technique she learned to use when her inner demons got out of control was to retreat to her room and crawl into bed. Once there, she would hide by staying under her blankets until, as she described it, she got herself *back on top of it.* The Wilsons did all they knew how to do to minimize and make less of this behavior, thinking that they were observing nothing more than the temporary petulance of an adolescent. They thought of her moodiness as part and parcel of being still somewhat troubled teenaged girl, something she would grow out of sooner or later, but it wasn't; it was much more than that. Her husband came to a somewhat similar conclusion later on, mainly because he never wanted to admit that anything was truly amiss in their relationship.

"Yet another coping technique Candice devised after her marriage was what she described as *talking to herself.* When a troubling problem or emotion really got her down, she would attempt to deal with it by mentally listing and then repeating aloud all of what she called the *pros and cons* or *bullet points* that could be identified. It was her way, she explained to her husband, of thinking matters through, of reasoning situations out in her mind. 'Sometimes it worked,' she explained, 'and sometimes it didn't.' She didn't even realize it when, later on, she began talking to herself any time she was under stress. Her husband should have gotten help for her right then, but he did not.

"Some of Candice's coping techniques were well established by the time she got married," said Foley, "and continued throughout her married life. Others, though," he said, "came into being as pressure continued to mount over the years.

"The Wilsons talked with her about this behavior again and again while she was with them, but, in the end, they dismissed too much of it being what moody, immature teenage girls sometimes do to draw attention to themselves or to get their way. Basically, they thought she'd grow out of it in time. In turn, her husband dismissed all her problems by characterizing all of it as what he wished it to be — the carrying on of a moody married woman. He just couldn't bring himself to admit to the truth.

"Regrettably for Candice," Foley sighed, looking down and slowly turning his head from side to side, "the Wilsons as well as her husband were wrong on all counts; her coping behaviors really were extreme and far out of the ordinary. Her condition didn't get better as time went by; instead, it got worse, much worse.

"Candice's problem didn't come to a crisis while she was with the Wilsons, probably because they watched after her so carefully and were so attentive to her needs. With her husband, though, different dynamics were at play. He was always so busy, and moving all over the country the way they did clearly made matters worse. He was so absorbed in his career that he wasn't as acutely attuned to what was going on within her. In addition, she was always so anxious to please him and support him, to be accommodative to his needs, that she never dared to describe what really was going on with her. When it came to gauging her innermost feelings, anyone else, I regret to have to say, would have been ten times more sensitive and attentive than her own husband."

When Foley made that comment, I couldn't help but cringe and sink even lower into my seat, especially after noting that the attention of multiple jurors once again shifted over to where I was sitting. Several of them looked as if they'd have liked nothing better than to give me a few swift kicks of their own. As our defense attorney, he had to do what he was doing, but, again, knowing that this was so didn't make his comments any easier to bear.

"The end result," said Foley, speaking in a sorrowful tone, "was that Candice lived her entire life subconsciously believing that her deepest feelings and needs ought to be kept hidden from others, always out of fear that revealing them might have unbearable effects on herself or on people she loved. This was blatantly true when she was at home with her birth parents, clearly true when she lived with various members of her own extended family, confusingly true when she was with her adoptive parents, and, regrettably and painfully true through all her years of married life."

“The deep-seated problems that had plagued her since childhood never went away,” he said, “not even after she was adopted by a wonderful couple or after she married a man who loved her dearly and who was able to provide her with a comfortable living and a respectable middle-class lifestyle. Her behavioral problems were ingrained well before these great changes in her life took place, and they never ceased to be the major component of her basic psychological make-up.”

“One inevitable consequence of her unusual condition was that much of her own inner self — her wants, needs, desires, abilities, aspirations, and so on — was never dealt with or even brought out into the open. All her needs were simply repressed, until she evolved into a person who learned to live by becoming what others wanted and expected her to be rather than what she would have or could have become in her own right. The monsters that plagued her never went away; they were just pushed down deep inside, without any true awareness on her part about what was happening.

“Candice, therefore, grew up never feeling free to be her own true self. She turned into two different people, one who always acted and behaved and believed the way people she loved expected her to and another who remained private and internally tortured. She never got to travel in her own space, so the speak, to become whatever she would have and could have become if she hadn’t been traumatized as a child. Lost potential and underdeveloped talent and a huge amount of internal frustration created her condition, and these were only a few of the many tragic consequences of being raised as a child who was not loved or properly nurtured from the beginning of her life.

“She ended up a highly inhibited person, one who was unhealthily fearful of honest self-expression or of disappointing anyone about anything but whose outward beauty and a glowing personality created exactly the opposite impression. Inside, she was entirely different from what she appeared to be on the outside. Fear of saying or doing anything that could be taken as being wrong or offensive by others became a powerful force in her life.

What she really wanted to create was a picture-perfect way of life, one that was as far removed as possible from the way she grew up as a child.

"Her suffering was caused by deep-seated and mysterious problems," said Foley, "problems that were unknowingly masked from external view. You could think of it as an inner darkness so carefully concealed that it rarely ever saw the light of day. It was always there, though, and it couldn't have been more real. If you had to judge her as an actor, you'd have to give her an honorable mention for an academy award." As he said this, Foley smiled sadly, and most everybody smiled back at him, equally sadly.

"The depths of her inner feelings were not even imagined by the people she was around, not during the time she lived with the Wilsons and not even during the thirty-plus years she lived with her husband. It's hard to believe, I know," said Foley. "It certainly was for me, back when I first figured it out. It makes me sigh every time I think about it. For all those years of married life she lived right beside a husband who loved her, but she remained afraid to letting herself *be herself*, fearing that demons would be let loose if she did. It had to have been a torturous existence.

"It seems obvious," he continued, "that if her condition had not been diagnosed by Dr. Koch and brought out in the open through the analysis we had to do in preparation for this trial, Candice would most likely have lived this way for the rest of her life or until she went off the deep end altogether. She alone knew it was possible for her to swing from one extreme to another in an instant — from, for example, feelings of great love to mind-numbing anxiety or to the blackest form of outright anger. In a strange and unexpected way, therefore, it could be argued that what happened that day at the club has been a boon to her as well as to her husband.

"Dark impulses lay buried in her mind, forces that could produce an emotional outburst at any moment. Most of her outbursts were too inconsequential for others to notice, but she lived on the verge of behaving in ways that most definitely could be offensive or dangerous. To be more precise about all this, there's a great difference between a crying jag as an emotional outburst and exploding in an absolute rage over something. The key point to be made here is that an unexpected reaction could be triggered in an instant, by a wide range of stimuli, over matters big or small. When I finally figured this out, the question of what had driven her over the edge that day at the country club ceased to be a mystery.

"No," said Foley, "it wasn't her interaction with the Stackhouses that did the trick; that was only an effect, not the ultimate cause. She lost control back when her own husband, the one person who loved her above all else, unwittingly maneuvered her into reliving so many of the miserable, degrading, and depressing agonies of her childhood in order to complete the family history project he had done in secret, ignoring her expressed wishes. If he hadn't done that, her condition might never have disintegrated to a breaking point, most assuredly not in a public setting. It was more painful for her that most of us can understand to be surprised by actual photographs of people and events she had struggled for a lifetime to forget."

Once again, eyes seemingly shooting angry daggers shifted back and forth from Foley and Candy over to my location, where I slunk even further down in my chair. *God*, I thought as I absorbed his comments, *what an idiot I'd been.*

"Candice," continued Foley, "didn't want anyone to know about her past, especially not her husband. When he so forcefully but thoughtlessly brought all her private agony out into the open by thrusting that family history in her face in such a clumsy and unexpected way, it didn't make her happy; it humiliated and embarrassed her. It made her sick at heart to learn that the past she considered too pitiful and shameful to be known by anyone had been found out by the one person she wanted not to know about it at all. Worse still, he forced her, through the seemingly never-ending series of private conversations that followed, to reveal what she considered to be a whole string of dirty little secrets, secrets that made her feel miserable as a human being and unworthy of being considered a beloved wife."

Lowering his voice even more and coming across if he were speaking confidentially and off the record, Foley then said to the court: "Those of us who worked on Candice's defense thought her first reaction to preparing for this trial was totally unjustified, since nothing that had happened while she lived with her birth family had been caused by anything she'd said or done herself. She told us that she was ready and willing to accept any sentence this court might render, to admit defeat without putting forth a defense. That," he said, "was totally unacceptable to any of us. Her husband, in particular," he confided, "really blew his top the first time he heard Dr. Koch say what she wanted to do. To be more specific, what he shouted out was 'What in the hell has she ever been guilty of? She's always been on the receiving end of misery, not the cause of it, and how much of that sort of thing can any human being tolerate?'"

And, as it turned out, this seemed to be the same conclusion that everyone else in the courtroom had arrived at as well. Asking how much of the kind of torment Candy had been exposed to one person could stand came across as a notably just and reasonable question.

Dr. Koch's thoughtfully arrived at observations seemed so logical that near visible changes of heart seemed to have taken place after he and Foley articulated them in court. There was no way to actually *know* this, of course; it just *felt* that way.

Dr. Koch, as if sensing the collective response that had taken place within the courtroom, went on to add the following comments: "It is clearly true that the ordeal she and her siblings went through was not her fault, but that didn't stop her from feeling guilty about it just the same. Her guilt stemmed from thinking that somehow or another she could have or should have done something to keep all of her brothers and sisters together, to have protected them in some way, especially the younger ones, to keep her family as safe and sound as families are meant to be. Her guilt," Koch asserted, "came from a form of protectiveness. Down deep inside, she instinctively wanted to do what her own mother had not been able to do; she wanted to save her family. At that moment, she became something beyond the child she really was; she became what might be thought of as a *sister-mom.*

"Even before Candice said goodbye to her husband and headed over to the clubhouse restaurant the morning of the shooting," said Dr. Koch, "her emotional condition had deteriorated to a crisis level. She had become a truly sick person, a powder keg ready to be set off by the right spark. Well, her interaction with Carl and Emily Stackhouse provided just the kind of spark that was needed. To be even more pointed about it, what set her off that day was when Emily Stackhouse slapped her hard in the face. That, as I see it, was an assault, as well as the first blow that was struck as a result of their argument, and I feel certain being struck as forcefully as Candy was would have upset anyone." Then, quietly, Foley added, "I know it would have upset me."

As soon as these statements were made, every eye in the courtroom instantly shifted over to Emily Stackhouse, and every person in the room immediately recalled the snarling frowns, condescending behavior, and attitudes of superiority she and Carl had displayed throughout the trial. Their demeanor made it easy for others to imagine how being slapped in the face by people like them would most definitely have made anyone angry, just as Foley had pointed out. It couldn't have been any more obvious that the couple had wanted to humiliate Candy and make her grovel in the same way as they had the young waiter, Derrick, earlier that morning. Upon realizing this, most jurors and spectators stopped viewing the victims with anything close to the degree of sympathy they had had for them at the beginning of the trial.

Emily Stackhouse, who immediately realized that everyone was seeing a whole new side of herself and her husband, suddenly, and of course, involuntarily, flushed bright red. Her husband Carl, as soon as he noticed his wife's reaction, flushed red as well. They had been forced to admit, most likely for the very first time, that their own behavior had been pivotal in terms of causing the argument to get out of hand that day at the club. Until this point in the trial, I don't think that possibility had ever occurred to them.

"If she had not been suffering from severe inner turmoil," Foley then continued, having brought about the impression he had intended all along, "this girl would not have lost all composure and all control over her thoughts and actions like she did that morning. Something had to spur it happen, something that was beyond her ability to manage. Had she been her normal self, it is highly unlikely that anything that untoward would have taken place.

"But," said Foley, pausing briefly so that the jury would wonder what he was going to say next, "her mental state was anything but normal that morning. As I have said, I think she was dealing with severe emotional distress, and I am as sure of that as I have been of anything since I became an attorney.

"The incident in the clubhouse restaurant that morning just happened to occur at a time when she had reached her own personal flash point, a day when the unspoken emotional toll exacted by dreams of her childhood agonies on top of the deteriorating situation taking place in her home had finally forced her, so to speak, to her knees. You can liken the way she reacted to some of the incidences of so-called *road rage* that occasionally appear on the evening news — mindless blowups that occur when normal people experience extraordinary personal anxiety and stress. When people get into that frame of mind, a minor incident can be more than enough to make them behave in ways that, under normal circumstances, they wouldn't even have dreamt of.

"We all know what this girl did wasn't right," said Foley, "but I think it ought to be equally obvious that it was neither premeditated nor intentional, and it certainly wasn't malicious. In fact," he said, "now that I've gotten to know her as a human being, I don't believe there's a spiteful bone in her body. She was simply overcome by the sadness and unfairness of all that had taken place in her past. In her mind, she was fighting back against the devil at last, something she thought she ought to have done — in the proper way, of course — a whole lot earlier in life. If she had, I don't think this incident would ever would have happened."

FOLEY'S *COUP DE GRÂCE*

THEN, JUST AS EVERYONE thought his defense of Candy had ended, Foley did what no one in the courtroom dreamed he would do; he called his own client, the accused, the beloved daughter of Ernest and Jewel Wilson, my own sweet wife, Candice Lee *Candy* (Caine) (Wilson) Holder, up to the stand to testify in her own defense. When she rose to head up front, my heart pounded so hard I thought I was going to fall off my chair.

Every eye in the room was welded on Candy as she walked forward to speak for herself in court, knowing that, as the judge had pointed out from the beginning, she wasn't obligated to do so. Everyone knew her coming forward meant much more than that she would be able to address the court under the guidance of Harry Foley, her own attorney; it also meant that District Attorney Preston Walker would have a crack at her as well. Everyone knew she'd be subjected to an unforgiving grilling of the kind he was famous for, so the fact that she had readily and willingly agreed to testify on her own behalf came across as a highly courageous act.

Because it was obvious that whole outcome of the trial could hinge on how Candy came across on the stand, everyone in the courtroom waited with bated breath to hear from her directly. Foley first looked directly at the audience and then over toward the jury and quietly commented: "I'm not one bit worried; I've gotten to know this girl."

This girl, I thought. *He's still calling her a girl, when we've been married for over thirty years.* Somehow, though, by this point in the trial, the use of the term didn't seem so out of place anymore; in fact, it seemed to fit the situation quite well, due to the revelations that had come out about her past. Now, no one batted an eye when the expression was used, which meant that most everyone else had come to think of her as a girl as well. He had made her the girl of our trial, a girl who had been so severely wounded in childhood that she'd suffered throughout her life and finally been driven to commit an act of desperation.

It was at this moment when I first began to believe that Foley really did have a chance of winning our case in court. It had become obvious that he was not just an expert at his craft, but that he also was a man who understood people exceedingly well. His practice of employing skillfully chosen expressions and quotations was a powerful weapon in his hands. He used words as a brush and the courtroom as a palette to paint a strikingly vivid picture of how every one of Candy's significant others had let her down over the years, and how her basic emotional needs had never been met. He made everyone understand how she had fought with all her might to keep her darker instincts in check, only to fail in desperation on one single occasion.

Now, with Foley guiding her, Candy went on to explain in court how she had lived her whole life afraid of her own emotions, repressing them for fear of what they might lead her to do or to say. She explained herself this way: "I've never been able to tell anyone, especially my husband, about the feelings that came over me at times, sometimes right out of the clear blue sky and without any warning. It's something I've struggled against all my life. My feelings were sometimes so strong that they scared me. They'd have scared you too, if I had told you about them, and you'd have been right to be scared of them, because there were many times when I thought I could say or do something truly harmful." Around the room, mouths opened wide in unconscious fascination as she continued to describe her own condition.

"There were times when I felt so much anger, I knew I could hurt someone under the right set of circumstances. This was something, though, that I just did not want to believe of myself. Again, it scared me. I didn't want to talk to my husband about it because I thought it would have wrecked our marriage. He wouldn't have believed what I wanted to say, and he would only have made light of the problem by making a joke of it. That's his way, you know; he means well, but sometimes he just doesn't hear what people are telling him, *especially* what *I* try to tell him."

Feeling small and more than a little bit sick inside and, again, slinking down as far into my chair as I could, it seemed obvious that everyone considered her point to be well taken. I wanted to forget about the hole I'd dug earlier, just so I could slash my wrists and therefore more immediately put an end to feeling so damned rotten about myself. I couldn't, though; I had to sit there, knowing that I richly deserved a few hard knocks on the head and a whole series of swift kicks in the butt. Judging from all the eyes that glared at me from around the room, most everyone fully agreed.

"I just boiled with anger at times," she continued, "and at other times I felt overwhelmingly sad; why, I didn't know. Feelings like mine, I knew all too well, if they were to come out, could have ruined us, you know, my husband and I, due to his holding such a visible public position. My outbursts were caused by emotions I couldn't explain, feelings that, if I had acted on them, could have destroyed our whole relationship, our entire lives together."

"You know," she said, "there are times when it is appropriate to be angry, when anger cries out to be expressed, when something should be done about the cause of it. It's just that it has to be dealt with in a constructive way, not in a way that makes matters worse, the way I expressed it that day at Pecan. The doctor who's been working with me, Dr. Koch, who has been a wonderful and helpful man, has made that perfectly clear, and I know in my heart that he's right. Being able to talk with him has meant more to me that I know how to say. I can't thank him enough."

Twelve sets of eyes, some of them glistening, briefly shifted over to Koch, who smiled at Candy as if to say through his expression: *You're welcome.* I sure as hell thanked him; I truly did, even though he and Foley had and were still in the process of excoriating me for being a major initiator of her overall emotional meltdown. He was absolutely right, so I could not disagree.

"Wherever I was, my environment was such that I could never do anything about how I felt, even when I had a perfect right to be troubled or angry. Keeping your feelings bottled up inside hurts more than you can imagine. It squashes and constrains and ties you into a knot, until you get where you think you just can't stand it any longer.

"It's a feeling that bounces you in one direction and then another, for reasons you can't understand. You think you're going crazy. Eventually, you start to feel so guilty about the anger you're feeling that you get to a point where you think you have no right to be angry about anything, that anger is never justified, and then, finally, you lose your ability to stand up for yourself. You just squeeze it all in. It's like giving up a basic human right.

"There's something truly sick about constantly having to see everybody else's side of things, but never being able to come up with a side of your own. My doctor pointed that out, and I immediately knew that what he'd said was absolutely right, just because I *felt* the truth of it. If you don't have a right to have opinions of your own, it's like you don't even matter, like you're not even there. Being *nice* can be nothing more than an excuse for not taking a stand on anything, for being so accommodative and understanding that you are, in fact, living a lie. Sometimes, people who appear to be calm on the outside are actually boiling over on the inside, and that's the way it got to be for me.

"I never felt free to speak up for myself, first because I wasn't allowed to and later on because I wouldn't allow myself to. It's humiliating to feel like everyone else matters but you. When you let people abuse you and take advantage of you and you don't say anything, just to keep everything harmonious, you become a traitor to yourself. That's how it was for me.

"Why," she cried quietly, dabbing her eyes with a tissue, "were my father and mother so unforgivably neglectful of me and my brothers and sisters when we were all so young and innocent and helpless? Why wasn't their abuse of us noticed and dealt with sooner? Why didn't the county or the state or someone give us more meaningful help, when our family was so clearly in crisis? Why did that woman at the club have to be hateful enough to scream in my face and slap me around like she did? Did anything I said or did warrant that extreme of a response? Our whole situation was so unbelievably unfair that it was absolutely outrageous."

The way in which Candy unwittingly juxtaposed past and

recent events and then spoke of them so openly using wording that clearly could have prejudiced the court against her made it obvious to every listener that she truly had been traumatized by her past. She couldn't have made it any clearer if she'd put up a neon sign. Foley hardly said a thing; he simply asked a question from time to time, just to keep her on track. Beyond that, he simply let her keep on talking, trying to explain herself.

"I was never able to forgive my parents, especially my dad, for the destruction of our family, no matter how hard I have tried. The misery they put us kids through, especially my little brothers, before our family broke up was just too hurtful to be forgiven. I hated them, no matter how hard I tried to put it all behind me. I've been trying to do so for as long as I can remember, without any lasting success."

Candy's own words enabled everyone in the courtroom to see that her subconscious problems had existed long before that fateful day at the Pecan Plantation Clubhouse dining room and well before she was presented with the project I had done about her family. Learning more about her family history had been nothing more than a trigger, yet another force to accelerate the long and torturous process of emotional unraveling that had been going on throughout her life. Viewing the words and pictures I presented had been such a poignant experience for her that she had literally absorbed the pain her elders must have suffered during their own times of trial. Hearing about the indignities they had to deal with had hurt her deeply, mainly because their stories amounted to yet another reminder of how much she herself had suffered in the past and how much she was still suffering at the time.

"Looking at those old pictures and hearing my relatives' stories really tore me up inside. It seemed so terribly unfair," she said, "that so many members of my family had to experience so much misery. Looking at those old photographs and thinking about all those tragic stories was more than I could stand. I just couldn't take it anymore."

She had to have felt, in fact, that she was just another in a long series of losers, one of a whole line of people who had failed in life because they never had a chance to compete on a level field. This thought surely had to have occurred to her, and it just as surely had to have been debilitating. It was what I was thinking as she spoke, and I think everybody else in the room was thinking the same thing. Reading her family history had been a final straw, a trigger that released the floodgate holding back her long-subdued emotions.

"My mother," she said, "after recovering from her suicide attempt, made a few half-hearted attempts to reestablish contact with me and, as I understand it, with some of the other kids, but her guilt-motivated and insincere efforts never came to anything. I refused to have anything to do with her. Later on, I heard through indirect sources that she had divorced our dad and remarried sometime thereafter. Basically, she just moved off somewhere to start a second life. As far as I know, she made no further effort to stay in contact with any of us kids. I never heard from her again, nor would I have cared to."

When Candy mentioned her father, anger and bitterness as well as anxiety became palpable in her tone of voice. Without the slightest bit of hesitation, she said that she had never wanted to see him or talk with him or even to think about him ever again. "Even if he had begged for reconciliation," she said, "it would have done no good. Nothing he could have said or done would ever have made up for his neglect and abuse. My memories of him amount to a dark dream, an ongoing nightmare that has done nothing but drag me down my entire life. As far as he is concerned, all I want is to forget him altogether."

"As it turned out," Foley interjected, "Candice needn't have worried about future contact with either one of her parents. Pirley, after her one half-hearted and token attempt to reestablish contact with her kids, just disappeared from their lives, making it quite clear that her interest in them really wasn't all that strong. And, after Luther disappeared that last time, the kids ever heard from him again, either. Only a handful of members of his extended family had had any further contact with him. When he died, authorities somehow managed to inform a few of his relatives, who then took it upon themselves to bring others up to date. Somehow, one of them talked with somebody who knew the Wilsons, who, in turn, felt that it was their duty to notify Candice, and that was how she happened to be present for his service."

"Yes," said Candy, "a ragged handful of people turned up for his pauper's funeral, but nobody there cried over his passing. He was just gone, and that's all there was to it. I cried, but not for him; I cried in memory of what he'd done to my brothers and sisters and me."

"Candice," Foley added, "was the only one of his twelve kids who was there to see their father off. We don't know if any of the others were reached; we just know that none of them showed up."

Jesus, I thought as I listened, *her story is so damned unbearably sad that I can hardly bear to hear it,* even though I had heard it many times before, during our preparation for trial. Even so, listening to it being repeated in a public setting made it sound all the more pathetic and disheartening.

"I considered my birth parents dead," Candy continued, "just as soon as they abandoned my brothers and sisters and me." It was just as well, especially as far as her dad was concerned. As it turned out, his alcoholism had eventually progressed from bad to worse, until his addiction ended up affecting his brain. After his last disappearance, he stayed gone for good. Until his funeral years later, no one in his immediate family had ever saw him again, as far as we knew. We learned later on, after the trial, that word of his whereabouts and activities occasionally reached a few of his relatives through incidental and secondhand sources, but that was about it.

"I might eventually have been able to forgive my mother for neglecting us kids," said Candy, "if our problems hadn't been caused as much by her behavior as by his. What I could never forgive nor forget is that she had, in effect, abandoned us in more ways than trying to kill herself, in that she made only a half-hearted effort to get us all back together again after she recovered. When you're little, you don't want people to know you are *in the system*, that you got taken away from your parents. What became clear was that she really *didn't want us back.* That," Candy said, with bitterness clearly evident in her voice, "is something no mother can ever justify, not even in the most desperate of circumstances. A mother," she said, "never has the right to take the easy way out, leaving innocent children behind to suffer. She should have been willing to die, rather than abandon us.

"I just decided," she said, "that my birth parents no longer existed. As far as I was concerned, Ernest and Jewel Wilson were my real parents, beginning back when they rescued me from the horrible way I had been living up to then, and they became all the parents I would ever need.

"Life," she said she had decided, "is too short and too precious to be spent worrying about birth parents whose only impact on me and my brothers and sisters had been to keep us living in wretchedness and misery. I made up my mind that nobody was ever going to take advantage of me like that again, and that I was going to live the rest of my life the way it was meant to be lived, the way I knew it could and should be lived.

"I decided after I went to live with the Wilsons that I was not only going to take charge of my own situation, but that I was also going to demonstrate through my own behavior how much good one person can do for others when their mind is truly put to the task. What I wanted was to become the exact opposite of what my birth parents had been for me."

She had done it too, I realized as she spoke, to the extent that she had been able to, right up until the day of the shooting at Pecan. As a beneficiary of her mindset for over thirty years, I could attest to her having done all she knew how to make our lives a good as they could be. It couldn't have been any clearer that her resolutions had been heartfelt, and that she'd honorably and dutifully done her best to keep them. Noting the sincerity written all over her face and that literally dripped from every word she said, I think everyone who listened to her testimony that day came to an identical conclusion.

THERE'S NO NEED TO GILD A LILY

"WELL, LADIES AND GENTLEMEN," said Foley to the jurors when Candy finished her comments, "that's all we have to say in this girl's defense. I said I'd explain to you why she behaved the way she did that morning at the country club, and I've done the best I could to do so. Now, you know as much about what happened as I do, as much as of her defense knows. It's up to you to decide where we go from here, but I sure know what I'd do if I were in your shoes." With these final comments, Foley's defense of my dear, sweet, lovely, fragile, wounded, precious wife came to an end.

Silence filled the courtroom for a while as she left the stand and a recess was called by the judge. Several people blinked, appearing reflective as well as taken aback by the information that they'd been asked to absorb; others seemed lost in thoughts unfathomable to anyone but themselves; and still others started glancing around with *what now?* looks on their faces. The room stayed quieter for longer than usually would have been the case.

As for me, all I felt was relief. I was glad Candy's initial testimony was over; I don't know if I could have endured much more of the raw truth that had to be placed on the table. With respect to Candy herself, my only thought at the time was *blessed be the pure of heart; they do indeed show the rest of us the right way.*

MUTED THUNDER FROM THE OTHER SIDE

AFTER THE COURT RECONVENED, the prosecutor, who seemed frustrated by the fact that the trial was not going as he had expected, aroused my fears anew by saying loudly and clearly for all to hear: "Well, even if her parents tortured her as a girl until she was thirteen years old and even if she tortured herself for another thirty years, that doesn't give her a right to try to kill two innocent people. Hellfire, if I gave in to that impulse any time I felt it, I'd have murdered half the people in Hood County by now."

Walker's stinging words immediately made me cringe, and I don't think they come across to anyone in the room in the jocular way he had hoped they would. The testimony already presented made his wording seem unduly coarse and hollow. His comments were worrisome anyway, mainly because we were in Texas, a state well known to be one populated by people who are intent on making sure guilty parties receive the punishment they deserve. Worse still, we were in Hood County, right in the center of one of the more conservative, law–and–order areas of our state. We knew we were up against a highly capable prosecutor, a man who was well known for having swung juries in his direction on many occasions, even when it appeared that he didn't have much of a chance of doing so. Before it was all over, there was no of telling what our jury would decide.

Despite my worrying, most of what Walker said and did from that point forward came across as petty stages of an anticlimactic ending to a play an audience had not enjoyed. Candy was cross-examined and excoriated at great length, but a die had been cast. Minds had been made up after Foley, Koch, and the rest of us and then Candy spoke, and nothing that was said thereafter made much of a difference.

Maybe, I thought at the time, *I was seeing and hearing only what I want to see and hear.* But there seemed to be no way in the world the jury was going to come down hard on Candy after the testimony that had been presented, if, indeed, they came down hard on her at all. As worried as I was, I sensed that our defenders Koch and Foley had made it abundantly clear that a harsh judgment against her would be unwarranted and would serve no useful purpose.

It was highly noticeable that there had been few overtly favorable responses to Walker's many stinging remarks, even though he had clearly hoped to quash the spell Foley had cast over the jury. Although he intended to interject *some old-fashioned commonsense* into the proceedings, he came across more like Teddy Roosevelt on a rant, encouraging his troops to charge up San Juan Hill. As emphatic as he tried to be, few listeners seemed to be on his wavelength. He came across as if he were trying hard to be more indignant than he really was, as if he wasn't fully convinced by his own arguments. These were no more than my personal thoughts about his remarks, but I thought sure others had taken them the same way.

Basically, Walker's tactics backfired. Foley and Koch's findings had touched everyone just as deeply as they had touched me, and Candy's own comments about her tortured childhood had sealed the deal. Jurors had formed opinions that could not be changed by theatrics or caustic accusations. Foley had so clearly explained why she folded up on that fateful day at the country club that they could not be swayed against her.

In the strangest and most unexpected twist of the proceeding, even Candy's victims — the two people she chased after with a loaded gun, Carl and Emily Stackhouse — had been sufficiently touched by her testimony that you could see their hatred melting as Foley and Koch's defense unfolded. Throughout the trial they had shown up smartly clothed, decked out in bejeweled affluence, seemingly fully composed, and showing no visible ill effects from the injuries they suffered that day at the club. Their only observable wound seemed to be to their sense of pride; their physical injuries, which were never as serious as they appeared, had healed to the extent that they didn't appear to have ever been hurt.

Their psychic wounds, however, had been real enough to cause them to do whatever they could to make sure Candy got the punishment they thought she damned well deserved. Getting even had been their primary reason for pursuing the case all along, as opposed to seeking redress for their actual physical injuries, which really weren't apparent to anyone. They stayed angry anyway, right up until Foley and Koch presented Candy's defense. After that, their overall take on what had happened that day in the dining room was swayed, in the same way as everyone else's.

In marked contrast to Carl and Emily Stackhouse, Candy

remained a picture of remorseful suffering throughout the trial. Clearly repentant about what she had done, she made a ready confession of guilt, willingly accepted personal responsibility for her actions, displayed heartfelt contrition, offered an abject apology, and earnestly pleaded for forgiveness — all without regard for any personal punishment she might receive. She had also testified on her own behalf, voluntarily accepting the risk of opening herself up for cross examination, when everyone in the courtroom knew that she wasn't obligated to go down that slippery slope. What more could any prosecutorial team have asked?

The stark contrast in demeanor the two sides exhibited made Candy a sympathetic figure in everyone's eyes. It couldn't have been any more obvious who was really suffering, and it was just as clear that her emotions were not a pretense; she was truly miserable.

The truth of the matter is that all four of us came across as far more pitiful than dangerous, and, in the end, that was the view of our culpability that prevailed; basically, the judge and jury ended up pitying us far more than they wanted to see us punished. And yes, it was appropriate at this point to use the pronoun *us* rather than *her*, since any punishment meted out to Candy would affect all of us in equal measure.

People today express a lot of cynicism about our criminal justice system, but for the most part, the people who turn its wheels are far more sensitive to human needs than high-profile cases heard about in the media make us think. What happened during our trial was that opinions that were well fixed at the beginning were turned around by the truth, until a collective reassessment of Candy's culpability occurred. Jurors who started out grimly determined to see the guilty punished were surprised when their initial sentiment was replaced by an overwhelming sense of sadness over what had happened to Candy as a child. Eventually, even her victims, the person she'd shot, Carl Stackhouse and his wife Emily, begun to feel somewhat ashamed of the way they'd behaved that day at the club. The fact that Candy had repeatedly apologized and begged the couple for forgiveness swayed everyone all the more.

Little by little as Candy's story was revealed, bitterness drained out of those who were involved in the proceedings. In the end, everyone realized that the cause of the shooting that day at Pecan had been nothing more sinister than the wounded psyche of an innocent child, a child who had suffered more than her accusers or anyone else in the courtroom could possibly have imagined. Eventually, it became clear to everyone who was present that the defendant they saw before them was not the flighty, craven person the press and prosecutor made her out to be, and it became equally obvious that she would be of no further danger to the general public.

Even the injured couple eventually stated that they had forgiven her for what she did. They weren't bad people; they were just totally self-focused, like so many people in our society are.

The Stackhouses' turnaround was not just a tremendously positive turn of events in terms of Candy's defense; it was also an enormously uplifting moment for everyone involved in the trial. Although their change of heart was totally unexpected, everyone seemed to consider is as somehow *appropriate*, for lack of a better word, upon hearing Candy's heart-wrenching childhood story. Her trial ended up becoming a sobering reminder of how true it is that life isn't always fair. I thought I'd long since cried myself out, but, when Carl and Emily Stackhouse accepted Candy's apology, I discovered I hadn't, not by a long shot. For those who were present, their turnaround was a deeply moving event. *God*, I thought, *hadn't forgotten us after all.*

The judge and jurors alike concluded that Candy was one of the most unlikely criminals they had ever seen. It had been made clear to them that what she did that day at the club was neither intentional nor in any way premeditated. She had simply buckled under the pressure of forces she didn't understand and, therefore, could not begin to control. It was obvious that she posed no threat to anyone, and there was no way under the sun that she would ever do such a thing again.

OUR FUTURE GOES TO THE JURY

IMMEDIATELY AFTER GIVING the jury instructions and directing them to depart for deliberations, the judge dismissed us to await our fate. We knew Candy would be found guilty, since she had indeed shot at Carl and Emily Stackhouse on that horrible day in the dining room of the Pecan Plantation Country Club in Granbury, Texas, and she had, in fact, wounded Carl Stackhouse, not just once but twice. Our best hope was that any sentence she received would be mitigated by the amazingly effective defense Foley had delivered on her behalf. We were convinced the jurors had been touched by his comments, but we also knew she had done what she was accused of doing. Waiting for a verdict was a nerve-wracking experience, no matter what we thought.

Knowing that a guilty verdict could lead to her being taken away for years left me feeling half nauseated; her sentence, it goes without saying, would be my sentence as well, no matter what it turned out to be. I was worried enough to fanaticize about begging the judge to let me stay in prison with her, to assure him that our living together in a tiny cell wouldn't be a bother for either of us. Whenever I thought about what might happen to her, my spirit sank a little deeper.

One finding that came out during the trial was so worrying I couldn't get it out of my mind, one that had to do with the gun that was used in the shooting. Its revolving chamber held nine bullets, but some of the shells I found with it were so corroded, they wouldn't fire when the trigger was pulled. Our old gun, it had been discovered, had misfired multiple times. Nine casings were found in the chamber afterwards, but three of them were unspent. All nine shells, as it turned out, had been struck by the firing pin, even the three that hadn't gone off. It was also proven through forensic examination that the trigger actually had been pulled more than nine times. What this meant, of course, is that Candy had been trying her level best to shoot the Stackhouses as many times as she could. Lordy, did that ever come across as damning, back when Walker pointed out in court. For this reason alone, I thought the jury might throw the book at her.

Of the six bullets that had been fired, only two of them hit their mark — the first two, which were fired at close range. The other four shots went wild, but only because they were fired while Candy was chasing the Stackhouses out of the clubhouse and up onto the greens. It was confirmed through forensics testing that the gun was too rusty to be fired by simply pulling the trigger, which meant that she had had to use her thumbs to force back the hammer. A good amount of force was required to pull back the hammer, and more was required to pull the trigger.

Some jurors didn't appreciate the full significance of these facts at first, but the prosecutor made sure that they caught on in short order. What this information meant, Walker carefully pointed out, was that if Candy could have fired the gun easily, two people might be dead or maimed today. When Walker made this particular point, he no doubt thought it would be his major blow against us. We agreed; it was truly damning evidence against her.

Thank God, I recall thinking to myself back when this ground was covered during trial, *that our old gun was as rusty as it was*. I also remember berating myself for not having gotten rid of the damned thing, back when I found it hidden under our attic insulation.

Foley did what he could to mute the point that the bullets in the gun were what are called *.22 caliber shorts*, a low-powered shell more commonly used for target practice or scaring away birds than for anything else. We were relieved and thankful for this small fact, knowing that a gun loaded with the higher-powered ammo most homeowners favor for self-protection would have inflicted a whole hell of a lot more damage than the lower-powered shells.

If Candy had had any intent to hurt anyone, Foley pointed out, she would have had high-powered rounds on hand. "I'm a gun owner myself," he said, "and we all know that. Besides," he pointed out, "the bullets that were used were purchased by the previous owner ten years or so before the shooting, long enough for the shells to have partially corroded. It couldn't be any clearer," he pointed out, "that there had been no advance intent to fire the gun."

Yet another highly worrisome argument Walker raised against Candy was that she had dropped the gun while sitting on the couch in the clubhouse foyer because she was aware enough to realize not only that a serious crime had been committed but also that she was in immediate danger of being clubbed over the head by the golfers who had walked toward her with clubs raised in the air. "She had been aware enough to fear for her own safety," he asserted, "which proves that was not as out of control of herself as she claimed. What this means," he declared, "that she was well aware of what she was doing all along." His point caused quite a stir during the trial.

Foley rebuffed Walker's contention by arguing that Candy dropped the gun and fainted because she was in an emotional daze, not because she was aware of what she had done or, for that matter, what would have happened if she had made a twitch as golfers walked toward her with their clubs raised. "If she had truly been aware of what might have happened," Foley conjectured, "wouldn't she have pointed the gun in their direction to keep them at bay? Not a one of those who were present, including the girl herself, had any way of knowing whether or not it could be fired again.

"During her testimony," he pointed out, "she said she had no idea why she dropped the gun and fainted, but that it had had nothing to do with her having been, as the district attorney has claimed, *suddenly paralyzed by fear*, either as a consequence of what she had done or due to the danger she knew she was in. '*My mind just went blank*,' she said, '*and I really can't explain why.*' Given what she'd just done," said Foley, "I really don't think she was afraid of anything at the time."

My impression during the trial was that Foley's points had resonated with the jury, mainly because I saw no skeptical expressions or rolling of eyes to indicate that they hadn't. In truth, though, their reaction was impossible to gauge, not with any degree of certainty. That, unfortunately, is how jury trials tend to go.

A UNANIMOUS VERDICT

THE MORNING OF THURSDAY, May 8, 2003, began like any other, but Candy and the Wilsons and I knew it would be the first day of the rest of our lives because it was on this date that our jury returned to the courtroom with a decision in hand. Waiting to hear what they had to say was a terribly anxious time for us, just as it was for Harry Foley and Walter Koch, even though we had a generally positive feeling that a reasonable verdict would be rendered.

As it turned out, the jury decided even more favorably on our behalf than we thought they would; they found Candy not guilty, on grounds that the shooting had been committed during a moment of temporary insanity. We were delighted, of course, even though their verdict flew in the face of public opinion throughout our highly conservative area, which was that she was as guilty as sin. Our jurors had made a gutsy decision, in view of the prevailing local sentiment.

After accepting and then announcing the jury's decision, the judge thanked the members for their diligent effort on behalf of the people of our Hood County. After that, he went on to offer a few carefully worded comments of his own as a means of summing up the proceedings. He'd formed some strong opinions during the trial, and he seemed eager to share them.

The judge began by saying that he fully agreed with the jury's opinion, then went on to make a series of additional observations about what he'd noticed during the trial. Turning his attention to where our team sat huddled near the front of the room, still red-eyed and teary but yet at the same time smiling in relief, he said to Harry Foley, "Mr. Foley, I couldn't agree more with the arguments you made in the courtroom; there's no way in the world a fine person like Mrs. Holder could have been herself when she hurt Mr. and Mrs. Stackhouse. She didn't know right from wrong that morning, and that clearly was why she wasn't able to appreciate the consequences of her actions. Because she wasn't herself during the shooting, holding her criminally responsible would have served no meaningful public purpose. The plaintiffs' own words helped confirm that she wasn't in control of her faculties on the day of the shooting, when they repeatedly stated that *she looked and acted like a crazy woman.*

"Furthermore," he said, "I fully agree that it was indeed most fortunate how Dr. Koch was able to ferret out what really drove Mrs. Holder's behavior that day, since his excellent work not only explained to the satisfaction of the court why she behaved as she did but also has been of immeasurable personal benefit in terms of assuring her full recovery. His excellent analytical work made the course of events so understandable that even the fine couple who suffered at her hands and filed the charges that brought about this trial were persuaded by the logic of it. Back when we first got under way, I'd have put up good money against anything like that happening, and I'd have had a lot of takers, too. That the plaintiffs allowed their hearts to be moved by the facts showed great strength of character on their parts.

"Mrs. Holder," the judge continued, looking directly at Candy, "if Carl and Emily Stackhouse have been able to forgive you for what you did to them, then surely you should be able to forgive yourself for anything you may feel you did or failed to do as a child — if, indeed, you ever did anything wrong, and it is my belief that you did not. In addition, as an officer of a court, I feel compelled to offer an apology on behalf of all the social service agencies that failed you during your young life. What happened to you and your brothers and sisters should never have been allowed to happen; I couldn't agree with you more about that. You were innocent children. The adults who were around failed you; you didn't fail any of them. Those of us who work in public positions do the best we can, but there are times when the ball is dropped in the worst of all possible ways, despite everyone's best intentions. That's clearly what happened in your case; not just once, but time and time again."

Then, smiling benignly due to being fully aware of how mortified I had been made to feel during the trial, he turned his attention directly to me, saying, "Mr. Holder, I think it would be a good idea for you to try to be a little more attentive to your wife. She's a wonderful woman, you know, and you're lucky to have her. I wouldn't want her to get mad at me; that's for sure."

Everyone in the room laughed at this remark, even me, despite the fact that I flushed red in the face. Nearly beside myself with joy, I responded by saying, "You don't have to worry about that, judge; my eyes have been opened, just like everyone else's," and I meant it for all I was worth.

Finally, with a smile on his fact and a demeanor that matched it, he said he hoped everyone in the courtroom would depart feeling just as good as he did about how our case had been concluded, then exercised his judicial prerogative to make a more summative comments to the assemblage as a whole.

Clearly relishing the fact that a highly sensational trial had ended on such an uplifting and positive note, he went on to say, "I want everyone in the courthouse today to know that I am closing these proceedings believing that I am a fortunate judge indeed. First of all," he said, "I couldn't be prouder of the way our judicial system enabled us to get to the truth through the vehicle of this trial. Our system never ceases to amaze me; I've always felt honored and proud to be a part of it, but never any more than today.

"Secondly," said the still smiling judge, "I feel compelled to say that I feel privileged to live among neighbors such as the Stackhouses and the members of this jury, people who have demonstrated that they are not only open-minded and conscientious but thoughtful and merciful as well. I applaud each one of you. Doing what I do, it's common to hear all kinds of negative comments about our system, but, when it works like it did in this instance, it's wonderful to be a part of. It feels good to be so lifted up.

"Finally," he said, and in my opinion to his own great credit, "I also want to add that I feel honored to have had an opportunity to meet our out–of–state visitors, Ernest and Jewel Wilson, two people who did the right thing at a time when no one else was around to step up to the plate." He was well aware of the Wilsons, too, having been raked over the coals during the trial. "I hope you folks come back and visit us again some time real soon," he said. "I think you'd really like our state, and, as you have seen, some truly good people live out here in Texas. Based on what I've seen and heard, you'd be welcome among them at any time. With that, ladies and gentlemen," he said, "I declare these proceedings closed."

THANK GOD, IT WAS FINALLY OVER

WE WON THE DAY, not because we had a shyster lawyer to twist the truth on our behalf, play pre-planned tricks in the courtroom, or engage in offbeat and questionable antics designed to sway a misguided and intimidated jury; we won because two determined professionals labored diligently within defensible legal and ethical guidelines to explain what really happened that day at the Clubhouse. The evidence our attorney and psychiatrist presented was carefully examined and thoughtfully evaluated by jurors whose minds were, if anything, more likely than not tilted against us at the beginning. In the end, though, all parties ended up believing that a just and reasonable verdict had been rendered.

When Candy and I walked out of the county courthouse after the verdict was rendered, we felt like we'd just sprouted wings and that we could have flown off to wherever we wanted rather than simply drive away in our car. Ernest and Jewel Wilson were just as ecstatic as we were. Because a ton of bricks had been lifted off all our backs, the four of us were so effusive in our praise of Harry Foley and Walker Koch that we didn't want to stop hugging them or shaking their hands.

For as long as we live, we will remain thankful to Dr. Koch for helping Candy contend with her childhood demons. We'll remain equally thankful to Harry Foley as well, for having so skillfully guided us through the legal process. What these two men accomplished on our behalf was a genuine blessing, and we still thank God on a daily basis for their excellent work. There's no doubt about it; having Candy's case decided in our favor was the first step in a whole new stage of our lives.

25

AT LONG LAST, WHOLE

AS QUICKLY AFTER CANDY'S trial ended as we could make it happen, we left the city of Granbury and Pecan Plantation behind for good. We wanted to move far away before starting a new life, not because of the way we were treated by the legal system — that, clearly, had worked out in our favor — but because residents of Pecan and the community of Granbury passed judgement on us based on the distorted stories about Candy that appeared in local media outlets. They condemned us, in other words, while we were down and out, well before we had a chance to be heard, and that's what both sides would never have forgotten and forgiven.

We were ridiculed, belittled, and rejected out of hand, while we were unable to defend ourselves. It got so bad that no one had anything good to say about us at all. Our reputations were destroyed, and that's what made trying to hang on at Granbury unthinkable. No matter what we might have tried to do, we would never have been able to live down what happened.

Despite all this, it was truly painful to drive away from the little town for the last time. Given that we really hadn't lived there for long and the appalling way we were treated, you'd think it would have been a relief to get away, but it wasn't; it was genuinely upsetting to sever the only genuine commitment to a community and home we had ever made. We had hoped to live out our lives in our beautifully restored home at Pecan Plantation, despite my own past indifference to staying put anywhere.

We moved from Granbury to where we have lived ever since,

a small place — a cottage, really — situated on a hillside lot on the outskirts of Kennewick, Washington, a home distinguished only by the fact that it has an excellent view of the Columbia River. On our small fixed monthly retirement income, a modest place was all we could afford. What I bring in each month, I regret to have to say, is not even close to the income I would have received if I had stayed put at any one location and my career had come to a conventional end.

Lawyer Harry Foley and psychologist Walter Koch were well worth the cost of their services, but their expertise didn't come cheaply. We're flat broke now, due to having had to spend nearly every dollar we had on Candy's intensive psychiatric treatment, her legal defense, living for a long time off our limited savings, the costs of relocation, and all the other expenses that had to be covered in the wake of the shooting at Pecan Plantation.

From here on out, we'll have to be content with living in the lean and modest way we're still in the process of getting used to. There aren't many luxuries in our lives anymore, but we're getting by quite well. Considering what we've been through, we're thankful to have as much as we have.

Having had to deal with a huge calamity brought us to a deeper level of understanding of each other than would have been the case otherwise. Our life together remains a process of discovery, of learning more about one another with every day that passes. As simple as it is, our relationship is a true delight.

Among the most fundamental of our many discoveries is that unexpected tragedies can be followed by unimaginably positive changes; good fortune, that is, can spring from events that at first appear to be hopeless disaster, in the same way that what at first appears to be to unquestionably good fortune can be followed by unexpectedly negative long-term results. A lottery winner who overnight becomes wealthy beyond his wildest dreams can end up becoming a miserable human being in fewer years than would ever be thought possible, while people who are forced to contend with unimaginable calamities sometimes end up happier than they've ever been before. Our own lives provide tangible evidence of this notable truth.

A typical day for us begins with reading two daily newspapers as we enjoy a quiet breakfast sitting at a small table located beneath a large picture window in the dining area of our kitchen and ends with evenings (when the weather is good, that is) that often find me sitting outside on our deck as I read a novel or work on a project of one kind or another and listen to Candy preparing dinner inside. We live a quiet life in our modest residence, which she has transformed into a warm and wonderful home.

We have a beautiful view of the deep, green-tinted, swift flowing water of the Columbia River as it rushes past us on the way to the ocean, a vista stirring enough to inspire us on a daily basis. We think of the Columbia as *our river*, and we never tire of looking at it from our hillside vantage point. Looking at it as it flows through the valley, *our river* provides a panorama as soothing to the soul as it is pleasing to the eye.

The smaller activities of everyday life are of greater satisfaction to me today than they've ever been in the past, including the kinds of things I spent far too little time enjoying back when I was caught up in the unnecessarily aggressive pursuit of a long list of highly nebulous career goals. I thoroughly enjoy, for example, the sense of peace that accompanies quiet evenings spent sitting on our deck, listening to the clatter of pans, dishes, and silverware in the kitchen as Candy prepares our dinner. Savoring the aroma of a roast in the oven, smelling coffee freshly ground and brewed, and anticipating a dessert she's made as our after-dinner treat are great pleasures for me.

We've never tired of doing things together. Lately, for example, we've truly enjoyed listening to the creative, original music of our favorite Indi band, Proverbial Cool Aid, especially their songs entitled "The Stand," "Grandpa (Tell Me 'bout the Good Old Days)," "Sick," and "West LA." They're a pleasure to listen to, and we wish them every success.

The process of revealing the trauma of her childhood years through examining it in great detail has taken an enormous load off her shoulders, and she is a happier person now than she's ever been before; there's little doubt of that. Now that her peace of mind has been restored, cooking has become one of her greatest pleasures. Today, she is nobody's victim.

We treasure every evening we have together, but what I find most pleasing about ordinary occurrences of the kind that have been described is knowing that they will be enjoyed in the company of a human being whose presence never ceases to make me smile and be thankful for our everyday existence. If there's anything better in life than loving and being loved in return, I don't know what it is.

Because an enormous burden was lifted off our backs, we know each other even better today than we did in the past. The best relationship that can exist between a man and a woman is one that has been strengthened through the tests of time and trial, leaving behind two people more firmly committed to each other than ever before. A bond of this kind is fuller and deeper than romantic love alone, so special that it must be described as a magnificent gift. Candy may remain suspect in the minds of those who have been unwilling to take a deep look into what really happened that day at the Pecan Plantation Country Club, but their failure to get to know her is their own great loss; they are missing out on an opportunity to become acquainted with a truly worthy human being, a person just as beautiful on the inside as she is on the outside. Regardless of the trials of her past and no matter what new challenges we have to face in the future, I'm back where I've wanted to be since the first day I met her, arm in arm with my blue girl, Candy Lee Caine.

Ω Ω Ω Ω Ω

www.ingramcontent.com/pod-product-compliance
Lightning Source LLC
Chambersburg PA
CBHW030350310726
48979CB00001B/242

* 9 7 8 1 7 3 7 1 4 0 6 3 4 *